Poppy's War

By Lily Baxter

THE SHOPKEEPER'S DAUGHTER
POPPY'S WAR

Poppy's War

LILY BAXTER

AVONIMPULSE
An Imprint of HarperCollinsPublishers

First published in Great Britain in 2010 by Century, a division of Random House.

Excerpt from *The Shopkeeper's Daughter* copyright © 2013 by Lily Baxter.

EPub Edition APRIL 2015 ISBN: 9780062412126

Print Edition ISBN: 9780062412133

10 9 8 7 6 5 4 3 2 1

For Jackie and Alan with love.

Poppy's War

Chapter One

Barton Lacey, Dorset, August 1939

THE WHEEZY NOISE made by the steam engine as it chugged out of the station was the saddest sound that Poppy had ever heard. She bit her lip, trying hard not to cry as her last link with the East End of London and home disappeared into the hazy afternoon sunshine.

The woman who had been put in charge of the school-children was not their teacher, and she had warned them before they boarded the train at Waterloo that she was not a person to be trifled with. They were to address her as Mrs Hicks and woe betide anyone who called her miss, although miraculously no one had fallen into that trap during the journey, which had taken three long hours. Poppy could tell by their silence that the other children were also feeling tired, hungry and scared as the formidable Mrs Hicks herded them into a semblance of a crocodile while she performed a roll call on the station platform. She was a big woman, and the buttons on her blouse seemed to be in danger of flying off in all directions when her large bosom heaved with impatient sighs. Her tweed skirt was stretched tight across her bulging stomach, and when Bobby Moss had asked her if she had a baby in her tummy he had received a swift clip round the ear. That had quietened him down a bit, which was a relief to Poppy as he had been a pest throughout the long journey, pulling her hair and calling her silly names, but she had felt a bit sorry for him when she saw him huddled in the corner of the carriage nursing his ear, sniffing and wiping his nose on his sleeve.

'Poppy Brown, stop daydreaming and follow the others outside into the forecourt where the billeting officer will deal with you all as he sees fit.' Mrs Hicks' stentorian voice echoed round the empty station as Poppy fell in step beside Bobby. They were marched through the station ticket hall to stand outside on the forecourt, labelled like parcels and carrying their meagre belongings in brown paper bags, together with that mysterious but compulsory object in a box, a gas mask. Some of the children were snivelling miserably, others hung their heads and stared at their boots, while a few of the bigger boys fought and scrapped like wolf cubs attempting to establish a pecking order in their pack.

Poppy wanted to cry like Colin, the ragged boy standing next to her who had wet his pants and was plainly terrified of being found out. She patted him on the shoulder. 'It's all right,' she whispered. 'I expect they'll take us somewhere nice and give us a slap-up tea.' She did not believe that for one moment, but she was not going to admit to being scared stiff. She held her head high and stuck out her chin. 'Up guards and at 'em' was what Grandad always said, taking his pipe out of his mouth and spitting into the fire as if to underline the importance of his words. 'Don't you let them country folk put one over on you, petal. If they does I'll come down on the next train and give 'em a good seeing to. Chin up, Poppy. You come from a long line of brave soldiers, and don't forget it.'

Poppy did not feel like a brave soldier or a brave anything at that moment. Mrs Hicks had vanished. Maybe she had eaten one too many biscuits and exploded somewhere out of sight, but she had been replaced by a man with a clipboard. He wore a pair of tortoiseshell-rimmed glasses through which he peered at them like a myopic owl.

'I'm Mr Walker,' he announced as if this was something they ought to know. 'I'm the billeting officer and I will find good homes to take care of you for the duration.' He turned to a small group of people who had gathered behind him. None of them looked particularly enthusiastic at the prospect of taking on youngsters from the East End, and the raggle-taggle line of children began to fragment as some collapsed on the ground in tears and several others were sick. Probably from fright, Poppy thought, as she eyed their prospective hosts, recalling Mum's last words to her as they had said a tearful good-bye outside the school gates at five thirty that morning.

'Look at their shoes and their hats, Poppy. Good shoes and a nice hat will mean a clean home and no bed bugs or lice. You be a good girl, wash behind your ears and say your prayers every night before you go to bed. Always remember that your mum and dad love you, ducks. And so does Joe, although he ain't always the best at showing his feelings. That goes for your gran and grandad too. We'll all miss you, love'

Poppy said a small prayer now as she met the eyes of a tight-lipped little woman wearing a felt beret and a mean scowl. Her shoes needed a polish and were down at heel. Poppy looked away and moved her gaze down the line until she came upon a smart pair of high-heeled court shoes, two-tone in brown and cream. Glancing upwards she noted a jaunty brown velour hat spiked with a long feather that reminded her of a film poster she had seen of Errol Flynn playing Robin Hood. The face beneath the hat could have been a female version of the film star's, but the woman's expression was neither charming nor kind. Poppy's heart sank a little as she read boredom and indifference in the hazel eyes that stared unblinkingly into her own. But the shoes were good and the hat was quite new. The woman wore a well-cut tweed costume with a gold brooch on the lapel. Poppy did her best to smile.

The lady in the Robin Hood hat turned to the billeting officer. 'What's the name of that one?' She waved her hand vaguely in Poppy's direction.

Mr Walker scanned the list on his clipboard but he frowned as if confused by the names and ages of the children. He moved a step closer to Poppy. 'What's your name, dear?'

'Poppy Brown, sir.'

'Poppy,' he said with an attempt at a smile. 'Named after the flower, were you, dear?'

'No, mister. I was called Poppy after me mum's favourite perfume from Woollies. Californian Poppy.'

The smart lady cast her eyes up to heaven. 'My God, what an accent.' She looked Poppy up and down. 'But she does look the cleanest of the bunch and she's old enough to be useful. She'll do.'

'You're a lucky girl, Poppy Brown.' Mr Walker took her by the shoulder and gave her a gentle shove towards her benefactress. 'You must be very grateful to Mrs Carroll and I hope you'll behave like a good girl at Squire's Knapp.'

'Follow me, child.' Mrs Carroll strode away towards a large black car, her high heels tip-tapping on the concrete, and as the feather in her hat waved in the breeze it seemed to be beckoning to Poppy. She followed obediently but shied away in fright as a big man dressed entirely in black from his peaked cap to his shiny leather boots leapt forward to open the car door.

'Don't loiter, girl,' Mrs Carroll said impatiently. 'Get in the car.'

Poppy glanced up at the chauffeur but he was staring straight ahead of him. She climbed into the back seat and made herself as small as possible in the far corner. The unfamiliar smell of the leather squabs coupled with the gnawing hunger that caused her stomach to rumble made her close her eyes as a wave of nausea swept over her. The jam sandwiches that Mum had made in the early hours of the morning had all been eaten before the train got to the Elephant and Castle. She had saved the piece of ginger cake until last, but she had shared it with the small girl from the infants class whose nose was permanently dripping with candles of mucus that grew longer each time she opened her mouth to howl.

'We'll go straight home, Jackson,' Mrs Carroll said in a bored tone. 'I've changed my mind about going to the library.'

The car picked up speed as they left the village and a cool breeze coming through the open window revived Poppy to the point where she could open her eyes. She craned her neck to look out of the window.

'You're very small,' Mrs Carroll said, lighting a cigarette that she had just fitted into a green onyx holder. 'How old are you?' She inhaled with obvious pleasure and exhaled slowly as she replaced the gold cigarette case and lighter in her handbag.

Poppy was impressed. Her dad smoked cigarettes but he always rolled them himself and lit them with a match from a box of Swan Vestas. Sometimes when she had earned a bonus at the glue factory, Mum would buy a packet of Woodbines for him as a special treat. Gran said it wasn't ladylike to smoke in the street. Poppy wondered what Gran would say about a lady smoking in her car.

'Well?' Mrs Carroll shot her a sideways glance. 'Have you lost your tongue, girl?'

'No, miss, I'm thirteen. I had me thirteenth birthday in April.'

'You're very undersized for your age, and you say *my* thirteenth birthday, not me thirteenth birthday. You call me Mrs Carroll or ma'am, not miss. Do you understand, Poppy?'

'Yes, mi— ma'am.'

Mrs Carroll smoked her cigarette in silence, occasionally tapping the ash into an ashtray located somewhere by her side. Poppy remembered that Gran also said it was rude to stare and she turned away to gaze out of the window. Through gaps in the hedgerows she could see fields of ripe corn, spiked with scarlet poppies and dark blue cornflowers. She had read about the countryside in books and she had seen the flat fields of Essex from the train window on the annual family August Bank Holiday trip to Southend-on-Sea, but the gently rolling countryside of Dorset was something quite new to her. She moved forward in her seat as they passed a field where a herd of black and white cows grazed on rich green grass, and she was amazed by their size and a bit scared, especially when two of them poked their heads over a five-barred gate and mooed loudly as the car drove past. She began to feel sick again and was relieved when Jackson brought the big limousine to a halt outside a pair of tall wrought iron gates. He climbed sedately out of the car and unlocked the gates, which protested on rusty hinges as they swung open. He drove slowly along an avenue lined with trees that formed a dark tunnel of interwoven branches heavy with wine-red leaves.

'This is like the park at home,' Poppy said appreciatively. 'Really.'

Mrs Carroll's voice sounded remote and mildly bored. Poppy accepted this as a matter of course. Grown-ups never took much notice of what children had to say, and she had just spotted a small lake with an island in the middle and a white marble folly in the shape of a Roman temple. It was like something out of a film and she was about to ask Mrs Carroll if all this belonged to her when she heard the thundering of horse's hooves and the car came to a sudden halt. Seemingly appearing from nowhere, the rider drew his mount to a halt on Poppy's side of the car. The animal whinnied and rolled its great eyes. Its nostrils flared and Poppy thought it was going to put its huge head through the open window to bite her. She screamed and ducked down, covering her eyes with her hands.

'Good God, who have you got there, Mother?'

The voice was young, male and well spoken but Poppy did not dare look up.

'Guy! Do you have to ride as if you're in a Wild West show?' Mrs Carroll said angrily. 'Get that beast away from the Bentley before it does some damage.'

'Have you kidnapped a little girl, Mother? I thought you hated children.'

The humour in the voice was not lost on Poppy. She struggled to sit upright, but as she lifted her head she saw the horse's huge yellow teeth bared as if it was going to snap her head off. Everything went black.

SHE WOKE UP feeling something cold and wet dripping down her neck. A fat, rosy face hovered above hers and for a moment Poppy thought she was at home in West Ham.

'Gran? Is that you?'

'Gran indeed. What a cheek!'

'Well, you are a grandma, Mrs Toon.'

'That's as maybe, Violet. But I'm not grandma to the likes of this little 'un, come from goodness knows where in the slums of London.'

Poppy was raised to a sitting position and the younger person, who she realised must be Violet, shoved a glass of water into her hands. 'Take a sip of that, for Gawd's sake.'

Poppy gazed in wonder at her surroundings. She was in a kitchen, but it was enormous. The whole ground floor of her home in West Ham would have fitted into it with room to spare.

'We thought you were dead,' Violet said cheerfully. 'But now we can see you're alive and kicking.'

Poppy drank some water and immediately felt a little better. 'I thought for a moment I was back at home.'

Mrs Toon cleared her throat noisily and wiped her hands on her starched white apron. 'There, there! You're a very lucky little girl to have been taken in by Mrs Carroll. I hope you're not going to give us any trouble, Poppy Brown.'

'I never asked to come here, missis.'

Mrs Toon and Violet exchanged meaningful glances, as if to say 'I told you so'.

'None of your lip, young lady,' Mrs Toon said sharply. 'You're a guest in this house, although I'm not sure what we're supposed to do with you. Are you going to be kept below stairs or upstairs? Mrs Carroll never said one way or t'other. But whatever she decides, you must keep a civil tongue in your head, or you'll answer to me.'

'Yes ma'am,' Poppy said, recalling Mrs Carroll's lesson in manners.

'La-di-dah!' Mrs Toon said, chuckling. 'Better give her a bowl of soup and some bread and butter, Violet. And then you can take her upstairs and run a bath for her.'

'It's not Friday.' Poppy looked for the tin tub set in front of the black-lead stove, but there was none. Come to that there was no stove either. There was a large gas cooker and some sort of range with shiny metal lids on the top, but that was all. She breathed a sigh of relief. 'Well, seeing as how you got no hot water, I'll skip the bath, ta.'

'People in proper houses have baths every day,' Mrs Toon said firmly. 'And I don't know what gives you the idea we haven't any hot water. We have the very latest in everything at Squire's Knapp.'

'That's right,' Violet said, nodding. 'We had central heating before even Cook was born, and that's going back some.' She placed a bowl of steaming soup on a stool which she set beside Poppy. 'I daresay you don't have proper bathrooms in the slums. Eat up and I'll show you how posh folks live.'

The soup was as good as anything that Gran could make, Poppy thought appreciatively as she bit into the hunk of freshly baked bread liberally spread with thick yellow butter. She had not tasted butter before as they always ate margarine at home. She stopped chewing as she thought of her family and suddenly it was difficult to swallow. She had lost track of time but a sideways glance at the big white-faced clock on the kitchen wall told her it was teatime. Dad and her elder brother Joe would be home from their jobs on the railways, and Mum would be stoking the coke boiler to heat water for them to wash off the grime of the day, while Gran peeled potatoes ready to boil and serve with a bit of fat bacon or boiled cod. Grandad would be out in the back garden smoking his pipe and keeping an eye out for the neighbour's pigeons. The birds were supposed to fly straight home, but were inclined to stop off in order to sample the tender green shoots of cabbage and a Brussels sprout or two.

'What's up with you?' Violet demanded. 'Don't you like proper food? I bet your family lives on rats and mice up in London.'

Apparently overhearing this remark, Mrs Toon caught Violet a swift clout round the ear. 'Don't tease the kid, Violet Guppy. How would you like it if you were sent away from home and had to live with strangers? You go on upstairs and run the bath water and don't dawdle.'

Uttering a loud howl Violet ran from the kitchen clutching her hand to her ear. Poppy swallowed hard and blinked, determined that whatever happened she was not going to disgrace herself by bursting into tears. Gran said tears were a sign of weakness, like not being able to work a pair of scissors with your left hand in order to cut the fingernails on your right hand. Gran said if you couldn't control your emotions or your left hand, it was just weak will and not to be tolerated.

'Eat up, little 'un,' ordered Mrs Toon. 'I haven't got all day to waste on the likes of you, you know.'

'Mrs Toon. I've got a message from her upstairs.'

Poppy twisted round in her chair to see a maid wearing a black dress with a white cap and apron standing in the doorway.

'Mrs Carroll wants to see you and the evacuee in the drawing room as soon as she's been fed and bathed.'

Mrs Toon tossed her head causing her white cap to sit askew on top of her silver-grey hair. 'All right, Olive. She's nearly finished her food. You'd better take her up to the bathroom and watch your cousin Violet. That girl's got a spiteful streak in her nature and I don't want her trying to drown young Poppy here. Mrs Carroll wouldn't like it.'

'Mrs Carroll says to burn the evacuee's clothes because they'll probably be – you know.' She winked and nodded her head, lowering her voice. 'She says to find some of Miss Pamela's old clothes and see if they fit.'

'As if I haven't got enough to do.' Mrs Toon clicked her tongue against her teeth. She sighed. 'Dinner to prepare and an evacuee to feed and clothe; I just haven't got the time to go poking about in Miss Pamela's room. You'll have to do that, Olive.'

Poppy leapt to her feet. 'You ain't going to burn my clothes. My mum sent me with my Sunday best and I haven't got fleas. It's only poor folk's kids that have fleas, not people who live in Quebec Road, West Ham.'

Olive reached out a long, thin arm and grabbed Poppy by the scruff of her neck. 'Less of your cheek, young lady. Mind your manners or Mrs Carroll will send you back to London to be bombed by them Germans.'

Poppy felt her heart kick against her ribs. If Olive had punched her in the stomach it couldn't have hurt more. 'They won't bomb West Ham, will they?'

'Why do you think the government sent all you kids out to pester us in the country? Silly girl!' Olive gave her a shove towards the door. 'Now get up the stairs and we'll make sure you haven't brought any little lodgers with you.'

AFTER AN EXCRUCIATING time half submerged in what felt like boiling water while Violet scrubbed her back with a loofah that felt more like a handful of barbed wire and Olive shampooed her hair, digging her fingers spitefully into Poppy's scalp, she was eventually deemed to be clean enough to be taken down to the drawing room. Dressed in clothes that were expensive but at least two sizes too large for her small frame, Poppy waited nervously outside the door while Olive went inside to announce that she was ready for inspection. Moments later she reappeared. 'Go in. Speak only when you're spoken to.'

Poppy entered the room as nervously as if she were venturing into a cage filled with wild animals. Mrs Carroll was seated in a large blue velvet armchair with her feet raised up on a tapestry-covered footstool. In one elegantly manicured hand she held a glass of sherry and between two fingers on the other hand she balanced her cigarette holder. She was talking to a thin, white-haired man seated in a chair on the opposite side of the huge fireplace. She stopped speaking to stare at Poppy. 'She looks cleaner, Olive. It's fortunate that I hadn't found time to send Miss Pamela's old clothes off to the orphanage. They fit Poppy quite nicely, considering she's so small and thin.'

Olive bobbed a curtsey. 'Mrs Toon would like to know where she's to put her, ma'am.'

Mrs Carroll took a sip of sherry and sighed. 'I don't know. There must be a spare room in the servants' quarters.'

A sharp intake of breath told Poppy that this suggestion was not popular with Olive.

'The ones that aren't used have been shut up for years, ma'am.'

The kindly-looking gentleman had been silent until now but he frowned, shaking his head. 'You can't put the child up there, Marina. What about the old nursery?'

'Don't be silly, Edwin. Pamela will need to put Rupert in there when they come to stay.'

'Well, just for the time being then, my dear. The girl will feel more at home in the children's room.'

Poppy cast him a grateful look. He seemed nice and had kind eyes.

'So you are Poppy Brown,' he said, holding out his hand. 'How do you do, Poppy? My name is Edwin Carroll.'

'Pleased to meet you, mister.' Poppy gave his hand a shake and thought how soft his skin was, not a bit like Dad's which was calloused by years of manual labour.

Marina Carroll groaned audibly. 'The reply to how do you do is simply how do you do, Poppy. Not pleased to meet you.'

The lines on Edwin's forehead knotted together in a frown. 'I think the lessons in etiquette might wait until the child has settled in, Marina.' His eyes, magnified by the thick lenses, smiled kindly at Poppy. 'Now you go with Olive, Poppy, and she'll make you comfortable in the nursery. Tomorrow we'll have a chat and you can tell me all about your family in, where was it? Caterham?'

'West Ham, Edwin,' Marina snapped. 'Take her away, Olive. We'll have dinner at eight o'clock whether Guy gets home on time or not.'

'Yes'm.' Olive seized Poppy by the arm and dragged her out of the room.

MRS TOON SAID she was too busy with dinner to think about minor details like Poppy's comfort and she put Olive and Violet in charge of settling Poppy in the old nursery.

Grumbling all the way, Olive trudged up three flights of stairs with the reluctant Violet carrying a pile of clean bed linen and Poppy following wearily carrying nothing but her gas mask and toothbrush, which was all that was left after Mrs Toon had incinerated her few possessions in the thing they called an Aga.

Olive and Violet made up a bed in the night nursery. After a great deal of bickering and a little half-hearted flapping around with a duster, they agreed that they had done enough for one day, and Olive flounced out of the room followed by Violet, who popped her head back around the door and poked her tongue out at Poppy. 'Sleep tight, Popeye. Don't worry about the ghost. The white lady don't do much more than tug off the bed-clothes and throw things about the room.'

The door slammed shut and Poppy remained motionless listening to their footsteps retreating down the staircase, and then silence closed in around her. She was unused to quietness. In the cramped living condi-tions of number 18 Quebec Road, the house reverberated with the sound of men's deep voices and the clumping of Dad's and Joe's heavy boots on bare linoleum. Mum and Gran chattered noisily as they pounded washing on the ridged glass washboard, riddled the cinders in the boiler or beat the living daylights out of the threadbare carpets as they hung on the line in the tiny back garden. Poppy's eyes filled with tears as she thought of her mum with her tired but still pretty face and her work-worn hands. The smell of Lifebuoy soap hung about her in an aura unless she was going to the pictures with Dad, and then she splashed on a little of the Californian Poppy perfume that Poppy had saved up for and bought from Woolworth's to give her as a birthday present.

The day room was furnished with what looked like odd bits of furniture that were no longer needed in the reception rooms. A child's desk and chair were placed beneath one of the tall windows and a battered doll's house stood in one corner of the room. A tea table and two chairs occupied the centre of the room and two saggy armchairs sat on either side of the fireplace. It was not the most cheerful of places and Poppy shivered even though the room was hot and stuffy. She could imagine the white lady sitting in one of the chairs or coming to her in the middle of the night. She had read about haunted houses and they were always old and large, just like Squire's Knapp.

She hurried into the night nursery, closing the door behind her. This room was slightly smaller and more homely. A baby's cot stood in one corner, with a large fluffy teddy bear lying face down on the pillow. Twin beds took up the rest of the floor space, separated by a white-painted bedside cabinet that some bored child had scribbled on with wax crayons and pencil. Momentarily diverted, Poppy climbed on the bed beneath the window and dangled her legs over the side as she tried to read the scrawled writing. Apart from matchstick men with six fingers on each spiky hand, the only word legible after many applications of Vim was the name **GUY**, printed in thick block capitals and repeated over and over again. Poppy lay down on the pink satin eiderdown and closed her eyes, too exhausted to go into the nursery bathroom and clean her teeth or to put on the flannelette nightgown that Olive had left under her pillow.

WHEN SHE AWAKENED next morning Poppy thought for a moment that she was back in the boxroom at home, but the brightly coloured cretonne curtains that floated in the breeze from the open window were not her bedroom curtains. The Beatrix Potter prints on the walls were nothing like the pictures of film stars that she had cut from movie magazines and pinned over her bed at home. She sat up, rubbing her eyes as memories of yesterday flooded back in an overwhelming tide of misery.

She strained her ears for sounds of life in the house but there was silence except for the birds singing away in the garden below. She knelt on the bed and rested her elbows on the sill as she looked out of the window. Her room was at the back of the house overlooking a wide sweep of green lawns, just like the cricket pitch in West Ham Park. She caught a glimpse of the mirror-like sheen of the lake between a stand of silver birch trees and a dense shrubbery. A movement down below caught her eye as a disembodied hand shook a yellow duster out of a window and was withdrawn almost immediately.

She slid off the bed and made a brief foray into the white-tiled bathroom with its huge cast iron bath standing on claw feet, a washbasin big enough to bathe in and a willow pattern lavatory. The toilet at number 18 had its own little house situated just outside the back door, which the Brown family considered was quite superior to the back-to-back terraces in the poorer part of town where the lavatory was at the bottom of the yard if you were lucky, and at the end of the block if you were not. She cleaned her teeth and washed her face in what Gran would have called a cat's-lick, deciding that she could not possibly be dirty after the scrubbing she had received at Violet's hands. Reluctantly she dressed in Miss Pamela's cast-offs, and after an unsuccessful attempt to get the comb through the tangles she tied her hair back with a piece of string she found in the day nursery.

She wondered what she was supposed to do now. Her stomach rumbled and she realised that she was extremely hungry, but it seemed that she had been forgotten. She might starve to death up here and her skeleton be found years later amongst the cobwebs in the disused nursery. She opened the door and made her way along the narrow corridor to the landing at the top of the stairs. Leaning over the banisters she strained her ears for sounds of life, and, hearing nothing but the tick of a slender grandmother clock on the floor below, she made her way down three flights of stairs to the kitchen. A wave of sound enveloped her as she opened the door and Violet flew past her carrying a dustpan and brush.

'I'd clean forgotten you, Popeye,' she said, grinning. 'Better keep out of Mrs Toon's way, she's on the warpath.' She slammed the baize door that kept the noise from below from disturbing the genteel calm of the family rooms.

'Oh, it's you!' Kneading bread dough as if she were pummelling her worst enemy, Mrs Toon glared at Poppy. 'I can't be doing with you under my feet today, there's too much to do.'

Poppy stood uncertainly at the foot of the stairs, creating patterns on the floor with the toe of her brown sandal. Mrs Toon's cheeks were bright red, the colour of the geraniums that Gran liked to grow in an old sink in the back yard. Strands of grey hair escaped from her white cap, bouncing about like watch springs as she wielded a floury rolling pin at her. 'I suppose you're hungry. Kids always are in my experience. There's some porridge in the pan on the Aga. Help yourself.'

Poppy approached the monster cautiously and was about to reach up to grab the ladle when Mrs Toon happened to glance over her shoulder. 'Not like that!' she screeched. 'For heaven's sake, girl, you'll scald yourself.' She bustled over and, snatching the ladle, she filled a china bowl with porridge and thrust it into Poppy's hands. 'There's sugar in the bowl on the table. Don't take too much! And there's fresh milk on the marble shelf in the larder. Don't spill it.'

Poppy tucked herself away in the corner of the kitchen and ate her porridge, watching in awe as Mrs Toon barked orders at two women who appeared from the scullery at intervals, carrying huge bowls of peeled vegetables. With a face that Mum would have described as a wet weekend, Olive looked distinctly put out as she clattered down the stairs carrying a tray full of dirty crockery.

'I hate bloody shooting parties,' she said bitterly.

'Language, Olive,' Mrs Toon muttered as Olive disappeared into the scullery.

There was a loud clatter and she flounced back into the kitchen wiping her hands on the tea towel. She stopped and her eyes narrowed as she spotted Poppy, who was trying her best to appear inconspicuous. 'You'd best keep out of my way today. I don't want madam making me look after you as well as doing all my other work.' She snatched an apple from a bowl on a side table and bit into it. 'By the way, Mrs Toon, best keep some breakfast hot for Mr Guy. He went out for his morning ride and hasn't come back yet.'

This piece of information did not seem to go down too well with Mrs Toon, and Poppy finished her food quickly. Taking her empty bowl into the scullery she made her escape through an outside door and found herself in a cobbled yard surrounded by outbuildings. The familiar smell of coarse soap and soda billowed out in clouds of steam from the washhouse, bringing a lump to her throat and a wave of homesickness as she listened to the washerwomen laughing and talking while they worked. She hesitated in the doorway, longing to go inside and find a motherly soul who would give her a cuddle and tell her that everything would be all right, but it seemed as if she was suddenly invisible. They were all too busy to notice her.

She was just wondering what to do when she spotted a gateway in the stone wall, and on closer examination she discovered that it led into the stable yard. The smell of horse dung, damp straw and leather was unfamiliar but not as unpleasant as she might have imagined. A horse stuck its great head out of its stall whinnying at her and stamping its hooves and she backed away. Those teeth looked as if they could bite a girl's head off with one great snap of the mighty jaws. She had been chased once by a carthorse that had seemed intent on trampling her underfoot, and she had been scared of the brutes ever since. She glanced round as a stable lad shouted something unintelligible at her and she panicked, thinking she must have done something wrong. She ran through the yard, past the carriage house and into the safety of a large clump of rhododendrons. The leaves slapped her cheeks and twigs scratched her bare legs as she forced her way through the tangle of branches. A large pigeon flew out of the bush close to her head and she screamed in fright as its wing feathers made a loud flapping noise.

Suddenly, she was out in the sunlight again and her heart was beating a tattoo inside her chest. Her feet crunched on the gravel as she ran headlong down the drive. Close by she could hear a dog barking. Too late she was aware of horse's hooves pounding on the hard-baked grass, and the shouted warning to get out of the way. She turned her head and was paralysed with fright at the sight of flailing hooves. The horse reared on its hind legs as its rider swerved to avoid her. She raised her arm to protect her face and plunged once again into a sea of blackness.

Chapter Two

POPPY REGAINED CONSCIOUSNESS slowly and found herself looking up into a pair of angry, hazel eyes, deep-set beneath dark brows that were drawn together in a frown. 'Are you Errol Flynn?' she murmured. His clean-cut features and strong jawline would have made him stand out in a crowd, but he looked decidedly cross.

'Oh God, she's concussed, Guy. Better send for the doctor.'

Poppy realised that she was lying on soft cushions and there was ceiling above her where the sky had been. A crystal chandelier dangled somewhere high above her and the female voice belonged to a young and attractive lady with blonde hair who looked just like Ginger Rogers.

'I'm a doctor. Well, halfway there, anyway,' Guy said, with a wry smile. 'And she's not concussed, she just fainted. She went down like a ninepin, having terrified poor old Goliath out of his wits and almost unseated me into the bargain.'

'Who is she anyway?' Pamela asked, staring curiously at Poppy. 'And aren't those my old clothes?'

'She's an evacuee from London. Mother has decided to do her bit for the war effort.' Guy raised himself from his knees, ruffling Poppy's hair with a careless hand. 'What's your name, kid?'

'Poppy Brown, mister.'

'How do you do, Poppy? My name is Guy and this is my sister, Pamela. I'm afraid you haven't had a very auspicious start to your time here.'

Poppy had not the faintest idea what auspicious meant, but he seemed to understand how she felt and he was really good-looking when he smiled. She remembered what Mum had taught her about manners. 'I'm quite well now, thank you. And I'm sorry if I frightened your horse, mister, but it scared me first.'

'We'll have to do something about your fear of animals, young lady. You can't live in this part of the country and go round fainting every time you see something on four legs.'

Poppy snapped into a sitting position. 'The greengrocer's horse chased me up the road and bit me bum. Don't make me go near them nasty things, mister.'

'Don't tease the child, Guy,' Pamela said, frowning. 'And we don't say bum in polite circles, Poppy. Your grasp of grammar is appalling. If you're going to stay here for a while I think you ought to be enrolled in the village school as soon as possible. I'll have a word with Mother when she gets back from the morning shoot.'

Poppy stared at her in amazement. 'Is she shooting Germans?'

Guy threw back his head and laughed. 'I'd back my mother against the Germans any day.'

'Don't encourage her, Guy. The child has a lot to learn and she'll get herself into trouble if she comes out with things like that in front of other people.'

'That's Mother's department, I'm glad to say.' Guy leaned down so that his face was close to Poppy's. 'And as for you, young lady, we have a date with Goliath when you're feeling better.'

She blinked up at him, intoxicated by the scent of damp Harris tweed and spice-scented cologne. She was suddenly the centre of attention and it seemed that at least someone cared about her. All right, she thought, so he isn't quite as handsome as Errol Flynn, but he's not half bad. The girls at school would be green with envy if they knew she was living in the same house as someone who looked like a film star. He strolled through the open French windows into the garden. She realised with a start that Pamela was saying something.

'You haven't heard a word I said, Poppy. Are you sure your head doesn't hurt?'

Poppy gazed up at Pamela, searching for some resemblance to her brother and finding none. 'I'm sorry, miss. What was it you said?'

'Never mind. I'll ring for Olive. She'll know what to do with you.'

Poppy did not think much of that idea and she scrambled to her feet. 'I'm all right now, honest.'

'Then you'd better go to the nursery and read a book, or go into the garden and play ball, or something,' Pamela said with a vague wave of her hands. 'Just make sure you keep to the servants' quarters while the shooting party have lunch in the dining room, and that goes for tomorrow as well. In fact the luncheon parties go on until the end of the week and you mustn't make a nuisance of yourself. If you don't know what to do, just ask Olive or Mrs Toon.'

Poppy eyed her warily. 'If you don't mind me asking, miss. Who are they shooting if it ain't the Hun?'

'It's way past the glorious twelfth, girl. The shooting season has begun. I thought everyone knew that.' Pamela hurried from the room leaving Poppy none the wiser.

'Ah, THERE YOU are, Poppy Brown. I've been looking for you.'

Guy's voice startled Poppy so that she almost fell out of the tree. She had thought she was well concealed amongst the greenery of the ancient oak where she had taken refuge from the house full of strangers. She had no idea how long she had been perched on the branch, but from her vantage point she had seen the return of the shooting party and the toffs in their tweeds, wearing flat caps that didn't quite look the same as the ones that Dad and Joe wore when they went to watch West Ham play at home.

'I can see you, kid, so you might as well answer me.'

'How did you know where I was?' She had bunched her skirt up into her knickers in order to make climbing easier and she was suddenly conscious of the fact that she was showing rather a lot of leg. Gran always said that ladies never showed their knees. She would have a fit if she saw her now.

Guy pulled himself up into the branches with the ease of an athlete and straddled the bough beside her. 'This is where I used to hide when I didn't want anyone to find me.'

'I didn't know it was your tree.'

'Well now you do, Poppy! But I give you permission to use it as and when necessary.'

'But you're grown-up. You don't need a place to hide.'

The smile on his lips did not quite reach his eyes. 'Everyone needs a place to hide sometimes, Poppy. Grown-ups are no exception.'

'I see.' She did not understand at all, but she was flattered to think that Guy had seen fit to confide in her. He seemed to have forgotten her for a moment and he took a cigarette case from his breast pocket, selected a cigarette and lit it with a flick of his silver lighter. Poppy watched him with open admiration as he blew smoke rings up into the branches. 'I wish I could do that.'

'Don't even think about it. Smoking isn't for little girls.'

'I'll be fourteen next April.'

'That makes all the difference, of course.'

'Now you're laughing at me. That's not nice.'

He shook his head. 'I didn't mean to hurt your feelings. I can remember what it's like to be sort of halfway between childhood and being an adult. No one takes you seriously.'

His smile would have melted an iceberg and Poppy was ready to forgive him anything. 'It doesn't matter,' she murmured, turning her head and hoping he had not seen the blood rush to her cheeks.

He tossed the butt onto the ground where it glowed for a moment before being extinguished by the damp soil. 'And now, Poppy,' he said seriously, 'I think it's time for your first riding lesson.'

She almost fell out of the tree in fright, but he had already lowered himself so that he could drop the last few feet, and he was standing below encouraging her to jump. She half climbed, half fell off the branch and was caught by a pair of surprisingly strong arms, stronger even than her dad's when he lifted her up on his shoulders to pick apples off the tree in their tiny back garden.

Guy set her on her feet and strode off in the direction of the stables. She trotted on behind, torn between the desire to follow him to hell and back or to run away and lock herself in the nursery bathroom. Forgiving him for teasing her was one thing; learning to ride one of those fearsome animals was quite another.

When they reached the stable yard he summoned a lad with a wave of his hand and told him to saddle up Goliath. Poppy sidled away, swallowing convulsively as the bile rose in her throat. She felt faint and sick and was about to make a bolt for the safety of the rhododendrons when Guy seemed to sense her fear. His hand shot out and caught her wrist in a vice-like grip.

'No you don't,' he said sternly. 'Goliath is as gentle as a lamb. I don't want you frightening him again.'

The notion of a gigantic animal like Goliath being scared of a person as small as herself struck Poppy as funny in spite of her rising panic and she giggled nervously. The stable lad brought the beast out of the stall and Guy stroked the horse's muzzle, speaking to it in a voice that made Poppy feel quite jealous. She took a step backwards as Goliath tossed his mane and pawed the cobbles with his huge metal-shod hoof, but Guy still had hold of her wrist and without saying a word he picked her up and set her squarely on the saddle. Poppy's legs were not long enough to reach the stirrups and she gripped the pommel while he adjusted the straps, closing her eyes and praying that she would not fall off. The ground seemed miles away, and when the horse moved she uttered a cry of fright.

'Hold tight. I'm going to lead Goliath around the yard. I won't let you fall off so there's no need to be scared.'

The bones of Poppy's pelvis bounced on the leather saddle and her stomach threatened to force its way up through her mouth as she clung on.

'There now, that's not so bad, is it?' Guy said as they completed a full circle of the yard, which brought a round of applause from the stable lad and one of the grooms.

'No-o,' Poppy muttered, opening one eye and sighing with relief when she realised that the ordeal was over.

Guy lifted her from the saddle and set her on the ground. He produced some lumps of sugar from his jacket pocket and put them in her hand. 'Hold your hand out and keep your fingers flat or Goliath will think your thumb is a bit of sugar and eat it.'

She held her hand out, keeping her eyes tight shut until she felt the soft, moist lips take the sugar gently from her hand. She opened her eyes and found herself looking into the limpid gaze of Goliath. For a moment she thought he was smiling at her. 'He's lovely,' she whispered.

'There you are, Poppy. I told you there was nothing to be afraid of.' Guy lengthened the stirrup leathers before mounting with the ease of long practice. Goliath pranced around excitedly, eager to be off, but Guy had complete control over the horse. He smiled down at Poppy. 'Cheerio, kid. See you later.'

She waved shyly as he urged Goliath into a trot and they disappeared from view. She sighed, feeling suddenly lonely and unprotected as she walked slowly towards the scullery, but she came to a halt as a shower of filthy water splattered her sandals and the hem of her skirt.

'Oops, mind out there, townie.' The stable lad stuck his face close to hers, revealing a set of uneven teeth with a large gap where one of the top front ones was missing. 'Oh dear, you're all muddy. You'll be in for it now.' He stood grinning stupidly at her, with the empty bucket still held in his hand.

The pent-up emotion that had been building in Poppy since she left home suddenly erupted in an explosion of blind fury. She gave him a shove that caught him off balance and sent him sprawling onto the pile of horse dung and straw that he had been raking out of the stalls. Floundering and winded, he gasped for air. A shout of laughter echoed round the yard as the other stable lads and grooms emerged from the tack room to watch the scene with evident enjoyment. 'Serves you right, Guppy,' one of them called out. 'We said you was too young to work here. Go back to the schoolroom where you belong.'

Poppy drew herself up to her full height, tossed her head and marched into the scullery. She managed to slip past the women who were washing crockery in the Belfast sink, and Mrs Toon who was having forty winks in a chair by the Aga, with her cap pulled down over her eyes. Violet was nowhere to be seen and Olive and a couple of women from the village were busy laying out trays in readiness for afternoon tea. Poppy's stomach rumbled as she realised that she must have missed the midday meal, but she dared not ask for food in case they saw the state she was in. No one at home had ever raised a hand to her, except for a swipe round the legs with a wet floor cloth once when she had cheeked Mum, but she was not so certain they would spare the rod in this house. If they went round shooting innocent birds, what might they do to a girl who had ruined a set of perfectly good clothes? Creeping up the back stairs, she managed to reach the nursery unseen, but as she closed the door behind her she came face to face with Pamela, who looked her at her as though she were something the cat had sicked up on the doormat.

'Just look at the state you're in!' Pamela said coldly. 'What on earth have you been doing, and where have you been all this time? Mrs Toon was going to send out a search party if you hadn't returned by suppertime.'

'Mr Guy taught me to ride,' Poppy said truthfully.

'Well, it looks as if you were thrown into a peat bog. You'd better change your clothes. No, on second thoughts you'd better have a bath first. You smell awful.'

'Yes, miss.'

Pamela ground her teeth. 'You don't say yes miss. You say yes Mrs Pallister. And before you go and clean yourself up, Poppy, I want you to say hello to my son, Rupert, and this is his new nursemaid, Nancy Guppy.' With a nod of her head she indicated a young girl seated at a low table with a toddler on her knee. 'Nancy lives in the village and is only going to be here during the day.'

Another blooming Guppy, Poppy thought, eyeing the girl warily.

'You'll be sharing the nursery with Rupert until we've decided what to do with you. I'm sure you are quite old enough to keep an eye on Rupert at night. Do you think you can be trusted to do that, Poppy?'

'Yes, M-Mrs Pallister.' Poppy nodded vigorously. She didn't much like the look of Nancy, who had freckles and a spiteful, foxy look about her, but Rupert smiled happily at her as he munched bread and butter soldiers dipped in his boiled egg.

'Good,' Pamela said with a hint of relief in her voice. 'Now go and take that bath and I'll have a tray of supper sent up for you later on. Mrs Toon won't want you getting in her way while she's preparing dinner.'

Poppy ran her bath, thinking while the water gushed into the big iron tub that these people were obsessed with cleanliness in a way that would even impress her gran, who prided herself on having the cleanest whites in the street. Gran was a great believer in Persil powder and not only used it to boil the whites but made it into a paste and scrubbed her own wrinkled skin with it and even used it to wash her hair. Poppy could never smell Persil without thinking of Gran and the tiny kitchen in Quebec Road on Monday, which was washing day, as opposed to Friday which was bath night. As she undressed, Poppy drifted into a blissful reverie about the home she was missing so much that it hurt.

Tuesday was the day when Mum black-leaded the boiler and on Wednesday Dad always brought home sprats for tea. On Thursday Mum and Gran had a baking day and the whole house was filled with the aroma of warm sponge cake and bubbling jam tarts. Joe had taken one off the wire cooling tray once and had burnt his mouth. Gran had said that was what you got for pinching things, but Mum had given him a cup of cold water and a kiss on the cheek. Friday was fish and chip night, after everyone had taken a turn in the tub. She was the youngest, and therefore the last in the queue. She was used to tepid water and floating islands of soap scum. Poppy tested the water with the tip of her big toe and climbed in. The bath was as big as the Serpentine; the water was hot and clear as crystal and she had it all to herself. No gritty bits in the bottom now. This was luxury, but it didn't make up for being away from home and family. She lay back in the bath and closed her eyes. Tears forced their way beneath her screwed-up eyelids and trickled down her cheeks to plop into the bath water.

'Have you gone down the plughole to the sea?'

Nancy's shrill voice made her sit up with a start, and she clutched the flannel to her bare chest. 'What do you want?'

'I want to use the lav, fathead! What do you think?'

'I'm getting out now.'

'You'd better hurry or I'm coming in ready or not!'

Poppy leapt out of the bath and had just wrapped herself in the white bath sheet when Nancy flew in and began to take down her navy blue knickers. Poppy hurried into the bedroom, and still damp around the edges she had just managed to struggle into her clothes when Nancy breezed back into the nursery.

'Whew! That was nearly a nasty accident. You took long enough in there, Popeye. I thought you'd drownded yourself.'

'Don't call me Popeye! That's not my name.'

'It's what Violet calls you,' Nancy said, smirking. 'And Violet's me cousin, so you'd better be nice to me, Popeye, or I'll set Violet on you.'

Before Poppy had time to think up a suitably cutting remark, the door opened and Violet stomped in carrying a heavy wooden tray which she dumped down on the nursery table, startling Rupert who opened his mouth and began to wail.

'I've got enough to do without having to wait on you two,' she grumbled.

'There now, Vi. You've made Master Rupert cry,' Nancy said, putting her arm around him, which made him wail even louder.

'It's your job to keep him quiet then, isn't it?' Violet snorted. 'Me, I've got to wait on you lot as well as everything else. I'm run off me feet, and there's still dinner to get through with all them snooty toffs. Think yourself lucky, Nancy Guppy. You've got it easy.' She left the room, slamming the door behind her.

'Bitch,' Nancy muttered. 'I hate her. Stuck-up cow.'

Poppy stared at her in astonishment. 'I thought you said she was your cousin?'

'She is, but that doesn't mean to say I like her, does it?' Nancy dumped Rupert on the floor as if he were a sack of potatoes. 'Go and play with your toys like a good boy while me and Poppy here have our tea. I'm flipping starving.'

Rupert sat where he had landed, plugging his thumb in his mouth and staring wide-eyed at Nancy. Poppy felt instantly sorry for him. He was only little, after all, and he seemed to be scared of foxy-face. She bent down and picked him up, settling him on her knee while she shovelled bread and milk into her mouth, but having taken the edge off her appetite she broke off a piece of shortbread and gave it to him. 'There you are, Rupert,' she said gently. 'You're a good boy, aren't you?'

He curled his stubby little fingers around the biscuit and grinned at her as he stuffed it in his mouth.

After they had finished their supper, Nancy picked up the tray and headed for the door. 'Keep an eye on Rupie for me, Popeye. I'll take the tray down before they send Vi up again. I need to keep in with her because I want to borrow her new blouse for the dance in the village hall on Saturday night.'

She flounced out of the room. Relieved to be on her own with Rupert, Poppy went to sit beside him on the floor where he was quietly playing with some wooden bricks. 'I'm Poppy, and I'm going to look after you at bedtime.' She lifted him onto her lap.

'Poppy,' he said, chuckling. 'Poppy.' He wrapped his chubby arms around her neck. He felt soft and warm like a puppy and it was wonderful to feel loved and needed, even if only for a moment as Rupert grew bored and wriggled until she set him down on the floor and he toddled over to continue playing with his bricks.

She was helping him build them into a tower when the door opened and Pamela entered the room. 'Where's Nancy?'

'She took the tray downstairs, Mrs Pallister.'

'Tell her she can go home as soon as she's put Master Rupert to bed. You must stay with him then, Poppy. I trust you to keep an eye on him.'

Poppy nodded her head, lost for words as she gazed in admiration at Pamela's elegant silk dress, which clung to her slender figure and swirled out around the hemline just like the ones that Ginger Rogers wore in the films. It must, she thought, have cost a bomb, not including the double row of gleaming pearls that she wore round her neck. As Pamela bent down to drop a kiss on the top of her son's curly head, Poppy caught a waft of expensive perfume that was nothing like the scent they sold in Woollies. Miss Pamela's husband must be worth a fortune, she thought enviously. One day maybe if she saved up enough she could afford to buy some of that perfume for Mum. She loved nice things, and although she never complained Poppy had often seen her leafing through the old fashion magazines she brought home from her cleaning job at the newsagent's in the High Street.

'Goodnight, darling,' Pamela crooned. 'Give Mummy a big kiss.'

Rupert obliged and then turned his attention back to the tower of bricks.

'I'll leave you to it then,' Pamela said, pausing by the mirror above the fireplace to pat an imaginary strand of hair into place.

Poppy was impressed. She had seen upswept hairstyles like that in *Picturegoer* magazine. 'You look pretty,' she said shyly.

'Thank you, Poppy. It is rather a special occasion tonight.'

'WHAT'S THE SPECIAL occasion?' Poppy asked when Nancy returned almost half an hour later. 'What's going on downstairs?'

'None of your business, Popeye,' Nancy snapped, seeming to regret her previous attempt at conversation. 'Come on, Rupe old man, let's get you bathed and put to bed and then I can get off home.'

'But what's going on that's special? Mrs Pallister was done up like a film star. She's ever so pretty.'

Nancy paused in the doorway of the night nursery with Rupert, red-faced and protesting loudly, tucked under her arm. 'Well it's not to celebrate you coming to pester us, Popeye. But if you must know, it's Mr Guy's young lady, Amy Fenton-Jones. She's been in Switzerland for her health for over a year, and now she's come home all fit and well. It's all right for some, that's what I say.'

Poppy said nothing as she registered with a shock that her idol was stepping out with a young lady, just like Joe, who had been courting Mabel for nearly six months. Nancy barged through the night nursery and banged the bathroom door behind her. Poppy could hear Rupert's protests and loud splashing noises together with a stream of bad words coming from Nancy's lips, which made her long to go into the bathroom and rescue him. Thankfully it was over in a few minutes and Rupert was dumped in his cot and left to sob. Nancy picked up her cardigan and headed for the door. 'I'm off then. Best of luck with his nibs. They say downstairs that he's a terrible sleeper. I bet she didn't tell you that.'

She was gone, leaving Poppy alone with nothing but the sound of Rupert's occasional muffled sob for company. She peeped round the door, but he was lying on his back and sucking his thumb, and his eyelids were heavy. She waited until he was asleep before closing the door. A long and lonely evening stretched ahead of her and she turned her attention to a more thorough exploration of the day nursery. She walked slowly around the room, opening drawers and lifting up the lid of the wooden desk that stood beneath the window. Amongst the jumble of rubber bands, bits of used sealing wax, coloured pencils and crayons, she found an exercise book and a pencil with a broken lead. After a further search she discovered a pencil sharpener and she sat down at the table to write a letter home.

An hour later she had laboriously filled two sides of the lined paper and had nowhere near finished telling the family about her first long day in exile, but her head had begun to ache and the shadows in the room were growing deeper. She crept into the night nursery, took off her sandals and undressed. She found her nightie under the pillow where she had left it that morning and slipped it over her head. Without bothering to wash or clean her teeth, she slid into bed. She fell asleep almost immediately, but was awakened by the sound of sobbing. She sat up only half awake and realised that it was Rupert, standing at the end of his cot, wailing dismally. She scrambled out of bed and picked him up in her arms, rocking him and crooning until he stopped crying. 'You'd best come in with me, little 'un,' she whispered, climbing back beneath the covers with him snuggled up against her. She rested her cheek on his tousled curls, inhaling the fragrant scent of Johnson's baby powder, and, lulled by his rhythmic breathing, she drifted off to sleep.

'POPPY, POPPY!'

She opened her eyes as the small voice penetrated her dreams and then something heavy landed on her stomach. Rupert was bouncing up and down chuckling and gurgling and calling her name. 'Come, Poppy.'

She pretended to be asleep, but Rupert was not so easily fooled and he tugged her hair.

'You little monster,' she said, sitting up and giving him a cuddle. 'Oh, Rupert, you've got a wet bum. I mean bottom.' She set him down on the floor, and climbing out of bed she went in search of clean clothes and nappies. She took him into the nursery bathroom and managed with a bit of a tussle to wash his hands and face. Master Rupert did not appear to appreciate the advantages of cleanliness, she discovered, but eventually she succeeded in getting him dressed, although he obviously felt the same about having his hair brushed as he did about being washed.

'You're a right 'un, Rupert,' Poppy said with a satisfied smile as she surveyed her handiwork. 'You'll be a real heartbreaker one of these days, my lad.'

'Hungry, Poppy.'

She glanced at the wall clock. 'It's long past your breakfast time, and mine too. I think they've forgotten all about us stuck up here.'

She dressed herself and was brushing her hair when Rupert began to whimper. She picked him up and gave him a hug. 'Don't cry, love. We'll go down to the kitchen and I'll make them give you some breakfast. I ain't afraid of Mrs Toon. Well, not much anyway.'

DOWNSTAIRS IN THE kitchen, Mrs Toon was not pleased. 'Violet,' she bellowed. 'Come here, girl.'

Violet skittered into the room looking apprehensive. 'Yes, Mrs Toon?'

'Where's that good-for-nothing cousin of yours?'

'Nancy's poorly, Mrs Toon. She was sick all night.'

'And for the Lord's sake why didn't you tell me that first thing, stupid girl?' Mrs Toon cast her eyes up to heaven and sighed. 'Do something useful and make up a tray for the nursery. You, Poppy! You take Master Rupert back upstairs and Violet will bring your breakfast when it's ready.'

Violet grunted and glared at Poppy as if it were all her fault. She mumbled something under her breath, but luckily for her Mrs Toon's attention had been diverted by Olive who staggered down the stairs with a tray heaped high with dirty crockery.

'Take that to the scullery and then you'd best tell Miss Pamela that Nancy's gone sick. And what are you hanging around for, Poppy? I told you to take Master Rupert up to the nursery. Get going, girl, or you'll feel the weight of my hand round your ear.'

Galvanised into action, Poppy took Rupert up to the nursery and attempted to keep him occupied by getting out the box of bricks. They had just completed building a rather rickety house when she heard heavy footsteps on the stairs. Violet kicked the door open, scowling as she dumped the tray on the table.

'You're more trouble than you're worth, Popeye. You probably gave Nancy the runs and sickness. I expect you brought your dirty germs down from London with you.'

Poppy leapt to her feet. 'That's a wicked thing to say. We're not dirty where I come from and I didn't make Nancy sick.'

'Hoity toity. I'm really scared!' Violet struck a mocking pose which she dropped just as quickly when Pamela walked into the room.

'Get back to work, Violet. Your family has caused me enough inconvenience already.'

'Yes, Miss Pamela. Sorry, I'm sure.' Violet backed out onto the landing, giving Poppy a murderous look as she went.

'And close the door behind you. I don't want Master Rupert catching his death of cold.' Pamela fixed Violet with a stern look as she waited for her instructions to be followed. 'And don't slam it, or you'll be looking for another job.'

The door closed with just a whisper as wood met wood. 'Wretched girl,' Pamela said, crossly. Her expression lightened as she watched Poppy scoop Rupert off the floor and settle him in his high chair. 'He seems to like you, Poppy. Have you brothers and sisters at home in London?'

'No, Mrs Pallister. Well, only Joe but he's nineteen. Although Mum says he's more trouble than a six-year-old.' Poppy turned her attention to Rupert, who was clamouring for his food and she fed him a spoonful of scrambled egg. 'You're a little love, ain't you, Rupert?'

'And did you dress him this morning?' Pamela asked casually. 'I suppose you must have done if Nancy failed to turn up.'

'Yes, ma'am.'

'You seem to be good with children, but you're little more than a child yourself.'

'I'm thirteen, miss. I mean, Mrs Pallister. I'll be fourteen in April. Anyway, I've looked after lots of nippers. I help Mrs Blackwell next door sometimes with her little 'uns. She has one a year regular as clockwork and my dad says that Mr Blackwell should tie a knot in it.'

'Yes, thank you. I don't need to know that.' Pamela twisted her pearl necklace thoughtfully. 'I wonder if I can trust you to look after Rupert all day today, Poppy? I've really got an awful lot to do, but it's a big responsibility for a girl of your age.'

'I can do it, miss.'

'Ma'am or Mrs Pallister, Poppy. I thought we'd got over that. I really must speak to my mother about sending you to school. However, you may look after Rupert this morning, and if I find I can depend on you then I may allow you to take care of him until Nancy returns, or until we go back to London. Do you understand?'

'Yes, ma'am.'

'Good. Well, we shall see. Bring him to the conservatory after he's had his breakfast and I'll give you your instructions then.'

POPPY BECAME HOPELESSLY lost during her attempt to find the conservatory. The house seemed as big and grand as a palace, and there were no clues to tell her which door led where. 'They should give you a blooming map,' she said, addressing the remark to Rupert as he trotted along at her side. His little fingers tightened around her thumb and he seemed to sense her agitation as his bottom lip started to tremble. She gave him an encouraging smile. 'Don't worry, kid. We'll pretend we're explorers looking for the source of the Nile. I learned about that chap Dr Livingstone in school. Let's see what we can find in here.' She opened a door but it was just a linen cupboard, and she closed it again. 'Come on, Master Pallister,' she said cheerfully. 'We ain't done for yet.'

She tried to make a game out of it by opening doors, peeping in and pretending there was something exciting on the other side, but after what seemed like hours she was beginning to feel quite desperate. She could imagine being lost forever in this maze of passages, some of which ended with a huge cupboard or another large room filled with heavy furniture. One of them was lined with book-shelves crowded with leather-bound tomes of every shape and size.

'Looks like they robbed the local library, Rupert,' Poppy said, closing the door hastily. By this time she realised that they were hopelessly lost. She was beginning to panic when she spotted a door at the far end of the long corridor. 'Come on, Rupie. This must be it. Home at last.' She flung it open, coming face to face with a man holding a shotgun. She screamed in terror. 'Oh my Gawd. It's the Germans come to get us. Run, Rupert!'

Chapter Three

THE CONSERVATORY WAS filled with potted palms and exotic plants the like of which Poppy had never seen, but this was not a nature lesson; it was an interrogation by a stern-faced Marina Carroll. Poppy stood in the middle of the black and white marble tiled floor with her fingers knotted together behind her back. Mrs Carroll was sitting in an ornate rattan chair and she was glaring at her as if she had just committed a capital offence. Any moment now Poppy was convinced that Mrs Carroll was going to point at her and shout 'Off with her head' just like the Queen in *Alice in Wonderland*. She glanced anxiously at Pamela in the hope of finding an ally, but she had Rupert on her knee and was half-heartedly trying to keep him amused by feeding him lumps of sugar from a silver bowl on the coffee tray. Guy was standing by the open French windows and was staring outside as if he wished he were anywhere but here. Poppy stared down at her feet listening in silence while the fair-haired young man who had brandished the gun in her face gave his account of what had occurred.

'And the best part of it was,' he said, chuckling, 'the poor little moppet thought I was a German.'

Guy turned away from the view with an amused smile. 'Well you are a bit of a Hun, Algy. Frightening little girls! What next?'

'At least I didn't run her down on horseback,' Algy said cheerfully. 'I'm not certain I want my little sister marrying a brute like you.'

'Then I'm glad that Amy doesn't share your poor opinion of me, old boy.'

'Come here, Poppy,' Marina said, beckoning to Poppy. 'You were supposed to be looking after Master Rupert. That wasn't a very good start, was it?'

Poppy stared at Mrs Carroll's slender finger with its talon-like nail varnished in blood red. The image it conjured up in Poppy's mind was that of the wicked queen in Walt Disney's *Snow White*. She felt a shiver run down her spine. 'I was lost, ma'am. You need a bloody map to find your way around this place.'

Marina's pencilled eyebrows rose in twin arcs of disapproval but Guy and Algy laughed out loud.

'Don't encourage her.' Marina quelled them with a single look before turning her steely gaze on Poppy. 'That's quite enough of that kind of language. You're not living in the slums now.'

'She's probably in shock, Mrs Carroll,' Algy said hastily. 'The poor little scrap got one hell of a fright when she blundered into the gunroom and saw me with the twelve-bore. I don't suppose they do much game shooting in the East End. No wonder she thought I was the enemy.'

'They'll be here soon enough if we don't do something about it, in spite of what Chamberlain tells us.'

'And we'll be ready for them,' Algy said eagerly. 'You'll wish you'd had a bit of practice with the shotgun then, Guy old thing.'

'I'll do what I have to, but in the meantime I don't see why all of you have to take it out on the innocent pheasant population.'

'There's no need to be so patronising, Guy,' Marina said sharply. 'We all know what you think about hunting and shooting and frankly I'd prefer not to hear it all again.'

'Yes, Guy. Do shut up. Just because you don't enjoy field sports doesn't mean that everyone else has to follow suit.' Pamela abandoned her attempts to entertain Rupert, who was patently bored with sitting on her lap and struggling to get onto the floor. She allowed him to slide off her lap and he ran straight to Poppy. Pamela brushed the creases from her skirt. 'The question is, Mummy, whether Poppy is responsible enough to look after Rupert while Nancy is sick. I'm not sure she can be trusted.'

Marina leaned forward, fixing Poppy with a stern gaze. 'What do you have to say for yourself, young lady?'

'I'll do me best, ma'am.'

'Then we'll give you another chance to do better. You may look after him for the rest of the day, but if anything should happen to him you'll be in very great trouble. Do you understand?'

Poppy nodded her head. 'Yes, ma'am.'

'And on Monday we'll see about enrolling you in the village school. If you're a good girl and behave properly, I'm sure we'll get along splendidly. But if you are a bad girl and misbehave, I want you to know that I can be very severe indeed.'

'For God's sake, Mother,' Guy said angrily. 'This is a thirteen-year-old child you're talking to, not one of your stable lads.'

'The principle's the same, Guy.'

He shrugged his shoulders. 'Have it your way, Mother. Anyway, I promised to pick Amy up at the station, so I'd better be off. I won't be in for lunch. See you later, Algy.' He strolled into the garden.

Poppy watched him go with a panicky feeling in the pit of her stomach. It felt as though her one ally in the house were deserting her. She waited nervously, wondering if she was free to leave or if she should wait until she was dismissed. It was just like being back in school, she thought, eyeing Mrs Carroll warily, but she need not have worried, as Algy had obviously become bored with domestic trivialities. He cleared his throat, turning to Marina with a beguiling smile. 'We're wasting time, Mrs Carroll. What say we leave the scrap to look after young Rupert and get going right away, or we'll miss the best of the day's shoot.'

Marina rose to her feet. 'You're right, Algy. Pamela, tell the girl what to do. We'll wait for you in the car.'

POPPY SPENT THE rest of the day keeping Rupert amused. She fastened him into his leather leading reins and took him for a walk in the grounds, taking care not to let him go too near the lake when they fed stale bread to the ducks. She managed to finish her letter to her mother while he took his afternoon nap, and she tucked it carefully into an envelope she had found in the desk. It had a bit of scribble on the back, but she did not think that their postman, Ted Johnson, would mind. He had been doing their round for as long as she could remember, riding his red bicycle no matter what the weather, and he lived next door. He kept pigeons in his back yard and she knew that Grandad shared his passion, although he pretended that the birds were a bit of a nuisance when they ate his pea crop. Gran said they were nasty feathered things and spread disease, and so Grandad had to make do with second-hand pigeon fancying. Poppy wondered if she ought to write a note to Mr Johnson on the back of the envelope, but then she decided that he might think it a bit cheeky and the men in the sorting office would think he had a girlfriend in the country. Mrs Johnson would not be amused. She was a force to be reckoned with, so Mum said. Poppy licked the sticky bit on the flap and pressed it down with her fist. She wondered if she dared ask Mrs Pallister for a postage stamp, and then she decided that Guy would be a safer bet.

She settled down to read a copy of *Treasure Island* that she had found in a cupboard. She had read it before but she loved the tale of the high seas and adventure and she was just getting into the story when Rupert woke up. She put the book aside and went into the night nursery to lift him from his cot. She gave him a cuddle and took him into the bathroom to change his nappy. After that there was nothing to do other than to wait for Violet to bring them their tea, which she delivered with a few personal and rather spiteful remarks. She stomped off when Poppy refused to retaliate and they were left alone until Pamela came to the nursery to kiss her son goodnight.

'He seems well enough,' she said, patting Rupert's head as if her were a puppy rather than a twenty-month-old toddler. 'Did he eat his meals, Poppy?'

'Yes, ma'am.'

'Did you bath him properly and wash behind his ears?'

'Yes, ma'am.'

'Good. If Nancy is still unwell, you may look after Master Rupert tomorrow, which of course is Sunday. We all attend church in the morning, except Rupert, who is too young, and so you will have to keep him amused until midday. You must bring him down to the dining room in time for luncheon, and I want you to make certain that he's wearing his best clothes, as his father should have arrived from London by then.'

Poppy blinked and said nothing; she had lost all idea of time and had not even realised today was Saturday. Mum would have gone down the road to the shops to get food in for Sunday dinner, or luncheon or whatever it was called; she was becoming confused. And Joe would be home from work and getting washed and smartened up ready to take Mabel out to the pictures.

'Have you listened to a word I said, Poppy?' Pamela's voice was as scratchy as an old needle on a gramophone record.

'Yes, ma'am.'

With an exasperated sigh, Pamela glanced at her watch. 'Heavens, I'll never get changed in time for dinner at this rate. Good night, Rupert darling.' She blew him a kiss and as she hurried from the room Poppy heard her murmur. 'I think that girl is a bit simple.'

NEXT MORNING, POPPY took Rupert to the lake where they fed the ducks with scraps of bread saved from their breakfast. The early September sun turned the surface of the water into molten gold, and across the sweep of green parkland the gently rolling hills were blue with morning mist. Poppy sat on the daisy-studded grass while Rupert chased butterflies. He was at a safe distance from the water's edge and she allowed her attention to wander, attracted by the purring sound of the big black car which had collected her from the station yard. It was a Bentley, unless she was very much mistaken. Joe had a passion for cars and the walls in his room were covered with pictures cut from glossy magazines. It was his ambition in life to own a car but unless he won the football pools it was very unlikely. The Bentley glided along the tree-lined avenue, stopping outside the lodge. The chauffeur climbed out and opened the tall wrought-iron gates.

Losing interest in the family's progress towards the village church, Poppy lay back on the grass looking up at the sky through the branches of a horse chestnut tree.

Out here in the open, the sky looked bigger and bluer than it did when viewed through the tightly packed terraces in London. There seemed to be more of everything here in the sweet-smelling country air. The grass grew thicker and greener here than it did in West Ham Park. Dandelions and daises were allowed to riot in profusion instead of being viciously beheaded by the park keeper's mower. She had picked little posies of the flowers to take up to the nursery when they went indoors, but sadly they were already wilting in the warmth of the sun.

She sat up, calling to Rupert, who had strayed a little too near the water for safety. He toddled back towards her clutching a dandelion in his chubby hand and beaming as though he had just struck gold. She took it from him and gave him a hug. 'Is that for me?'

He nodded his head but his attention was distracted by the sound of a car engine. Poppy turned her head to see a smart yellow and black open-top roadster roaring up the drive. She leapt to her feet as she recognised Guy at the wheel and she waved frantically, trying to attract his attention, but then she saw that he was not alone. His companion was a pretty young lady with a halo of golden curls. Poppy's hand dropped to her side as the car shot past them. Neither of its occupants had noticed her and the wheels spun on the gravel as Guy turned in the direction of the stable block.

'I might as well be blooming invisible,' Poppy said, catching hold of Rupert and fastening him into his reins despite his loud protests. 'Let's go for a walk before dinner and maybe you'll sleep all afternoon.'

After a complete circuit of the lake, Poppy's stomach was rumbling and Rupert was a dead weight on her back. His little legs had given out before they were halfway round the large expanse of water, and she had had to give him a piggyback. His arms were too short to reach round her neck and he had not quite mastered the art of hanging on. He had fallen asleep before they reached the house and Poppy's muscles were beginning to ache. The sound of the Bentley's engine confirmed her suspicions that it was getting late, and another car was following close behind. She had a nasty feeling that this must be Rupert's father, the man who expected to see his son spruced up in his Sunday best, not covered in grass stains with muddy knees and jam on his face. She broke into a run, heading for the servants' entrance.

She had just managed to get Rupert washed and dressed when the nursery door opened and Violet erupted into the room. 'They want Master Rupert in the drawing room double-quick.'

'Show us the way,' Poppy said boldly. 'There'll be trouble if I get lost again.'

'For Gawd's sake, Popeye. Haven't you heard the news? We've declared war on the Germans. They're all at sixes and sevens below stairs, and there's Sunday lunch to serve. I haven't got time to pander to the likes of you.'

Poppy stood her ground. At this moment she was more scared of Mrs Carroll than she was of Violet. 'I don't care about all that. Please, you must show me the way.'

'Oh, all right then. Get a move on.' Violet grabbed her by the sleeve and pulled her roughly towards the door.

'Let me go.' Poppy wrenched her arm free. 'What's the matter with you? Why are you being like this? I haven't done anything to you.'

'I don't like you,' Violet said, pinching her arm. 'You're a dirty city kid from the slums, that's what they're all saying. I bet you got lice in your hair and fleas too.'

Rupert had begun to snivel and Poppy picked him up, giving him a cuddle. 'Shut up, Violet. You're frightening him.'

'You think you're something special because Miss Pamela lets you look after Master Rupert, but you're not. She'd let the cat take care of him if she could get away with it. You're just convenient, that's what you are.' Violet turned on her heel and stalked out of the room with Poppy hurrying after her.

'Don't go so fast, Violet. Rupert's heavy and I can't keep up.'

'See if I care. It's you who'll get into trouble, not me.' Quickening her pace, Violet ran down the first flight of stairs, pausing on the landing to glance up at Poppy and cock a snook at her.

Incensed, and worried that she might lose her way for a second time, Poppy hurried after her. She was unfamiliar with the main staircase, having grown accustomed to using the back stairs, and Violet obviously knew this. She wanted her to be late, Poppy was certain of that, and she was equally determined to arrive in the drawing room on time. She hefted Rupert over her shoulder, ignoring his loud protests, but halfway down the stairs she slipped and fell against Violet, catching her off balance. With a loud scream, Violet missed a step, tottered on the next one, lost her footing and fell down the remaining stairs bumping off each tread. She landed on the polished parquet floor with a sickening thud and there was an eerie silence.

Poppy stopped, frozen to the spot, thinking that she had killed her, but with a sudden intake of breath Violet began to howl as if all the demons in hell were after her. A door flew open and Mr Carroll emerged followed by the rest of the family. Violet was suddenly the centre of attention.

'What is the meaning of this?' Edwin Carroll demanded angrily.

'She pushed me down the stairs.' Violet pointed a shaking finger at Poppy. 'She's a wild thing, sir. She attacked me.'

Poppy stared aghast at the sea of faces. Violet had lied and now she was going to take the blame. Mrs Carroll's expression of cold rage was far more frightening than anything Violet could do to her, and she knew that if she did not speak up she would get the blame for Violet's accident. Rupert was holding on to her for dear life and any moment now he was going to set up a wail equal to anything that Violet could produce. She hurried down the remaining stairs. 'I never did, sir. I tripped and almost fell down them bloody stairs meself.'

Pamela hurried forward to snatch her son from Poppy's arms. 'I won't have that sort of language used in front of Rupert.'

'Get up, Violet.' Mrs Carroll's voice was icicle sharp. 'Stop that noise at once and get back below stairs, and as for you, Poppy Brown, come into the drawing room. I want a word with you.'

Everyone filed back into the drawing room and Marina took her seat, folding her hands in her lap. 'What was the meaning of that disgraceful outburst? I won't tolerate that sort of behaviour in my house.'

'It weren't my fault, ma'am,' Poppy said with a defiant lift of her chin. 'I never pushed her.'

'So you say, but I only have your word for it. This really is the last straw, my girl. Tomorrow morning I'll contact the billeting officer and have you taken away. You're not fit to live in a civilised household.'

Poppy stood alone in the centre of the room holding her head proudly, filled with righteous indignation, and raging inwardly against the injustice of being blamed when it was not her fault. She wished her dad were here to sort these people out, or even Joe; he was big and strong and could shout much louder than Mrs Carroll. Gran could be fierce too; Mrs Carroll might think twice before taking her on, and Mum would stand up for her even though she didn't like arguments and fights.

Rupert was crying loudly and resisting all his mother's efforts to calm him.

'What were you thinking of, Pamela?' The man who Poppy thought must be Miss Pamela's husband was glaring at her as if she had just crawled out from under a stone. She knew she had it right when he turned away to frown at his wife. 'How could you entrust our son to the care of a street urchin?'

'That's not fair, Hector,' Guy said calmly. 'Give the poor kid a chance. She's done all right so far. I never did like that girl Violet, or her foxy-faced family come to that.'

Poppy could have rushed over and kissed him. She resisted the temptation but she would be eternally grateful to him, and he obviously shared her dislike of the Guppy family.

'Don't encourage her, Guy.'

Mrs Carroll sounded slightly calmer to Poppy's ears. It was obvious that she thought a lot of her son, but then that's what mums did in Poppy's opinion. Joe could get away with murder.

'Poppy, go to the nursery and stay there until the billeting officer comes for you tomorrow.' Mrs Carroll dismissed her with a wave of her hand. 'Pour me a large sherry, Edwin. My nerves are shredded.'

'Mother, this isn't fair,' Guy protested. 'Don't you think you should give Poppy a chance to explain?'

Marina shook her head. 'Such conduct is indefensible. Get out of my sight, Poppy.'

'Just a moment, Mrs Carroll.' A light, girlish voice coming from somewhere behind the tall figure of Hector Pallister caused everyone to turn their heads to look at the petite and pretty blonde whom Poppy had seen earlier in Guy's car.

'My mind is made up, Amy.'

'I understand your feelings, Mrs Carroll,' Amy said, moving swiftly to Poppy's side. 'But haven't we enough trouble with war being declared just this morning? Isn't this poor little girl one of the first victims, torn away from everyone she knows and loves and thrown in amongst total strangers?'

'Steady on, sis. You'll have us all in tears in a minute,' Algy said, grinning.

Guy nudged him in the ribs. 'Put a sock in it, Algy. Let Amy speak.'

Amy slipped her arm around Poppy's shoulders, giving her a comforting squeeze. Looking up at her, Poppy was lost in admiration. She was prettier than Joe's girlfriend, and even lovelier than Ginger Rogers who was Poppy's favourite film star at the moment, although not so long ago she had thought that Olivia de Havilland was quite beautiful.

'You all know that I've just come home from Switzerland,' Amy said in a voice that shook with emotion. 'I went into the sanatorium a year ago and I was alone, away from those I love. Mummy and Daddy were away in Singapore and Aunt Jane was too old and crippled with arthritis to cope with travelling all that way to visit me. I was scared stiff, just as this child must be now. I was amongst strangers and I hardly spoke any French and no German at all because I was a complete duffer at school.'

'That was quite different, Amy,' Marina said, raising her voice to make herself heard above the sympathetic murmurs. 'You were ill and you were there to be cured.'

Edwin frowned at her over the top of his spectacles. 'Let Amy finish, my dear.'

'Go on,' Guy said with an encouraging smile. 'You're doing splendidly, darling.'

Amy took a deep breath. 'I think all that Poppy needs is someone to spend a little time with her. I had to learn the rules and regulations in the sanatorium and it made things easier when I had grasped a little of their language. I think it's terribly unfair to take a child out of her own environment and expect her to fit in immediately.'

'Well said, Amy.' Guy took her hand and raised it to his lips.

Pamela bent down to snatch Rupert up in her arms as if he were in imminent danger. 'I don't trust her to look after Baby.'

'She's only a child herself,' Amy said angrily.

'She's a wildcat,' Pamela argued. 'If she's prepared to push Violet down the stairs who knows what she might do to my son?'

'Absolutely,' Hector said, ruffling Rupert's hair in an absent-minded way. 'Can't be too careful when there's a little one involved.'

'I think you're being very unfair,' Amy protested. 'I feel very sorry for Poppy.'

Marina reached for her glass and put it to her lips. 'So may I take it that you are offering to tame the wild beast?' She drained the glass and held it out to her husband. 'I'll have another, Edwin. I can feel one of my heads coming on.'

Obediently, as if he had been trained to obey the slightest command, he poured her another drink and placed it in her hand. He turned to Amy with a worried frown. 'My dear girl, are you willing to give up your time and spend it with one young evacuee when there are so many more important things to do now?'

'You are supposed to be resting, sweetheart,' Guy added gently.

'I haven't forgotten, but if Poppy is prepared to let me help her, I'll be glad to spend some time with her.'

'Do you hear that, Poppy?' Edwin said sternly. 'Will you be guided by Amy and do just as she tells you?'

'I'll do anything she says, sir. She looks like an angel.'

'She is an angel, kid,' Guy said, smiling. 'And if you play her up or tire her out you'll have me to answer to.'

The awkward silence that followed was broken by a squawk of protest from Rupert who began to wriggle violently in his mother's arms. 'I'm taking Rupert back to London with me,' Pamela said, setting him down on the carpet. 'I've changed my mind about leaving him here. I'd sooner risk the bombs, Mummy.'

'Quite right, my dear,' Hector said, eyeing his son, who was trying to climb up his pinstripe trouser leg. 'Perhaps someone should ring for Violet to take him back to the nursery. Has the boy been fed?'

'He's eating with us, darling. It's Sunday.' Pamela tucked her hand in the crook of Hector's arm. 'And Rupert hasn't seen his father for almost a fortnight.'

Olive poked her head round the door, peering in nervously as if she expected to find that the invasion had begun and the room was filled with German soldiers. 'Luncheon is served, ma'am.' She retreated hastily, closing the door behind her with a dull thud.

'You'd better return to the nursery, Poppy,' Marina said, rising from her chair. 'Violet will bring you your lunch on a tray.'

Poppy made a move to leave but Amy had her firmly by the hand. 'If you wouldn't mind too much, Mrs Carroll, I think it would be a nice gesture to allow Poppy to eat lunch with us today.'

Marina looked as if she was about to argue, but Guy forestalled her. 'It's not every day we declare war on Germany, Mother. I'm sure that the kitchen is in such an uproar that the poor child wouldn't get fed if she had to rely on Violet.'

'The damned Germans have a lot to answer for already,' Marina said bitterly. 'Come along, Edwin. The rest of you can do what you like.' She stalked out of the room followed by her husband.

The rest of the family filed out of the drawing room in a respectful crocodile, which reminded Poppy of the animals going into the ark two by two. She was considering this when Amy took her by the hand.

'Come along, Poppy. You shall sit next to me.'

'Thank you, miss.'

'You call me either Amy or Miss Fenton-Jones, but as I call you Poppy, which is a very pretty name by the way, I think it only fair you should call me Amy.'

POPPY FELT OPPRESSED by the Carrolls' formal dining room. The vast mahogany table seemed to stretch into eternity. The cutlery was confusing and she watched Amy carefully to see which spoon she used for the soup and which knife and fork was right for the fish course. By the time the roast lamb was served, accompanied by an astonishing array of vegetables, Poppy was feeling more at ease, although she had never seen anything as grand as the feast set before her. She memorised each small detail, from the cut crystal wine glasses which she was not allowed to use, and had to make do with a beaker of water, to the delicately patterned bone china dinner service, which must have cost an arm and a leg. She would write about it in her next letter to Mum and Gran.

After lunch Poppy would have been quite glad to slink away to the nursery but Amy insisted that they go for a walk as the doctors had stressed that she needed plenty of fresh air and exercise. Poppy plucked up courage to ask if they could post her letter and Amy not only agreed wholeheartedly but also persuaded Mr Carroll to donate a postage stamp. Amy and Guy walked hand in hand with Poppy following a discreet distance behind them, clutching the envelope in her hand. She could not hear what they were saying to each other but it was obvious that they were stepping out together in the same way as Joe and Mabel. By the time they reached the post box in the village Amy was breathless and had to sit down on the nearest wall.

'You've overdone things,' Guy said anxiously. 'We shouldn't have walked so far.'

'Nonsense, Guy. I'm perfectly well. It's just a little stitch.'

He took her slender wrist in his hand and consulted his watch. 'Your pulse is racing.'

'Oh, so you're a qualified doctor now, are you, Guy?'

'Not for another two years, but I can tell a racing pulse when I feel one.'

Poppy gazed up at him lost in admiration, but his attention was focused on Amy. She did look very pale and Poppy wondered if she was going to faint. 'My gran sniffs smelling salts when she has a funny turn.'

Amy smiled and squeezed her hand. 'Thank you, but I'm quite all right, really.'

'We'll get you home at once.' Without a by your leave, Guy swung her effortlessly into his arms, and despite Amy's protests he strode off down the lane with Poppy hurrying along at his side. It was like something out of a film, she thought, quickening her pace in order to keep up with him. He was Errol Flynn carrying Maid Marian into Sherwood Forest. Poppy stole a sideways glance at his determined profile. I wouldn't make a fuss like Amy, she thought enviously, but Amy looked far from happy.

'Put me down, please, Guy. I'm fine, honestly.'

'You're not fine and this is good for improving my biceps, which I need if I'm going to be selected for the hospital rowing eight. Keep up, Poppy. We don't want to have to come back to find you.'

Amy laced her fingers together behind Guy's neck. 'I didn't know you liked rowing, Guy. I've missed so much this last year, and you're a terrible correspondent.'

'And you may look as if a puff of wind would carry you away, Amy, but you're quite a weight, my girl.'

Poppy jogged along at his side, wishing that she was fair and lovely like Amy, instead of being sallow-skinned and dark-haired. She made a firm decision to include Amy in her prayers that night, along with Mum, Dad, Joe, Grandad, Gran and little Rupert. She was still burning with shame that the family thought she was unfit to look after him. She would miss his small body cuddling up to her in bed at night.

When they arrived back at the house Poppy was dismayed to see Miss Pamela standing by their car with Rupert clutched in her arms, while Jackson loaded luggage into the boot. Rupert chortled with delight when he spotted her and began to struggle but his mother gave him a sharp reprimand and he started to cry. Poppy longed to rush over and comfort him, but she did not dare.

Guy set Amy down at the bottom of the stone steps leading up to the main entrance. 'I'd better drive you home, Amy.'

She reached up and kissed him lightly on his cheek. 'Not yet, Guy. I'm going to see that Poppy is settled in the nursery, and I'll have a word with Cook to make sure she gets some tea or otherwise I'm afraid they're in such turmoil below stairs that they may forget all about her.'

'Tell Mrs Toon she'll have me to deal with if anyone takes it out on Poppy. I'll just go and say cheerio to Pam and Hector.' He strolled off in the direction of the Pallisters' car leaving Amy and Poppy to negotiate the steps.

Inside the entrance hall, Poppy stopped at the foot of the stairs. 'You shouldn't walk up all them stairs if you're tired, miss – I mean Amy. I know the way now, ta.'

'You're a sweet girl, Poppy. I am a bit tired but I wouldn't admit it to Guy. He worries about me.'

With one foot on the bottom tread, Poppy hesitated, turning to Amy. 'You won't forget about me, will you?'

'Don't worry about anything. I'm going to speak to Mrs Toon now, and tomorrow morning I'll be here bright and early to take you to school. You'll soon settle in, and you'll feel happier when you've got some friends of your own age.'

'Will Guy come too?'

'No, I'm afraid not. He's going to London tonight and he may not be back for quite a while.'

Chapter Four

THE HEADMISTRESS OF the village school greeted Amy and Poppy with an air of tired resignation. 'I don't know how we'll cope, Miss Fenton-Jones. We're terribly over-crowded, and with more evacuee children expected. I think we'll have to work out some sort of shift system for teaching.'

'Poppy's had a particularly difficult time, Miss Dobson. She needs friends of her own age.'

'Well, I'm not sure that's going to happen. You haven't seen the rest of my new pupils.' Miss Dobson eyed Poppy as if she were about to bite a chunk from her plump leg. 'I've never seen anything like it. Most of them are vermin-ridden and I doubt if half of them are literate, let alone toilet-trained. I just don't know how we'll cope.'

'I'm certain you'll manage splendidly, but I'd be most grateful if you could keep an eye on Poppy. If anything goes wrong this is my phone number at home. I don't want Mrs Carroll to be troubled unnecessarily.' Amy scribbled something on a page torn from her diary and handed it to Miss Dobson, who was immediately called away by a summons from an apparently desperate younger teacher.

Amy gave Poppy a hug. 'There are lots of children in the same situation as yourself, and I'm sure by the end of the day you'll have made new friends.'

Poppy nodded dumbly and swallowed hard. There was a subdued but menacing babble of noise emanating from the classroom and she was not convinced, but she managed a weak smile and opened the door. Something flew past her head and as it hit the wall she realised that it was a pellet of blotting paper soaked in ink. It exploded in a blue-black starburst and slid down the brown paint-work to land in a dark puddle on the bare floorboards. As she stepped into the room she found her way barred by a boy with an unpleasant expression on his foxy face. 'I know you,' he said in a whisper. 'You're the kid what pushed Violet downstairs. Could've killed her.'

Poppy backed away and found herself pinned to the ink-covered wall. 'It was an accident.'

'Sid Guppy, I won't tell you again. Sit down.' There was a note of resignation in the young teacher's voice.

'Better watch out for me at break-time, Popeye,' Sid hissed.

'I won't tell you again, Sid Guppy.'

'Yes, Miss Morris.' He slithered onto a seat, pulling a face at Poppy under cover of wiping his nose on his sleeve.

'What's your name?' Miss Morris pointed a ruler at Poppy. 'I've called the register and you don't seem to be on it.'

'Poppy Brown, miss.'

'Sit down and I'll take your details later. Now, children, Miss Dobson is going to divide you into groups according to age. Come to the front when your name is called.' She handed the register to the headmistress.

To her dismay, Poppy found herself sharing a desk with Sid Guppy. She tried to protest but she found herself ignored by the hard-pressed teachers as they marshalled their classes together and herded the younger children into another room. Making her way to her seat Poppy was met by grinning faces and subdued sniggers.

Vera Brice, who had been in Poppy's class at school, shot her a sympathetic glance. 'Look at your back,' she whispered. 'You've got ink all over your blouse.'

Poppy acknowledged this piece of information, biting her lip. Mrs Carroll would kill her when she got home. The blouse had belonged to Miss Pamela and probably cost a small fortune.

'Hurry up and sit down, Poppy. We'll begin with reading.'

Poppy put as much distance between herself and Sid as was possible. She knew that he was laughing at her, but she refused to look at him.

Miss Morris placed a pile of books on the front desks, and they were passed backwards in an orderly fashion by the girls and a disorderly one by the boys, who earned a sharp rebuke. The story was *Treasure Island* and Poppy sighed with relief. She was more than familiar with the adventures of Jim Hawkins and Squire Trelawney. Here she was on familiar ground and she began to relax. The reading began with the front row and some of the children stuttered and stumbled over the words, mumbling tonelessly. Some of the evacuees could read well but there were some, including Colin, who found it almost impossible. He had to be taken to the boys' toilets by one of the older girls when he suffered yet another little accident.

When it came to Poppy's turn, she stood up and began to read, but she was nervous and the words leapt about the page like a mass of squiggly tadpoles.

'Speak up, Poppy,' Miss Morris said sternly. 'We all want to hear the story, but we can't hear if you whisper.'

A snigger from Sid made Poppy even more determined to do her best. As she launched once again into the story she forgot that she was in a hostile environment. Ignoring the stares of the village children and the smirking face of Sid Guppy, she forgot that the room smelt of unwashed bodies and blackboard paint with overtones of dust and chalk. She became enthralled in the tale of pirates and buried treasure, and as she read the class quietened down and began to listen. Poppy was transported to another world and it was almost a shock when Miss Morris told her to stop.

'Thank you, Poppy. That was very good indeed. You may sit down.'

Poppy sat down but an excruciating pain made her leap from her seat with a yelp of pain. Sid sniggered and a ripple of laughter ran through the class. Poppy found a drawing pin embedded in her right buttock and she wrenched it out, gritting her teeth and blinking hard in an effort not to cry.

'Good heavens, girl. What's the matter?' Miss Morris hurried along the aisle between the desks. 'What's wrong?'

'I was stung, miss,' Poppy said, clutching the drawing pin in her fisted hand.

'It must have been a wasp. Children, you must be careful. Wasps get very sleepy at this time of year. Poppy, you'd better come into the kitchen and we'll find something to put on it.'

Poppy followed Miss Morris into the tiny kitchen.

'Now what is best?' Miss Morris said, opening a cupboard and peering inside. 'Vinegar or blue bag? It will have to be vinegar. Show me where it hurts.'

AMY WAS WAITING at the school gate when Poppy flew out of the building ahead of the rest of the children. She had managed to kick Sid Guppy on the shins before he got the first punch in at break, and although she had been severely reprimanded Miss Morris seemed to have a fair idea who had started the fight.

Amy greeted her with a sweet smile. 'How was your first day, Poppy?'

'I'm never going back there.' Crossing her fingers, Poppy hoped that Amy would not notice the ink-stain on the back of her blouse.

'Oh, surely it can't have been as bad as that?'

'It was worse! I'd rather be bombed in West Ham than go back in there.'

Amy stood aside as a stream of children poured out of the school and raced off in different directions shouting and screeching as if they had just escaped from the zoo.

'What happened to upset you so much?'

'I can't tell you.'

'We'll see about that. It's my guess you've been bullied and I won't stand for it.' Taking Poppy by the hand Amy marched her back into the school. 'Wait here by the coat racks. I'm going to sort this out once and for all.'

Poppy watched in amazement as sweet and gentle Amy turned into an avenging angel and stormed into the classroom, slamming the door behind her. Sid poked his head round the outer door and grinned at her. 'I'll get you tomorrow, Popeye. See if I don't.'

'Bugger off, Sid Guppy.'

His shocked face was reward enough for Poppy. He turned and fled as Amy and Miss Dobson strolled out of the classroom, smiling and obviously on good terms.

'I don't care what you say. I'm not coming back,' Poppy said before either of them had a chance to speak.

Amy took her by the hand. 'There's no need to worry, Poppy dear. Miss Dobson and I have had a chat about you and we both agree that you're in the wrong school. I'll take you home now and tomorrow we'll go and see the headmistress at the girls' grammar school in Fairford.'

Sid was leaning against the wall outside the playground with his hands stuffed into his pockets, whistling tunelessly as he kicked windfall crabapples through the school gate posts. Holding her head high, Poppy walked past without looking at him. She heard him mumble something under his breath, but a frown from Amy was enough to silence him and he ambled off towards the village.

Guy's roadster was parked in the lane at an eccentric angle. 'Hop in,' Amy said, peering into her large brown suede handbag. 'As soon as I've found the wretched car key we'll be on our way.'

The golden September sun had warmed the leather seat, and Poppy settled down, waiting patiently while Amy fumbled in the bottom of her handbag.

'Got it,' Amy said, climbing in beside her and stowing her bag on the floor by Poppy's feet. 'I should either get a smaller handbag or stop putting everything in it but the kitchen sink.' She slanted a mischievous smile at Poppy. 'Hold on. I can't promise to drive this thing as well as Guy, but I'll do my best.' She started the engine and after a few bunny hops they were speeding through the lanes, sending up clouds of dust and dry leaves. Poppy admired the way that Amy handled the car, but all the same she could not help wishing that it was Guy in the driving seat. She was immediately ashamed of herself for harbouring such mean thoughts when Amy had shown her nothing but kindness. Even so, she could not hold back the question that was tingling on the tip of her tongue. 'Has Guy come home?'

'No. He left the car so that I could have use of it while he was away in London.'

'But he will come home soon?'

Amy was silent for a moment as she concentrated on the road ahead. She changed gear in order to negotiate a steep bend, and once they were back on the straight she glanced at Poppy with a smile. 'If I tell you a secret, will you promise on your honour not to tell anyone else?'

'Cross me heart and hope to die.'

'Guy has gone up to London to enlist in the Royal Air Force. He doesn't want Mr and Mrs Carroll to find out until it's a fait accompli.'

'What's that?'

'Guy will tell his parents when it's too late for them to try to stop him. He's had some flying experience at university, and he's keen to join up.'

'Hell's bells and buckets of blood,' Poppy said with feeling.

A gurgle of laughter escaped Amy's lips. 'It's not considered polite for young girls to use that sort of language, Poppy. I don't give a tuppenny damn, and don't repeat that either, but I'm afraid others might find it offensive.'

'I'll button me lip in future.'

Amy crunched the gears as they reached the crossroads and the engine stalled. 'Bloody thing! One day I'll get the hang of driving this beast, but don't you dare tell Guy that I made a mess of driving his precious car.'

Poppy's heart swelled with pride. She shared a secret with Amy, and, for the first time since she had arrived in Dorset, she felt a sense of near belonging.

THE HEADMISTRESS AT Fairford Girls' Grammar School was reluctant to consider taking Poppy as a pupil unless she passed the common entrance examination. Most of the conversation during her initial interview passed over Poppy's head. She perched on her seat and whiled away the time looking round the oak-panelled study, which was lined with bookshelves and group photographs of past and present hockey teams. A glass-fronted cabinet was filled with silver cups, which was depressing as she was not very keen on sport. Amy's voice never rose above a pleasant murmur but she countered every excuse that the headmistress put before her as skilfully as any lawyer. The conversation turned to talk about fees and Poppy, only half listening, thought she heard Amy promise to be responsible for the financial obligations, but the interview was suddenly over and the headmistress was shaking Amy's hand. Poppy realised with something of a shock that she had been enrolled as a pupil at the posh girls' grammar school.

Without giving her a chance to protest, Amy whisked her off to the school outfitters in Fairford and Poppy was kitted out with a navy blue gymslip, three white blouses, two navy blue cardigans, and several sets of underwear including hideous navy blue knickers with a pocket for a hanky. Who in their right minds would want to tuck their hanky in their bloomers, Poppy thought in amazement? She was still puzzling over that when she tried on a school blazer and a black barathea overcoat. Amy told the shop assistant to pack everything and have it taken to the car, which impressed Poppy no end, but she could not help worrying. This must be costing Amy a fortune. Her worst fears were realised as she peered over Amy's shoulder as she was about to sign the bill.

'That's an awful lot of money.'

'What's the matter?' Amy hesitated with her pen poised above the invoice book.

'My mum and dad can't afford all this stuff. I don't think Dad earns that much in a week.'

Amy smiled. 'You mustn't worry about things like that. I can easily afford to treat you, and anyway this is wartime and we must all do our bit.' She wrote her signature with a flourish. 'Come along, Poppy. You need new shoes. You can't go to school in sandals with the toes cut out.'

'Mum does it with a razor blade,' Poppy said, hurrying after her as Amy made her way out of the store. 'It stops me toes from bending double inside the sandals and they do another season. Shoes cost money, a lot of it, and you've already spent a fortune on me.'

'As I said, that's not your problem, Poppy. I'm not letting you start school at a disadvantage.'

The next stop was the shoe shop, and by this time Poppy was past protesting. She sat in silence while her feet were measured and she was fitted with a pair of black lace-up shoes, plimsolls and hockey boots. She felt quite faint when the assistant handed the sales slip to Amy but, as in the other store, it appeared that Amy had something mysteriously called 'an account' and no money changed hands.

Poppy wished that Mum and Gran could see her now as she carried her parcels to the car. She promised herself that she would go to the nursery as soon as they arrived home. She would sit down to write a long reply to Mum's letter, which had arrived that morning. She had read it and wept, even though Mum's words had been encouraging and filled with the hope that they would be together again by Christmas. It was only a few months away, but that seemed like a lifetime to Poppy.

POPPY STARTED AT the prestigious girls' school on the following Monday. The girls in her class were neither friendly nor unfriendly. She was the first evacuee to attend the school and the girls treated her with a certain amount of reticence, but at least no one attempted to bully her. She actually preferred to be left alone as she struggled to learn the rules and regulations. She threw herself into her studies with an enthusiasm that brought plaudits from her teachers, and her days drifted into a set routine.

Breakfast in the nursery was delivered by a silently resentful Violet. Poppy left the house alone and unnoticed as she began the long walk to the main road where she caught the bus to Fairford. She returned in the afternoon on the four o'clock bus, and after tea, also eaten in solitary state, she set about her homework, after which she was free to read or write long letters home.

Her residence in the house was barely acknowledged by Mr and Mrs Carroll, unless they happened to pass her on the stairs. Edwin always enquired solicitously about her schoolwork, and Marina spoke politely but always looked faintly surprised to see her, as if she had forgotten that Poppy was living in the same house. If it had not been for Amy's faithful visits on Saturday afternoons,

Poppy would have lived a monastic existence, suspended between the two worlds of upstairs and below stairs, and belonging to neither. Amy always came armed with a new letter from Guy which she read to Poppy as they ate lunch in the Cosy Corner Café in Fairford or took afternoon tea in Nan's Pantry on the other side of the High Street. When she came to some passages, Amy would blush rosily and skip the next few lines, leaving Poppy in no doubt that these must be very personal and filled with love and kisses and all that stuff. If Amy had not been her friend, she would have been deeply jealous.

With Christmas not far off, Amy decided that Poppy should have some pocket money, something unheard of in the Brown family. Poppy had tried to refuse but Amy gave her a shilling every Saturday afternoon, telling her that it was hers to save or spend as she pleased. Poppy hoarded it faithfully, hiding the coins in the toe of an old sock under her mattress in the night nursery.

September quickly faded away into October. The days became shorter and the leaves were whipped off the trees by the boisterous south-westerly gales. The hedgerows grew bright with scarlet berries, and the newly ploughed fields stretched as far as Poppy's eyes could see in a rolling patchwork of ribbed umber earth, tipped with white chalk where the subsoil pushed to the surface. The undulating countryside looked so peaceful from the bus as Poppy travelled to and from school that it was almost impossible to imagine that the country was at war. Mum's letters were filled with hope that they might be together again very soon as the expected bombing of London had not occurred, and everyone said that the war would soon be over.

By the end of the first week in December Poppy had saved up the magnificent sum of twelve shillings, which she intended to spend on Christmas presents. She could barely control her excitement as she set off with Amy on their customary Saturday outing to Fairford. Amy left her in Woolworth's while she visited the hairdressers in South Street, and Poppy spent a happy hour browsing amongst the counters heaped with exciting things. It was the first time she had ever had money to spend as she pleased, and she walked up and down the aisles, her feet echoing on the bare wooden boards, carefully working out how far her money would go. After much deliberation, she bought a white lace-trimmed hanky for Gran and a brooch in the shape of a flower for Mum; a woollen scarf each for Dad and Grandad and a pair of gloves for Joe. She selected a string of pearl beads for Mabel and a book of nursery rhymes for Rupert. Mr and Mrs Carroll obviously lacked for nothing, and she decided on a colour photograph of Durdle Door with a calendar suspended from it by two pieces of pink tape. For Amy she chose a blue chiffon headscarf, and for Guy she purchased a St Christopher medallion which claimed on the label to be *genuine nine carat gold-plated*. It took her last penny to buy it, but Poppy was so proud of her purchase that she ran all the way to the hairdressers and burst into the cubicle where Amy sat beneath the hairdryer reading a copy of *Modern Woman*.

Poppy dangled the St Christopher in front of her eyes. 'Look what I got for Guy. D'you think he'll like it?'

'It's beautiful.' Amy raised her voice to make herself heard over the din of the hairdryer. 'He'll be absolutely thrilled with it.'

'I've got heaps more to show you, but not yours, of course.'

'Excuse me, miss.' The hairdresser pulled back the curtain. 'If you'd like to wait outside, I'm just about to brush out Modom's hair.'

Amy smiled at Poppy's reflection in the mirror. 'I'll meet you in Nan's Pantry.'

Feeling very grand and grown-up, Poppy made her way to the tearoom and was delighted to be recognised by the waitress who showed her to their usual table in the window. She ordered tea for two and pastries, and she sat looking out into the drizzly gloom of a December afternoon, surrounded by her packages. As she waited for Amy, she felt happier than she had for months. Christmas was just three weeks away and Mum had written to say that she hoped they would all be together by then as the threat of air raids seemed to have passed. She waved as she spotted Amy making her way towards the tearoom. She entered on a gust of cold air and threaded her way between the packed tables to join Poppy just as the waitress brought their order.

'You can be mother,' Amy said, taking off her mink jacket and tossing it onto an empty chair.

Poppy poured the tea but she was shocked by Amy's casual treatment of what must have been a very expensive garment. However hard she tried, she could not get used to the way that rich people seemed to take their expensive things for granted. She recalled how Mum always put her clothes on hangers as soon as she took them off, even if the dress or the cardigan was patched and darned. The thought of seeing Mum and everyone brought a smile to her lips as she passed Amy a cup of tea. 'I can't wait to show you what I bought for my family. If what Mum said in her letter is true, I'll be able to give them their presents in person.'

'I know I'm being selfish, Poppy,' Amy said, as she sipped her tea, 'but I'll miss you terribly when you go home. Living with my Aunt Jane is terribly dull. She's a dear, of course, but if it hadn't been for my silly old illness I'd have gone to Singapore with my parents.'

'I'll miss you too, Amy. You're my best friend in the whole world.'

'I'm very flattered, but surely you must have some friends at school by now?' Amy's blue eyes darkened with concern.

'Not really.' Poppy eyed the plate of fondant fancies. 'May I have another one?'

'Of course you may. You don't have to ask.'

'I do. You said I must always ask before I take anything.'

'That's in polite society. You can do more or less what you like when you're out with me. I haven't forgotten what it's like to be your age.'

'How old are you, Amy?'

'I'll be twenty-one in February and Guy will be twenty-two in December.' Amy's eyes softened as she mentioned Guy's name, and a tender smile curved her lips. 'Shall I tell you another secret, Poppy?'

Poppy leaned forward, the cakes forgotten. 'Oh please.'

'Guy writes that he's almost finished his initial pilot training and he's expecting to be posted soon. We don't know where, and I doubt that he'll be able to tell us, but he hopes to get some leave before Christmas. And then . . .' Amy broke off, blushing prettily.

'And then?' Poppy held her breath.

'You're not to breathe a word of this, Poppy. But we're going announce our engagement on Guy's first home leave.'

'Oh!' The shock of Amy's words hit Poppy like a blow to the heart.

'Aren't you pleased for us?'

'Of course I am. It's a surprise, that's all.'

'I knew you would be happy for us, and I want you to be one of my bridesmaids.' Amy paused, eyeing Poppy anxiously. 'What's the matter? Don't you want another cake?'

Poppy forced a smile. 'No, I'm quite full after all.' She swallowed a mouthful of tea and her eyes watered as the hot liquid burnt her mouth.

'And when we have a home of our own, you must come and stay with us. We'll keep a bedroom especially for you and you may choose the wallpaper and curtain material too.' Amy hesitated and leaned towards Poppy. 'Are you sure you're feeling all right? You've gone quite pale. Perhaps we should get you outside into the fresh air.'

BACK IN THE nursery, Poppy wrapped her gifts in brown paper tied with scraps of red knitting wool that she unravelled from an old cardigan. She was just packing them all away in the chest of drawers when Violet burst into the room. She put the supper tray down on the table with a loud thud. 'Mrs Carroll wants to see you in the drawing room, Popeye. Better go double-quick; I expect you're in for it. What've you done this time?'

Refusing to retaliate, Poppy closed the drawer and hurried from the room. She raced downstairs and arrived outside the drawing room breathless and expecting the worst. It must be something serious if Mrs Carroll sent for her, but try as she might she could not think what she had done wrong. It was cold and draughty in the hallway despite the central heating, and Poppy was shivering as she raised her hand to knock on the door.

'Enter.' Marina's voice did not sound welcoming.

The warmth in the drawing room almost took Poppy's breath away. Marina was seated in her usual chair by a roaring log fire with her feet resting on a footstool. The curtains were drawn, shutting out the bleak chill of the December evening, and the room was bathed in lamplight.

'Don't stand in the doorway,' Marina said sharply. 'Come over here where I can see you.'

Her tone and the tight-lipped expression on her well-moulded features did nothing to inspire Poppy with confidence. Her palms were moist as she moved closer.

'You wanted to see me, Mrs Carroll?'

Marina drained the last of her drink, and set the glass down on a side table. Unsmiling, she met Poppy's anxious gaze. 'I received a telephone call from your mother today.'

'Is something wrong?' Her lips were so dry that Poppy could hardly frame the words.

'Yes and no.' Marina hesitated, as if unsure how to break what must be terrible news. Poppy had visions of their home having been flattened by a bomb or one of her family having fallen ill with an incurable disease. She felt sick and faint all at the same time. 'For heaven's sake sit down, silly girl. There's no need to look so terrified. The good news is that your mother will be arriving by coach tomorrow with other parents who have come to take their children back to London with them.'

'Mum is coming here?' Poppy could hardly believe her ears. Her hands flew to her face as she uttered a gasp of delight. 'I'm going home for Christmas?'

Marina shook her head. 'No. I'm afraid not, but I'll leave it to your mother to explain why.'

Chapter Five

THE COACH WAS late. Poppy stood like a statue amidst
the group of evacuee children who were stamping their
feet and flapping their arms in an attempt to keep warm.
Small powdery flakes of snow swirled around them and
their shouts of excited laughter echoed off the buildings
in the village square.

'It's wizard, isn't it?'

Poppy turned slowly to look at Vera, who was standing beside her. 'What is?'

'Us going home, of course. My mum will be on one of
them buses and I can't wait to see her again. I ain't never
coming back to this place, I'll tell you that for nothing.'

'So you're going home then,' Poppy said dully. She
had not yet recovered from the shock of being told that
Mum was coming to Squire's Knapp for a brief visit
only, and that she was planning to return home without her. The decision had been taken without asking her

opinion. It had not made sense then and it did not make sense now.

'Are you stupid or something?' Vera muttered, frowning. 'They ain't coming down on a day trip with kiss-me-quick hats on their bonces.'

A cheer went up as a coach nosed its way into the square and Vera surged forward with the rest of the children. Poppy remained standing at the back of the crowd, craning her neck as the occupants clambered stiffly down the steps. Despite the bitter cold there was a carnival atmosphere in the square as children were reunited with their parents. Poppy was becoming anxious when the last passenger alighted with no sign of her mother, but then a second coach drew up. The driver climbed down onto the pavement. 'You've got two hours, ladies and gents. Then we've got to set off back to London. Don't be late or you'll get left behind and have to thumb your way back to town.' He strolled off to speak to the other driver, leaving the passengers to alight and seek out their offspring.

For a horrible moment, Poppy thought that her mother was not amongst the second wave of eager parents, but then she recognised the top of Mum's grey felt hat, the one she wore for best, which was skewered in place by a mother of pearl hatpin. When she was little, Poppy had thought that the vicious-looking pin went straight through Mum's head, and she had expected to see the tip covered in blood. It was a long time before she realised that the pin only went through her tightly curled hair. 'Mum,' she cried, raising her voice to a shout in order to make herself heard above the babble of voices.

'Over here.' Standing on tiptoe, she waved frantically until her mother spotted her. Poppy forgot about manners and pushed and shoved with the rest of the eager children and parents as they surged towards each other.

'Poppy, love. I hardly recognised you!' Mary held her daughter at arms' length before enveloping her in a warm hug. 'You look so smart and grown-up.'

'I'm just the same, Mum.' Poppy kissed her mother's soft cheek, inhaling the familiar scent of Californian Poppy and Lifebuoy soap tinged with the camphor smell of mothballs. She could not help comparing her mother's old and slightly threadbare woollen coat which had seen at least ten winters with her own outfit. The well-cut camel three-quarter-length jacket, grey flannel skirt and coral-pink jumper might have belonged to Miss Pamela when she was much younger, but they were the sort of classic style that stayed in fashion for years. Poppy felt suddenly ashamed for taking pride in her appearance, particularly when she glanced down at Mum's shoes, which were well polished but sensible rather than smart, and slightly down at heel, whereas Poppy was wearing a pair of fur-lined suede ankle boots that Amy had bought for her on one of the shopping sprees in Fairford.

'You look ever so posh,' Mary said, gazing at Poppy with a delighted smile. 'Quite a young lady, in fact.'

Poppy shook her head. 'It's only the clothes that make me look different.'

'Of course you are, and I'll swear you've grown an inch at least. Are they treating you well? Are you happy here, love?'

'I'm feeling much better for seeing you, Mum.' Poppy linked her hand through her mother's arm. 'Let's get back to Squire's Knapp. Jackson is waiting with the car, and Mrs Carroll has arranged for us to have some lunch. You must be starving after that long bus ride.'

'Oh, Poppy, love, I'm not dressed to have dinner in a posh house.'

'Not dinner, Mum,' Poppy said, chuckling. 'Dinner's what the family have at night. Lunch is what they eat midday.'

'I know that, but it's not what we say at home.' Mary shot her a sideways glance as they made their way towards the Bentley which was parked on the far side of the square. 'If you carry on like this I expect we'll have to pay to speak to you soon.'

Stung by the inference that she was showing off, Poppy felt the blood rush to her cheeks. 'I didn't mean it that way, Mum. It's just that they do things different at Squire's Knapp. I'm still learning and I make mistakes all the time. Anyway, there's Jackson with the car. We're riding in style to the big house.'

'So I see.' Mary folded her lips in a thin line as Jackson stepped out of the limousine and opened the door for them. 'Very nice I'm sure.' She climbed inside and sat on the edge of the seat, clutching her handbag. 'Do you always travel like this?'

'No. Hardly ever. Usually I go with Amy in Guy's roadster. She's lovely, Mum, and such a kind person. She's done everything for me.'

'So I believe.' Mary stared straight ahead as the car purred forward and Jackson drove carefully through the narrow streets, which were thronged with reunited parents and children.

Poppy stared down at her gloved hands, knotted tightly in her lap. 'Mrs Carroll said I wasn't to come home with you, Mum. It's not true, is it? You wouldn't leave me here and go home without me?'

Mary seemed to shrink in size as she slumped back against the leather squabs. She eyed Jackson warily through the glass that separated the chauffeur from his passengers. 'Can he hear me?'

Poppy shook her head. 'Not unless you speak to him through the tube thing. Mum, what's going on? You've got to tell me.'

'Your dad and me had a letter from that lady what's taken you under her wing; Miss Amy something double-barrelled.'

'Amy wrote to you?'

'She said she'd heard on the news that some parents were taking their nippers back to London and she asked ever so nicely if you could stay on in Dorset. She said you were getting on well in that posh school, and that she'd be only too happy to keep an eye on you. She said she'd talked it over with Mrs Carroll and they were both in agreement.'

'But I want to come home, Mum. I miss you all and I don't belong here.'

'Aren't you happy here, ducks?'

'That's not the point, Mum. If there isn't going to be any bombing, I don't see why I can't come home with you.'

Mary reached out to hold Poppy's hand. 'You're a bright girl, Poppy. You were meant for better things than going into service like I did. I want you to make the most of yourself and not end up a dreary housewife scrimping and wearing yourself out bringing up a family on a working man's wage.'

'I don't understand.'

'You don't now, but you will in the fullness of time.' Mary lifted Poppy's gloved hand to the light. 'That's real glacé kid unless I'm very much mistaken. I haven't seen anything so fine since I worked at the manor house in Epping.'

'I don't care about the blooming gloves. All I want is to go home with you. Why won't you tell me what's going on?'

'Poppy, love. You'll be fourteen in April, old enough to leave school. If you come home you'll end up in a munitions factory or doing some kind of war work that they're all talking about. Your dad thinks that this is only a lull in the offensive and that if Jerry starts bombing London we'll be in line for everything he can drop on us, being so close to the docks. We only want what's best for you. Stay here and you'll get a good education and be safe. Come home and who knows what might happen?'

'But I belong with you, Mum.'

'Of course you do, and we'll be waiting for you when the war's over. They say it can't go on for long.'

'Mrs Carroll doesn't like me, and I know she thinks I'm a nuisance. The only person who's been kind to me is Amy, and of course Guy.'

'And it was Miss Amy who begged us not to take you home, not yet anyway. She sounds a really lovely lady, and you should be grateful to her and her young man. She said that he thought it was a good idea for you to stay.'

Poppy was temporarily lost for words. If Guy wanted her to remain in Squire's Knapp she could hardly refuse, even if it meant putting up with snide remarks from the likes of Violet, Nancy and Olive. 'You're sure the war won't last long then, Mum?'

Mary leaned forward, peering out of the window. 'Oh my Gawd, it's a bleeding palace.'

They had just passed through the tall wrought iron gates leading to the arrow-straight drive lined by copper beeches. Their bare branches were iced with snow and the whole of the parkland glittered like a Christmas card.

'I can't believe it,' Mary whispered. 'I thought the manor was grand, but this is like one of them stately homes you see at the cinema on Pathé News, in between the feature film and the adverts.'

At any other time Poppy would have been amused by her mother's astonished expression, but her feelings were too raw to find anything amusing. 'It's just a house, Mum.'

'And bigger than anything I've ever seen before. Just wait until your gran hears about this. She wanted you to come home today, but I know she'd change her tune if she could see this place.'

For once Poppy did not care what Gran or anyone else thought about her temporary home. 'Mrs Carroll won't want me hanging around, Mum.'

'Nonsense,' Mary said, craning her neck to get a better view of the imposing façade and with a wide flight of steps leading up to the main entrance. 'When I spoke to her on the phone she was very polite and she left the final decision up to me and your dad. This is a chance of a lifetime, Poppy. With a good education you could get a job in a bank or an office up West.'

The Bentley slid to a halt and Poppy waited for Jackson to open the door with a feeling of doom. She could tell by the rapt expression on her mother's face that she was carried away with the notion that her daughter was going up in the world, and everyone knew that when Mum got an idea in her head there was nothing anyone could do about it.

She scrambled out of the car, remembering to thank Jackson as he stood stiffly to attention holding the door for Mary, who slid off the seat displaying an embarrassing amount of stocking with a ladder running from the top of her shoe well past her left knee.

'Thank you,' she said, bestowing a beaming smile on Jackson. 'Nice place you got here.'

'Yes, ma'am.' He accepted the compliment with a nod.

'Come on, Mum.' Grabbing her mother by the hand, Poppy led her up the steps and into the house.

'Don't they lock their doors round here?' Mary looked round the entrance hall wide-eyed and obviously impressed. 'And shouldn't we have used the servants' entrance round the back?'

'No, Mum. I'm allowed to come in this way now, and I can use the main stairs. Mrs Carroll said so.'

'Well, I never did.' Picking her way delicately as if walking on thin ice, Mary followed Poppy across the gleaming expanse of the polished parquet floor and up the staircase. She stopped halfway to the first floor, and glancing over her shoulder Poppy was amazed to see her mother take a clean hanky out of her pocket to wipe a real or imagined mark off the banister rail.

'Mum, what are you doing?'

'Sticky fingers,' Mary said tersely. 'I'd have a word with the charlady if I was Mrs Carroll.'

'Come on up to the nursery,' Poppy said, hoping that none of the servants had witnessed her mother's action. 'There isn't much time if you've only got an hour and a half before the bus goes.'

'And I'm supposed to see your Mrs Carroll at one o'clock. It was good of her to make the time to speak to me. I'm sure she's ever so busy running a big house like this.'

In the day nursery a fire had been lit and the room was unusually warm and cosy. On a normal day Poppy would have had to put on an extra jumper and wrap her eiderdown round her knees when she wanted to sit and study. This was the first time she had been treated to such a luxury. Obviously someone was out to impress, she thought wryly, and, judging by the expression on Mum's face, it had worked. A clean white cloth covered the table and a spread of cold boiled ham and pickles with bread rolls and a dish heaped with pats of butter had been laid out in readiness, as well as a whole apple pie accompanied by a jug of cream. Poppy was not certain if it was Mrs Toon or the mistress who had authorised such an extravagance, but Mum was smiling delightedly as she struggled out of her coat. 'I wish your dad could see this, Poppy. He'd tuck in and no mistake. As for Joe, he could finish off that pie in one sitting.'

Poppy took the coat from her and hung it on the row of pegs behind the door. 'Sit down, Mum. Let's eat before we have to face Mrs Carroll.' She pulled out a chair for her mother.

Mary sat down, smiling appreciatively. 'Ta, ducks. You've developed lovely manners since you come here. You're halfway to being a lady already.'

But I'm not, Poppy thought miserably, as she took her seat. I'm still me; I haven't changed. Why can't you see that, Mum? I don't want to go to that posh girls' school where most of them look down on me because I don't speak like them. I want to go back to being plain Poppy Brown from West Ham. 'Bloody war,' she muttered beneath her breath.

'Did you say something, ducks?' Mary paused with a forkful of meat halfway to her mouth. 'This is a lovely bit of ham. I don't know when I last tasted anything like it.'

The meal dragged on but Poppy had lost her appetite.

When they finally went downstairs she was surprised to find Amy waiting for them outside the drawing room. She extended her hand to Mary with a beaming smile. 'Mrs Brown, how nice to meet you at last.'

'Pleased to meet you, I'm sure, miss.'

Poppy stared at her mother in surprise. She did not recognise this subdued version of the woman who could take on all of Mr Hitler's army single-handed.

'Poppy has done so well at school, Mrs Brown,' Amy said enthusiastically. 'She's a real credit to you and your husband.'

'I know that, miss.'

'Anyway, here am I chattering on and you have so little time. What must you think of me? I'm sure Mrs Carroll would like to see you before you go.' She opened the door and ushered Mary into the room.

Poppy was about to follow but her mother shook her head. 'No, ducks. Wait outside for me. I want to speak to Madam in private.'

ALTHOUGH IT WAS only just after three in the afternoon, the snow clouds had brought about an early dusk and the wind whipped snowflakes into tiny shards of ice as it slapped their faces. Amy had insisted on driving Mary and Poppy to the village square and they huddled together with their backs to the wind while they waited for the drivers to unlock the coaches and allow the waiting families to board.

'Let me come with you, Mum,' Poppy whispered. 'I'm not afraid of the bombs. I want to see Dad and Joe and Gran. Please take me home.'

There was a sudden rush and scuffling as the coach doors flew open and adults and children jostled to clamber up the narrow steps. Mary stumbled as a man barged her without any apology but she regained her balance and took Poppy's face between her hands.

'It's not sensible, love. Miss Amy will look after you and you'll be ten times better off and a hundred times safer down here in the country.'

Poppy clung to her mother's arm. 'But if they don't start bombing London will you let me come home after Christmas?'

'As soon as it's safe you shall come home with bells on.' Mary gave a wintry smile and, with an obvious effort, turned away to take her place in the queue.

It was only then that Poppy remembered the brown carrier bag in her hand. She plucked at her mother's sleeve. 'I've got your Christmas presents here. There's one for each of you. I chose them all myself.'

Mary looked at her in amazement. 'Well, I'm blowed! I don't know what to say, Poppy.'

'Don't open them till Christmas Day.'

'We won't, I promise.' Mary took the bag as if it were the most precious thing she had ever been given and her eyes brimmed with tears. 'There now, look at me getting all sentimental and slushy. But I got nothing for you, Poppy. In the rush to come down here I never had the time to wrap your present.' She wiped her eyes on her sleeve. 'But there's something I've always intended to give you on your twenty-first birthday.' Her face was a study in concentration as she fumbled with the clasp, finally managing to unhook the slender silver chain that hung around her neck. She seized Poppy's hand in hers and folded her fingers around a small glass pendant in the shape of a heart. 'There, Poppy love. I want you to keep this. It's all I got to give you.'

Poppy's cold fingers opened and she stared at the tiny pendant, her eyes wide and her bottom lip trembling. 'But, Mum, I can't take this. It's yours and you always wear it.'

'Your dad gave that to me, Poppy. He said he was giving me his heart. It was fragile like glass and could break just as easily. I've worn it ever since that day, but now it's yours.'

Poppy gulped and sniffed. 'That's really lovely, Mum.'

'Take good care of it, and remember that I loved your father with all my heart.'

Mary was about to board the coach but the parting seemed suddenly final and Poppy clutched her arm. 'Don't go, Mum. Please don't leave me.'

'I got to go, love.' Mary cast an anguished look at Amy who stepped forward and put her arms around Poppy.

'Take care of my baby, miss,' Mary murmured as she was hustled into the crowded vehicle.

'Don't let your mother see you crying,' Amy whispered. 'Next time she comes I'm sure it will be to take you home.'

Poppy hiccuped and blew her nose into the handkerchief that Amy produced from her coat pocket. Standing on tiptoe she craned her neck in an attempt to catch a last glimpse of her mother. The first coach started off with a roar of the engines and cheers from the passengers inside, followed quickly by the second coach. Poppy was rewarded by the sight of her mother's white face in the rear window, and her pale hand fluttering against the pane like a butterfly trapped behind glass.

That night Poppy cried herself to sleep. The fire had gone out and the temperature in the night nursery had plummeted so far that there was frost on the inside of the windows. Curled up in bed, Poppy clutched the glass heart, vowing that she would wear it for ever and ever.

THERE WAS THE smell of woodsmoke in the air, mingling with the fruity fragrance of damp earth as Poppy leapt off the bus which always dropped her in the lane outside Squire's Knapp. The great iron gates were unlocked and she squeezed between them, breaking into a jogging run in order to keep warm. It was bitterly cold but the snow had melted, which was disappointing as she had been hoping for a white Christmas. There were still patches of snow icing the rounded tops of the hills surrounding the village, and in places where it had not had a chance to thaw beneath north-facing hedgerows, but the gravel drive was clear and there was only a thin sheet of ice on the lake. She could see the ducks slithering about on their webbed feet as they searched for open areas of water and their comic antics made her smile. She sprinted up the stone steps and burst into the entrance hall where she was met by a rush of warm air filled with the scent of pine needles and resin. She came to a sudden halt, staring up at the huge tree that almost touched the ceiling. The dark green feathery branches contrasted sharply with the ivory background of the hand-painted Chinese wallpaper. Small red candles were clamped securely into metal holders and Amy was balanced precariously on top of a pair of ancient wooden stepladders as she attempted to fasten a silver star on the topmost branch. She looked down at Poppy with a rueful grin. 'I was hoping to get the tree finished as a surprise for you when you came home from school.'

'I've never seen such a big tree. Not indoors anyway.'

Amy climbed down the steps and rested on the bottom rung. 'I'm not too good at heights, Poppy. Perhaps you'd like to finish decorating the top of the tree and I'll do the easy bits at the bottom.'

Tossing her school beret, coat and gloves on a nearby chair, Poppy was only too pleased to have something useful to do. 'I'd love to. We never had a tree this size at home.'

'I must sit down for a moment,' Amy said, leaning against the newel post. 'Don't look so worried; I just felt a bit dizzy.'

'Can I get you a cup of tea or something?'

Amy sank down on the nearest chair and fanned herself vigorously with the cardboard lid off one of the boxes that contained glass baubles. 'I'm fine, Poppy. I'm just excited, that's all.'

A shiver of anticipation ran down Poppy's spine. 'It's Guy, isn't it? He's coming home?'

'Yes, he'll be home for Christmas. Isn't that absolutely wonderful?'

'Spiffing. I can't wait to see him in his uniform.'

'Shh.' Amy put her finger to her lips. 'No one knows that he's enlisted in the RAF but us, Poppy. It's going to come as an awful shock to Mr and Mrs Carroll when they find out that he's left medical school. It's our secret until Guy sees fit to tell them.'

'I won't tell a soul,' Poppy said, touching the glass heart which was now her talisman against all evils. 'When will he be here?'

'On Sunday; Christmas Eve,' Amy said happily. 'This is going to be the best Christmas ever.' She paused as she was about to hang a large red ball on the tree. 'I'm so sorry, Poppy. What an idiot I am. I'd quite forgotten that this will be your first Christmas away from home.'

'That's okay. I was upset at first when Mum told me I was to stay on here, but at least I know they're safe and well at home.' Poppy curled her fingers around the glass pendant that hung around her neck. 'Mum thinks the war will be over soon.'

'Let's hope so, Poppy. I sincerely hope she's right.'

THE HOUSE SEEMED to burst into life on Christmas Eve, and even Violet seemed less surly than usual when she slapped Poppy's breakfast tray down on the day nursery table. 'I'm off as soon as I've cleared the dining room, so you won't get waited on hand and foot until Wednesday when I'm back on duty. You'll have to look after yourself for once, Popeye.'

'I'd be quite happy to fetch my tray from the kitchen,' Poppy said warily. 'It wasn't my idea to eat on my own up here.'

Violet shrugged her thin shoulders. 'But you're one of them now. Look at you, all dolled up in them nice clothes Miss Amy bought for you. I wish I had a fairy godmother to spoil me like that.'

'She's very kind,' Poppy said quietly. 'I never asked for any of this.'

'No, but you got it anyway. I wish I'd been evacuated from bloody Barton Lacey and sent somewhere glamorous like Hollywood. I'd love to be in pictures; maybe I will one day.' She whisked out of the room without giving Poppy a chance to reply, although she had given up sparring with Violet long ago. She found it easier to ignore the silly nickname and her constant sniping.

When she had finished her bowl of porridge laced with brown sugar and cream, and eaten two slices of toast covered in Mrs Toon's homemade strawberry jam, Poppy decided to take the tray back to the kitchen and save Violet's legs. In any case, she had purchased small presents in Woolworth's for the servants below stairs with the half-crown that Amy had slipped into her hand telling her to spend it on herself.

The aroma of boiling ham and hot mince pies floated up the back stairs as Poppy made her way to the kitchen. The fierce heat hit her like a slap in the face as she pushed the door open with the toe of her shoe. Mrs Toon was up to her elbows in bread dough while Nancy, who had been taken on to help in the kitchens during the Christmas festivities, was stirring something in a pot on the stove and Olive was busily polishing silver cutlery and placing it on a tray. Violet clattered in from the scullery carrying a tray laden with clean plates. 'I never meant you had to start today, Popeye,' she muttered.

Mrs Toon stopped kneading the dough. 'What's going on, Violet?'

'I didn't tell her she had to bring the tray down, honest, Cook.'

Mrs Toon wiped the sweat from her forehead with the back of her floury hand, leaving streaks of white on her flushed skin. 'We're a bit busy as you can see, miss.'

'I haven't come to disturb you,' Poppy said, looking around for a clear space in which to place the tray, but all the work surfaces seemed to be covered with plates of food and baskets of vegetables waiting to be peeled. 'I brought you a small present each,' she added shyly.

'That was kind, miss.' Mrs Toon nodded to Violet. 'Take the tray from Miss Poppy and put it in the scullery.'

Violet sidled forward to snatch the tray from Poppy's grasp. 'Bet you didn't get nothing for me,' she hissed.

Poppy put her hand in her skirt pocket and pulled out two small packages. 'I did as it happens.' She placed one of them on the tray. 'I hope you like it.'

Violet's mouth formed a small circle of surprise as she peeled off the paper to reveal a pair of clip-on earrings. 'Oh, thanks. You shouldn't have.'

'It's Christmas,' Poppy said, walking past her to give the larger present to Mrs Toon. 'It's only small, I'm afraid. I couldn't afford a big bottle.'

Wiping her hands on her large white pinafore, Mrs Toon tore off the paper and her face crumpled into a smile. 'Evening in Paris, my favourite scent.'

Olive left the tray she was preparing to take upstairs and glanced critically at the gift. 'Very nice too,' she remarked stiffly.

Poppy plunged her hand in her pocket and brought out another package. 'For you, Olive.'

Olive sniffed and took the present gingerly, as if she were afraid it might bite her fingers off. 'I didn't expect anything neither.'

'Well, open it, you silly girl,' Mrs Toon remonstrated cheerfully.

'And where's mine, Popeye?' Nancy demanded with a curl of her lip. 'Don't suppose you got anything for the likes of me.'

'Why don't you wait and see?' Poppy kept her hands in her pockets while she waited for Olive to rip the paper off her present.

'Very nice too.' Olive held up the string of glass beads for the others to admire. She smiled. 'Thanks, Poppy.'

'All right for some,' Nancy muttered beneath her breath as she stashed the clean crockery away in the oak dresser.

'I almost forgot,' Poppy said, making her way round the table to hand a small flat package to Nancy. 'Here's yours.'

Ripping off the brown paper, Nancy stared at the diary, frowning. 'Ta! Very nice I'm sure.'

'I thought you could keep your dates with young gentlemen from getting muddled up,' Poppy said sweetly.

'Who told you about that?'

'Sally Pitman's in my class at school. Everyone knows you stood her brother up last week.' Poppy had the satisfaction of seeing Nancy looking distinctly put out. She opened her mouth to reply but a loud jangling from the bell board made everyone turn with a start.

'Olive, front door,' Mrs Toon said, straightening her white cap. 'They've started arriving already and here am I, all behind like the cow's tail.'

Poppy's heart did a convulsive leap inside her chest. She had kept the secret so well that she had almost forgotten that Guy was due today. She raced after Olive as fast as her legs would carry her.

Chapter Six

To Poppy's intense disappointment it was Pamela who entered first, resplendent in a sable coat with a matching Cossack-style hat and high-heeled shoes that were totally unsuitable for walking anywhere, let alone on stony country lanes. Hector followed her with Rupert in his arms and their chauffeur, Harper, brought up the rear with their luggage. Marina emerged from the drawing room, holding out her arms. 'Pamela, darling.'

Leaving a waft of expensive perfume in her wake, which Poppy guessed had cost more than a shilling in Woollies, Pamela glided across the floor to kiss her mother. 'It's good to be home, Mummy.'

Hector put a squirming Rupert down on the floor. 'Go and say hello to your grandmama, there's a good chap.'

But instead of toddling towards his grandmother Rupert flung himself at Poppy with a cry of delight. 'Poppy.'

Marina bristled visibly. 'As the boy seems to prefer you, Poppy, I suggest you take him upstairs to the nursery.' She beckoned to Hector. 'Come into the drawing room where at least the temperature is above freezing. Olive will see to your luggage.'

They disappeared into the drawing room, and Olive picked up the suitcases. 'Olive do this; Olive do that. Where's their Christmas spirit, that's what I'd like to know?' She pushed a smaller valise towards Poppy with the toe of her shoe. 'Make yourself useful and take this one. It looks like it might belong to the kid.' She stomped off, hefting the cases up the main staircase with a mutinous look on her face that dared anyone to challenge the fact that she had not taken the back stairs.

Left alone in the entrance hall with Rupert and the huge Christmas tree, Poppy realised that as far as Mrs Carroll was concerned she would always be on a par with the servants. In fact she was probably less valued than Violet or Olive because she had no useful part to play in the day to day running of the house. Rupert tugged at her hand and she smiled, swinging him up in her arms. 'You're pleased to see me at any rate. Look at the pretty tree, Rupert.'

'Poppy,' he said, tugging her hair.

'Come on then,' she said, settling him on her hip as she picked up the valise. 'Let's take you to the nursery. They've lit a fire in your honour, which is more than what I get.'

It was a reluctant Nancy who brought them their lunch, grumbling that she had to do Violet's work as well as her own and it wasn't fair. Poppy said nothing.

When they finished their meal, she took Rupert into the bathroom and changed his nappy. She washed his hands and face put him down for his nap. Even though he fought sleep he succumbed quickly. She gazed down at him and felt a tug of something like love even though he was not related to her in any way. His eyelashes formed golden crescents on his rosy cheeks and his soft fair baby curls spread out on the white pillowcase. She crept out of the room, leaving the door ajar so that she could hear him when he awakened.

She went to sit on the window seat, gazing down onto the driveway at the front of the house. The Pallisters' car, a large black limousine, was where they had left it but there was no sign of Guy's roadster. She sighed and picked up a copy of *Vanity Fair* that she had borrowed from the school library, but she could not concentrate on the exploits of Becky Sharp, even though their situations were in some way similar. She found herself wondering what Mum and Gran were doing now. She could imagine them sitting round the kitchen table peeling spuds for roasting with the bird next day. Dad would come home later with a goose or a turkey that he had bought last thing from Smithfield Market where bargains were to be had if you waited until closing time. Joe would bring beer for himself and Dad, and a bottle of gin for Mum and Gran. Tea would be toasted crumpets and margarine with mince pies to follow, and afterwards they would sit round the fire and roast chestnuts on the coal shovel. She could smell the fragrance of red hot chestnuts and the spicy aroma of mince pies. She always left one out for

Santa Claus with a glass of beer, which was empty next morning. She knew now that it was Dad who drank the beer and probably Joe who ate the pie, but when she was younger she had firmly believed that the jolly old man in the red hat had come down the chimney to fill her stocking.

A whimper from the nursery made her jump to her feet. Outside a pale watery sun had fought its way through the clouds. On an impulse she decided to dress Rupert in his outdoor clothes and take him to his favourite spot by the lake to feed the ducks. Visiting the kitchen first, she was relieved to find that Mrs Toon seemed more kindly disposed towards her after the gift of perfume, and she gave them some stale bread for the ducks and two fingers of freshly made shortbread for themselves.

Outside, as Poppy had hoped, the air was crisp and cold and the threat of snow seemed to have blown away on the westerly wind. Their feet crackled on the dead leaves underfoot and the sun's feeble rays reflected off the dark water of the lake. The ducks quacked and waddled over, greedily snapping up the chunks of bread as Rupert tossed them inexpertly into the water. When the last crumb had been swallowed the ducks paddled their way back to roost on the small island in the middle of the lake. A cold wind whipped through the bare branches of the trees as the sun plummeted towards the horizon and Poppy took Rupert by the hand. 'Time to go indoors, love.' He looked up at her and grinned, licking the last crumbs of shortbread from his lips. 'More ducks,' he said hopefully.

'More ducks tomorrow.' They set off walking slowly towards the house, but the sound of a car coming up the drive made her stop. She did not have to look to know it was Guy's roadster, but as she turned slowly her heart gave a great lurch as she saw him at the wheel resplendent in his RAF uniform. Amy was sitting beside him in the passenger seat with Algy balancing precariously on the dicky seat. Snatching Rupert up in her arms she ran towards the drive, waving frantically. Guy smiled when he saw her and she felt as though she was going to burst with happiness. By the time she caught up with them they were unloading the car.

Light from the entrance hall spilled onto the steps as Pamela emerged from the house, closely followed by Hector. She paused on the bottom step, staring at Guy in astonishment. 'You idiot, Guy, why didn't you tell us you'd enlisted? Just wait until Mother finds out.'

'I didn't say anything because I knew there'd be a fuss, Pam. This way it's a fait accompli.'

'I know what that means.' The words tumbled from her lips before Poppy could stop herself. Everyone turned to look at her and she felt the colour rush to her cheeks.

Guy ruffled her hair. 'It's good to see you again, Poppy. Amy's told me how well you two have been getting on.'

'For heaven's sake come indoors,' Pamela said, folding her arms about herself with an exaggerated shiver. 'It's freezing out here. Poppy, take Master Rupert upstairs to the nursery; I don't recall giving you permission to take him out.'

Hector put his arm around her shoulders. 'The boy needs fresh air and exercise, Pam. You mollycoddle him.'

'I do not.' Pamela broke away from him and mounted the steps, tossing her golden hair so that it caught the light.

She has a pageboy bob just like Ginger Rogers, ~~Polly~~ Poppy thought wistfully. She wished that her hair was that shade of blonde instead of being dark. Even when it was confined to two long plaits she could not quite control the strands that escaped to curl in tendrils round her face. She jumped at the sound of Amy's voice.

'Do go indoors, Poppy dear; it really is getting very cold.' She lowered her voice. 'And don't take too much notice of Pamela. She doesn't mean to be sharp with you.'

Algy staggered past them with his arms filled with packages tied with coloured ribbon. 'Give me a hand, old girl. There's more in the car. I think Guy's bought up the whole of Oxford Street.'

With a suitcase in each hand, Guy followed him up the steps. 'Don't listen to him, Amy. You're the one who shouldn't be standing outside in this weather. Take the children indoors.'

Poppy stared after him in dismay. She was not a child. Her hand went automatically to the glass heart around her neck; she could feel its shape through her woollen jumper.

'Guy's right. We must be mad standing out here when there's a lovely fire inside. Come on, Poppy.'

Holding Rupert's hand, Poppy followed Amy into the house, but she knew there was going to be trouble the instant she saw the expression on Mrs Carroll's face. Her smile of welcome had been replaced by tight-lipped disapproval. 'Are you completely insane, Guy?'

'Merry Christmas to you, Mother.'

'Don't Merry Christmas me. How could you do such a thing without consulting your father and me?'

'Oh dear, she is upset,' Amy murmured, clutching Guy's arm as if she wanted to shield him from his mother's wrath.

'Perhaps we'd better make tracks for home, sis,' Algy said in a low voice. 'I think Guy needs time alone with his family.'

'Nonsense,' Guy said firmly. 'You're both family as near as damn it, anyway, and we won't allow this to spoil Christmas, will we, Mother?'

'We'll see what your father has to say.' Marina stalked off in the direction of the drawing room.

'What did I tell you just now?' Pamela hissed in Poppy's ear. 'Take Master Rupert to the nursery and make sure that he eats his supper. I'll come up and kiss him goodnight when he's ready for bed.'

Finding herself left alone with Rupert yet again, Poppy picked him up and carried him to the nursery, but he was fractious and all her attempts to amuse him failed. She could not stop thinking about Guy and wondering what was being said in the drawing room. He looked so handsome in his uniform, and she simply could not understand why his mother was not bursting with pride to have such a brave son.

Rupert had begun to snivel, but his attention was diverted when the nursery door flew open, helped by

Nancy's foot. 'What a way to spend Christmas Eve,' she muttered, eyeing Poppy as if it were all her fault. 'Here's your supper, Popeye. I hope it chokes you.' She dumped the tray on the table, causing Rupert's milk to slop onto the cloth.

'Thank you,' Poppy said, lifting Rupert into his high chair.

Nancy hesitated in the doorway. 'I suppose you're happy now?'

'I don't know what you mean.'

'Your heart-throb has come home all dolled up in uniform.'

'Mr Guy is a brave man, fighting for his country.'

'And you're a stuck-up little bitch.'

'Go away, Nancy. You're upsetting Master Rupert.'

Nancy hovered in the doorway, seemingly unwilling to let matters lie. 'You think you're the bee's knees since Miss Amy took you under her wing, but you're still common like the rest of us. The family won't never accept you as one of them. Put that in your pipe and smoke it, Popeye.' She slammed out of the room, leaving Rupert staring after her with his mouth open.

Poppy scooped up a spoonful of chicken broth and put it to his lips. 'Don't take any notice of her, Rupert. She's a mean old fox-face.'

EARLY NEXT MORNING, Poppy saw to it that Rupert was washed and dressed with a feeling of resentment gnawing inside her. His mother had not come to kiss him goodnight as promised and no one had thought to hang a stocking at the end of his cot. If Poppy had been at home the smell of bacon frying and hot toast would be wafting up from the kitchen. Cooked breakfast was a special treat reserved for birthdays and Christmas. Even though she was too old for toys, there would have been a stocking filled with nuts, sweets, an apple and an orange and some small gifts. It seemed callous to treat a little kid this way, but the Carrolls did everything differently all round. A wave of homesickness washed over her. She fingered the silver chain and the glass heart, closing her eyes and picturing Mum's face when she had said goodbye. In her pocket she had an envelope that had come on Christmas Eve bearing a London postmark. Inside, tantalisingly enough, was another smaller envelope with the inscription *Do not open until Christmas Day.*

Olive delivered the breakfast tray with an air of resignation. 'Merry Christmas, Poppy.' She left the room without giving Poppy a chance to respond in kind.

Half an hour later, Pamela collected Rupert and Poppy was alone at last to open her letter. Her fingers trembled as she ripped the envelope apart and a card dropped onto the tablecloth. On examination it was a book token to the value of seven and six. She could hardly believe her eyes. Mum and Dad must have been saving up for weeks to give her such a magnificent present. She snatched up the slip of paper that had fluttered out with it.

Dear Poppy,
   Knowing how you love to read we all clubbed together to get you this book token so you can choose

something you really want. Joe has joined up because the papers say that he'd be called up soon anyway. Your dad is disappointed that he is too old to go back in the army, but as you can imagine, love, Gran and I are very pleased. Anyway he does important work on the railway and we all have to do our bit.

Take care of yourself, love, and let's hope it'll all be over soon and you can come home. Give my kind regards to Mr and Mrs Carroll and that nice Miss Amy.

Lots and lots of love,
Mum.

Poppy's eyes filled with tears as she read and reread the note, but she swallowed hard and braced her shoulders. Mum would tell her not to cry and Gran would say, 'Keep your chin up, girl.' But it was not that easy. A large teardrop splashed onto the paper causing the ink to smudge. Mum's writing brought home closer and yet her family were as far from reach as ever. She dashed her hand across her eyes as she heard the latch click and the door opened. She looked up and saw Guy standing in the doorway. The letter fell from her nerveless fingers but he moved swiftly and caught it before it fluttered to the floor.

'News from home, Poppy?'

'Yes.'

'Not bad news, I hope?'

'Not really. Except that my brother Joe has joined the army.'

'Good for him. You must be proud.'

She raised her eyes to his face and his sympathetic smile brought a rush of tears that simply refused to stop. He sat down at the table and taking a starched white handkerchief from his pocket he pressed it into her hand. 'Chin up, Poppy.'

She blew her nose into its soft folds. 'My gran always says that.'

'Your gran sounds like a very wise woman. You must tell me all about your family when there's more time, but now I want you to dry your eyes and come downstairs with me.'

Poppy slanted a sideways look at him. He is handsome like a film star, she thought, but just now his face had a touch of hardness about it that had not been there before he went away. His thick, wavy hair, which was more or less the same colour as Rupert's, had been cut very short. She realised that he was regarding her with a smile on his lips. 'Penny for them, Poppy.'

'They've cut your hair too short.'

He stood up to look in the mirror above the fireplace. 'You know, I think you're right. Next time I'll tell the barber not to be so keen.'

She stared at him in amazement. 'Will you really?'

'I certainly will. And now we'd better hurry or we'll be late for morning service.'

She stared at him, thinking that she must have misheard. 'I'm going to church with you?'

'Absolutely, and then you're going to have Christmas lunch with the family.'

'Really and truly?'

'Really and truly. Get your coat and hat.'

She jumped to her feet, but then she remembered that she had his handkerchief clutched in her hand. She offered it to him but he shook his head. 'You keep it, Poppy. I've got plenty.'

SHE WAS ALLOWED to sit in the roadster's dicky seat all the way to the village and again on the return from church. She had sat in between Amy and Guy during the service and when they got back to the house she could hardly believe her luck when Guy took her firmly by the hand and led her into the dining room. Her eyes opened wide as she gazed around at the usually sombre room, which had been transformed with swags of holly and ivy. At home they would have put up paper chains she had made at school and maybe there would be a sprig of mistletoe hanging from the lightshade in the hall, but only when Joe was bringing a girlfriend round for Christmas dinner. The gleaming mahogany dining table was set with silver cutlery and candelabra with tapering candles throwing a soft light onto the crystal glasses. If the Ghost of Christmas Past had suddenly appeared Poppy would not have been at all surprised.

After lunch Poppy was prepared to take Rupert back to the nursery, but Amy guided her into the drawing room. Beneath a much smaller Christmas tree than the one in the great hall was a pile of boxes wrapped in brightly coloured paper and tied with ribbons and tinsel. Poppy's small gifts wrapped in brown paper paled into insignificance beside such opulence.

Poppy was amazed when Guy placed one of the largest boxes at her feet. 'For me?'

'All for you, Poppy,' Amy said, smiling. 'It's from the whole family. We wanted you to have something special.'

Poppy began to take the paper off very carefully without tearing it but Guy leaned forward and gave the paper a tweak so that it fell from the box, causing Poppy to gasp with delight. 'It's a wireless. There must be some mistake. This can't be for me.'

'It certainly is,' Amy said happily. 'We thought you spent far too much time doing nothing but study.'

'I don't know what to say,' Poppy murmured, completely at a loss.

'Well, we're looking forward to opening our presents from you,' Amy said gently. 'Why don't you give them out yourself, Poppy? Everyone else has had theirs now.'

Poppy got up feeling very self-conscious as she crossed the expanse of Persian carpet to the tree. She gave out her small packages, apologising to Pamela and Hector and then to Algy because she had nothing for them.

'Never mind,' Hector said cheerfully. 'It was more than good of you to think of Rupert, Poppy.'

'And I certainly didn't expect anything,' Algy said, tweaking her plaits. 'Though of course I'll never speak to you again.'

She thought for a moment that he was serious, but a quick glance at his smiling face reassured her. For the first time, she could see a likeness between him and Amy. Maybe it was the china blue eyes or the way they crinkled at the corners when he laughed, or simply the abundant good nature that they both possessed. Poppy grinned back at him and he responded with a cheery wink.

Edwin thanked her enthusiastically for the calendar, which he said he was going to hang in his study. Amy immediately knotted the blue chiffon scarf around her neck and kissed Poppy on the cheek. Guy unwrapped his present and taking great care he opened the little cardboard box and took out the St Christopher medal, holding it by its chain for everyone to see. 'Thank you, Poppy. This is the best present ever.'

'It's to keep you safe in your plane. St Christopher looks after travellers.'

'I'll wear it and think of you,' Guy said, smiling. He rose to his feet. 'And now I've got an announcement to make.' He cleared his throat and smiling down at Amy he took her by the hand. 'This brave girl has done me the great honour of agreeing to be my wife.'

In the sudden, deathly silence Poppy was certain that the clock on the mantelpiece stopped ticking, the flames in the grate froze in fiery spikes and she held her breath.

Marina sprang to her feet. 'You damn fool, Guy!'

Hector cleared his throat with a nervous cough and Rupert started banging the drum that some thoughtless person had given him as a present.

Amy stood up, moving close to Guy so that to Poppy's eyes they seemed to be welded together.

'Well, aren't you going to congratulate us?' Guy said, slipping his arm around Amy's waist.

The clock started to chime the hour, the fire spat a lump of burning coal onto the hearth and everyone began talking at once. Poppy looked helplessly at Guy but he was staring at his mother with his jaw set in a hard line.

'You're completely mad, Guy,' Marina said furiously. 'First you give up medical school and decide to become a fighter pilot in some immature, misguided attempt at heroics, and then, without any apparent thought, you engage yourself to a sick girl. I won't allow it.'

Before Guy could retaliate, Amy stepped forward, glaring angrily at her future mother-in-law. 'Don't speak to Guy like that, Mrs Carroll. You should be proud of him for joining up to fight for his country. I think he's terribly brave.'

There was a moment of silence as everyone stared in amazement at Amy who was visibly trembling with anger. Poppy thought vaguely that it was as if a toy poodle had attacked a tiger.

'Brave?' The word fell from Marina's lips like acid. 'Guy hates the sight of guns. He refuses to join our shooting parties. What chance would he have against the Luftwaffe? And what does a silly young girl like you know about anything anyway?'

'Just because he doesn't enjoy blood sports doesn't make him any less of a man.' Amy's voice throbbed with passion. 'In fact, in my eyes it makes him ten times the braver for sticking to his principles. And as for him saddling himself with a sick woman, let me assure you that I'm perfectly well. The sanatorium cured me completely and even if it hadn't, I'd rather spend a few short years as Guy's wife than live to be a hundred without him.' She burst into tears.

Guy hooked his arm around her shoulders. 'Mother, unless you apologise to Amy this minute, I'm walking out of the house and I won't return until you beg her forgiveness.'

'It's Christmas and you're upsetting everyone, Guy,' Pamela said angrily.

Edwin rose to his feet. 'Marina, my dear, I think you should put an end to this before things get completely out of hand.'

'That's right, Edwin. Side with the children as you always do. When did you ever agree with me on any subject?'

'Almost every day, my dear. But in this instance I think you should apologise to Amy and to our son. Guy is almost twenty-two and he can run his life as he sees fit. For myself, I'm proud that he's going to do his bit for King and country. And as to the engagement, if I had to choose my daughter-in-law, I don't think I could find a sweeter or more courageous young lady than Amy.'

'Bravo,' Algy said, clapping his hands.

With an impatient shrug, Marina resumed her seat by the fire. 'I can see I'm outnumbered. I think you're utterly reckless on both counts, Guy, but I didn't mean a personal slight on you, Amy. Heaven knows, I've always been very fond of you.'

Amy gulped and sniffed and had to borrow her brother's handkerchief because Guy's was nestling in Poppy's pocket. She managed a watery smile. 'I'm sorry for flying off the handle.'

Guy crossed the floor to drop a kiss on his mother's forehead. 'Maybe I should have broken the news more tactfully, Mother. But I never want to hear you speak like that to Amy again.'

That night, Poppy slept with Guy's handkerchief tucked under her pillow and, in the cold hours just before dawn, she had the comfort of Rupert's little body cuddling up to her for warmth.

IT SEEMED TO Poppy that nothing, not even war or family crises, could prevent the Fairford Boxing Day hunt from taking place. She watched Marina and Edwin ride off early next morning resplendent in their hunting pink. Pamela and Hector took Rupert to see the meet on the forecourt of the Stag and Hounds pub in the village square, and that left Poppy free to do as she pleased. But she was restless and still coming to terms with the fact that Amy and Guy had announced their engagement. Now that the secret was out she must face the truth. On his marriage to Amy, Guy would be lost to her forever. He would belong heart and soul to Amy, and they would have no room in their lives for a girl from West Ham.

Violet was back on duty with a vengeance and making it plain that there were places she would rather be than pushing the carpet sweeper around the day nursery. With her copy of *Vanity Fair* clutched in her hand, Poppy made her way to the peace and quiet of the conservatory. The ribbed iron radiators belched out heat and the air amongst the potted palms was warm and moist. Poppy curled up in a rattan chair close to the window where she could sit and read unseen by anyone who entered the drawing room. She was so deeply engrossed in the book that she did not realise that she was no longer alone until she heard raised voices. She was about to make her presence known when she realised that Amy and Guy were in the middle of a fierce argument. She froze, unable to move a muscle.

'No, no, a hundred times no, Guy. I've told you before, there's no way I'm going to live with your parents while you're off fighting the war.'

'Be reasonable, darling. You can't stay with your aunt forever. You said so yourself.' Guy's tone was calm but there was an edge to his words, as if he were trying hard to be patient.

'I'm sick and tired of being reasonable. You heard what your mother said to me, and I'm sorry I went for her, but if I had to live here it would only get worse. She may think I'm a soft touch but I've got a temper too, and I won't be put on.'

'You're being overdramatic, darling. Mother isn't an ogre; she just finds it hard to express her feelings.'

'Not hard enough it seems where I'm concerned. She virtually told you that I'm going to spend my life on a couch dying slowly of consumption like Garbo in *Camille*. Well, it's not true. I'm well again now, and I want a husband, my own home, and babies.'

'Of course, sweetheart, but I think we should wait a while to get married. You must face the fact that I could get killed. I don't want to leave you to bring up a family on your own.'

'No, I understand that, but I'll inherit a small fortune under the terms of my grandfather's will when I'm twenty-one, which is only two months away. I could afford to buy our dream cottage not too far from here, and we could have a June wedding.'

'Darling, I don't know where I'll be in June. I might be stationed in the Outer Hebrides for all I know. It's just not possible.'

'Then let's get married in a register office with a special licence. What's to stop us? Lots of people do that nowadays.'

Poppy stuffed her hand in her mouth to prevent herself from speaking out. The angry young woman did not sound the least bit like sweet, agreeable Amy who never raised her voice to anyone. She wanted to stand up for Guy and tell Amy that she was being selfish, but a small part of her sympathised with Amy's plight. Who in their right mind would want to stay with Mrs Carroll if the alternative was to have a home of their own and Guy for a husband?

'No, Amy. That's not the way to go about this. Marriage is a serious step and I refuse to rush you into something you may regret later.'

'Oh my God, Guy, you sound just like your mother.'

'That's not fair. I'm trying to do the right thing, but you're making it very difficult.'

Poppy could hear light footsteps pacing up and down the tiled floor. She crossed her fingers, hoping that Amy did not suddenly come round the stand of palms and see her crouching in the chair. They would never forgive her for spying on them, albeit unintentionally.

The pacing stopped as suddenly as it had begun. 'I had a letter from Mummy just before Christmas,' Amy said breathlessly. 'She wants me to join them in Singapore. Daddy says it will be safer for me to be away from England for the duration.'

'What's going on in your head, Amy? Why didn't you mention any of this sooner?'

'Because it was Christmas and you had your first leave. I wasn't thinking seriously of going, but if you want to wait until the war is over to get married, there doesn't seem to be anything stopping me.'

'So you've already made up your mind? Why the hell didn't you tell me?'

'Don't shout at me, Guy. I hadn't decided, until now.'

'What are you saying, Amy? Are you breaking off our engagement?'

Chapter Seven

POPPY SUFFERED AGONIES of embarrassment tinged with jealousy each time she remembered the sound of Guy and Amy kissing as they made up after their quarrel. She had covered her ears but she had been compelled to remain in her seat until they left the conservatory. It had seemed like hours but it had probably only been minutes and the pain of knowing she had lost Guy forever lasted much longer.

Marina had relented enough to arrange a large party for the newly engaged couple before Guy returned to his squadron. Pamela and Rupert stayed on at Squire's Knapp while Hector returned to his job in the War Department and the house buzzed with telephone calls and visitors. Guy had taken Amy into Fairford as soon as the shops opened after Boxing Day and they had returned with Amy brandishing a solitaire diamond ring. Poppy admired it dutifully but thought privately that it would have been prettier if it had had a nice coloured stone in it, like her mother's ring, which was red like strawberry jelly.

Mrs Toon was permanently in one of her warpath moods as she prepared mountains of food for the guests, and Violet was kept too busy to bother with carrying trays upstairs to the nursery. Poppy was quite happy to collect the meals for herself and Rupert. It broke up the day and she was able to watch Mrs Toon flinging dough around and basting huge joints in the ovens with sweat pouring off her brow, while Violet scuttled in and out of the scullery looking agitated. Sometimes Poppy was allowed to go into the larder and choose her own food, and on these rare occasions she and Rupert crammed themselves with cake and biscuits and hardly touched bread and butter at all.

On the night of the party, Poppy waited until Rupert had settled down to sleep and she crept downstairs to the first landing, peeping through the banisters to watch the guests arrive. She would write and tell Mum about the gorgeous dresses worn by the ladies and the smart black evening suits worn by the gentlemen. In spite of the war and winter, the hall was filled with hothouse flowers and an orchestra played the sort of music Poppy had only heard on the wireless. The strains of Viennese waltzes and Ivor Novello songs wafted through from the conservatory.

Standing at Guy's side as they welcomed their guests, Amy looked ethereal in a silver slipper-satin dress that skimmed her slender figure and fishtailed on to the ground just above her high-heeled silver shoes. The diamond ring sparkled like white fire on her left hand and she was all smiles. No one seeing her tonight would imagine the fierce argument that had passed between her and Guy just days previously.

The stream of guests seemed endless and Poppy clung to the banisters overawed at the splendour of it all until pins and needles forced her to stand up and stretch her cramped muscles. Everyone was moving into the drawing room and there was nothing much to see anyway. She wished that she had been invited to the party, but that would be expecting too much, and anyway she had nothing suitable to wear. Guy and Amy might treat her like family, but she knew that to the others she was still an outsider.

She dragged her feet as she climbed the two flights of stairs to the nursery and it was a long time before she managed to get to sleep that night. She was awake well before dawn, and, checking to see that Rupert was sleeping soundly, she took her clothes into the day nursery and dressed hurriedly. She knew that Guy was leaving early to rejoin his squadron and she was determined to see him to say goodbye. She crept down the stairs feeling her way in the dark but the whole house seemed to be sleeping and there was no sign of activity even below stairs. There was a strong smell of alcohol mixed with stale cigarette smoke, and although the servants had cleared up most of the debris there were champagne glasses in odd places and plates of congealed food left on the staircase and tucked beneath the spindly chairs in the entrance hall. The floor was strewn with pine needles where the Christmas tree was shedding its foliage and someone had knocked over an ashtray, spilling its contents on the floor. She let herself out of the house through the front entrance and tiptoed down the wide flight of steps. The moon was still high in the sky, lighting her path across the frost-covered gravel, and each breath she took was like swallowing iced water. She made her way through the stable yard to the coach house where the cars were garaged. In the light of a paraffin lamp she could see Guy bending over the engine, but he straightened up as she approached, staring at her with a look of surprise. 'Poppy? What on earth are you doing up at this ungodly hour?'

'I wanted to say goodbye and I didn't get the chance last night.'

He wiped his hands on a piece of rag, regarding her steadily. 'No, it was rather a busy evening. Why weren't you there?'

'Nobody invited me.'

'I'm sorry, I didn't know. I leave that sort of thing to Mother and Amy, but I really thought they'd include you.'

She shrugged her shoulders, staring down at the ground. 'It doesn't matter.'

'But it does. My sister is happy to treat you like family when it comes to looking after young Rupert. I'll have a word with my mother. It's not on, Poppy.'

'Please don't.' She looked up and met his worried gaze with an attempt at a smile. 'I know I'm just the evacuee and I'm very grateful for . . .'

'Stop that.'

The harsh note in his voice made Poppy jump, but he tempered his anger with a rueful grin. 'I'm sorry, I didn't mean to shout, but you are just as important as any of us and it makes me angry to see you hidden away in the nursery as if they were ashamed to have you in the house.'

'I don't mind, honest. My mum was a servant in a big house, she understands.'

Guy stared at her, shaking his head. 'This war is going to change all that, Poppy. Heaven knows I'm as guilty for neglecting you as the rest of my family, and I'm sorry.'

'You don't have to be. I know you've just got engaged.' Memories of that morning in the conservatory flooded back and she looked away, biting her lip.

'You heard us, didn't you?' Guy's tone was suddenly gentle. 'I know you were there because you left your book in the chair by the window. I went back to find Amy's scarf which fell off during our rather heated discussion, and found it caught on one of the palm fronds. I saw your book and picked it up. The cushion was still warm.'

'I didn't know what to say,' Poppy murmured. 'Are you very angry with me?'

He put his arms around her and gave her a hug which was as unexpected as it was overwhelming.

'Don't be silly. I know you well enough to realise that you must have almost died with embarrassment. I'm the one who should apologise to you for putting you in such a situation.'

Poppy met his gaze and felt suddenly as though they were equals. She smiled. 'I'd hate it if you went away mad.'

'I don't think I could be mad at you if I tried.' He released her and turned away to lower the bonnet so that it clicked into place. 'The old girl's ready to take me back to Upminster, which is a hell of a long drive, so I'd better be going.'

Poppy laid her hand on his sleeve. 'Is Amy going to move in with us?'

He shook his head. 'We talked it over sensibly, and I can see it would be best for her to join her parents in Singapore. Let's hope this bloody war doesn't go on too long.'

'You will be careful, won't you?'

He patted his breast pocket. 'I've got your St Christopher medal, Poppy. It will go with me on every sortie and keep me safe.' Hooking his uniform jacket out of the passenger seat he shrugged it on. 'I've got to go or I'll be late reporting for duty and then I'll be in real trouble.'

She nodded her head wordlessly. If she opened her mouth to speak she knew she would cry and make a complete fool of herself. He vaulted into the driver's seat and started the engine. With a last smile and a casual wave of his hand he drove slowly out of the stable yard. She followed the car, breaking into a run so that she could watch him until he was out of sight. She waved frantically as he gunned the engine and the car shot off down the avenue. She could just see the brake lights as he stopped to open the gates, and then he was gone.

The first iron-grey band of dawn lit the sky in the east and Poppy could hear movement in the house as lights began to appear one by one below stairs. She made her way quietly up the staircase and almost bumped into

Amy as she came out from one of the bathrooms on the first floor.

'What time is it?' Amy asked, running her hand through her tousled hair. 'I think I overslept. I meant to get up and see Guy off.'

'He's gone.'

Amy peered at her in the half-light. 'You look upset. What's the matter?'

'Nothing. Well, Guy told me that you're going away. Is it true?'

'Darling Poppy, I have to go. You understand that, don't you?'

'Not really. If I was engaged to Guy I wouldn't go off to the other side of the world and leave him.'

Angling her head, Amy laid her hands on Poppy's shoulders. 'You're very fond of him, aren't you?'

'I suppose so.'

'I'm not planning to stay in Singapore a moment longer than necessary and I'll come back as soon as the war's over. I'll marry Guy and we'll have a big white wedding with you as our chief bridesmaid and Rupert as pageboy. In the meantime I want you to promise to look after Guy for me. He already thinks of you as a little sister, and so do I.'

Amy's breath smelt of toothpaste and her eyes were red-rimmed with fatigue, but the smile on her lips seemed suddenly false in Poppy's eyes. The person she had thought to be an angel was as flawed as any other human being. Amy was running away from danger and deserting the man she was supposed to love above all others. Poppy swallowed hard but there was still a bitter taste in her mouth. Her last ally in Squire's Knapp was about to desert her.

Amy left a week later, and it seemed to Poppy that the weather matched her mood. According to the wireless it was the coldest January for over fifty years and the Thames actually froze over, as did the lake. Jackson and Sid Guppy went daily to the water's edge to break holes in the ice to allow the ducks to dredge the icy waters for any remaining plant life. It became part of the daily routine for Poppy and Rupert to take the stale crusts of bread to feed the mallards, coots and moorhens and they were often mobbed by flocks of hungry seagulls.

Mrs Toon was even grumpier these days as rationing had been introduced and she had to adjust their daily menus accordingly. Olive had left for better pay and shorter hours in a munitions factory, leaving them short-handed, which made Violet even more dissatisfied than usual. Nancy had been kept on as there did not seem to be any village girls willing to take Olive's place, and that had not gone down well with Violet as the pair were constantly bickering. There was not so much activity on the estate as in normal times. The younger male workers had received their call-up papers, leaving just the boys and the older men to cope with the grounds and stables.

What surprised Poppy most of all was the fact that Mrs Carroll dropped her habitual air of boredom and was sitting on numerous committees. She was also the local controller in charge of recruitment to Women's Land Army. She was filled with enthusiasm for turning the parkland into fields of corn, and the ornamental gardens into vegetable patches. Poppy felt quite sorry for Mr Carroll, who was relegated to the background when it came to running the estate as the day to day decisions were being made by his wife. It was fortunate for him, she thought sympathetically, that he had plenty to occupy him as a magistrate.

Letters from home were few and far between, and even though her mother tried to sound positive Poppy could not help worrying about her family, especially now they had to live on the meagre rations allowed each week. There was still the threat of air raids, and her mother described huge shelters being put up all over the city. What with that and the blackout, life was getting a bit trying in West Ham, Mum admitted, but Grandad had joined the ARP and Dad had taken a night watchman's job at the munitions factory as well as doing shifts on the railway. Joe was stationed in Kent at present but expecting to be sent abroad soon. Mum ended, as always, by telling her to be a good girl and to work hard at school.

She kept the letters safely tucked away from Violet's prying eyes in the battered school desk where Guy had once carved his initials and had probably received a sound telling off for doing so. She read and reread the missives from home in the quiet of the early morning before school, or in the evenings when she had just the wireless for company. Pamela had taken Rupert back to London, leaving Poppy very much to her own devices. She studied hard and read voraciously, losing herself in the novels that she borrowed from the school library, but she could not stay in her room for an entire weekend, and driven by loneliness she occasionally ventured down to the kitchen.

If Mrs Toon was on her own she was only too pleased to let Poppy help her by peeling vegetables or performing other menial tasks. If she was in a particularly good mood she allowed her to make pastry under strict supervision. But if Violet or Nancy were working in the kitchen, Poppy took refuge outside and she found an unexpected friend in Jackson. He was only too pleased to have someone to help him wash the Bentley and Mrs Carroll's MG, although as he gloomily prophesied petrol would be the next thing to be rationed, and then he would be out of a job.

Each visit to the coach house entailed a walk past Goliath's stable and quite often an exchange of words with Sid, who had left school and was now the only groom in the Carrolls' employ. The upside of this was that he had plenty of work to keep him busy, and the downside was that he had developed an exaggerated idea of his own importance. Whenever he thought that Poppy was looking he strutted around the stable yard like a rooster showing off his bright plumage. Mindful of her first day in the village school when Sid had placed a drawing pin on her chair, Poppy avoided him as much as possible, but she could not help feeling sorry for Goliath. The large animal would stick his head over the stable door and whinny hopefully when he heard her footsteps. She had not previously ascribed human emotions to horses, or any animal if it came to that, but the doleful look in Goliath's huge brown eyes made her think that he might actually be pining for Guy. She could sympathise with that, as the house seemed lifeless and dull now that he had gone and no one knew when he might return. She would have liked to stroke the horse's patrician nose and feed him sugar lumps as she had done when Guy was there, but she could not quite pluck up the courage.

One blustery Saturday afternoon in March, she walked to the village to post a letter to her parents. It was over a mile away and the narrow lanes were flanked with hedgerows just beginning to show signs of life after a long hard winter. Clumps of late snowdrops lay like patches of forgotten snow amongst the dead leaves, and fluffy catkins hung from the hazel trees. Cows grazed on the lush grass in the meadows but she no longer leapt back in fright when they rushed to the five-barred gate as if expecting her to bring them fodder or to take them to the milking parlour. The lane widened as she drew nearer to the village and there was the occasional thatched cottage set in gardens that had been filled with flowers when she first came to Barton Lacey. It seemed like years rather than six months since she arrived at the station with the rest of the evacuees. Only a few remained, and she saw Colin hanging upside down over a rickety-looking gate. He had been billeted with Jack, the aged potman who worked at the Rose and Crown pub in the village centre. Colin did a back flip and landed inexpertly at her feet. 'Hello, Poppy. Where are you going?'

'To post a letter home. Are you okay, Colin?'

He grinned, exposing two missing top teeth. 'Got a halfpenny for me tooth. It come out last night. Wanna see it?' He shoved his hand in his trouser pocket and produced a blood-stained rag. He opened it carefully to reveal a small tooth. 'I was ever so brave when Jack pulled it out. I didn't cry.'

'You're very brave,' Poppy said, smiling. 'You like being with Jack, do you?'

He nodded emphatically. 'I like it here. I don't want to go back to London, not never.'

'But your mum will want you home when the war's over, Colin.'

'She ain't me mum. Me mum run off with the window cleaner, and me dad took up with Florrie. She hates me and I hates her.'

'Oh dear.' Poppy was at a loss for words. 'Well, goodbye for now, Colin. I must be getting along.'

'Ta-ta.' Colin threw himself over the gate and resumed his upside down position, grinning at her like a monkey.

Poppy walked on, quickening her pace. She was shocked to think that young Colin preferred living in a tumbledown cottage with a man old enough to be his grandfather than with his real father in Hoxton, and yet she could see an improvement out of all recognition in the frightened little boy who had wet his pants on his first day at school. His clothes might be on the grubby side, and he looked as though he had not seen soap and water for several days, but he was obviously happy and healthy. That must count for something in the world of grownups. She posted her letter, but on her way home she had to stop several times to speak to the people she had come to know on her weekly trip to the post office, including Miss Dobson, the headmistress of the village school.

'How are you getting on at the grammar school, Poppy?' Miss Dobson took off her horn-rimmed glasses and wiped them on her scarf before setting them back on her nose.

'I'll be leaving in the summer, miss.'

'No, surely not, Poppy. You're a bright girl, you could stay on another year and maybe even go to university.'

'Oh no, miss. I don't think so. I'll be going home soon and then I'll get a job. My mum and dad couldn't afford to send me to university.'

'That's a great pity. You have the potential to do well academically, but I'm sure you know best. Good day, Poppy.' Miss Dobson sallied off to speak to a group of women standing outside the village shop.

Poppy continued on her way home, mulling over Miss Dobson's words. She had never considered the possibility of further education; that was for people like Guy and Miss Pamela, not for the likes of her. Mum might have high hopes for her, but a few months at the posh girls' school was not going to take her to university or turn her overnight into a doctor or a lawyer. Now that Amy had gone she doubted whether Mrs Carroll would be willing to pay the fees for another year at school, and anyway she would rather get a job. With money in her pocket she could pay for her train fare home and cock a snook at old Hitler and his bombs. Once she was there she would forget about posh people who didn't really want her, and about Guy. She dug her hands deep into her pockets. No. She would never forget Guy, not if she lived to be a hundred, but he was spoken for and she was just a schoolgirl.

The house was eerily silent as she let herself in through the conservatory, which was never locked during the day. It was as cold indoors as it was outside as Mr Carroll had turned off the central heating and, in order to save fuel, fires were only lit at night and then only in certain rooms. Coal was needed to fuel ships, or something like that. She was becoming confused with all the instructions that were being given out. Careless talk costs lives was one of them, although she had so few people to talk to that it really did not count in her case. She went upstairs to the day nursery, but she could not settle down to read. The mad March wind had made her restless, and she needed to be out of doors, doing something useful. She changed out of her grey flannel skirt and pulled on a pair of Pamela's old jodhpurs which she wore when helping Jackson clean the cars. At least Jackson talked to her. He told her about the glory days before the Great War, when the Carrolls employed many more servants than they did now and had hosted large house parties that went on for days. She hurried downstairs, peeping into the kitchen in the hope that Mrs Toon had left a tray of jam tarts to cool, but the only smell of cooking was from the oven where something savoury was stewing. There were no tarts and no sign of cake either. Her stomach rumbled but she dared not go into the pantry in case she awakened Mrs Toon, who was sitting in a wheelback chair by the range with her feet up on an old milking stool. Her cap had slipped over one eye and her ample breasts rose and fell as she snoozed by the fire.

Tiptoeing past her, Poppy snatched an apple from the bowl of fruit set aside for dessert. It was slightly wizened, having been stored since harvest time, but it would fill a gap. She slipped out of the house through the back door and made her way to the coach house, but as she walked past the stables Goliath stuck his great head out and whinnied. It was almost as if he was calling out to her. Lifting her hand she wiggled her fingers at him and smiled. Did horses respond to human facial expressions? She did not know, but Goliath flicked his ears and pawed the ground. Maybe he was not so dumb after all. She hurried on to the coach house but both cars were out and there was no sign of Jackson.

Walking back past the stables, she stopped to take the apple from her pocket. She was about to bite into it when she realised that Goliath was watching her. 'Hello, old boy.' Her voice faltered but she was determined to conquer her fear of horses. 'I'm not scared of you.' She cleared her throat. 'Would you like an apple?'

Goliath moved his head up and down as if nodding in assent. Poppy's hand shook as she stared down at the apple. She was tempted to run away, but she thought of Guy and how much he cared for his horse. Taking a deep breath she laid the piece of fruit on the palm of her hand and moved just close enough for Goliath to take the offering. His lips were soft and his breath warm on her skin as he took the apple. She did not particularly like the look of his long yellow teeth as he munched the fruit, but at least she had stopped shaking.

A slow handclap made her spin round to see Sid standing in the doorway of the tack room, grinning at her. 'And I thought you was too chicken to go near a big nasty beast like him.'

'I'm not scared any more.'

'Bet you aren't brave enough to ride him.'

'I can't ride.'

'There's nothing to it. Unless you're chicken, of course.'

Sid's crooked smile was annoying but not irritating enough to make her reckless. 'I don't want to ride him.'

'Mr Guy would be ever so grateful. Poor old horse badly needs exercise and I've got enough on me hands with being the head stable lad, groom and general dogsbody all rolled into one. There is a war on, you know.'

'Yes, of course I know, but I can't ride. I don't know how.'

Sid opened the stable door and stepped inside. 'Give me a minute or two and I'll saddle him up. You can have a go at walking round the yard. See how you like it.'

Poppy shook her head. 'No, I don't think so.'

'Want me to tell Vi what a little yellow-belly you are?'

There was something in Sid's sly expression that reminded Poppy yet again of that awful first day in school, when he had tormented her and ruined a perfectly good blouse by pushing her against the inky wall. 'I'll do it,' she said through gritted teeth.

He led the horse to the mounting block. 'Come on then, Popeye. Let's see what you're made of.'

It was a challenge that she could not refuse. Getting on the horse was comparatively easy but once she was in the saddle she realised just how far off the ground she was and fear took over. She clutched the pommel, hanging on for dear life as Goliath pranced about. She could hear almost nothing other than the pounding of her heart.

'He's a bit fresh,' Sid said dubiously. 'Don't dig your heels in or nothing like that, or he'll be off like a shot.'

'Dig my heels in?' Poppy murmured, closing her eyes. It did not sound like good advice but she did it anyway. The result was even more terrifying than she could have imagined. With a lurch that almost unseated her, Goliath moved forward, his hooves striking sparks off the cobblestones as he cantered out of the yard.

The breath was knocked from Poppy's lungs and there was nothing she could do other than cling on. She had lost the reins and they flapped around the horse's head, causing him to go even faster. The gravel flew in all directions as he headed down the drive. 'S-stop, p-please stop,' Poppy cried in desperation, but either Goliath was deaf or she was using the wrong words. He galloped towards the gates, and to her horror Poppy saw that they were open. Mrs Carroll's MG was heading towards them. Certain that she was going to die, Poppy closed her eyes just as Goliath swerved onto the grass and she felt herself flying through the air.

She landed with a sickening thud that winded her. Unable to breathe she fought to get air into her lungs.

Someone was shouting in the distance, and she realised dimly that it was Sid.

'What the hell were you doing on that animal?' An angry voice close to her ear made Poppy open her eyes. She found herself looking up into Mrs Carroll's furious face. 'Are you hurt, Poppy? Speak to me, damn it.'

Every breath was agony but gradually she managed to fill her lungs enough to be able to speak. 'I'm all right. I think.'

Marina straightened up. 'Guppy, catch that animal and take it back to the stables. I'll have words with you later, young man.' She helped Poppy to her feet. 'Nothing broken, I think. Get in the car and I'll drive you up to the house. Get yourself out of those muddy clothes and then I want to see you in the drawing room.'

Bruised and mortified, Poppy climbed the stairs to the day nursery. It was almost dark and she flicked the light switch. Without a fire in the grate the room looked cold and uninviting. She would have liked to climb into a hot bath to ease the ache in her back, but she put her soiled clothes into the laundry basket. Violet would have something to say about that when she emptied it in the morning. Rifling through the chest of drawers, Poppy found a clean jumper, which was a bit short in the arm and stretched over her budding breasts. She would soon need a bust bodice, but she did not know how she was going to pluck up the courage to ask Mrs Carroll to buy her clothes. Now that Amy was no longer here she was going to find things very difficult. She stepped into her skirt and changed her shoes.

In the drawing room she found Mrs Carroll seated by a roaring log fire with a glass of sherry in her hand. 'Well, what have you got to say for yourself, Poppy? Were you trying to commit suicide riding that damned horse?'

'I'm sorry, Mrs Carroll.'

'Sorry isn't good enough. You might have broken your neck or been paralysed for life, or worse still Goliath might have been seriously injured. He's not only a valuable horse but Guy thinks the world of him. He would never have allowed you to ride such a spirited animal.'

'He let me ride him once,' Poppy said, staring down at her brown lace-up shoes. 'He led me round the stable yard.'

'Which is a different matter altogether. What made you do such a stupid thing?'

Once again, Poppy found herself having to cover up for Sid Guppy, but for some strange reason she could not bring herself to tell Mrs Carroll the truth. 'I don't know. Well, I suppose I just wanted to make Guy proud of me. I thought he'd be pleased if I could ride properly and show him I wasn't scared of horses.'

'Heaven help us.' Marina drained her glass and set it down on the side table with a thud. 'There are a hundred and one other ways to impress my son, and none of them include the possible maiming of his favourite horse. If you want to ride, there are farm horses in the stables. You could work on the land and earn your keep.'

'I'd be pleased to do something useful,' Poppy said earnestly. 'I could be a land girl, just like the one on the posters in the village.'

'Nonsense, you're too young.' Marina rose from her seat and went to the table where a selection of cut glass decanters sparkled in the firelight. She refilled her glass. 'What am I going to do with you, Poppy Brown?'

It was obviously a rhetorical question and Poppy remained silent, clasping her hands tightly behind her back.

'You ought to know that Amy paid your school fees up until the end of the summer term, but she left in such a hurry that we didn't discuss what would happen in the future.' Marina sipped her sherry, eyeing Poppy over the rim of her glass. 'Well, say something, girl.'

'I–I'm very grateful to Amy. She was very kind to me.'

Marina's lip curled in a sarcastic smile. 'Yes, when it suited her. My future daughter-in-law was most eager to show herself off in the best possible light, if not for my benefit then most certainly for Guy's.'

'She was very generous to me, Mrs Carroll.'

'Yes, money is no object when you've got your sights set on a husband with prospects. Not that you'd understand, but it seems I'm the only one who saw through Miss Amy Fenton-Jones. She was always a little schemer even as a child. She had her hooks into my son from the start, but she may have made a mistake by running away to Singapore.'

Poppy shifted from one foot to the other. She wanted to stand up for Amy, but the martial look in Mrs Carroll's eyes made her wary and she thought it safer to say nothing.

'I don't know why I'm telling you all this. All you need to know is that I have no intention of paying for your education, and if I'm to be saddled with you for the duration you will leave school at the earliest opportunity and find work even if it's in the munitions factory. Do you understand me, Poppy?'

Chapter Eight

THE COMING OF spring coincided with the arrival of the land girls; three of them, to be exact. It was a sunny Saturday in April, and with nothing better to do Poppy was sitting on the steps outside the main entrance watching in a mixture of horror and fascination as the parkland was put to the plough. The avenue of copper beeches looked oddly out of place marooned between ribbed expanses of dark earth, and the deer had migrated to the spinney on the far side of the lake. Seagulls flocked to scavenge amongst the dark ridges of bare soil, their noisy cries almost blotting out the sound of the tractor's engine.

'Hello there.'

Poppy turned her head with a start to see three young women teetering up the gravelled drive on their high heels, each of them carrying a suitcase, with the obligatory gas mask cases slung over their shoulders. She leapt to her feet and ran down the steps to meet them. 'Hello, I'm Poppy. Have you come to work here?'

'Well we ain't come on holiday, ducks.' The tallest of the three held out her hand. 'I'm Edie. Do I hear a hint of a cockney accent there, Poppy, or are you one of them posh kids who like to pretend they're one of us?'

'Shut up, Edie. She's only a kid.' A smaller girl, who could not have been a day older than seventeen, managed a tight little smile but Poppy could see from her red-rimmed eyes that she had been crying. 'Mavis Thompson.' She sniffed and produced a soggy-looking hanky from her coat pocket. 'Got a bit of a cold.'

'She's been blubbing since she got on the train at Winchester,' Edie said with a pitying glance. 'She's never been away from home before. Anyway, since we're doing introductions, I'm Edie Blake from Hackney, and the skinny one with the plum in her mouth is Jean Hodge from Carshalton. We're a mixed bunch, as you can see.'

'I wish you'd stop that,' Jean said, tossing her long blonde hair. 'We're all in the same boat as far as I can see and it doesn't matter what sort of family we come from, we're all going to get our hands dirty.'

'And you'd know all about that, I suppose?' Edie curled her lip. 'My dad's a coalman. I suppose your dad's a bank manager.'

'No,' Jean said evenly. 'As a matter of fact he's a bank clerk. Does that satisfy your snobbish prejudices?'

'My dad's a lay preacher,' Mavis said softly. 'But that doesn't make me a saint. I wish you two would shut up.'

Poppy could hardly contain her excitement. The prospect of having company close to her own age was thrilling. Suddenly what had started out as an ordinary and rather boring Saturday was turning out to be quite an event. 'Are you really going to work here? Does Mrs Carroll know you're coming?'

'We ain't here for our health,' Edie said, chuckling. 'This seemed a better idea than working in a factory or joining the services, but looking at that bloody great field I ain't so sure.'

'It's war work,' Mavis murmured through the folds of a clean white handkerchief. 'We've all got to do our bit.'

'Don't take no notice of her, she'll soon learn that high ideals don't count for sweet F A in the real world.' Edie took off her navy blue felt hat and raised her face to the sun. 'I'm going to treat it like a holiday in the country.'

'Then you'd be making a huge mistake.' Marina walked slowly down the steps, looking the girls up and down. 'I'm Mrs Carroll, the district organiser of the Women's Land Army, and you three have been detailed to work my land.'

'How do you do?' Jean said, smiling and holding out her hand.

Although she was a good few inches shorter, Marina was standing on a higher step, gaining the advantage in height. She ignored the polite overture. 'You will be billeted in the rooms above the stables. We only employ one stable lad these days and he lives in the village. Poppy will show you where to go and then she'll take you to the kitchen where Cook has laid on a meal for you.' Without waiting for their comments, Marina ascended the steps and disappeared into the house.

'Snooty bitch,' Edie muttered, pulling a face. 'Who does she think she is?'

'She's our boss for the duration,' Jean said with a resigned sigh. 'But I do think she could have been a bit more civil.'

Poppy felt compelled to stand up for Mrs Carroll. 'That's just her way. She's not so bad when you get to know her.'

Edie picked up her battered suitcase, which was held together by a length of cord. 'Well I think she's a stuck-up cow and I can see us falling out if she don't drop the attitude.'

'I'll take you to the stables,' Poppy said hastily. 'I don't know what the rooms are like, but the stable lads and grooms used to live there, so they can't be too bad.' She led the way to the stable block, bracing herself to walk past Goliath's stall without flinching.

'Oh, what a lovely horse,' Jean breathed, stopping to stroke his nose. 'Who's a beautiful boy then?'

'For God's sake, Jean. It's just a bloody animal,' Edie said impatiently.

Goliath rolled his eyes and nuzzled Jean's hand. She responded by dropping a kiss on his muzzle. 'He's gorgeous. I hope I get a chance to ride him.'

'He's Guy's horse.' Poppy was not certain she liked the way Jean seemed to have an instant rapport with something that belonged to Guy, or the way that Goliath was patently enjoying the attention.

'Who's he?' Edie's eyes lit up as she turned a curious face to Poppy. 'Who is Guy when he's at home?'

Poppy felt the blood rush to her cheeks, and she walked on. 'He's Mrs Carroll's son and he's in the RAF.'

'I think I'm going to like this dump after all,' Edie said, chuckling.

Mavis quickened her pace in order to keep up with Poppy. 'I wouldn't fancy your chances, Edie. If he's anything like his mother he'll be a snooty type who looks down on the likes of us.'

Regretting the fact that she had brought Guy's name into the conversation, Poppy hurried on towards the tack room. The accommodation was reached by a stairway which was little more than a ladder at the back of the room and Poppy was frankly curious. She had seen the lads coming and going but she had never ventured any further than the doorway. She went inside, blinking as her eyes grew accustomed to the gloom. There was a strong smell of saddle soap, leather and stale tea. Ashes spilled from the grate onto the floor and the table was littered with old newspapers and cups that Sid had forgotten about or had been too idle to wash.

'What a mess. It looks like the *Mary Celeste*,' Jean said, gazing round the room in disgust.

Edie picked up a yellowing newspaper. 'September the first 1939. *Poland Invaded*. Well that proves how long it is since anyone cleaned up in here.'

'I think your rooms are up here,' Poppy said, making her way round the table and heading towards the rickety-looking stairs.

Mavis followed close on her heels. 'What are you doing here, Poppy? You obviously don't come from these parts.'

'I'm an evacuee. My mum and dad live in West Ham, but I don't suppose you know that area.'

'I've never been to London.' Mavis negotiated the stairs, heaving her suitcase from step to step.

'Get a move on. I'm busting for a pee.' Edie's voice rose to an agonised shriek.

'I'm going as quick as I can.' Mavis stumbled as she caught her toe on the top step, cannoning into Poppy. 'Sorry. She pushed me.'

Tossing her case onto the bare boards, Edie bounded into the room. 'Where's the bloody bathroom? Don't tell me it's an outside lavvy.'

Poppy peered into the large open space beneath the rafters. There were three small windows beneath the eaves but they let in precious little daylight. A paraffin lamp hung from a beam and she could just make out four single beds lined up against the back wall.

'So this is country living,' Jean said as she joined them. 'Are we really expected to live up here without so much as an electric light or a bathroom?'

Poppy frowned. 'I think there's a toilet in the head groom's office next door.'

'Now she tells me.' Edie flew past her and almost fell down the stairs in her haste.

'How do we keep warm in winter?' Mavis asked faintly. 'Did the stable lads really live like this? There's no lino on the floor and not even a rug to make the place look a bit more like home.'

'I believe it's called roughing it,' Jean said drily. 'All part of the country experience. I think I might get the next train back to Carshalton and enlist in the WAAF.'

Poppy's heart sank; she did not want to lose her new friends so soon. 'Don't go yet. I'm sure there must be things in the big house that they don't need which would make it much more comfortable for you. I'll ask Mrs Toon if she can help.'

Jean put her suitcase on the nearest bed with a sigh. 'You're a good kid, Poppy. Perhaps you could ask for a few more blankets or a nice feather eiderdown.'

'There's a wood burner,' Poppy said, pointing to a soot-blackened pot-bellied stove at the far end of the room. 'And there's plenty of trees growing on the estate. There's a log store at the back of the kitchen, and it's always piled high with firewood.' She glanced over her shoulder as Edie thundered up the stairs.

'Flaming hell,' she said, wiping her hands on her skirt. 'Those stable lads lived like pigs. I've never seen such a mess, and there's only a cold water tap in the toilet. I wouldn't wash my dog in that sink, and I'll swear that the water has legs.'

Poppy could see a rebellion brewing. 'I'll take you to the kitchen if you've seen enough up here. Mrs Toon is a very good cook. Maybe you'll feel better about things when you've had something to eat.'

'She's probably boiling up eye of bloody newt as we speak,' Edie muttered, dragging off her beret and tossing it across the room.

Mavis had already started to unpack but she looked up at the mention of food. 'I could murder a cup of tea.'

'Let's go then,' Edie said, scowling. 'Anywhere would be better than this dump. It's like a setting for a horror film.'

Jean patted Poppy on the shoulder. 'You're a saint for putting up with this place. I'm not sure I can stand it, though.'

When they reached the kitchen it was obvious that Mrs Toon had been primed about the arrival of the land girls. Nancy had laid the table for tea and the aroma of freshly baked bread made the girls stop in their tracks and sniff the air like gun dogs scenting the kill.

'Cake,' Edie said, licking her lips. 'I ain't seen one like that since they brought in rationing.'

'Jam tarts.' Mavis took a seat at the table and was reaching out to take one when Mrs Toon cleared her throat.

'Bread and butter first, ladies. Cake and jam tarts later.'

Edie sat down next to Mavis. 'It's like being back in bloody school.'

'And no swearing,' Mrs Toon said sternly. 'Don't bring your city ways here. Remember there are young ears taking in every word you say.'

Mortified by the inference that she was too much of a child to mix with adults, Poppy decided to beat a hasty retreat. Her new friends were too busy eating to pay any attention to her and Mrs Toon was bustling about like a mother hen. Unnoticed, Poppy went outside into the stable yard and found Sid leaning against the wall, smoking a roll-up cigarette. She approached him cautiously. 'You're just the person I wanted to see.'

He flicked the butt onto the cobblestones and stamped on it. 'Oh yeah?'

'I need riding lessons, Sid. I know the last time was a disaster, but if you can teach me to ride Goliath then I might be allowed to help the land girls. I'm fed up with doing nothing.'

'You were rubbish last time you had a go.'

'I know, and I'm sorry I got you into trouble. It wasn't your fault.'

He eyed her suspiciously. 'What's all this about, Popeye?'

'I'm too young to be a land girl, but if I can prove to Mrs Carroll that I can do something useful she might let me join up. She says I've got to leave school at the end of term and I'm desperate to do something for the war effort.'

'I tried to enlist but they didn't believe me when I said I was eighteen, so I'm stuck here with all you blooming females.'

'You could work in the munitions factory.'

'Not me. I like the outdoor life.' Grinding the dog end in with the toe of his boot he eyed her thoughtfully. 'All right, I'll teach you to ride, but don't you dare breathe a word of it to me sister Violet. She'd think I gone soft.'

'I don't want Mrs Carroll to find out until I've got it right, so we'd have to do it on the quiet.'

Sid's small eyes lit up and he grinned. 'It would be us peasants taking a swipe at the ruling classes.'

'Well, not quite,' Poppy said, trying to be fair, but seeing the downcast look on Sid's face she nodded enthusiastically. 'Yes, you're right, Sid. It's us against them. Will you do it?'

He spat on his hand and held it out. 'Shake on it, comrade.'

She shook his hand. 'When can we start?'

'There's no time like the present. I've nothing better to do and I just saw Jackson driving the missis out in the Bentley. She's gone to one of them committee meetings and then they'll wait and bring the master back from the court house, so we've got plenty of time and no one will be any the wiser.'

'Give me a few minutes to change.'

'Okey-dokey. I'll saddle up Goliath, or maybe you ought to start on Miss Pamela's old nag, Romeo?'

Poppy shook her head. 'No, it's got to be Goliath. I won't let this thing beat me.'

'Suit yourself. See you in the paddock behind the Dutch barn in ten minutes.' Sid strolled off towards Goliath's stall, whistling an out of tune rendition of 'Run Rabbit Run'.

Twenty minutes later, dressed in jodhpurs and an old jumper that was in need of darning, which was not in Poppy's field of expertise, she went to the paddock and found Sid waiting for her with Goliath pawing the ground. Close to he seemed even larger than before and Poppy had to use a couple of bales of hay as a mounting block.

Once in the saddle she felt sick with fear, but she gritted her teeth and did her best to follow Sid's instructions.

Having shown her how to hold the reins and to sit with her back straight and her toes pointing upwards in the stirrups, Sid held the leading rein, walking the horse until Poppy was at ease in the saddle. Goliath behaved like a perfect gentleman, plodding sedately so that after a few circuits of the paddock she felt confident enough to allow Sid to stand back and watch.

'Back straight, elbows tucked in, heels down,' he said with a smile of approval as she rode past him for the second time. 'You're doing well, but I think that's enough for today, Popeye.'

She reined in beside him and dismounted. 'How did I do, Sid?'

'You done well today. Tomorrow I'll teach you how to rise and fall in the trot, and when you've got that I'll saddle up Romeo and we can ride out together.'

Poppy returned to her room flushed with pride and excitement. She had ridden Goliath and not been afraid; well, not much anyway. Guy would be proud of her, and if she could show Mrs Carroll that she was a competent rider and had conquered her fear of large animals, she might allow her to work alongside the land girls. Suddenly life seemed full of possibilities. She settled down to write a letter to her mother.

Next day after church, Poppy could not wait to see how the girls had fared overnight in their new environment. As she entered the stable yard it was obvious from the pile of rubbish on the cobblestones that something was afoot. The tack room door was open and she went inside to find Mavis enveloped in a pinafore, scrubbing the deal table. The chairs were stacked in the corner and Jean, with her hair tucked up in a turban, was busy sweeping the flagstone floor. Dust flew up with each pass of the broom and eddies of dry leaves and straw were then trapped in a dustpan and deposited in a bucket. Sounds of water running and Edie's high-pitched soprano voice singing rather plaintively 'Somewhere over the rainbow' emanated from the office next door.

'I came to see how you're getting on,' Poppy said lamely. It was obvious that they were working hard to make a home for themselves, but she could not think of anything else to say.

Jean paused, leaning on the broom handle. 'We're getting there, Poppy. But there's plenty to do. You can give a hand if you want to, but not in those clothes.' She eyed Poppy's outfit doubtfully. 'Why are you wearing school uniform? It's Sunday.'

'I've been to church with Mrs Carroll, and she sent me to say that she expects you three to come with us next week, unless your religion forbids it, whatever that means.'

'I'll go,' Mavis volunteered. 'I would have made the effort today, but as the Bible says, cleanliness is next to Godliness, and this place needs a lot of hard work.'

'I can't speak for Edie,' Jean said, smiling, 'but I don't mind showing up in church. At least it will be a chance to get out and meet the locals.'

Mavis winked at Poppy. 'All the decent men will be away in the forces. You'll be wasting your time, Jean.'

'Well, there must be some social gatherings in the village, or at least a decent pub or two. We can't live like nuns for the duration.' She resumed sweeping the floor. 'Move your feet, Poppy, and I suggest you go and change into something more suitable. This place is worse than a rat's nest. Anyway, it's almost midday. I assume we get fed at regular intervals.'

'Mrs Toon usually does a roast on Sunday,' Poppy said eagerly. 'Although with rationing there's more veg and less meat.'

'How does she manage at all with rationing as it is?' Mavis exchanged a puzzled look with Jean. 'We're only allowed one and tuppence worth of meat each a week at home. Is it different in the country?'

Poppy shook her head. 'I don't know, but there are always plenty of vegetables to go round and sometimes she makes treacle pudding and custard for dessert.'

'Don't tell me our holier than thou district organiser stoops to the black market,' Jean said, smothering a giggle.

'I don't know what that is, but I'm sure Mr Carroll wouldn't allow anything like that. He's a magistrate.'

'They're often the worst,' Mavis said, grinning. 'Oh, don't look so worried, Poppy. We're just kidding. I'm sure we'll get super food if Mrs Toon's cakes are anything to go by.'

Jean wiped her hands on her apron. 'She was quick enough to ask for our rations books, and we'll be the ones helping to produce the food, so I should hope we get fed well.'

The clattering of a bucket and the sound of water swishing on the cobblestones outside preceded Edie as she burst into the tack room, red-faced and obviously out of sorts. 'What a God-awful mess in that toilet. Anyway it's clean now and I expect we'll get rid of the brown stains in time as long as they don't put bleach on ration.' She paused, staring at Poppy with raised eyebrows. 'Is it fancy dress or something? Why are you dressed like a posh schoolgirl?'

'Shut up, Edie,' Jean said crossly. 'Poppy came to see if she could help us. She's just been to church with Mrs Carroll.'

'Oh, yes. The Sainted Marina. Well, I hope she doesn't expect me to toe the line. I'm strictly nonconformist and I'm blowed if I'm going to waste my Sunday mornings sitting in a cold and draughty church.'

'Not even if the vicar is a bit of a dish?' Mavis asked innocently.

'That may be your husband of choice, my girl, but I prefer my men a bit more worldly. I think I may go for the Sainted Marina's son if he turns out to be a looker. I fancy a rich husband with a landed estate.'

The reference to Guy made Poppy feel distinctly wary and she backed towards the doorway. 'I think I'll go and change.' She hesitated, wondering if she ought to explain why she was wearing her school uniform. It certainly was not from choice. 'I had to wear this because it's all I've got that's suitable for church. I seem to have shot up since I came to live here and nothing fits. Even Miss Pamela's cast-offs are getting a bit tight up here,' she indicated her budding breasts, 'and I'll soon need a bras.'

Edie snorted with laughter, covering her mouth with her hand as she received a withering look from Jean. 'Sorry, kid. But we generally call it a bra now. Bras is a bit old-fashioned.'

'My gran calls it a bust bodice,' Poppy said, frowning. 'Anyway, I could do with one, especially in gym at school. Everything bounces when I have to vault the wooden horse.' She stopped, staring at the red faces as the girls stifled their laughter. 'What have I said that's funny?'

Jean slipped her arm around Poppy's shoulders. 'Nothing, darling. We're just in a silly mood. It must be all the bleach we've been sniffing. You go and get changed and after lunch perhaps you'd like to put in a good word with Mrs Carroll. We desperately need some mats or rugs upstairs and more blankets. My teeth were chattering in bed last night.'

Relieved to have something to do and glad that the embarrassing subject of undergarments had been forgotten, Poppy smiled. 'Of course I will. But it will have to wait until after lunch. I'll see you in the kitchen.'

'Hang on a minute, kid,' Edie said, frowning. 'Don't you eat with the family?'

Poppy shook her head. 'I did once, at Christmas. I used to eat in the day nursery, but since Olive left to work in the munitions factory Violet has more work to do and anyway she never liked having to wait on me. I eat in the kitchen, or if Mrs Toon is very busy I take a tray upstairs.'

'You poor little sod,' Edie said with feeling.

WHETHER IT WAS from innate generosity or the fact that she had enjoyed a few sherries before lunch and a glass of wine with her meal, Marina gave Poppy permission to search the attics for anything that the land girls might need to make them more comfortable, and Poppy could not wait to pass the information on. Edie, Mavis and Jean were only too delighted to spend the afternoon exploring the top floor of the house, which had once been the servants' quarters but was now disused, as Mrs Toon had a small flat on the third floor adjacent to the nursery suite, and Violet went home each evening.

After a happy couple of hours foraging they found a cedar-lined chest filled with woollen blankets, several oddments of carpet and a couple of threadbare but useable rugs. Edie whooped with glee when she discovered a zinc bath hidden beneath a dust sheet and Mavis found some enamel ewers and a china washbowl set patterned with cabbage roses and violets. Jean uncovered a Victorian burr walnut dressing table mirror, which she insisted would come in handy if and when they had time to put on makeup, and Poppy almost trod on a small oil painting of Squire's Knapp in the days when people rode about in carriages. She tucked it under her arm, intending it for her room. She was certain that no one would mind as it was dusty and obviously long forgotten.

It took several trips to ferry everything down four flights of stairs and across the stable yard to the tack room. It was dark by the time they fetched the last rug and the bathtub, but there was a general feeling of a job well done. Mavis had proved to have a knack with combustibles and had the fire roaring up the chimney in the tack room, and had even managed to light the pot-bellied stove in their dormitory. In the glow of the paraffin lamps the room looked almost homely with a patchwork of carpet and rugs on the newly swept and scrubbed floor, and the blankets neatly folded on the beds.

Poppy felt quite envious as she left them to finish unpacking their things in readiness for work next day, but she had the painting to put on the wall by her bed. She could look at it as she drifted off to sleep and pretend that it was her home with Mum and Dad, Gran and Grandad living there too, and of course Guy.

It was hard to return to school next day knowing that the girls were being put to work on the home farm, but Poppy had no alternative. She had let slip to Mavis, in a burst of confidence while they were sorting through the cedar chest for blankets that were not too moth-eaten, that she would be fourteen next Saturday. Of course Mavis had told Jean, who immediately passed the news on to Edie, and they had wanted to know if she was going to have a party. Mavis had been quite upset when Poppy shrugged her shoulders and said that she doubted if anyone in the big house would be the least bit interested. It was at times like these that homesickness took over and she felt a million miles from her family.

After school Poppy could barely contain her excitement as she travelled home on the bus. She was eager to see the girls again and instead of going straight to her room, as she would normally have done, she ran to the stables. But the only person there was Sid, who was looking distinctly gloomy.

'What's up?' Poppy asked breathlessly. 'Why the long face?'

He continued shovelling a mixture of straw and dung into a wooden handcart. 'Mr Carroll has bought a new shire horse and he expects me to work with it. I'm a stable lad, not a bloody farm hand.'

'It's still a horse, and you like working with horses.'

'That don't include pulling a plough and towing a hay wagon. I wanted to get a job in a racing stable and train to be a jockey. Now they're going to turn me into a farmer.'

'I'm sorry,' Poppy murmured. 'I really am, Sid, but I was looking for the girls. D'you know where they are?'

'Powdering their noses, I expect. It'll be me who does the heavy work while they sit back and watch.' He stomped off into the stall and resumed sweeping, sending flurries of straw smelling strongly of ammonia onto the cobblestones.

Poppy was not dressed for walking across muddy fields and she decided to change out of her school clothes before going in search of the girls. As she entered the house by the back door she could hear the sound of voices in the kitchen. She hurried through the scullery and found her new friends seated round the table munching thick slices of bread and jam. The aroma of freshly baked bread and hot tea, with just a hint of sweet strawberry jam, made Poppy's mouth water.

Jean saw her first and she waved. 'Come and join us, Poppy. How was school?'

'I hated school,' Edie said, pointing a jammy knife at Poppy. 'Don't tell me you like it, kid.'

'Sit down and have a cup of tea.' Mrs Toon took a cup and saucer from the dresser. 'Don't take any notice of her, Poppy. You'll need a good education if you're to get on in the world.'

'My back is killing me,' Mavis said, moving her head from side to side and frowning. 'We've been picking huge chunks of chalk out of the soil all day. I'm sure I must have done myself an injury.'

'Never mind that now.' Jean patted the empty chair beside her. 'Sit down, Poppy. Were your ears burning today?'

Poppy slid onto the hard wooden seat, shaking her head. 'No, why?'

'Because we was talking about you,' Edie said, cutting in before Jean had a chance to explain. 'We're going to celebrate your birthday on Saturday. We're taking you to the pub.'

Mrs Toon put the teapot down on its stand with a thud. 'She's too young for that sort of thing, miss. Don't you lot go leading her astray.'

ON SATURDAY EVENING the sun came out in between the April showers and raindrops sparkled on the hedgerows like diamond necklaces. Poppy waited in the lane outside the wrought iron gates. It had been decided by the committee of three, Jean, Edie and Mavis, that it would be best if Mrs Carroll was kept in ignorance of their little jaunt. Not, they said, that they were doing anything wrong, but she might not think it appropriate to take a fourteen-year-old to the pub.

Suddenly nervous, Poppy shifted from one foot to the other. She felt incredibly grown-up and smart in the dress that Mavis had altered to fit her. The pale green crêpe de chine afternoon gown, which had once belonged to Miss Pamela, was almost the exact shade of the new shoots on the blackthorn, and Mavis assured her that it brought out the colour of her eyes. She had helped to tame Poppy's dark curls so that when released from the plaits she normally wore her hair floated around her head and shoulders in a cascade of shining waves. Poppy did not possess any stockings but Mavis had filched some gravy browning from the pantry and had shown her how to rub it on her legs so that it was a fair imitation of silk stockings. She had produced an eyebrow pencil and proceeded to draw a line up the back of Poppy's legs, although it had been difficult not to laugh and wriggle about as it tickled. At the sound of approaching voices, Poppy peeped round the corner and a shiver of excitement ran down her spine as she saw the girls, dressed to the nines, strolling arm in arm along the avenue of budding copper beeches.

'Happy birthday, Poppy.' Edie grabbed her round the waist and gave her a twirl. 'My, you look the bee's knees. Doesn't she, girls?'

'She certainly does,' Jean agreed, smiling. 'You look super, Poppy.'

'Thanks to Mavis,' Poppy said shyly.

Mavis shook her head. 'Nonsense. I just did a few tweaks, that's all. Who does she remind you of, Jean?'

'I don't know, but she looks terribly grown-up.'

'Yes, you do,' Mavis insisted. 'I bet Edie can guess who I mean.'

Edie angled her head, staring thoughtfully at Poppy. 'Well, it ain't Harpo Marx.' She slapped Poppy on the shoulder. 'Don't look so worried, kid. I was only joking.'

'Vivien Leigh,' Mavis said impatiently. 'Vivien Leigh in *Fire Over England*. I saw it at the Odeon three times. She could be her double.'

'Well, come on, Viv,' Edie said, linking her hand through Poppy's arm. 'Let's celebrate your birthday in style.'

'Let old Hitler invade now,' Mavis said happily. 'We'll show him who's who round here.'

Edie began to sing a rather rude song about Hitler's anatomy which struck Poppy as being terribly daring and very funny, and she hardly noticed that they walked the best part of two miles to the Rose and Crown. Situated on the edge of the village green, surrounded by thatched cottages and facing the duck pond, the pub boasted two bars: the public bar for the farm labourers and working men and the saloon bar for passing trade.

'You'd better not come inside, Poppy,' Mavis said, glancing round as if she expected Marina to leap out of the pond like Venus rising from the sea. 'It's a lovely evening. We can sit outside.'

Poppy was disappointed but she did not want to spoil things by acting like a baby. She perched on a wooden bench, taking care not to move about too much in case she snagged her skirt on a splinter. Edie, Jean and Mavis had disappeared into the pub, and it seemed to Poppy that they were taking their time over buying drinks. Perhaps there was a queue at the bar, although the other tables outside were empty, and there was a definite chill in the air as the sun sank in the west. She shivered, wrapping her arms around her body in an attempt to keep warm. She was determined to enjoy her first real taste of freedom since Amy had left for Singapore. She had hoped to hear from her but so far there had been nothing in the post. She wondered if Amy had written to Guy and then chided herself for being so silly. Of course Amy would have corresponded with her fiancé; she loved Guy and it was only the war that had caused them to separate.

Just as Poppy was beginning to think she had been forgotten, Edie breezed out of the pub and thrust a half-pint mug in her hands. 'It's only cider, love. It'll warm the cockles of your heart.'

Mavis took a seat beside Poppy. 'Are you sure it's not alcoholic, Edie?'

'Nah! They give that stuff to babies. Here's to you, Poppy. Happy birthday.'

Jean shivered and wrapped her cardigan around her shoulders as she sipped a glass of something dark and red. 'Yes, happy birthday, Poppy. Here's how.'

Poppy had not the faintest idea what 'here's how' meant, but she echoed it anyway and took a long draught of cider. It was refreshingly tangy and tasted of apples. She drained the glass. 'Thank you all, that was lovely. Can I have another?'

'I don't think so,' Jean said warily.

'Oh, don't be such a spoilsport,' Edie said, laughing. She took Poppy's glass. 'Okay, kid. But drink it a bit slower this time.'

Poppy felt pleasantly muzzy as she sipped her drink. Edie was telling jokes, most of which she did not get, but the others were laughing, and Poppy did her best to join in, but suddenly she began to feel very strange. She rose to her feet, but the world began to spin around her and she fell back onto the bench.

'Oh heavens, she's drunk.' Jean leapt to her feet. 'We'd best get her home, girls.'

'Don't look now but there's a bloody great limo pulled up,' Edie said in a low voice. 'And there's two chaps in uniform getting out. I think someone must have phoned the cops. Now we're for it.'

Chapter Nine

'I'M PERFECTLY ALL right,' Poppy said, rising unsteadily to her feet. She peered into the gathering gloom and for a moment she thought she must be extremely drunk. 'It's not the police,' she murmured, waving frantically. 'Guy, it's me. Over here.'

'Guy!' Jean and Mavis spoke as one.

'That's torn it,' Edie said gloomily. 'The boss's son complete with reinforcements. Bloody hell.'

Guy strode towards them with Algy hot on his heels. Behind them, Poppy could just make out Miss Pamela and her husband. She wondered why they were staring at her and decided it must be her posh frock. She lurched towards Guy, holding out her arms. 'It's my birthday, Guy. Have you come to join the party?'

'What's going on here?' he demanded. 'Who are these people, Poppy?'

Jean slipped her arm around Poppy's shoulders. 'Excuse me, Mr Carroll, but I resent your tone. We brought Poppy out to celebrate her birthday, which everyone in your house seemed to have overlooked. The poor kid would have been totally ignored but for us.'

Guy recoiled, staring at Jean in surprise. 'I'm sorry, who are you?'

'Jean Hodge, and my friends are Edie and Mavis. We're in the Land Army and we work for your mother.'

'How do you, Miss Hodge?' Algy said, shaking Jean's hand. 'You'll have to excuse my friend; he's a bit overprotective of young Poppy, but then she's just a kid and she really shouldn't be drinking alcohol, so he has got a point.'

'Thanks, Algy,' Guy said, frowning. 'I can speak for myself.'

'Guy, what on earth is going on?' Pamela's voice was shrill and impatient. 'Mummy will be wondering what's happened. She was expecting us half an hour ago and Rupert should have been tucked up in bed an hour ago.'

'Rupert,' Poppy said, smiling. 'Where's my boy?'

'We're coming, Pam.' Guy took Poppy by the hand. 'I think you've had enough excitement for one day. I'm taking you home.'

Edie stepped forward, sticking her chin out. 'What if she don't want to go, mister? Doesn't she get a say in this?'

'She's drunk,' Guy said drily. 'I don't think she knows where she is or what she's doing. Come along, Poppy.'

'But Guy, we were having a good time.' Focusing on his face with difficulty, Poppy could see that he was not going to take no for an answer. 'Oh, all right, but you're being mean.'

'That's a good girl,' Algy said, nodding his head and smiling. 'You go with Guy, and I'll stay here and see the ladies home. It's not safe for young women to walk the country lanes alone at night.'

'I never could resist a man in uniform, but I think we might be safer without you, mate,' Edie said, chuckling. 'Don't let that put you off, though. Mine's a gin and water. Make it a double seeing as how it's turning a bit chilly.'

NEXT MORNING POPPY woke up with a dry mouth and the hint of a headache. The beautiful silk dress was lying in a crumpled heap on the floor, and as she swung her legs over the side of the bed she thought for one horrible moment that she had contracted some hideous skin disease. She stared in horror at her mottled skin, but then she remembered that it was simply gravy browning which was smudged and streaked. Gradually it was all beginning to come back to her, including the humiliating car journey home with Pamela going on and on about the evils of drink, which was a bit hypocritical coming from someone whose family drank wine at almost every meal and were not averse to a sherry or two before dinner. Poppy had made herself as small as possible in the corner of the back seat, hoping that Miss Pamela would grow tired of berating her, but Mr Pallister had also gone on and on until her head was spinning. She had taken a little comfort when Guy held her hand, giving it a squeeze as if to say everything was all right, even though she knew it was not and she hadn't heard the last of this by a long chalk.

She rose from the bed, taking care not to awaken Rupert who was still sleeping soundly in his cot. She crept over to take a look at him and she smiled, thinking how much he had grown since Christmas. She had to resist the temptation to pick him up and give him a cuddle, but he looked so peaceful and angelic that she let him sleep on. She went into the bathroom and closed the door. The linoleum was cold underfoot and steam filled the room as she ran her bath. It was difficult getting used to having only five inches of water to bathe in, and she was beginning to realise that living in the big house had encouraged her to take things that once would have seemed like a luxury for granted. She could barely imagine going back to a zinc tub in front of the kitchen fire, and she felt a wave of sympathy for the girls living above the stables who had to do just that every time they wanted to take a bath. She lay back, watching the gravy browning dissolve into the warm water and float to the surface forming small islands of scum. Last night had been a disaster. Guy had been awfully cross, but not with her. He had been quite sweet in the car on the way home, but he must think she was a silly child for getting drunk on two glasses of cider. She could not imagine Amy ever doing anything so stupid or undignified. She had longed for him to come home on leave, but after making such a fool of herself last evening she doubted if she could ever look him in the face again.

Breakfast was brought upstairs by a reluctant Nancy. She dumped the tray on the table. 'I'm only doing this because Miss Pamela insisted that Master Rupert had his boiled egg and soldiers in the nursery. Don't think you'll get this treatment when they've gone home, because you won't.'

Poppy said nothing. She chopped the top off Rupert's egg with a decisive cut of the knife and dipped the finger of buttered toast into the golden yolk. He opened his mouth obediently and she gave him the bread to hold in his chubby hand.

'You can give me the cold shoulder,' Nancy hissed, 'but Mrs Toon said you was drunk as a lord last night. Made a real show of yourself, so I heard.'

'Go away, Nancy,' Poppy said tiredly. 'Leave me alone.'

'I'll leave you alone all right. I'm going to join Olive and Violet in the munitions factory. I'll earn several times what I get here for less work.'

'Good luck then,' Poppy said wearily.

Nancy paused in the doorway. 'You'll end up scrubbing floors and washing dishes when they can't get anyone else to work for next to nothing. Don't think you're one of them because you're not. They'll put up with you while you're useful and when they don't need you any more you'll be out on your ear.' She whisked out of the room, slamming the door behind her, causing Rupert to jump.

'Don't mind her,' Poppy said with a reassuring smile. 'She's silly.'

'More,' Rupert said, pointing to his egg.

ALTHOUGH POPPY HAD been dreading a further encounter, Pamela seemed to be in a hurry when she breezed into the nursery to collect Rupert. 'We're going to visit my mother-in-law in Sherborne,' she said, scooping him up in her arms. 'But I want you to look after Rupert tomorrow morning. I'm having my hair done in Fairford and meeting Mummy for lunch, so I won't be home until mid-afternoon at the earliest.'

'I can't, Miss Pamela. I have to go to school.'

Pamela pursed her lips and frowned. 'Bother. Mummy said you'd be willing to help look after him, and since we're staying here for a few weeks I was counting on you.'

'I'm leaving school in July.'

'That's not much use to me now, is it? I suppose I could ask one of those females who are supposed to be working the home farm, although they looked a fairly common crowd from what I saw last evening.'

Poppy bowed her head. She was not about to argue with Miss Pamela, as she knew she would lose hands down.

'Oh, well, we'll see. Anyway, you will be here this evening, I suppose?'

'Yes, Miss Pamela.'

'Good. You can take care of Rupert while we're at dinner and put him to bed. Unfortunately I had to leave Nanny behind in London. The silly girl was going to enlist in the women's army.' She paused, setting Rupert down and seizing him by the hand as he was about to run back to Poppy. 'And you must stop calling me Miss Pamela. It's a relic of the past and it annoys me.'

'Yes, Mrs Pallister.'

'And I don't want you taking my clothes, even the old ones that I never wear any more. There's a rumour that clothing might be rationed in the future, so leave my things alone.'

'Yes, Mrs Pallister.'

'Good, I'm glad we had this little talk.' Dragging Rupert behind her like a model trailing a fur coat on the catwalk, Pamela left the room.

Poppy picked up the breakfast tray and took it downstairs to the kitchen. She knew it would be left to moulder if Nancy had any say in the matter. Mrs Toon was busy preparing Sunday lunch and Poppy could hear Nancy's voice raised in protest as she argued with someone in the scullery. She was about to make her escape when a bell rang. Mrs Toon glanced up at the board on the wall where a light was flashing. 'Nancy, come here. Where is that dratted girl?'

There was the sound of scuffling in the scullery. The daily woman put her head round the door. 'She's gone out to fetch the eggs from the dairy, Mrs T.'

Mrs Toon frowned. 'Well you can't go, Ada. It'll have to be you, Poppy. Go and see what the mistress wants. I just don't know how we're going to manage when Nancy leaves. I can't do the running up and down stairs.'

'Well, don't look at me,' Ada said hastily. 'My rheumatics couldn't cope with all them stairs.'

'I'll go.' Poppy left them discussing their ailments. She did not particularly want to see Mrs Carroll, but she might as well get it over and done with.

'Oh, there you are, Poppy,' Marina said as Poppy entered the drawing room. 'Why aren't you ready yet? We're leaving for church in five minutes. Go upstairs and get your hat and coat.'

'Yes, Mrs Carroll.' Poppy had forgotten that it was Sunday, but the fact that Mrs Carroll either did not know about last night or had chosen to ignore it made her feel light-headed with relief. Now all she had to do was face Guy.

He did not accompany them to church. Jean, Edie and Mavis were in the back pew and Edie winked at her as Poppy followed Mr and Mrs Carroll up the aisle to their family pew. She suspected that the only reason she was allowed to sit with them was so that the villagers would see how well the Carrolls treated their evacuee. Hardly any of the other children attended church, although she knew that some of the younger ones went to Sunday school.

When the congregation filed out after the service ended, Marina stopped to compliment the vicar on his sermon and Poppy stood outside to await further instructions. She had learned never to take anything for granted where Mrs Carroll was concerned.

'You may walk home with the girls,' Marina said graciously, as though bestowing a huge favour on Poppy. 'The exercise will do you good.' She walked briskly to the Bentley where Jackson stood to attention by the open passenger door. He winked at Poppy and she smiled. At least she had one friend at Squire's Knapp. She heard someone call her name and she turned to see Mavis waving at her.

'Hello, birthday girl. How's the head this morning?'

'It's fine now.'

'Where's your boyfriend,' Edie asked, chuckling. 'He's a bit of all right.'

'If you mean Guy, he's not my boyfriend.'

Jean tucked Poppy's hand in the crook of her arm. 'Don't take any notice of Edie, she's teasing you. But I must say that Guy is very good-looking, and he seems very fond of you.'

'Algy's more fun,' Edie said, hitching her gas mask case over her shoulder. 'He's a laugh and no mistake. We had a really good time after you'd got carted off, even though Flight Lieutenant Fenton-Jones seemed to prefer Jean's company to mine.'

'Shut up, Edie,' Jean said, blushing. 'Don't make more of it than it was.'

Edie pulled a face. 'Hark at her; you'd think butter wouldn't melt in her mouth. Well, I tell you, Poppy, she was anybody's after a couple of gin and tonics. It's a pity you missed it all.'

'Are you in a lot of trouble?' Mavis asked sympathetically.

'No, it's okay.'

Jean gave Poppy's arm a squeeze. 'Forget about it. I have, and I don't suppose I'll see Algy again. He's spending the day with his rich aunt and meeting up with Guy at the railway station this evening. Anyway, I'm starving. I wonder what Mrs T has got for our lunch today.'

Everyone enjoyed Mrs Toon's rabbit pie, although Mavis demurred at first, saying that she had kept a pet rabbit when she was a girl and it would be like eating one of its relations, but eventually hunger won and she cleaned her plate like the rest of them. Poppy managed to eat most of hers although the food stuck in her throat and she was relieved when Edie offered to finish it off for her. There was bread and butter pudding for dessert, although as Jean said the search for raisins was like hunt the thimble. Mrs Toon took offence at this remark and scolded her, reminding them all that there was a war on and dried fruit was scarce and likely to be unobtainable by Christmas. She was saving what she had in the store cupboard for the Christmas cake.

'Anyway, it was jolly good,' Jean said as she left the table. 'You're a great cook, Mrs T, and we love you.'

Mrs Toon flushed with pleasure. 'Well, I do me best,' she murmured modestly.

'Anyone got any shampoo?' Mavis asked as they wandered outside into the yard. 'My hair feels like coconut matting.'

'I've got a bit of Amami left,' Edie said warily. 'What will you give me as swops?'

'Oh, never mind. I'll use soap powder instead. I hate this war.'

'What are you going to do this afternoon, Poppy?' Jean angled her head. 'Are you washing your hair too?'

Poppy had just caught sight of Guy going into Goliath's stall and suddenly her legs refused to move. 'I've got homework to do. I'll see you later.'

'You can help us bring the cows for milking later on,' Edie said, strolling across the stable yard with her hands in her pockets. 'That's if you want to.'

'I do. I'll be there.' Poppy hurried off in the opposite direction. She had done her homework but now she wanted to get as far away from the house as possible. She simply could not face Guy after her humiliating experience last night. She crossed the field which had once been the deer park and found herself at the edge of the spinney where the old oak tree spread its crooked branches. Hitching her skirt up into her knickers, she climbed the tree. The tender green leaves did not offer much cover but she did not expect anyone to come past this secluded spot, particularly on a sleepy Sunday afternoon, when only the absolutely necessary farm work would be done. From up here she had a wonderful view over the brow of the hill to the distant sea. The sky was a perfect shade of azure as if an artist had washed it with watercolour and dotted it with puffball clouds made of cotton wool. She leaned back against the trunk and thought how wonderfully peaceful it all was and how hard to imagine that they were at war. The air smelt of damp earth with a hint of a salty tang blown in on a warm westerly breeze. Silence enveloped her, interrupted once or twice by the distant call of a cuckoo deep in the woods.

She closed her eyes and was drifting in the pleasant place between waking and sleeping when a voice below made her look down with a start.

'I thought I might find you here, Poppy.'

Peering through the branches, she saw Guy seated on Goliath's back, and he had Romeo on a leading rein. He smiled up at her. 'A little bird told me that you had learned to ride.'

She nodded wordlessly.

'Come down then and show me. Romeo could do with a bit of exercise.'

'I'm wearing a skirt.' It seemed an obvious statement but she could not think of anything else to say.

'That didn't stop you shinning up the tree.' He turned his head away. 'I'm not looking.'

With an almost euphoric feeling of relief, Poppy lowered herself until she could drop safely to the ground. She mounted Romeo with ease, glancing at Guy to make sure he was not looking as she arranged her skirt so that not too much leg was showing. 'All right then. I'm ready.'

They rode for a while in silence with Guy leading the way across the park and out through a gateway that led into a narrow lane bounded by high hedgerows. It was a steep descent to the rocky cove overlooking the wide expanse of the bay. The island of Portland loomed above a line of low-lying cloud, giving it the appearance of floating on the calm ultramarine sea. They dismounted and Guy tethered both horses to a five-barred gate leading into a field.

'Guy, about last night,' Poppy began hesitantly. 'I'm sorry . . .'

He held up his hand. 'Don't be. If anyone should apologise it's I and my family. We should have known it was your birthday and done something about it. At least your friends had the right idea, even if they were a bit misguided in their attempts to entertain you.'

'Amy would have remembered,' Poppy said, watching his expression closely. 'You must miss her a lot.'

He walked to the water's edge and picked up a stone, flinging it so that it bounced several times before sinking beneath the waves. 'She was keen to join her parents, and I can't blame her for wanting to get away from the war.'

It was hardly an answer to her question but Poppy could tell by the set of his shoulders that she had touched on a raw subject. She attempted to emulate his action with a pebble but it sank to the bottom.

'Sunk without trace,' Guy said, turning his head to grin at her.

'Don't say that. It might come true.'

'Not a chance. I'm fireproof.'

'Don't say that either, it's like tempting fate.' Her hand went automatically to the glass heart hanging on its silver chain. She had not taken it off since Mum gave it to her and the simple act of touching it brought the family closer and made her feel safe.

'What's that, Poppy?'

She displayed it proudly. 'Mum gave it to me last time I saw her. She said my dad had given it to her years ago, but I have to be careful as it's fragile and breaks easily.'

'That's true of all hearts, I suppose.' His serious expression melted into a smile. 'Easily broken, I mean. But not yours, I hope, Poppy. You've borne everything like a real trooper. Don't think I haven't noticed.'

'Oh, well, I don't know about that.' Suddenly shy, Poppy stared down at the wet sand as she traced a wavy line with the toe of her shoe.

'I mean it,' he said emphatically. 'You must miss your home and family but I've never heard you complain. You've been neglected by my mother and largely ignored by the rest of my family, and yet you still come up smiling. I don't think I would have had as much guts at such a young age.'

Poppy shrugged her shoulders. 'There's a war on.' She looked up and met his worried gaze with a chuckle. 'That's what everyone says when things go wrong, isn't it?'

He threw back his head and laughed. 'You've got a wicked sense of humour, Poppy Brown.'

'Have I?' She experienced a thrill that was even more intoxicating than the cider she had drunk the previous evening. Guy was speaking to her like an adult and an equal. 'No one ever told me that before.'

Hooking his arm around her shoulders, he gave her a hug. 'I wish I'd had you as a little sister. If it was possible to adopt siblings, I'd choose you.'

A cloud blotted out the sun and Poppy shivered. 'Ta,' she murmured, although inside she felt as though an ice-cold hand had clutched her warm heart.

'Of course I would, but I think your parents might object if anyone tried to take you away from them. You're special, Poppy, and don't you ever forget it.'

'I'll be going home soon, I expect.'

He frowned. 'I thought Amy had arranged for you to stay on at school.'

'It's complicated, and anyway I'd rather join the Land Army and work with the girls. I love it here, although of course I miss my family, but I don't miss brick and concrete, the thick smelly fog in winter, or pavements so hot in summer you could fry an egg on them.'

Guy stared at her as if seeing her for the first time. 'I had no idea you felt like this.'

'Why would you? I'm just an evacuee. I'll go home when the war is over and we'll never see each other again.

I don't fit in with your lot.' The bitter words came tumbling out unbidden, but she was surprised to see the look of shock on Guy's face. 'It's the truth,' she added.

'You make me ashamed of myself and my family.' He lifted her onto Romeo's saddle. 'But it's only the truth as you see it, Poppy. I'm truly sorry if that's the impression you've been given, but I don't think of you in that way, and neither did Amy. My parents are dinosaurs, living in a bygone age that began to fragment during the Great War, and will be gone forever by the time this one ends.' He vaulted onto Goliath's back. 'You're the future, and my family will have to get used to the idea. Now let's get home before it rains. I can see clouds forming over the island. We're in for a storm unless I'm very much mistaken.'

Guy left that night, taking the train to Waterloo, having left his car at the Pallisters' London home in order to save petrol. The family stood on the steps to see him off, but Poppy stood apart, as if separated from them by an invisible barrier. Guy brushed his mother's cheek with a brief kiss, gave Pamela a hug and ruffled Rupert's curls. He shook his father's hand and just when Poppy thought she was forgotten, he turned and walked over to her. The dying rays of the sun caught the crystal hanging round her neck, and he touched it gently with his finger. 'Take care of that glass heart, Poppy. Don't let anyone break it.' He wrapped his arms around her and held her for a brief moment before turning away and striding down the steps to the waiting car. Jackson made a move to open the rear door, but Guy shook his head and climbed into the front passenger seat.

As the Bentley pulled away, Poppy clasped the glass heart in her hand. She was certain the imprint of Guy's touch would be stored in it forever like a fly trapped in amber.

The family had gone indoors without acknowledging her presence, and Nancy's spiteful words rang in Poppy's head.

'Cooee.'

Poppy turned to see Mavis was waving frantically from the entrance to the stable yard. 'D'you fancy a cup of cocoa?'

Poppy ran down the steps to join her. 'I'd love some.'

'Edie's heating some milk on the stove in our room, and that Algy Fenton-whatshisname gave Jean a packet of chocolate biscuits that he'd bought as a present for his aunt but he decided that our need was greater. Jeannie obviously made a hit with him.'

'Algy's all right,' Poppy said vaguely. 'Guy's engaged to his sister. She was really good to me.'

'I heard that she'd scarpered off to Singapore to join her parents. If I was in love with a bloke like Guy I'm blowed if I'd leave him a prey to man-hungry females. Anyway, that's not our problem. Let's go and get some biscuits before those two greedy pigs scoff the lot.' Mavis hesitated, eyeing Poppy with a sympathetic smile. 'You're fond of him, aren't you?'

Poppy nodded her head. Her throat felt tight and tears stung the backs of her eyes. 'It's dangerous flying planes.'

'Guy's a survivor if ever I saw one. He's not the sort to get into a flap and panic. I'll bet he can keep a cool head in the worst situations. He'll be all right, I promise you.'

IN THE MONTHS that followed Mavis's confident prediction often sprang to mind, but that did not stop Poppy from worrying. Keeping busy was one way to allay her fears for Guy and for her family in London, although as yet there had been no air raid. Mum wrote once a week at least and Poppy sent a reply by return of post.

Life settled into a daily routine. On her return from school she would rush up to her room and change into something more suitable. She helped Mavis to milk the cows, collected eggs and cleaned out the hen houses. She ate her tea in the kitchen with the girls, and they helped Mrs Toon by washing up afterwards. Mr Carroll had thoughtfully installed a wireless so that they could keep up to date with the news, and they listened in awed silence to the broadcast describing the evacuation of British troops from the beaches at Dunkirk, and the heroic actions of the men in small and large craft who saved many thousands of lives. Then there was the occupation of the Channel Islands, which brought the war even closer to the Dorset coast. Mrs Toon was certain that they were all going to be murdered in their beds by German spies, and Edie said she would like to see the spy brave enough to take on three land girls with pitchforks and a set of red-hot curling tongs heated on the pot-bellied stove. Poppy prayed every night for Guy's safe deliverance. She did not know exactly where he was stationed, but when it was too dark to do any work in the fields she listened to the wireless in her room. Accounts of attacks by the Luftwaffe and the retaliatory strikes by the RAF Spitfires and Hurricanes made her break out in a cold sweat.

But the real nightmare began for her at the end of September, when the harvest had been gathered in and the trees in the orchard were groaning beneath the weight of apples ready to be picked and stored for winter. In the midst of this seeming bucolic idyll came the news of the savage air raid attack on London, and in particular the East End. They called it the Blitz, and in the days to come Poppy began to dread the mere mention of the word. She cried with relief when she received a letter from her mother making light of the terrors they faced and assuring her that they were all fine. They were all well and Poppy was not to worry, but she must remain in Dorset and not think of coming home until it was all over.

Poppy had been working full time on the land since she left school at the end of July, and Mrs Carroll had seemed content to allow this state of affairs to continue, but Edie urged her to get things on a more formal basis. Although Poppy had been putting it off, she knew that what Edie said made sense. If she was officially enrolled as a land girl she would be paid for her labours, and there would be no chance of her being compelled to do war work. Sid, although he was only just sixteen, was making noises about enlisting in the army. He did not, he told Poppy, want to work with a lot of silly women who thought they could boss him about, but in the end he departed for the munitions factory, no doubt encouraged by the fact that he could earn a great deal more money there than he did working for the Carrolls. This left the care of the horses, including the hefty Percheron, to the girls, who were already working from dawn until dusk on the farm.

Poppy had completely conquered her fear of horses, and had made it her business to learn as much as she could from Sid before he left. Armed with this knowledge, she plucked up the courage to speak to Marina.

'So you want to be a land girl, Poppy?'

'Yes, Mrs Carroll.'

'How old are you? I'm sure I should know, but I've completely forgotten.'

'I'll be fifteen next April.'

'You have to be eighteen. I don't make the rules.'

'But I'm doing the same work as the girls, Mrs Carroll.'

Marina leaned her elbows on the desk in her small study, steepling her fingers as she eyed Poppy thoughtfully. 'Yes, that's true. I know you work hard, and you also help out with Rupert, but it doesn't alter the fact that you can't enlist in the Land Army until you are at least seventeen, although it's officially eighteen. I could bend the rules a little but I can't break them. I'm afraid until then you will have to continue as you are. Unless, of course, you want to return home to London, although I wouldn't recommend it with the bombs raining down on the East End and the docks almost every night, and I'm sure that your mother wouldn't wish to put you in harm's way.'

Disappointment cramped her stomach as if she had just eaten several unripe apples. 'No. She doesn't want me to go home yet.'

'Then you must abide by your mother's wishes.' Marina sat back in her chair, and a hint of a smile curved her lips. 'Keep up the good work.'

Poppy left the house muttering, 'Keep up the good work, my foot.' A cold wind whipped across the fields as she trudged over the muddy furrows to relieve Jean who was taking a turn at ploughing, but obviously having some difficulty in handling Bob, the Percheron, who had a mind of his own. Jean's nose was pink at the tip and her cheeks reddened by the chilly east wind as she turned her head to grin at Poppy.

'Thank goodness. I thought I'd have to drive this beast all morning. He knows that I'm a complete amateur and he's so stubborn I'm sure the horrible thing is part mule. You'd think that Mrs C would hire one of those steam tractors they use on Tatton Farm, wouldn't you, only she's too tight-fisted. This contraption is positively mediaeval.' Jean paused, eyeing Poppy warily. 'What's the matter? Didn't it go too well?'

Poppy shook her head. 'She says I'm too young.'

'It's more like she doesn't want to pay you. Edie would call it slave labour, and I'd be inclined to agree with her.' She handed the reins to Poppy. 'Here you are then. I'm going for a cuppa. See you later.'

Poppy flicked the reins, clicking her tongue to make Bob lurch into action. Concentrating on the art of ploughing a straight line kept her mind off her own problems and by the end of the day she was too exhausted to care one way or the other. Having put Rupert to bed and read him his favourite story about Goldilocks and the Three Bears, Poppy had a splash about in the obligatory five inches of water, and went to bed early.

She was awakened from a deep sleep by someone shaking her shoulder. She opened her eyes, blinking as she tried to focus on Mrs Carroll's face in the dim light of early dawn. 'What's the matter?'

'I'm afraid I've got some rather bad news for you.'

She was awakened from a deep sleep by someone shaking her shoulder. She opened her eyes. Blinking as she tried to focus on Mrs Carroll's face in the dim light of early dawn. 'What's the matter?'

'I'm afraid I've got some rather bad news for you

Chapter Ten

Poppy sat astride the strongest branch of the oak tree, now in its autumn finery with acorns formed and ready to fall to the ground. She stared at the peaceful scene below with unseeing eyes. It was more than a week since she had received the terrible news, and she was still finding it almost impossible to believe that what Marina had told her was fact and not some cruel fiction. Surely there must have been a mistake? She had remained numb with shock as she struggled to come to terms with the loss of her entire family in one cataclysmic night. The red-brick terraced houses in Quebec Road had been built at the beginning of the century by skilled artisans. They were not particularly handsome, but they were solid and might have provided homes for countless generations, if it had not been for the direct hit by a bomb that the Luftwaffe pilot had apparently intended for the docks.

POPPY'S WAR 189

Poppy could barely remember what had happened after Mrs Carroll had told her the facts in her calm, dispassionate manner. The rest of the day was a blur, but for the first time since her arrival at Squire's Knapp she had been the centre of attention, when all she had wanted to do was crawl into a hole and hide. But no matter how grief-stricken she was, or how appalling her loss, the clock still ticked on. Day turned into night and with each dawn came a fresh start, but the pain was still there and she doubted if it would ever go away. Nevertheless, she had to get up in the morning if only to dress Rupert and give him his breakfast. He was too little to understand what had happened, but in an odd way this had been a comfort. She did not have to pretend to be cheerful or to fend off well-intentioned questions about how she was feeling. Sometimes the sympathy of others was almost harder to cope with than the grief itself.

Everyone had been kind, even Mrs Carroll in her unemotional way. Edie, Jean and Mavis had done their best to raise her spirits, but it seemed that the whole village knew of her loss and she could not walk down the street without somebody coming up to her and giving her a hug or a pat on the shoulder. Colin had drawn a picture for her which he presented shyly, explaining that it was supposed to be a bar of chocolate, the thing he missed the most. He had written a request to Santa Claus, asking for a bar of Cadbury's milk chocolate in his stocking on Christmas Day; that was his dream and he hoped the picture would make Poppy happy. She had thanked him solemnly and promised to pin the slightly crumpled piece of paper on the wall by her bed. She had shaken his hand and hurried on her way, hoping that no one in the village shop mentioned her loss. She did not want to break down and make a fool of herself in public.

A cool breeze fanned her cheeks and the cloudless sky showed promise of a fine day to come. It was only here, in Guy's tree, that she felt safe from prying eyes. In this serene rural setting it was almost impossible to imagine the war raging across the Channel and in the air over Britain. She could see deer grazing at the edge of the spinney, and rabbits were hopping about on the brow of the hill oblivious to the fact that their lives were likely to be short unless they kept away from snares and men with shotguns. On the ground below Goliath was munching the sweet grass. If she closed her eyes she could visualise Guy sitting on his back, looking up at her through the branches and smiling. Her hand flew to the heart pendant that he had touched as he said goodbye. He was risking his life every day in this awful war. She felt her throat constrict as she recalled the snowy day in December when Mum had given her the pendant that had meant so much to her. She curled her fingers around the glass drop, which was still warm from her body. In her mind's eyes she could see Mum in her shabby grey woollen coat with the unflattering felt hat pinned to her head by the ridiculously long hatpin. If she closed her eyes she could see her mother's pale hand waving from the rear window of the coach. She bowed her head, wrapping her arms around her body in an attempt to hold herself together.

The tinny sound of a bicycle bell made her open her eyes and looking down she saw Jean pedalling frantically on the old sit-up-and-beg bike that they had found in a corner of the coach house. She was bouncing up and down as she rode across the furrows which were ready for sowing winter wheat. 'Poppy, come down quick. You've got a trunk call.'

Slithering off the branch, Poppy dropped to the ground. 'Who is it?'

'I dunno,' Jean said breathlessly as she swerved to a halt. 'It's a man. He had to ring off but he's calling again in five minutes.'

The telephone was in Edwin's study: a warm, book-lined room that smelt faintly of cigar smoke and beeswax polish. He was still in his dressing gown, looking tousled and sleepy as he picked up the receiver. 'Barton Lacey 349.' He listened intently. 'Hold on a moment, and I'll pass you to Poppy.'

She took it from him, and suddenly it was hard to breathe. 'Hello.'

'Poppy, is that you?' The achingly familiar voice sounded very far away.

Her heart missed a beat. 'Joe, is that really you?'

'It's me, kid. Are you all right?'

'Oh, Joe, you're safe. I can't believe it. I thought I'd lost you as well.'

'Not me, ducks. I'm bullet proof, but seriously, it was just luck on my part. My leave was cancelled or I would have copped it too. It's a bloody bad show, Poppy.'

'Why didn't you let me know before? It's been awful . . .'

'I thought Mum would have written and told you that my leave had been cancelled, and . . .' Three loud pips drowned his last few words.

'What did you say, Joe?'

'I said I've got compassionate leave. Mabel and me are getting married by special licence at the register office.'

'You're getting married?' Poppy could hardly take it all in.

'The pips will go again any second now and I've no more change. I know it's all a bit sudden but can you come up to London tomorrow? We want you to be there and I've only got thirty-six hours' leave.'

'Yes, of course I will.'

'Meet me at one under the clock at Liverpool Street station.'

'I'll be there, Joe. Joe, can you hear me?' She took the receiver from her ear. 'We've been cut off.' She turned to Edwin who was watching her with a worried frown. 'That was my brother. He's getting married and he wants me to go up to London tomorrow. May I go? Please say I can.'

SHE ARRIVED AT Waterloo station just before twelve thirty. The train had been packed with servicemen and women as well as civilians, and had stopped at every station en route, taking on more passengers until there was no standing room in the corridors, and in the compartments people were packed together like sardines. Revelling in the prospect of being reunited with her brother, Poppy had been oblivious to the discomfort. She had barely noticed the unpleasant body odour emanating from the fat woman sitting next to her whose bulk seemed to overflow, squashing Poppy into the corner of the compartment, or the constant coughing of the man sitting opposite who obviously had the most awful cold and was probably infecting everyone within range of his explosive sneezes. Every time he took his hanky from his pocket there was an overpowering smell of Vick's VapoRub, but that did not seem to curb the appetite of the girl who sat next to him munching an apple down to the core, which she also ate with apparent relish. The journey took over three and a half hours, but as soon as her feet touched the platform and she took a deep breath of the smoky London air, Poppy felt at home. She had never done this journey on her own, and as the Bakerloo Line beneath the Thames had been closed for safety reasons before the outbreak of war, she had to find a bus to take her to Liverpool Street. It took longer than she had anticipated and when she eventually reached the main concourse of the station she could see by the huge white-faced clock that she was over twenty minutes late. She scanned the faces in the crowd, praying that she had not missed Joe. Then she spotted him. There was no mistaking Joe. He reminded her forcibly of their dad with his slightly beaky nose, high forehead and determined chin. He looked thinner than when she had last seen him, but when he saw her and smiled he was the same old Joe: the big brother who had alternately teased and spoiled her as a young child, but had always been on her side when she was in trouble with Mum or Dad.

'Poppy? Cor blimey, mate. I hardly recognised you.' He wrapped his arms around her in a hug. 'Strewth, you've grown up a lot in a year.'

Halfway between laughing and crying, Poppy touched his thin cheek with the tips of her fingers. 'You haven't changed at all, Joe. Well, not much anyway. You're even better-looking than I remember.'

'Get off with you, girl.' He held her at arm's length, looking her up and down as if he could scarcely believe his eyes. 'I can see that you're the same cheeky little madam you always were beneath the posh voice and fancy clothes.'

Shocked, she stared at him in disbelief. 'I'm not posh. I'm just the same as I always was.'

'You've grown up into a proper lady, Poppy. Not that I'm saying that's a bad thing, not at all. But you are different, there's no two ways about it. Anyway, let's get moving and get the tube home. You can stay tonight, can't you?'

She patted her shoulder bag, slanting a look at him beneath her lashes and grinning. 'Got my toothbrush, nightie and clean knickers, Joe. I can stay as long as you like.'

'Saucebox. Lucky Gran can't hear you talking about unmentionables in public.' He took her by the elbow, guiding her towards the subway.

'What time is the ceremony, Joe?'

'Half past three. We'd best get a move on or Mabel will kill me before Hitler has a chance to have a go.'

THE WALK FROM the tube station took a good fifteen minutes through pleasant streets lined with modest semi-detached houses with neat gardens and well-trimmed hedges. The only difference from the one time when Poppy had visited Mabel's home was that the window-panes were criss-crossed with brown paper tape and there were piles of sandbags everywhere. She had to trot in order to keep up with Joe, but he kept her amused with stories about the catering corps, which was not a subject which she would have thought conjured up much mirth, but he had a way of putting things that made her laugh out loud; something she had not done for quite a while. It seemed that no sooner had they left the station than they arrived at the house, and Mabel was standing at the front door, wiping her hands on her apron and beaming a welcome.

She ran down the front path, which was bordered by strips of flowerbed overflowing with fading asters and stumpy dahlias.

'Poppy, love, it's so good to see you, you poor little scrap.' Throwing her arms around Poppy's neck, Mabel held her to her ample bosom. 'I was just going upstairs to change into me glad rags. I couldn't get the coupons to buy a proper wedding dress. Still, beggars can't be choosers, and I've got a nice new frock.'

Hustled into the small, rather dark hallway, Poppy blinked as her eyes grew accustomed to the dim light. The contrast between Squire's Knapp and this small sub-urban house was startling. She realised with a jolt of surprise that she had grown accustomed to enormous rooms, high ceilings and the trappings of wealth, but she was instantly ashamed of herself for making comparisons. So what if the staircase ended just a few feet from the front door? Did it really matter that the passage leading to the kitchen was narrow and the paintwork scuffed, and the wallpaper faded to a dull sepia tint? This was probably more of a home to Mabel and her mother than Squire's Knapp was to the Carrolls, who always seemed to be on the verge of falling out with each other.

'Come into the front room, Poppy, and dump your things down anywhere. Make yourself at home, ducks,' Mabel said, pushing Joe away with an embarrassed chuckle as he grabbed her round the waist. 'Lord, Joe. Not in front of your sister.'

He winked at Poppy. 'She's a big girl now, and we'll be man and wife in an hour or so.'

Mabel uttered a loud screech. 'And me with me hair still in curlers. I've got to go upstairs and get changed.' Dodging Joe's grasping hands, she opened the door and ushered Poppy into the front room.

A desultory fire burned in the grate and Mabel's mother sat huddled in an armchair with a crotchet blanket over her knees. She squinted at Poppy, peering at her through glasses with lenses as thick as milk bottle bottoms.

'It's Poppy, Mum. Joe's sister.' Mabel raised her voice. 'You know Poppy.'

'Never seen her before in me life.'

'Yes, of course you have, Mum.' Mabel exchanged resigned looks with Joe. 'I'm going upstairs. I'll leave you to explain.'

'It's my sister Poppy, Ma,' Joe said cheerfully. 'You remember little Poppy.'

'That's never little Poppy. You've got the wrong one there, Joe.'

Poppy knelt down beside her, trying not to stare at the whiskers growing out of Mrs Tanner's chin. 'No really, it is me, Poppy.'

'You don't talk like Poppy.' Mrs Tanner fingered the fine tweed of Poppy's jacket, passed on by a reluctant Pamela who had been forced to acknowledge that she had put on a few pounds in weight. Child-bearing she had cried dramatically, had ruined her figure forever.

'But I am Poppy, Mrs Tanner. I've only been away for a year.'

'That's what I call a good bit of cloth. Proper Harris tweed unless I'm very much mistaken. You done all right for yourself by the looks of things, young miss.'

'Sit down and tell us what's been happening to you in the country,' Joe said hastily. He leaned over Mrs Tanner's chair. 'How about a glass of stout, Ma? It's a special occasion after all.'

'Never mind the stout,' Mrs Tanner muttered, fixing him with a hard stare. 'Where's that girl hidden the sherry bottle?'

'Sherry it is then.' Unruffled, Joe went to a corner cupboard and took out a bottle which he set on a table in the bay window where a tray of glasses had been laid out in readiness for the coming celebrations. He filled three of them to the brim and handed one to his future mother-in-law and one to Poppy. 'How old are you now, ducks? Old enough to take a drop of sherry, I hope.'

'I'm fourteen and a half, Joe.'

He grinned. 'The half is important at your age. Anyway, down the hatch.' He tossed the drink back in one go. 'Sit down, Poppy. Make yourself at home.'

The settee was covered in slightly worn Rexine and Poppy sat down cautiously, half afraid she might slither to the floor if she made the wrong move. She sipped her sherry, looking round the room which she had once thought was huge, but now she realised that it was comparatively small. The dark brown three-piece suite might have been the in thing twenty years ago, but it was now outdated and extremely uncomfortable. She could feel a broken spring pressing into her buttocks and she shifted her position, hoping that it would not impale her as she moved. Joe and Mrs Tanner were seemingly in a contest to see who could down the most sherry in the shortest space of time, leaving Poppy free to study the Victorian prints on the walls, which were sombre and thoroughly depressing. She had not realised until now how much she had grown to appreciate the gilt-framed oil paintings of landscapes, family portraits, still lifes and studies of thoroughbred horses that hung on the walls in Squire's Knapp. Coming back to suburbia was like entering a forgotten world.

Joe refilled his glass and perched on the arm of the settee, gazing down at Poppy with an anxious frown. 'The reason it took so long to let you know that I was all right, was that I had a job tracing you, Poppy. I knew you'd been sent to a posh house in Barton Lacey, but I'd clean forgotten the name of the people who'd taken you in, so I got in touch with the billeting officer. After going through a load of red tape, I found you.'

The sherry had gone straight to Poppy's head. She had not eaten since breakfast and she was feeling distinctly muzzy. 'I couldn't believe it when I heard your voice, Joe. I thought I'd lost everyone.' Suddenly she was crying and she could not stop.

'What's the matter with her?' Mrs Tanner picked up her walking stick and prodded Joe. 'Do something, you big booby. Tell her to stop snivelling like a baby.'

'Shut up, Ma.' Abandoning his drink, Joe sat down beside Poppy and slipped his arm around her shoulders. 'There, there, kid. Let is all out. I howled meself when I heard the news, and I'm a bloke.'

Poppy fumbled in her pocket and found the handkerchief that Guy had given her. She had meant to return it to him, but somehow there had never been an appropriate moment. She buried her face in its soft folds. The familiar scent of him still lingered in the material, or perhaps it was simply wishful thinking. Whatever it was she felt comforted, and Joe was saying something. She blew her nose. 'I'm sorry. I didn't mean to cry all over you, Joe.'

He gave her shoulders a quick squeeze, clearing his throat. 'It's all right, kid. Understandable, but this is meant to be a happy occasion. Don't let Mabel see you crying. She was very cut up about what happened too. We don't want to spoil her big day.'

'Nobody bothers about me,' Mrs Tanner muttered, holding out her glass. 'What has an old woman got to do to get another drink round here?'

'Don't you think you've had enough, Ma?' Joe said anxiously. 'You'll be too squiffy to go to the register office if you drink much more.'

Mrs Tanner opened her mouth to reply but she closed it again as Mabel entered the room and did a twirl. 'How do I look, Joe?'

He shook his head. 'Bloody marvellous, ducks. You look a million dollars.'

'You look lovely,' Poppy said sincerely.

Mabel's cheeks glowed pink and she puffed out her chest. 'It took all my savings, and it's rayon not silk, but you'd never know, would you?'

Poppy shook her head. 'Of course not.' She would die rather than say that the blue and white floral dress with its padded shoulders and belted waist might be a clever high street copy, but it was nothing like the fashionable silk gowns that Pamela Pallister wore. If Poppy were to be completely honest she would have to admit that Mabel's dress emphasised her bulges and made her look rather podgy, but even under torture on the rack the truth would not be dragged out of her. She would not wish to see the happiness fade from Mabel's pretty face or the loving look in Joe's eyes wiped away by a careless word. 'You look absolutely beautiful, Mabel. Joe's a lucky man.'

Joe leapt to his feet as something in the street outside caught his eye. 'It's my mate Dennis. Our lift is here. I know it ain't done for the bride and groom to travel together, Mabel love, but needs must.' He moved to Mrs Tanner's side and helped her from her chair. 'Can you manage to walk or shall I carry you, Ma?'

She shook her stick at him. 'Get away from me, you big lump. I ain't so crippled I can't walk a step or two to the taxi.'

Mabel was in the middle of securing her blue straw hat with a hatpin. She paused, exchanging glances with Joe. 'It's not a taxi, Mum.'

Poppy's hand flew to her mouth as she smothered a giggle. Outside she could see a brewer's dray decorated with white ribbons. The sturdy Shire horse had bows tied to its mane and the driver wore a rather battered top hat. Suddenly everything settled into perspective and she put all thoughts of Squire's Knapp and the elegant Carroll family out of her mind. This was how things were done here in Ilford, and it was wartime when everything was topsy-turvy. This was her real family and she was determined to have fun.

The ceremony was simple and of necessity brief as there were two other couples waiting to be married. Poppy had a lump in her throat as Mabel, looking every inch the radiant bride, left the register office on Joe's arm. Mabel's Uncle Fred had a box Brownie and he took several photographs in the vestibule, making everyone stand in line and say 'cheese', which also made Poppy want to giggle. Outside it had started to spit with rain and, despite her protests that she was the eldest sister and in a poor state of health, Mrs Tanner was crammed in the back seat of Uncle Fred's Austin Seven with Auntie Dottie, while Auntie Ida sat in the front.

Poppy was relieved that there was no room in the car for her as she preferred riding on the dray. She made herself as comfortable as possible on an old mattress that had seen better days and was only fit for a rubbish tip, while Mabel and Joe sat on the driver's seat next to Dennis, who seemed to have something wrong with his legs and walked with a strange lop-sided gait. He had insisted on lifting Poppy onto the dray, but she did not like the way his hands had lingered around her waist or the look in his eyes as he glanced at her bare legs. She was beginning to wish she had worn the hideous lisle stockings that she had been compelled to wear to school in winter. No man in his right mind would ogle a girl in lisle stockings, unless he was completely desperate.

Back at the house everyone filed into the front room and there was an uncomfortable silence as if they were all waiting for someone to strike up a conversation. Poppy had seen more cheerful faces in the doctor's waiting room, but she could think of nothing to say. Mrs Tanner had ousted her sister Dottie from the chair by the fire and the pair of them were left glowering at each other after the battle of wills. Mabel left the room saying she was going to fetch the sandwiches, and it seemed that the party was doomed to be more like a wake until Joe produced a crate of brown ale from beneath the table. He poured sherry for the ladies and filled pint mugs with beer for the men.

'Down the hatch.' Uncle Fred took a hefty swig of beer.

Auntie Ida raised her sherry glass. 'To the bride and groom,' she said, staring pointedly at her husband.

Uncle Fred flushed brick red and cleared his throat. 'Yes, of course. The bride and groom, God bless 'em.'

'Well done, Joe.' Dennis slapped him on the back. 'You've got yourself a real smasher.'

Mabel had just come into the room carrying a plate heaped with sandwiches. She bobbed a curtsey. 'Ta ever so, Dennis. You tell him that often enough and maybe he'll believe you.'

Joe slipped his arm around her waist. 'I know it already, ducks. I'm the luckiest man alive.' He planted a smacking kiss on her cheek.

'Never mind the canoodling,' Mrs Tanner said crossly. 'I'm starving. Give us a sandwich, Mabel.'

It might not have been the best beginning to a party, but the ice was broken and as the beer and sherry went down, the conversation picked up. Mabel handed round meat paste sandwiches and slices of Victoria sponge cake. Auntie Dottie nibbled a sandwich having first opened it up and inspected the filling. 'Couldn't you get any tinned salmon, Mabel? We always had salmon and cucumber sandwiches at family weddings.'

'No, Auntie. They'd run out at the Home and Colonial.'

'You should try Waitrose, dear,' Auntie Ida said, helping herself to cake. 'I always shop there and have my order delivered.'

'Stop showing off, Ida,' Mrs Tanner said, scowling. 'I expect you get stuff on the black market anyway. I reckon that Fred's one of them spivs you hear talked about on the wireless; making money out of other people's hardship.'

'Hold on, Maggie,' Fred protested, gulping down a tot of brandy from a bottle that Joe had found at the back of the cupboard. 'I'm no spiv. I'm an auctioneer and businessman.'

'Same thing,' Mrs Tanner muttered. 'Fill me glass up, Joe.'

'Have you tried the cake, Poppy?' Mabel wafted the plate under her nose. 'I made it myself. I couldn't get any fat so I used liquid paraffin. It rose a treat in the oven. Do have a bit before the gannets eat the lot.'

'Thanks, it looks lovely.' Dutifully, Poppy took a slice. She bit into it and managed a smile. 'It's super. You'd never know the difference, Mabel.' She tried not to think of the feather-light sponges that Mrs Toon made without the aid of liquid paraffin, or the warm scones straight from the oven served with homemade raspberry jam.

It was getting dark, and the blackout curtains had to be drawn before Mabel switched on the light. The sandwiches had been consumed and there were only a couple of slices of cake left on the plate. Joe's crate of brown ale was emptying fast and the level in the sherry bottle had gone down considerably. Uncle Fred went out to his car and returned with a bottle of gin and another of whisky. 'Go easy on the measures,' he told Joe in a low voice. 'Dennis got me these.' He tapped the side of his nose and winked.

There was a sudden lull in conversation and Dennis leapt to his feet. 'Come on, folks, this is a wedding, not a wake. Let's have some music.' He limped over to a small upright piano that stood in the corner shrouded in a chenille cloth. 'The old harp in a coffin,' he said, laughing loudly. 'Any requests?' Without giving anyone time to answer he sat on the piano stool and began a rendering of 'Roll out the Barrel' with more enthusiasm than artistic merit.

Joe pushed the settee back against the wall and moved the armchairs into the bay window. He took the cake plate from Mabel and put it down on the table. 'May I have this dance, Mrs Brown?'

'Ooer, that doesn't half sound good,' Mabel said, flinging her arms around his neck. 'Delighted, I'm sure, Mr Brown.'

'There's nothing like a good wedding, I say,' Auntie Ida said, draining her glass. 'Get us a drop of mother's ruin, love.' She held it out to Poppy. 'Two fingers of gin and a dash of water.'

'Yes, ma'am.' Poppy went to fetch the bottle from the table.

Dottie nudged her elder sister. 'Ain't she got lovely manners, Ida? That's what comes of living with toffs.'

Ida peered at Poppy through narrowed eyes as if she were having difficulty in focusing. 'Yes, I heard you'd been evacuated to the country, dear. Nice place, is it?'

'Very nice.' Poppy poured the gin, guessing the amount, and added a splash of water. She handed it to Auntie Ida. 'I hope that's to your liking.'

'So tell us about the people who took you in.' Auntie Ida patted the empty seat on the settee. 'Sit down, dear. We want to know everything.'

NEXT DAY POPPY made the return journey to Dorset. She had left Ilford early in the morning and arrived at Barton Lacey station late in the afternoon. Trains had been cancelled or simply delayed. She was tired and hungry and it was a good two-mile walk to Squire's Knapp. This time there was no Jackson waiting for her in the Bentley and she had no other option than to go on foot. By the time she reached the house she had blisters on both heels and her small suitcase felt as though it was packed with bricks instead of a change of clothing and her toothbrush.

It was teatime and there was no one about on the estate. The sky was dark with rainclouds and the house looked shuttered and grey. The blackout curtains had already been drawn in the downstairs rooms and the front door was locked. She made her way round through the stables hoping to see one of the girls, but again there was no sign of life other than Goliath poking his great head over the stable door and whickering gently. She went to him and stroked his head, tickling his ears, which was what he seemed to enjoy most, but the rain had started in earnest and she hurried across the cobblestones to enter the house through the scullery. Again she seemed to have mistimed her arrival through no fault of her own. The table had been cleared and Cora, the girl from the village who had been hired to help out in the kitchen after Nancy's sudden departure, was sweeping the floor.

'Where is everyone?' Poppy asked, setting her case down on the floor and warming her hands in front of the range.

'Gone out. There's a film show in the village hall.' Cora continued sweeping.

'Is Mrs Carroll at home?'

Cora frowned, leaning on the broom. 'I think she wants to see you. That's right, she does. You're to go to the study as soon as you get here, that's what she said. I remember now.'

'Thanks.' Picking up her case with a sigh, Poppy went in search of Mrs Carroll. She tapped on the study door.

'Come.'

Mrs Carroll's voice did not sound too inviting. She was leafing through a pile of papers and she did not look up when Poppy entered the room.

'You wanted to see me, Mrs Carroll?'

Marina glanced at her, unsmiling. 'Yes. take a seat.' She set the documents aside. 'How old are you now?'

Surprised by the sudden question and Mrs Carroll's apparent loss of memory, Poppy sat down on the nearest chair. 'Fourteen. I'll be fifteen next April.'

'Now that you've been reunited with your brother and he is a married man, you have a family of your own again. You're too old to be kept here as an evacuee but you're much too young to be taken on as a land girl. I know that's what you wanted, but I'm afraid it's impossible.'

'But I do the same work as the other girls, ma'am.'

'Nevertheless, I'd be flouting the law if I allowed you to continue. I overlooked your age in the past because you were orphaned and homeless, but now everything has changed, and I have no alternative but to send you home.'

Poppy stared at her aghast. 'But it isn't my home. I hardly know Mabel and her mother. Joe has gone back to his regiment and you promised Mum that I could stay here.'

'That was a long time ago. Amy was paying for your schooling and you were helping to look after my grandson.'

'But I can still look after Rupert. I love him and he loves me.'

Marina frowned. 'Sentimental nonsense. I don't doubt that you're fond of the boy and he likes you, but then a two-year-old loves anyone who makes a fuss of them. Anyway, your room will be occupied by a professional nanny whom my daughter has employed to look after her son, and she will be starting at the beginning of next week. I've written a glowing reference for you to give to any future employer, and I've sent a telegram to your sister-in-law telling her to expect you tomorrow evening. I'm sorry, Poppy, I know you've settled down here and you've been very little trouble during your stay, but I have no choice. I wish you every success in the future, but you will leave Squire's Knapp in the morning.'

Chapter Eleven

'It's not bloody fair,' Edie said, hooking her arm around Poppy's shoulders. 'Mrs C is an old bat and I don't care who hears me say so.'

'Hush, keep your voice down.' Jean glanced anxiously up and down the railway platform. 'You'll get us all sacked if you don't watch your tongue.' She patted Poppy on the cheek. 'Not that I disagree with Edie. We'll miss you terribly.'

Mavis came hurrying through the ticket hall clutching a bar of chocolate which she thrust into Poppy's hands. 'I used all my coupons for this, so don't go sharing it around. It's for you and you alone, love.' Pushing Edie aside, Mavis gave Poppy a hug. 'I can't believe you're leaving us.'

Close to tears, Poppy sniffed. 'I don't want to go, but she said I'm too young to be a land girl.'

'She makes me sick,' Edie said bitterly. 'The old hypocrite. She was happy enough to let you slog away when it suited her, and play nanny to young Rupert, but now she's no use for you you're chucked out with the bath water.'

'Isn't that throwing the baby out with the bath water?' Mavis said with a puzzled frown.

'Don't be so literal.' Jean slipped her arm around Poppy's shoulders. 'We think it's a crying shame, and we'll miss you like billy-o.'

'I'll write to you,' Poppy said, sniffing. 'And you must write and tell me everything that's going on. Tell Algy to send my love to Amy, because I haven't got an address for her. I asked Mrs Carroll but she kept forgetting.'

'Typical,' Jean snorted. 'Never mind. I promise to mention it to Algy, if I ever see him again. We're not an item . . .'

'Just good friends,' Edie and Mavis chanted in unison.

'Shut up,' Jean said without malice. 'Anyway, here comes your train, Poppy.'

Amidst tears and hugs, Poppy somehow managed to board the London-bound train. She let the window down and leaned out waving until they were out of sight. She picked up her suitcase, slung her gas mask over her shoulder and trudged through the corridors in search of a non-smoking compartment. After being buffeted about and doing an involuntary cake-walk as she crossed the concertina-like area where the carriages were joined together, she found an almost empty compartment next to the guard's van. A young woman in Wrens uniform was asleep in the far corner next to the window and a thin woman with a baby in her arms was seated opposite, staring blankly out of the window while her child slept.

No doubt she was grateful for the rest, Poppy thought sympathetically. The poor soul looked exhausted.

Poppy settled down by the window next to the corridor and closed her eyes but she could not sleep. All she could think of was Squire's Knapp which had become her home, and the friends she was leaving far behind. If only Guy had been there he would have stood up for her. He would have seen how well she had looked after the horses and appreciated how hard she had worked on the farm. He would not have allowed his mother to send her away. Neither would Amy, who had done so much for her in the past, but at least she was safe in Singapore.

Poppy smothered a sigh and unwrapped the chocolate bar, breaking off a square and popping it into her mouth. The sweet scent of cocoa and cream had the effect of waking the Wren and the woman with the baby looked up, showing a spark of interest for the first time. 'I can't eat it all,' Poppy lied, breaking the bar into chunks and offering it round. 'Do have some. I don't want to make myself sick.'

'Ta, I don't mind if I do,' the thin woman said, smiling.

'Go on then,' the Wren said, taking a square of chocolate. 'I never could resist anything sweet. My name's Sally, by the way. What's yours?'

'I'm Poppy Brown, and I've got sandwiches too. Mrs Toon made enough to feed an army. Would you like one?' She passed round the packet of cheese and pickle sandwiches and Sally produced a Thermos flask of tea which they also shared. The thin woman, whose name was May, had three apples in a brown paper bag, although both

Poppy and Sally said they were too full to take advantage of her offer. Exchanging knowing glances with Sally, Poppy thought privately that the apples were probably the only food that May was likely to get that day. They parted at Waterloo in a spirit of camaraderie and went their separate ways.

Feeling as though she had been travelling for days, Poppy arrived at the house in Ilford just as Mabel was setting the table for tea.

'Well this is a turn up for the books,' Mabel said cheerfully. 'I wasn't expecting to see you again so soon, Poppy. When I got the telegram from that posh woman you could have knocked me down with a feather. I thought you was set to stay there for the duration.'

'So did I,' Poppy said tiredly. 'I hope you don't mind.'

Dropping a knife with a clatter, Mabel enveloped her in a warm embrace. 'Of course I don't, ducks. You're my Joe's sister and part of the family. You'll have to put up with Ma, who isn't such a bad old stick when you get to know her, but we'll rub along nicely, I'm sure.'

'I heard that,' Mrs Tanner said, glowering at Mabel. 'And who's going to pay for her keep, I'd like to know? Make sure you get her ration book off her.'

Poppy fished in her pocket and handed her ration book to Mabel. 'I'll go out tomorrow and look for a job. I won't be a burden to you.'

Mabel's mouth turned down at the corners. 'Oh, love. Don't talk like that. You're a good kid and I'm glad to have your company.'

'There is a war on,' Mrs Tanner said grimly.

'I'll find something, even if it's scrubbing floors.'

Mabel laid her hand on Poppy's arm. 'Tell you what; I do a cleaning job at the hospital. Perhaps they'll have something for you too. I've seen plenty of young 'uns doing all sorts of things from running errands to helping the nurses. I'm sure they'll be glad to have you.'

'I always wanted to be a nurse when I was little,' Poppy said with a sigh. 'But I'd need more qualifications, which I could have got if I'd stayed on at school.'

Mabel nodded sympathetically. 'Never mind, ducks. Sit down and have something to eat. You'll feel better after a good night's sleep. Let's hope the blooming siren doesn't go off tonight.'

'Even if it does I'm not getting into that damn Morrison shelter again, Mabel.' Mrs Tanner emphasised her words by striking the floor with her stick. 'I'll take me chances in me own bed. Bloody Hitler.'

LARGELY DUE TO Mabel's efforts, Poppy was taken on as a cleaner at the local hospital. She scrubbed floors, cleaned sinks, basins and lavatories, and returned home each day with rough reddened hands and the smell of disinfectant clinging to her clothes and hair. She was too young to train as a nurse but at the suggestion of one of the ward sisters she joined the Red Cross as a cadet, spending three or four evenings a week attending classes in first aid, home nursing, hygiene and even ARP training. In the winter evenings she not only had to contend with wind, rain and bitter cold, but also the blackout, which made the walk to and from the church hall where the classes were given quite hazardous. Sometimes it was impossible to see her hand in front of her face, and the newspapers said that the number of road traffic accidents had doubled despite strict petrol rationing. As the winter progressed, Poppy was beginning to feel like a mole. She left for work in the dark and returned home after dusk. She rarely had time to stop and look out of the windows at the hospital, unless she was cleaning them, and on her day off she slept.

A few days before Christmas, on a Sunday when Mabel's off duty happened to coincide with Poppy's, they had just finished washing the dishes after lunch when Mrs Tanner called out from the front room where she had retired to take her afternoon nap.

'Come and look, Mabel. There's a bloody big limousine pulled up outside.'

Mabel and Poppy hurried into the room to peer out of the window.

'It's chauffeur driven,' Mabel said in an awed tone. 'Maybe the King and Queen have invited themselves to tea?'

'Well, I hope they like fish paste,' Mrs Tanner said grimly. 'And liquid paraffin gives me the runs.'

Poppy's hand flew to her mouth as she recognised the car. Unless she was very much mistaken it belonged to the Pallisters, and when Harper stepped out to open the door she knew she was right.

'Good heavens. Just look at that coat.' Mabel grabbed Poppy by the shoulder, pushing her towards the window. 'That's mink or I'm a Dutchman.'

'It's Mrs Pallister.' Poppy hurried to the front door and opened it in time to see Pamela picking her way daintily over the cracks in the concrete path.

She looked up, twisting her scarlet lips into a smile. 'Hello, Poppy.' She turned to the chauffeur. 'Bring the basket, Harper. This is the right house.'

'Come in,' Poppy said, standing back to allow Pamela to step inside. The chauffeur had dutifully followed her up the path carrying a wicker basket which he handed to Poppy with a smart salute.

'Thanks,' she murmured. 'Won't you come in and have a cup of tea?'

'Harper will wait in the car,' Pamela said firmly. 'Close the door, Poppy. Your neighbours are staring at me. I can feel the fluttering of net curtains from here.'

Somewhat reluctantly, Poppy closed the door on Harper. She remembered the kindness that Jackson had shown her when she was ignored by everyone else at Squire's Knapp. If she lived to be a hundred she knew she would not be able to treat servants like lesser beings. She eyed Pamela warily, thinking that she looked distinctly out of place in her mink coat and matching hat. The crocodile-skin handbag that she clutched in her gloved hands was certainly not imitation, and her stockings were silk. No gravy browning for Mrs Hector Pallister.

'Are you going to keep me standing in the hall, Poppy? I thought we'd taught you better manners at Squire's Knapp.'

'I'm sorry. I'm just so surprised to see you, Miss Pamela.'

'Mrs Pallister. I've told you a dozen times if I've told you once.' Pamela turned to look at Mabel, who was standing in the doorway, staring at her in amazement. 'And you are?'

'Mrs Brown, madam. I'm Poppy's sister-in-law. Do come into the sitting room and make yourself comfortable. I'll put the kettle on.' Mabel hurried into the kitchen and closed the door.

'I can't stay,' Pamela said, shaking her head as Poppy made a move to show her into the front room. 'I'm not supposed to use the car this afternoon. Petrol coupons, you know. Even though Hector gets a special allowance because of his job, we have to use them judiciously. I simply came to wish you the compliments of the season from everyone at home and to bring you some gifts from the land girls. Mrs Toon baked a cake for you and asked to be remembered.'

'That was kind of her.' Poppy clutched the basket handle tightly in her hands, staring down at the starched white table napkin that covered the contents. 'Thank you. It was good of you to come all this way.'

'Well, I must confess I wasn't too happy when my mother sent you back to London without so much as a word to any of us. You were good to Rupert and he misses you. I'm afraid he hasn't taken too kindly to Nanny, although she's a most competent and experienced woman.'

'I'm sorry. I miss Rupert too. He's a lovely little boy.'

'Yes, well he's going through a rather naughty stage at the moment, but Nanny is very strict and doesn't allow him to get away with tantrums. I'm sure she's right.'

Before Poppy had a chance to say anything, Mabel stuck her head round the kitchen door. 'D'you take sugar, Mrs Pallister?'

'No, too kind, but I really can't stay for tea. I must be toddling along.' She turned to Poppy. 'I almost forgot to tell you. Guy sends his very best wishes.'

Suddenly Poppy was finding it hard to breathe. 'He came home?'

'He had a twenty-four-hour pass. I think he only wanted to see that wretched horse of his, but he was quite upset to think you'd been sent back to London with the Blitz and everything. But then he always took your side. I suppose it's his instinct to look after helpless creatures like animals and small children.'

'I'm glad he's all right anyway,' Poppy said, ignoring Pamela's patronising remarks.

'Yes, but I think they're sending him abroad. He didn't tell us, of course, that wouldn't have been the done thing at all, but Hector says there's going to be a push in the Western Desert, but don't you dare mention that to anyone else.'

Flattered to be taken into her confidence, Poppy shook her head. 'No, I won't say a word. Cross my heart.'

'Yes, well I really must go now. Good luck and merry Christmas, Poppy.'

Poppy stood in the doorway, watching Pamela teeter down the path. Harper leapt out of the car to open the gate for her. He moved swiftly to hold the door while she took her seat in the limousine. The net curtains in the house across the road fluttered as old Mrs Marshall peered out of the window. It would be all round the street by tea-time that the Tanners had a posh visitor. Poppy could not have cared less, but she imagined that Mrs Tanner would be secretly delighted. She stepped back into the hallway almost bumping into Mabel who was standing close behind her.

'Well, I never did.' Mabel snatched the basket from Poppy's hands. 'What a turn up for the books. Close the door, love, it's perishing freezing outside.'

Poppy did as she was told, but her mind was else-where. The fact that Guy was safe and had not completely forgotten her was the best Christmas present anyone could have given her. She did not know much about the Western Desert, in fact she was not quite certain where it was, but she had complete faith in Guy. If he flew a plane with the same dash and expertise as he rode a horse, then he would be a more than able pilot. She followed Mabel into the front room feeling much happier than she had done since she left Squire's Knapp.

Mabel placed the basket on the tea table. 'Let's see what they sent you. I must say that Mrs Pallister's a bit posh, but at least her heart's in the right place. It was decent of her to come all the way out here to bring you a present.' She gave Poppy a gentle shove towards the table. 'Open it up and let's take a peek inside. You go first. After all, it's for you.'

'I hope it's something to eat,' Mrs Tanner said, taking off her glasses and wiping them on her skirt. 'Why didn't you bring that woman in here to see me, Mabel? Anyone would think you was ashamed of your old mother.'

'Nonsense, Mum. She was in a hurry.' Mabel nudged Poppy in the ribs. 'Get a move on. Whatever's in there won't bite you.'

Poppy peeled off the napkin, passing it to Mabel who felt the cloth and passed it on to her mother for her inspection. 'Irish linen, Mum. I bet that cost a bob or two.'

Mrs Tanner laid it across her knees. 'It'll do nicely for me when I have me tea. I haven't seen anything as good as this since I was in service, which is when I met your mum, Poppy. She was a good bit younger than me, but we got on all right.'

Poppy was barely listening as she took out a Madeira cake wrapped in a tea towel and placed it on the table. Underneath there were three small packages wrapped in brown paper bearing labels from Edie, Jean and Mavis and a note bearing the legend *Do not open until Christmas*.

'How kind of them to remember you,' Mabel said softly. 'They sound like lovely girls, Poppy.'

'They were. I mean, they are. I really miss them.'

Mabel patted her on the shoulder. 'Is there anything else?'

The last item in the basket was a white envelope with Poppy's name written on it in bold italic script. She had seen his name written on the flyleaf of the books left in the nursery often enough to recognise Guy's handwriting. Her fingers trembled as she plucked the envelope from the bottom of the basket.

'Open it then,' Mabel said cheerfully. 'I expect it's a Christmas card.'

'A fiver would be more useful,' Mrs Tanner said, eyeing the cake. 'Let's have a taste of that cake. It's hours since we had our dinner.'

'Oh, Mum, it's ages until teatime,' Mabel protested, but a look from her mother sent her scurrying out of the room. 'All right,' she called from the kitchen. 'I'm just fetching a knife and some plates.'

Poppy went to sit in a chair by the window where the light was better. She opened the envelope and took out a single sheet of deckle-edged paper that must have come from Mrs Carroll's study. She doubted if you could buy anything of this quality now that paper was in short supply.

1940

Squire's Knapp

10 December 1941
Dear Poppy,
  I was very sorry to learn that you have had to return to London, but I hope you have settled in with your sister-in-law. Goliath misses you very much and I'm sending you something to remember him by.
  Very best wishes for your future.
  Guy.
  PS Your St Christopher has got me out of some tight squeezes.

She shook the envelope and a snapshot fell onto her lap. It was a photograph of Goliath standing beneath the oak tree at the edge of the spinney. She would have liked Guy to have been in the frame too, but knowing how much he cared for the horse this was the next best thing. She slipped it into her skirt pocket before Mrs Tanner had a chance to see it and demand to have a look.

Mabel brought plates and a cake knife and Poppy's letter was forgotten as the cake was cut and the tasting began.

'There's not a drop of liquid paraffin in this,' Mrs Tanner said happily. 'I can taste real butter.'

'They've got a farm, Mum,' Mabel said through a mouthful of cake. 'I expect they make their own butter and cheese. What a pity they threw you out, Poppy. You'd have had a better time down there and you wouldn't have had to slog away cleaning bedpans and lavvies.'

Poppy shook her head. 'It's hard work on the land too, and long hours. I love the countryside but I'm very grateful to you both for taking me in.'

'La-di-dah,' Mrs Tanner said, wiping her lips on the napkin. 'It's a pity they ever sent you to that place. You got ideas above your station, girl. I liked you better when you was plain Poppy Brown, not Poppy with a plum in her mouth.'

'Mum, that's not fair,' Mabel said in a low voice. 'You take that back. Poppy's a good girl and she works hard at the hospital. And you wouldn't be stuffing your face with Madeira cake if it wasn't for Poppy's friends in the country, posh or not.'

CHRISTMAS WAS A quiet family affair. Uncle Fred had somehow managed to get hold of a large capon, which

Poppy suspected had been bought on the black market, but he had done his usual thing of tapping the side of his nose and saying 'Ask no questions and you'll be told no lies.' Black market or not, it had tasted good, and Mabel said she planned to make the carcass into stew next day. Poppy washed the dishes while the others slept off their meal, which had included the best part of a bottle of port that Uncle Fred had produced from a poacher's pocket inside his greatcoat.

The presents were arranged on the table beneath the imitation Christmas tree that Mabel said had come out every year since she could remember. The branches were slightly twisted and there were bald patches where the fake pine needles had rubbed off, but these were mostly hidden beneath the tarnished tinsel. To Poppy it was a poor substitute for the real tree that had graced the hall at Squire's Knapp. What she missed most of all was the resinous smell of fresh pine, and the scent of apple logs burning on the fire in the entrance hall. She had tried to push aside the memories of a life that had never really been intended for a girl from West Ham, but then she remembered Christmases spent with Mum, Dad and Joe, and that was even more painful.

Although she was paid a mere pittance at the hospital, Poppy had saved every penny she could spare and had bought Mabel a Tangee lipstick in Woolworth's, and for Mrs Tanner a handkerchief with the initial *M* for Maggie embroidered on one corner. She had laboriously unpicked an old jumper that Mabel had bought in a jumble sale but never worn, and using the wool Poppy had knitted a scarf for Uncle Fred and a pair of mittens for the two aunts, although she doubted whether fussy Ida would stoop to wearing anything handmade. She had standards, as she was fond of telling anyone who would listen, but in Poppy's opinion Auntie Ida might change her mind about wearing woollen mittens during cold nights spent in the Anderson shelter in their back garden in Leytonstone.

Having finished her chores, Poppy was eager to open her presents from the girls, but she had to wait until the others woke up and even then they would do nothing until they had consumed several cups of tea and the last slice of Mrs Toon's cake.

Ida licked her fingers delicately. 'Now that's what I call a Madeira cake, but then you wouldn't expect anything less coming from a country house kitchen. I don't suppose they have to worry about ration books and coupons; so much for everyone being treated the same.'

'There's always a way round things if you have the money.' Uncle Fred patted his round belly and the bottom button flew off his waistcoat, landing on the hearth rug.

Mabel retrieved it and handed it to him. 'I expect that capon cost a bob or two, Uncle Fred.'

He grinned. 'I have my sources, ducks. Say no more.'

'You could do with cutting down anyway.' Ida stared pointedly at his corpulent figure. 'You always were a pig, Fred.'

'Don't start on him, Ida.' Mrs Tanner wiped her lips with the table napkin from Squire's Knapp. 'Irish linen,' she said, waving it under her sister's nose.

Mabel rose hastily to her feet. 'I know, let's open our presents. Poppy, love, will you do the honours?'

Poppy had been waiting for this moment. She handed round the gifts, all of which were in brown paper parcels, apart from the ones from Ida and Fred which were wrapped in tissue paper and tied with red ribbon.

'I save my paper from year to year,' Ida said smugly. 'Waste not, want not has always been my motto.'

'Some might call it being stingy,' Auntie Dottie muttered beneath her breath.

Poppy sat in a chair by the window to open her presents. There was a sparkly brooch from Edie, a woollen scarf from Mavis and a bottle of Evening in Paris perfume from Jean. Mabel had given her two pairs of Aertex knickers, which might not be the most exciting present she had ever received but were most welcome as the elastic had perished in the ones that Amy had bought for her, which were too small anyway. Auntie Dottie gave her a diary and Mrs Tanner said the panties were half from her as she was now a pauper living off her meagre life savings and could not afford the luxury of giving presents. Poppy noticed that she was not too proud to accept them. Auntie Ida and Uncle Fred gave her a fountain pen, which was quite a magnificent present, but Ida rather spoilt it by telling Poppy that she must work hard and take the examinations set for Red Cross cadets, and then maybe she would get a decent job and not spend the rest of her life scrubbing floors. This was so patently aimed at Mabel that Poppy felt like giving Auntie Ida a piece of her mind, but she knew it would lead to a row amongst the volatile Tanner sisters, and she said nothing.

The remainder of Christmas day passed without any upsets. There were mince pies for tea, although Auntie Dottie rather spoilt the treat by prophesying gloomily that preserves would soon be rationed and this was probably the last time anyone would see mincemeat until the war was over. Auntie Ida went in on the attack as usual and told her sister in no uncertain terms that she ate too much sweet stuff anyway, and that it would do her good to cut down on sugar and starch. At which Auntie Dottie stood up, her bottom lip trembling and the rolls of fat squashed between her corsets and her brassiere wobbling, and demanded an apology. Uncle Fred rose to his feet like a leviathan rising from the sea. 'Time to go home, ladies. I'll drop you off on the way, Dottie.'

The argument was forgotten in the ensuing rush to pick up presents and the scramble to find coats, hats and scarves. Suddenly everyone was hugging and kissing and wishing each other a happy New Year even though it was days away. Poppy said her goodbyes and went upstairs to the boxroom at the front of the house, which had been used for years as a junk room. Mabel had cleared away most of the battered old suitcases, disused handbags, odd shoes and an umbrella with broken spines, but it still did not feel like home to Poppy. The room was simply furnished with a bed and a chest of drawers. The narrow divan had a lumpy mattress but Mabel had seen to it that Poppy had as many blankets as she needed and an eiderdown covered in a rather sickly pink material which clashed with the orange and brown pattern on the linoleum. The curtains were floral cretonne in varying shades of purple and blue, and the bare walls, which were distempered in a particularly putrid shade of pink, cried out for adornment with pictures of film stars, but Mabel had warned her against sticking things on the walls and ruining the paintwork. Blushing, she had said that one day she hoped this room would be a nursery, but this remark only served to make Poppy remember the two large rooms she had shared with Rupert at Squire's Knapp. Old-fashioned and slightly shabby they undoubtedly were, but homely all the same with echoes from past generations of children who had occupied the nursery suite. She could imagine Guy and Pamela larking around in the day nursery when they were supposed to be doing lessons with their governess, or having pillow fights when they were supposed to be asleep in their beds.

But that was all in the past now. She must forget that part of her life, which was well and truly over. At least this small space was hers for the time being, and she had somewhere to store her few possessions, although these did not amount to very much. She had grown a couple of inches during her year in the country and none of her clothes fitted properly, apart from the tweed hacking jacket that had belonged to Pamela, a grey flannel skirt which was fashionably short, and a couple of jumpers that were a bit too tight across her bosom. Mavis had given her a brassiere, which was a bit on the large side but would do until she could save up enough to buy one that fitted properly. And when it came to shoes, the only pair

Poppy had were the stout lace-ups that Amy had bought for her when she started school. Luckily they had been too big then but now they cramped her toes and she could not walk far without getting blisters on her heels. If she wanted to buy a new pair of shoes she would have to save every penny she earned after deducting the amount of housekeeping money she gave Mabel each week.

Poppy flopped down on the bed. She would have to get used to being poor again, but her brief taste of life on a country estate had unsettled her in more ways than one. She knew that she would no longer be satisfied with the sort of life that her mother had accepted as being the lot of women; the daily drudgery of housework and eking out a living on a working man's wages, never thinking that there might be something better or that she could achieve anything on her own. She could see Mabel going down a similar path, but it was not for her. Even though such thoughts made her feel thoroughly disloyal and ashamed, Poppy could not help making comparisons. Whereas she had once felt like an alien in the Carroll household she was now experiencing a similar sort of feeling in the small suburban house that Joe and Mabel were happy to call home.

She took Guy's letter out and read it several times before folding it and putting it under her pillow with the photo of Goliath. The past was over and done with. Tomorrow she would be back at work and with an early start she needed to get her rest. Rising to her feet, she went across the landing to the tiny bathroom and did a quick strip wash in lukewarm water. Mabel was very strict about the amount of coke they burned each day, more out of necessity than for the sake of conserving coal stocks, but she said that it seemed almost inevitable that fuel would soon be rationed and they might as well get used to it.

Shivering, Poppy put on the winceyette pyjamas that Amy had given her and made a dash for her bed, cuddling down beneath the covers and grimacing as her bare feet touched the icy sheets. She closed her eyes, wishing that someone had thought to give her a pair of bedsocks for Christmas.

NEXT DAY, EVEN though it was Boxing Day there was no day off for the hospital workers. It was still dark when Poppy and Mabel left for work and dark when they trudged wearily home. Three days later, it was Sunday and Poppy's day off, but Mabel was not feeling very well and Poppy volunteered to take her afternoon shift. She was glad to have an excuse to get away from Mrs Tanner's constant moaning, which was always worse on Sunday when she had a captive audience.

Poppy enjoyed being at the hospital anyway. She was not thrilled by the repetitive nature of scrubbing and cleaning, but she derived a great deal of satisfaction from a job well done, and she took comfort from the thought that in a small way she was helping people recover from their illnesses and injuries. She liked the people she worked with; or most of them anyway. The exception was Sister McNally, who everyone agreed was a dragon masquerading in a starched white cap and apron. If the woman had breathed flames Poppy would not have been at all surprised. When Sister McNally was on duty there was a subdued hush on the wards. Probationer nurses trembled at the sight of her and she had been known to make a houseman cry. It was rumoured that her acid tongue could strip paint, but it would have been a brave or suicidal soul who dared to say it to her face.

It was late when Poppy finished her shift. She had stayed behind to tidy the broom cupboard in case Sister McNally became bored in the night and decided to do a few spot checks. She was just putting on her coat when the air raid siren sounded. For a moment she froze, wondering whether to leave or stay and help with the air raid drill in which all staff had been trained. The decision was taken out of her hands when one of the probationer nurses rushed into the changing room and grabbed her by the arm. 'Come on; don't stand there like an idiot. We've got to get the patients to safety in the basement.'

A loud explosion rocked the building, the lights flickered and the aftershock went on like a volcanic eruption. Poppy and the nurse were flung to the floor, where they lay covering their ears with their hands. In quick succession there was another crump and they were in complete darkness. The building seemed to be collapsing around them.

Chapter Twelve

FOR ONE TERRIBLE moment Poppy thought she was going to die. It was pitch dark and the dreadful noise seemed to go on forever. Then she realised that she was still clutching the nurse's hand. 'Are you all right?'

'I think so, but I can't see a bloody thing.'

There was a dull buzzing sound as the hospital generator cut in and the lights came on. Poppy scrambled to her feet. 'Are you hurt?'

The young nurse shook her head, sending a shower of plaster dust onto the floor. 'I don't think so. Are you okay?'

Poppy nodded. She was shocked and her head was ringing with the percussive sound of the bomb blast, but as far as she could tell she was unharmed. She moved shakily towards the door, which was hanging on one hinge. She pushed it open, and as she stepped outside into the corridor she was aware of shouts, screams and cries for help. The air was thick with dust and acrid smoke but this part of the building at least seemed relatively intact.

The nurse pushed past her. 'I can't remember the air raid drill,' she muttered. 'My mind's gone blank.'

'Evacuate the patients,' Poppy said hoarsely. 'Take the ones who can walk down to the basement.'

'Yes, that's it.' Straightening her cap, the girl hurried off, leaving Poppy alone and undecided. She was officially off duty but she could not walk away and leave people in pain and possible danger. She hurried towards the casualty department but came up against a wall of rubble. She turned and made her way towards the main entrance. A woman patient staggered out of a doorway, looking dazed and pale with shock.

'What happened?' she murmured. 'I thought the place was coming down around my ears.'

Poppy took her arm and hooked it around her shoulders. 'Let's get you somewhere safer.'

A scene of chaos met her eyes in the main corridor. Nurses and orderlies were pushing patients in wheelchairs, on hospital trolleys and even on their beds away from the damaged area of the hospital to a place of safety. Poppy helped the woman to the top of the stairs where a porter was assisting an elderly man in his descent to the basement.

'Can you take this lady as well?' Poppy asked anxiously. 'I'll go and see if there's anything else I can do.'

He nodded, giving the woman a cheerful grin. 'Okay, come on, love. Let's get you downstairs to the first class lounge. Tea and biscuits for all.'

Poppy left them and was threading her way through the crowd, not knowing quite where she was heading, when she saw Sister McNally marching purposefully towards her.

'You there.' Sister McNally pointed a finger at Poppy. 'Come with me.'

Poppy followed her tall figure as almost miraculously the beds, wheelchairs and trolleys moved aside to allow them to pass. Sister McNally had an air of authority that must be obeyed no matter what the situation. She appeared to have been untouched by the bomb blast. Everyone else bore marks of the disaster with bits of plaster stuck in their hair, blackened faces or uniforms covered in dust, but Sister McNally was immaculate as ever. Her starched white cap with its goffered frill was on straight and her uniform spotless. It was like walking in the footsteps of an avenging angel as Poppy followed her to the ward that was being used to treat the casualties.

Sister McNally pulled back the curtains around a bed where a young man lay looking deathly pale with one arm covered in a blood-stained gauze dressing. Lifting the corner she glanced at the wound. 'This will need stitching.' She turned to Poppy, eyeing the uniform that denoted her as a cleaner. 'Are you trained in first aid?'

'I'm a Red Cross cadet, Sister. I've done basic first aid.'

'This wound needs several stitches. It's very straightforward.' Sister McNally pointed to a sterile pack on the locker. 'You'll find everything you need there. You do know how to sew up a wound?'

'I've seen it done,' Poppy whispered, gazing anxiously at the pale-faced young man who looked as though he was going to pass out at any moment.

'You look like a capable girl,' Sister McNally said, filling a hypodermic syringe with local anaesthetic. 'What's your name?'

'Poppy Brown, Sister.'

'Watch and learn, Brown.' Sister McNally rubbed the afflicted area with cotton wool soaked in alcohol. 'This won't hurt,' she told the patient firmly and rammed the needle home.

His eyelids fluttered and he fainted.

'There's nothing to it. Simple interrupted sutures are all that's needed here. Carry on, Brown.' Sister McNally marched off to the next bed and had disappeared behind the curtains before Poppy had a chance to argue.

Taking care to scrub her hands first, Poppy gritted her teeth and prayed that the young man would not come round until she had finished stitching the ugly gash on his arm caused presumably by flying glass. She shut her ears to the sounds around her and concentrated on remembering everything she had learned in first aid classes. She had practised suturing on the arm of a rag doll donated for the purpose but this was quite different. She was sweating by the time she had finished and she looked up to find the patient staring at her. She managed a tight little smile. 'All done. How are you feeling?'

'Okay. I think.'

Sister McNally appeared as if from nowhere, leaning over to inspect Poppy's handiwork. 'That's very good work, Brown. Dress the wound and then report to me.' She slipped behind the curtains once again, leaving Poppy to finish off her work.

Feeling more confident now, she dressed the wound and bandaged the arm, which was something she had practised many times in class. 'Can I get you anything?' She heard the rattle of teacups, and pulling back the curtain she saw Florrie, one of the other cleaners, pushing the tea trolley into the ward.

'I could murder a cuppa,' the young man said with feeling. 'I was just walking past the hospital on me way home from work when there was this bloody great crump and next thing I knew I was on the ground covered in broken glass. I never even had time to get to an air raid shelter.'

Poppy signalled to Florrie. 'One tea here, please. Two sugars.'

'Make that three, love,' the young man said, raising himself on his good arm. 'I'm in shock don't forget.'

'Come here, Brown.'

Sister McNally's command made Poppy jump to attention. 'Yes, Sister.'

'I've another task for you.'

'Coming, Sister.' Poppy smiled at her patient. 'Florrie will bring your tea. I hope you feel better soon.'

'Ta, nurse.' The young man grinned up at her. 'You done a good job on me arm.'

IT WAS DAYLIGHT when Poppy finally left the hospital and she realised that it was Monday morning. People were already hurrying on their way to work; some stopping to look at the devastation caused by the German bomb which had razed the casualty department to the ground, and others seemingly oblivious to their surroundings, or perhaps they were getting used to seeing bomb sites even this far from the East End. Poppy was bone tired and every part of her body ached. She had worked alongside the doctors and nurses until she was almost too exhausted to stand. She had comforted distressed patients, handed out cups of tea, dressed wounds and plucked fragments of glass out of human flesh. She was almost too weary to put one foot in front of the other, but she was happy to have done something important for once in her life. She had been needed and felt appreciated for the first time since she had been forced to leave home almost sixteen months previously. If Mum and Dad were up there looking down on her, she was sure they would be pleased that she had not let the side down. Dad and Joe were great ones for playing fair. Grandad had always instilled in her that it did not matter whether you won or lost, it was how you played the game. She had believed him wholeheartedly and she knew that she had performed well and to the best of her ability. She could hear Grandma saying, 'You can't do any more than your best, Poppy.'

Someone was repeating her name and it was not Gran. She stopped, peering up at the man driving the brewer's dray. Her heart sank as she recognised Dennis, Joe's friend with the wandering hands. 'Oh, hello.'

'Are you okay?' Dennis peered down at her, his smile fading. 'You look done in.'

'I've been up all night. The hospital suffered a direct hit.'

'I heard.' He shook his head. 'That's really bad. Many hurt?'

'I don't know, but there seemed to be lots.'

'Hop on board, kid. I'll take you home.'

Poppy hesitated. 'I don't want to take you out of your way.'

He grinned. 'Don't worry about that. I make me own rules. Climb aboard.' Leaning down, he held his hand out to her. It was a large hand with capable square-tipped fingers and when he smiled his dark eyes twinkled with humour.

Too tired to argue, Poppy accepted his offer. He might not be tall, and she had noticed at the wedding that he walked with a distinct limp, but he was thickset and she discovered that he was much stronger than he looked when he hoisted her onto the driver's seat. 'So how've you been getting along?' He spoke as if they had just met at a social gathering rather than in a street covered with rubble and broken glass. 'Walk on.' He flicked the whip expertly just above the horse's ear and the animal lumbered forward at a sedate walk.

Despite her reservations about Dennis Chapman, Poppy found herself telling him everything that had happened during and after the bombing raid. She found that he was a surprisingly good listener and in no time at all they were pulling up outside the house in South Road. Before Poppy had a chance to alight from the driver's seat, the front door opened and Mabel ran down the front path, red-faced and breathing heavily. She was still wearing her dressing gown and slippers and had a scarf tied turban-style around her head with curlers poking out at the front. 'Where the hell have you been?' she demanded angrily. 'What sort of time do you call this to bring a young girl home, Dennis? What's she doing with you anyway?'

Poppy scrambled down from the dray, catching Mabel's arm as she shook her fist at Dennis. 'It's not what you think.'

'Oh, ain't it?' Mabel took a deep breath. 'He had his eye on you at the wedding. Any fool could see that.'

Dennis climbed down from the driver's seat with surprising agility. 'Put a sock in it, Mabel. Give the poor kid a chance to explain.'

Arms akimbo, Mabel glared at him. 'She's only fourteen and she's been out all night and now she comes home with you, looking like something the cat dragged in. I've got eyes in me head, Den.'

'But no brains if you ask me.' He grinned, exposing a row of even white teeth in startling contrast to his tanned and weathered skin. 'She's a heroine, that's what young Poppy is, so you shut up and give her a chance to speak.'

Mabel recoiled at the sharp tone in his voice, turning to Poppy with her eyebrows raised. 'Well? I'm listening.'

'The hospital took a direct hit,' Poppy said tiredly. 'I was just leaving but I had to stay and help out. I'm sorry if you were worried, Mabel.'

'A handsome apology and one you don't deserve.' Dennis put his arm around Mabel's plump shoulders and gave her a hug. 'Now instead of giving a show for the neighbours, how about you asking me in and putting the kettle on, Mabel, love?'

A reluctant smile curved Mabel's full lips. 'Oh, you are a one, Den. You'll get the sack from the brewery one day, you know that, don't you?'

'They can't afford to lose me. There ain't too many strong men left who can heave barrels of beer around. Even a one leg wonder like me has his uses.' He hooked a nosebag over his horse's head and patted him on the neck. 'Good lad, Napoleon. Enjoy your breakfast, old chap.'

Poppy hesitated as she was about to follow them into the house. 'What about your horse? Will he be all right on his own?'

'He's not going anywhere without me. We're a team, old Napoleon and me. Come indoors out of the cold, ducks. You're the one who needs looking after.'

The small kitchen seemed filled by Dennis's presence. Poppy accepted a cup of tea gratefully. She was exhausted and all she wanted was to go to bed and sleep, but it seemed rude to leave him after he had gone out of his way to help her, and his concern for her wellbeing had made her feel warm inside; all gooey like melted chocolate. Anyway, Mabel was firing questions at her as if she were interrogating a spy and Poppy could hear Mrs Tanner stirring in the dining room, where she now slept in a narrow bed next to the Morrison shelter.

At last Mabel was satisfied with Poppy's account of the happenings during the night, and she was generous with her praise, but then she remembered that she was doing an early shift and she hurried upstairs to dress and do her hair.

'And I'd best be on me way too,' Dennis said, placing his empty cup in the Belfast sink. 'Are you okay now, Poppy?'

'I'm fine. Thank you for giving me a lift, Dennis.'

He paused in the doorway, eyeing her speculatively. 'How about going to the flicks tonight, kid? *Goodbye, Mr Chips* is on at the Majestic. You know, Robert Donat and Greer Garson. What d'you say?'

'I–I don't know about that.'

'Not on duty, are you?'

'No, but . . .'

His cocky smile faded. 'Look, Poppy. I know we got off on the wrong foot, but Joe's my best mate. I wouldn't do anything that'd upset him, or you for that matter. I know you're just a kid, and I'd treat you just the same as if you was me little sister.' He held up his hands, twisting his face into a comical parody of sadness. 'Anyway, you can run faster than me with me gammy leg.'

Poppy covered her mouth with her hand in an effort to suppress a chuckle. 'What's wrong with your leg? I didn't like to ask until you mentioned it.'

'Polio, love, had it when I was five. Me sister, Joan, died but I was a tough little bugger and got over it, except for having one leg a couple of inches shorter than the other. That's why they won't have me in the forces. I'm a bit of a freak.'

'No, don't say that,' Poppy said, moved almost to tears by his admission. 'I'd love to go to the pictures with you,

Dennis. I haven't seen a film since I was evacuated to the country. It would be a real treat.'

THE TRIP TO the cinema exceeded Poppy's expectations and was just the thing to take her mind off the horrors of the Blitz, if only for a couple of hours. It was wonderful to step into the glitzy world of make-believe; purple carpets, gilded plasterwork on the walls and ceilings and the warm fug of cigarette smoke and damp overcoats as people packed into the auditorium under the surveillance of a commissionaire wearing more gold braid on his peaked cap than an admiral of the fleet.

Dennis bought her Rowntree's Dairy Box chocolates, which was an absolute luxury, and they sat side by side in the dark watching the heart-warming love story of the shy schoolmaster who fell in love with a beautiful young woman while on holiday. The stuffy schoolmasters at the public school were astounded when dull old Mr Chips turned up with a charming young bride, and it should, in Poppy's opinion, have had a happy ending and she sobbed into her handkerchief when Greer Garson died in childbirth. She consoled herself with the fact that Mr Chips went on to lead a worthy life and was much loved by everyone, but she could not quite get over the tragedy of his lost love. When the lights went up in the interval Dennis bought her a tub of Eldorado ice cream, and he sat and smoked Woodbines while she licked the creamy vanilla ice off the tiny wooden spatula. Pathé News followed and then the atmosphere lightened with a series of Mickey Mouse cartoons. Dennis walked her home and left her at the garden gate, thanking her for her company and saying they must do it again some time. Poppy watched him shamble off with his awkward gait and the glow of his cigarette was the last thing she saw before he was enveloped by darkness. Mabel had waited up for her, with the excuse that she had come downstairs for a cup of cocoa, but Poppy suspected that her sister-in-law was simply making certain that Dennis kept his word and behaved like a gentleman. She was able to reassure Mabel on that score, and they huddled round the dying embers of the fire in the front room sipping cocoa while Poppy described the scenario in detail.

When she finally went to bed she dreamed that Guy was Mr Chips, but now the schoolmaster was a dashing RAF officer, and it was she herself who was playing Greer Garson's role and not Amy who was conveniently absent, presumably living in style half a world away. In the morning she was still Poppy Brown and the reality was walking to work in the rain, clambering over piles of debris to get into the hospital, and pitching in to restore cleanliness to the undamaged departments and wards.

In the months that followed Poppy settled into a routine of work and evening classes, interrupted by frequent air raid warnings and dashes to the nearest shelter. Dennis was a frequent visitor to the house, and their trips to the cinema became a weekly outing for Poppy. He proved to be good company and there was never a hint of anything other than friendship in his attitude towards her. Mabel's initial worries seemed to have been forgotten, or maybe it had something to do with the small gifts that Dennis brought her every time he called at the house. It could be anything from a bar of milk chocolate to a bunch of flowers, and he always had a packet of Kensitas cigarettes for Mrs Tanner, who said that the doctor had advised her to smoke as it calmed her nerves. Poppy had grown familiar with Mrs Tanner's nerves, which Mum would have said were just an excuse for bad temper, but it would be a brave person who voiced that opinion to Mabel's irascible parent. Dennis was the only one it seemed who could charm her into smiling, and he even made her laugh on occasions. Mabel hung on every word when he recounted stories of his boyhood escapades with Joe. Poppy was amazed that Dennis and her brother had not been arrested for some of their less worthy capers, and she was glad that Mum and Dad had been blissfully ignorant of their son's activities.

On Poppy's fifteenth birthday, Dennis had offered to take them all out to dinner at the Seven Ways Restaurant, a mock Tudor building overlooking a busy roundabout at Gants Hill, which was within easy walking distance. He had borrowed a wheelchair, and although Mrs Tanner said she would not be seen dead in such a contraption, when faced with the alternative of being left alone and having to get into the Morrison shelter unaided in the event of an air raid she changed her mind, but that did not stop her grumbling. In the end, Dennis, who was limping badly himself, gave the chair a hefty push, shouting, 'Whee. Off you go, ducks. Let's see you get there under your own steam.'

Mabel uttered a shriek of protest. 'Catch her, Dennis. For the love of God, she'll be killed.'

Mrs Tanner's language was choice as Dennis caught up with the chair and drew it to a halt. Mabel clapped her hands over Poppy's ears, but it did not drown the string of expletives.

'Now, now, Ma. You enjoyed the thrill,' Dennis said, chuckling. 'Admit it, Maggie. You ain't had such fun since Granny was a boy.'

Wielding her handbag like a morning star, Mrs Tanner caught him a blow on the shoulder. 'Shut up, you hooligan. I'll have the law on you for mistreating a poor old woman.'

Dennis took a packet of Woodbines from his pocket and lit one, handing it to Mrs Tanner. 'Have a fag to calm your nerves, ducks.'

'Ladies don't smoke in the street,' Mrs Tanner said, snatching it from him. She inhaled deeply. 'Doctor's orders,' she added, glaring at Mabel. 'I've had a terrible fright thanks to that – that cripple, who ought to know better.'

'Dennis isn't a cripple,' Poppy cried angrily. 'That was a horrid thing to say.'

'It's okay, love.' Dennis took her hand and gave it a squeeze. 'I know what I am, and I have to live with it.' His serious expression melted into a grin. 'Come on, girls. This is meant to be a celebration. We're on a night out, no expense spared.' He seized the wheelchair handle. 'Okay, Maggie. I won't give you no more frights and on the way home you can push me.'

Puffing a smoke ring, Mrs Tanner glared at him over her shoulder. 'I'll push you into the boating pond, you bugger.'

'You two are awful,' Mabel said with feeling. 'I hope you're not going to spend the whole evening bickering like a couple of kids.'

'Not me, honey.' Dennis winked at Poppy. 'I'll be a gent just like Ashley Wilkes in that film we saw last week at the flicks.'

'It was wonderful,' Poppy said, sighing. 'Scarlett O'Hara was so beautiful and she had all the men falling at her feet. You must see it, Mabel.'

'I have seen it,' Mabel said breathlessly as she quickened her pace in order to keep up with them. 'Joe and I treated ourselves to a performance in the West End the night before our wedding.'

'Poppy looks just like her,' Dennis said, smiling. 'Vivien Leigh, I mean. She's our own little Scarlett.'

Mabel shot him a warning glance. 'Don't talk soft, Dennis. You'll give her ideas.'

'I'm starving,' Mrs Tanner said plaintively. 'Can't you go no faster, Dennis? There'll be nothing left on the menu if you lot don't stop gassing on about film stars and all that soppy rubbish.'

He made a move as if to send the wheelchair off on its own again, but Poppy caught the handle, shaking her head. 'Don't you dare,' she whispered, smothering a giggle. 'And stop teasing Mabel. You'll have her turning grey before her time.'

'Who says I'm joking?' For a brief moment his hand covered hers and the expression in his eyes startled

Poppy, but it also sent thrills running down her spine. She withdrew her hand hastily. There was an earthy quality about Dennis that, combined with his sense of humour and undeniable good looks, made it possible to forget his lack of stature and his physical disability. She found it all very confusing. 'I wonder what they've got on the menu,' she said, turning to Mabel. 'I hope there's cake.'

The restaurant was crowded but Dennis had reserved a table in the window and the waitress who served them, a buxom, dark-haired woman called Betty, obviously knew him as a good customer. As if to make up for teasing Mrs Tanner, he made a fuss of her, lifting her bodily from the wheelchair so that she could sit at the table. He took her coat and Mabel's, complimenting Mabel on her dress. It was the one she had worn on her wedding day, but Dennis did not appear to recognise it. He said that particular shade of blue matched her eyes exactly and Mabel blushed, giggling like a schoolgirl as she took her seat. Poppy had slipped off her tweed jacket, but Dennis took it from her with a smile that would have melted the hardest heart. 'You look a treat,' he said softly. 'You're a real smasher, Poppy Brown.'

'He fancies her,' Mrs Tanner said grimly as Dennis went to hang the coats on the stand by the door. 'You'd better watch him, Mabel. He's like a dog on heat.'

'Mum,' Mabel said in a shocked undertone. 'Stop it. You don't know what you're saying.'

Poppy picked up the menu, pretending not to hear them. She had felt a bit self-conscious in a dress that had belonged to Mabel before she began to put on weight. It had taken several evenings of painstaking needlework to alter it to fit Poppy's slender frame. The eau de nil figure-hugging rayon had the feel of silk. Gathering beneath the bust emphasised her tiny waist and the skirt ended just below her knees, swirling sinuously with every step she took. She might not be as gorgeous as Scarlett, but Dennis seemed to think she looked pretty. It was slightly embarrassing, but it was also flattering to be taken seriously by an older man. He must be all of twenty-three, the same age as Joe and Guy. Her heart did a funny little flip inside her chest.

She had done her best to put Guy from her mind. In her busy life working at the hospital and spending evenings at class, she had had little time to dwell on the past. It was still there, of course, tucked away in a secret compartment of her memory; a place sacred to her mind's eye to be savoured and relished in moments when she was alone. She had not always been happy at Squire's Knapp and the memories might be bittersweet, but they were still very much a part of her life.

'Well, now, ladies, what's your poison?' Dennis said cheerfully as he took his seat. 'A drop of mother's ruin for you, Maggie?'

'Cheeky blighter,' Mrs Tanner muttered. 'I'll have wine. White and sweet.'

'That will do for me too,' Mabel said hastily. 'You order, Dennis. You know what's what.'

Poppy sat back watching Dennis as he ordered their food and wine as if he did that sort of thing every day of his life. In deference to Mrs Tanner he chose a sweet white wine that tasted of grapes and sunshine, and although Mabel frowned when she saw him fill Poppy's glass he forestalled her by saying that a drop or two on her birthday was quite in order. 'She's fifteen, not five years old,' he said, topping up Mabel's glass. 'Give the kid a break and let her grow up.'

Mabel took a sip of her wine, shooting him a resentful glance. 'She's my responsibility while Joe's away.'

'I wish you'd stop talking about me as if I wasn't here,' Poppy said, frowning.

Dennis reached across the table to pat her hand. 'Sorry, ducks. We're just trying to look after you, although Mabel here thinks I'm a wolf in sheep's clothing.' He grinned and winked at Mabel. 'Don't worry, love. I'm a sheep in wolf's clothing. I wouldn't do nothing to harm a hair of her pretty head. My little Scarlett O'Hara.'

'Well, you ain't Rhett Butler,' Mrs Tanner said, glaring at Dennis with narrowed eyes. 'And don't look so surprised. I've read all about it in *Picturegoer*. Now where's that fish and chips I ordered? Call that waitress over, and tell her to hurry the food along before I faint from lack of nourishment.'

Luckily for everyone Betty appeared at that moment, expertly balancing four plates of food on her upturned arms. Poppy held her breath in case she dropped one, but Betty had obviously done this many times before and she served the food without mishap. Mrs Tanner had her cod and chips, and even though she complained that the peas were like bullets it did not prevent her from clearing her plate, downing three glasses of wine in the process. Mabel and Dennis both had the meat pie, although Mabel complained that there was more carrot and swede in it than meat. Dennis had no complaints. Poppy had fish pie. There was more potato than fish but the cheese sauce was tasty and she was hungry. They all chose the jam roly-poly pudding for dessert with a generous helping of custard. Whether it was the food or the second bottle of wine that had helped it go down, Mrs Tanner was in a spectacularly good mood. She even thanked Betty for waiting on them and complimented her on her clean fingernails, which Poppy found excruciatingly embarrassing, but Dennis made up for it by leaving a tip large enough to make Mabel's eyes widen.

'That's too much, Dennis,' she hissed.

'Makes his money on the black market I should think,' Mrs Tanner said in a voice loud enough to turn heads. She pointed at Dennis, mouthing 'spiv' and shaking her head as if to disassociate herself from him.

Dennis lifted her into the wheelchair. 'I love you, Maggie. Will you marry me?'

'You're only saying that because a wife can't give evidence against her old man, you cheeky blighter.'

'Let's get you home, Mum,' Mabel said, smiling apologetically at the woman on the next table who looked distinctly affronted. 'She's had a drop too much. Sorry.'

It was pitch dark by the time they reached South Road. A thick blanket of clouds hid the moon, but in the distance they could hear the crump of ack-ack guns, and then the wail of the air raid siren. 'Get inside quick,'

Mabel said, unlocking the front door. 'Into the Morrison shelter with you.'

Dennis lifted Mrs Tanner out of her chair and carried her into the hall. 'D'you need help, Maggie?'

She shook her head. 'I ain't a complete cripple, like some.' Grabbing her walking stick she hobbled towards the dining room where the Morrison shelter had replaced the table.

'Sorry about Mum,' Mabel said apologetically. 'It's just her way.'

Dennis kissed her on the cheek. 'I know. Go and sort the old besom out. You're a saint to put up with her, Mabel.'

'Come on, Poppy. You too, Dennis.' Mabel tossed her coat over the newel post at the foot of the stairs and hurried into the dining room.

Poppy made to follow her but Dennis caught her by the hand. He drew her into his arms and kissed her on the lips. 'Happy birthday, Poppy.'

Shocked, she pushed him away. 'What did you do that for, Dennis?'

His eyes darkened. 'Because you're lovely and I wanted to.'

'Well, I didn't.' She wiped her lips on the back of her hand. 'Don't ever do that again. Not ever.' She turned and ran upstairs, shutting her ears to Dennis as he begged her to take cover in the Morrison shelter.

Chapter Thirteen

IT WAS DAYS before Poppy could bring herself to face Dennis again. He had called at the house several times, bringing flowers for Mabel and cigarettes for Mrs Tanner, but Poppy always managed to be otherwise engaged. If she heard the sound of Napoleon's hooves on the road outside and the rumble of cartwheels, she either pretended to be asleep or slipped out of the house by the back door and climbed over the fence into the neighbour's garden. Old Mrs Kemp had been widowed for more than twenty years and was always glad of company. She invariably wore black and lived mainly in her sombre back room which also seemed to be in permanent mourning. The walls, once cream, were darkened to taupe by smoke from the coal fire and nicotine from the cigarette that habitually dangled from the corner of her mouth. The carpet and curtains were brown velveteen and the chenille cloth that covered the dining table was a similar colour. On the wall above the table was a sepia print of a choppy sea, unrelieved by any type of vessel or hint of land. Mrs Kemp's husband had gone down with his ship in the Great War, and Poppy wondered if this was supposed to be the spot where the tragedy had occurred. She had never liked to ask in case it brought back painful memories, but Mrs Kemp was always good for a cup of tea and a biscuit.

If Mabel or her mother noticed, surprisingly neither of them remarked on Poppy's reluctance to see Dennis, but it seemed that he was not going to be put off easily and a week after her birthday she found him waiting for her outside the hospital. He was leaning against the wall, smoking a cigarette. With a flick of his fingers he sent it arcing into the gutter. 'Hi. Haven't seen you for a while, Poppy.'

There was no way she could avoid him without being downright rude. She was on her own as Mabel had worked the night shift and would not be arriving at the hospital for another hour at least. 'I've been busy,' Poppy murmured, wrapping her coat around her as a bitter east wind hurled bits of grit into her face.

Dennis jerked his head in the direction of the dray parked alongside the kerb where Napoleon waited with an air of stoical resignation. Poppy could not help comparing the sturdy Shire horse with the thoroughbred Goliath. Both were beautiful in their own way, but she experienced a sudden wave of nostalgia for the green countryside and the rolling hills of Dorset. She could almost smell the damp earth and the salty tang of the sea. She jumped as Dennis wrapped his scarf around her neck. It was still warm from his body and smelt of Brylcreem, Gibbs Dentifrice and cigarette smoke. 'What's that for?'

'To keep you warm, ducks. You look perished and it's getting dark. I came to give you a lift home.' Without waiting for her response, he took her arm and guided her across the pavement, which was already slippery with a film of ice. He lifted her up onto the driver's seat as if she weighed less than a feather, and he clambered up taking his seat beside her. 'You've been avoiding me, Poppy.'

It was a statement said without rancour but she did not feel the need to defend her actions. She huddled deeper into the camel coat that she had purchased for a shilling at a jumble sale in the local church hall.

'All right,' Dennis said equably. 'I plead guilty to unacceptable behaviour and I'm sorry if I overstepped the mark. How's that? Are we friends again?' He flicked the reins. 'Walk on, Napoleon, old chap.'

His rueful expression was so comical that she found it impossible to keep a straight face. 'Yes, of course. Just don't do it again.'

'Don't you like being kissed?'

'Can we change the subject?'

'Or is it just me you don't like? I'm no Rhett Butler or Ashley Wilkes, but I'm not a bad bloke, Poppy.'

'I like you lots, but I'm not ready for that sort of thing. Perhaps you should find someone your own age, Dennis.'

'Ouch!' He pulled a face. 'I'm not that old, girl.' He reined in Napoleon as they came to a crossroads. It was almost dark, and with their headlamps partially obliterated it was difficult to see oncoming vehicles until they were almost on top of them.

'Perhaps I should get off and walk,' Poppy said uneasily. 'It's not fair to keep the horse out in this icy weather and it's dangerous. He might get knocked down. Anyway, shouldn't you have the wagon back at the brewery?'

'You worry too much, ducks. Napoleon can see in the dark and I've got mates in the brewery stables.'

'I'm used to walking home alone,' Poppy said lamely.

'If you don't want to see me again I'll understand. You're a great girl and I really enjoy your company, but if you think I'm too old or if it's because of the way I am . . .'

'Stop it, Dennis.' She laid her hand on his sleeve. 'Don't talk like that. I like you a lot, and age doesn't matter if two people get along well. I'm just not ready for anything other than being just friends.'

'Just friends it will be then.' He flicked the whip so that it tickled Napoleon's ear and encouraged him to walk on. 'But if Joe gets suspicious and thinks I'm after his Mabel, I want you to back me up and tell him that it's Maggie I fancy. I'm not too proud to admit I like older women, so you'll have to put on a few years before I start courting you.'

She linked her hand through his arm, giggling. 'Dennis, you are funny.'

'Funny's good. I'll settle for that, for now.'

IN THE WEEKS that followed Poppy was still a little wary of Dennis, but gradually they resumed something like their old easy companionship. He continued to take her on regular trips to the cinema or to the local pub where he drank shandy while she sipped lemonade. There was always someone who was prepared to strum away on the piano and more often than not it was Dennis who was called upon to play a tune. Everyone enjoyed singing the popular songs. Dennis had a good baritone voice and his renditions of 'Run Rabbit Run' and 'Any Old Iron' or 'Knees up Mother Brown' had the whole bar joining in. He was a born performer and Poppy could not help thinking that but for his disability he might have made a living on the music hall stage. Everyone knew Dennis Chapman and wanted to buy him a pint or two, but he was not much of a drinker and usually suggested that the money was put in the Red Cross collecting tin, or some other charity. Poppy felt a rush of pride when he did this, although sometimes his loud behaviour was embarrassing. She knew he would be mortified if she said anything, and she resisted the temptation, waiting until they were on their way home before giving him a piece of her mind. Unfortunately this only seemed to amuse him and he would slip his arm around her shoulders and whistle 'The Lambeth Walk', dancing along the pavement and exaggerating his lopsided gait until she saw the funny side of the situation and laughed.

Spring gave way to summer. In May the Blitz on London intensified, almost ripping the heart out of the city. Food became even scarcer. Cheese was put on ration and then eggs. Poppy often went to bed hungry and woke up to a meagre breakfast of toast and a scraping of margarine. Clothing coupons were issued in June although

Poppy earned so little that she could not afford to buy anything new, but Dennis had mates in Petticoat Lane who somehow managed to sell garments on their stalls without a single coupon changing hands. Mrs Tanner said it was against the law and they should be locked up in the Tower and shot, but Mabel said it was a godsend. Poppy was somewhere in the middle, and although she wrestled with her conscience when Dennis presented her with a summer frock in a floral cotton print with a sweetheart neckline and tiny puff sleeves, she had not the heart to refuse the gift. She had worn cast-offs for so long that she had almost forgotten what it was like to wear something new and pretty. She thanked Dennis and kissed him on the cheek, but she insisted that she would pay him back every penny it had cost. She did not want him to get the wrong idea.

'Nonsense, kid,' Dennis said, ruffling her hair. 'Can't let my Scarlett go round in second-hand duds. You're entitled to something nice every now and then. It's my pleasure and I got it at cost, so spend your money on something else.'

Mabel was not so guilt-stricken when he produced a crêpe blouse that looked almost exactly like the one Dorothy Lamour wore on the cover of *Picture Show*, and had worn it that evening when they went to the pub to celebrate Poppy having passed her first aid exam. She had continued to study even though work at the hospital was gruelling and the hours long. Sister McNally had been impressed by Poppy's actions during the air raid and had taken a personal interest in her from that day onwards.

She encouraged Poppy to train as a nursing auxiliary, merely raising an eyebrow and shrugging her shoulders when she discovered that she was under age. 'I doubt if anyone will ask to see your birth certificate,' she said. 'There is a war on, you know.'

For six weeks Poppy attended lectures and spent every evening studying and revising. To her intense relief she passed the examination which enabled her to apply for a position as a nursing auxiliary, and with Sister McNally's backing she was taken on at the hospital. Despite the long hours, almost military discipline and back-breaking work, Poppy was in her element. Her old ambition to be a land girl was superseded by her desire to become a fully fledged nurse. As soon as she was old enough she would apply to become a nurse probationer, and to that end she studied even harder, spending evenings in her room reading books borrowed from the Red Cross or the local library.

She barely noticed the passing of the seasons. The news on the wireless was depressing and it seemed that the fighting would go on forever. She was beginning to forget what it was like to live in peacetime and her memories of Squire's Knapp seemed like a distant dream. Jean wrote to her often, keeping her up to date with events on the estate. Mavis was stepping out with an airman from the air base at Warmwell, and Edie was spending all her spare time at the neighbouring farm. She said that the farmer's son, Howard, was giving her tips on animal husbandry. A line of exclamation marks followed this statement and Jean had written 'Ha ha!' at the end of the sentence.

There was a brief mention of Algy, who had been granted thirty-six hours' leave and seemed to have spent most of it with Jean, although she left the details to Poppy's fertile imagination. It was obvious from what she left unsaid that Jean had fallen headlong for Amy's brother, and it was not difficult to understand why. Algy was charming, good-looking in an under-stated English way, and had impeccable manners. He had a keen sense of humour and he was Guy's best friend; that fact alone made him almost perfect in Poppy's eyes. Poppy took some comfort from the knowledge that Jean would have been the first to tell her if anything had happened to him. No news in this instance was definitely good news.

One Sunday at the beginning of December Poppy was enjoying her first weekend off in weeks. Dennis had come to tea bringing with him a brown paper bag filled with sprats, which Mabel grilled, although Mrs Tanner complained that she did not like burnt fish skin and they should have been dipped in flour and fried in dripping or lard. Mabel's lips hardened into a thin line as Poppy had noticed they always did when she was struggling to keep back an angry retort.

Poppy was preparing to step in and change the subject but Dennis suddenly held up his hand for quiet. The wireless had been droning on in the background but something in the BBC news had caught his attention. Even Mrs Tanner remained silent as they listened to the newsreader's account of the Japanese air attack on Pearl Harbor.

'The Americans will come into the war now,' Dennis said, helping himself to a slice of bread and marg. 'The Yanks will be coming over here in their droves.'

'All those poor sailors,' Poppy murmured, staring down at the sprat on her plate that seemed to be peering back at her. 'So many killed. It's awful.'

'Hong Kong and Singapore will be next,' Dennis said, shaking his head. 'The Japs have already got French Indo-China, and now they've attacked America they'll have to keep on with the offensive.'

Poppy pushed her plate away, her appetite suddenly deserting her. Amy was in Singapore. She wondered if the Fenton-Joneses knew that they were in imminent danger, or perhaps it was just Dennis being dramatic again. She hoped so.

'What's up with your fish?' Mrs Tanner demanded. 'I'll have it if you don't want it. Pass it here.'

'I thought you didn't like burnt skin, Mum,' Mabel said pointedly.

'I don't, but I'm starving. I'm fed up with rationing and I want meat, but if this is all we've got then it'll have to do.'

Mabel raised her eyebrows and sighed. 'Give it to her then, Poppy. And don't complain you've got a bone stuck in your throat, Mum.' She rose from the table. 'I'll get the pudding. It's carrot cake made with dried egg. I'm only telling you that so some of us don't moan that it's not up to much. I do what I can with what I've got.'

'That's right, Mabel my duck. Make do and mend, that's the ticket.' Dennis winked at her and grinned.

'I'll make do and mend you in a minute, Dennis Chapman. And you can take that grin off your face. It won't be so funny when we're eating Woolton pie for Christmas dinner instead of turkey.'

Dennis threw up his hands. 'You've only to ask, ma'am, and I'll see what I can do. I've ...'

'Got a mate in Smithfield,' Poppy cut in before he could finish the sentence. 'I bet if you wanted a Spitfire, Dennis would have a mate working for the aircraft company that makes them and he'd have one parked outside in the road on Christmas morning.'

Dennis blew her a kiss. 'Wonders I can perform, love. Miracles take a bit longer.'

POPPY WAS ON duty on Christmas Day, but Dennis met her when she finished at eight o'clock in the evening and walked her home through the dark streets. Mabel had saved her some chicken and vegetables, which she had kept warm over a pan of hot water. She had made giblet gravy and the chicken carcass was already simmering away with carrots, parsnips and swedes to make soup which would feed them for the next couple of days. There was no Christmas pudding or cake but Dennis produced a box of fondant fancies and a bar of Cadbury's Whole Nut chocolate, which was shared around between them, even though Mrs Tanner complained that the nuts got stuck in her teeth. Dennis had also provided a bottle of ruby port, which put everyone in a good mood. Mabel had made paper hats out of newspaper and they sat around the wireless, sipping port and listening to Christmas carols on the Home Service.

After three glasses of port, Mrs Tanner fell asleep in her chair and Mabel brought out her knitting. She had recently taken it up and had only just mastered stocking stitch. The shapeless khaki object was intended as a balaclava helmet for Joe, who was still somewhere in England, but Poppy thought secretly it looked more like a scarf. She could tell by the twinkle in Dennis's eyes that he was thinking the same thing.

At ten o'clock, Mabel put away her knitting and roused her mother. 'Come on, Ma, I'll help you to bed.'

Mrs Tanner opened her eyes and blinked owlishly at her daughter. 'Is it Boxing Day?'

'No, Mum. It's bedtime.' She turned to Dennis. 'Give me a hand, please. She's always stiff as a board when she's fallen asleep in the chair.'

Dennis sprang to his feet and lifted Mrs Tanner bodily, which made her screech in protest. He carried her into the dining room and sat her down on her bed.

'I hate this room,' she complained bitterly. 'And I hate that damn Morrison shelter. It's like sleeping in the same room as a dog kennel.'

'You'd be glad enough of the shelter if we got a direct hit, Mum. Let's get you into bed.' Mabel turned to Poppy who was waiting by the door in case any extra help was needed. 'I'm going to bed as soon as I've settled her for the night. And, Dennis, don't keep Poppy talking until all hours. She's got to get up early in the morning and so have I.'

Poppy hesitated, reluctant to abandon Mabel to the whims of her difficult parent. 'Do you want me to refill your hot water bottle, Mrs Tanner?'

'D'you want to scald me?' Mrs Tanner demanded fiercely. 'Get him out of me room. I can't undress with a man looking on.'

'Don't be difficult, Mum,' Mabel said wearily.

Dennis shepherded Poppy from the room. 'I bet that's what her old man used to say every night when she went to bed in her liberty bodice.'

'Hush, she'll hear you.' Stifling a giggle, Poppy closed the door. 'I'll just see to the fire and then I'm going to bed, Dennis. I'm on the early shift tomorrow.'

Dennis followed her into the front room. 'Mabel's got the patience of a saint. I'd strangle the old girl if she was my mother.'

Poppy moved closer to the fire, standing with her back to the dying embers. The temperature in the room had plummeted and she was exhausted. Even though she had enjoyed her evening, it had been a busy week working with just enough staff to keep the hospital running smoothly. She smiled. 'No you wouldn't, Dennis. You talk tough but you wouldn't hurt a fly.'

His expression softened as he moved slowly towards her. 'I wouldn't do anything to harm you, Poppy. You do know that, don't you?'

Two glasses of port had made her feel warm and at peace with the world. She did not protest when he took her in his arms. 'Of course I do, silly.'

His hands caressed her back as she laid her head on his shoulder and she slid her arms around his neck. The experience of being held close to someone who cared about her was a joy that had been denied her for a long time, and she breathed in the scent of him. The smoky, sooty smell of the city on a winter night that clung to his jacket took her back to her childhood and the hugs that Dad used to give her when he returned home from working on the railways. She raised her head and was about to make the comparison, thinking it would amuse him, but the look in his eyes robbed her of speech. Slowly, as if they were drawn together by a strong magnetic force, his dark face moved closer until she could feel his breath on her cheek. He held her eyes like a modern-day Svengali. She could hardly breathe. Her lips parted as he took them in a kiss that left her in no doubt as to the depth of his feelings. This time she did not pull away from him. She could not even if she had wanted to, and to her astonishment she did not want this tender embrace to end. She gave herself up to the moment, allowing the new and exciting sensations to blot out the war, and all the terrible things she had witnessed at the hospital and the ghastly news that they heard every day on the wireless. For the first time in her life she knew what it was to feel like a woman with desires and needs of her own.

But all too soon it was over. Dennis released her gently, gazing into her eyes with a smile that almost melted her heart. 'Happy Christmas, Poppy darling.'

For a moment she was unable to catch her breath; then confusion set in and she moved away from the comforting circle of his arms, shivering as the chill in the room seemed to envelop her. Her hand flew automatically to the heart hanging around her neck and feelings of guilt assailed her. She had loved Guy devotedly since almost the first moment she had met him, and she had betrayed him with another man. Dennis was supposed to be her friend and now he had turned her small world upside down. Suddenly she was angry. Friends did not treat each other like this. He was standing very still, watching her with a wary expression. She closed her fingers around the pendant. It was cold as ice. 'I'm very tired, Dennis. I've got get up early in the morning.' She made for the door but he moved swiftly, bumping clumsily into the settee in his haste to intercept her.

'I'm sorry, love. I got carried away. I know I broke my promise, but . . .'

She could not look him in the eye. 'It's all right. It was my fault as much as yours.'

'But it meant something to me, kid. I can't go on pretending that I don't have feelings for you.'

'I know you do.' She raised her eyes to his face with an attempt at a smile. 'I like you a lot too, but there are more important things than us at the moment.'

A lock of hair had come loose from the confines of her snood and he twisted it round his finger. 'I know I'm not much of a catch and there'll be young doctors and grateful patients who'll be buzzing round you like flies around a honey pot, but I don't want to lose you, Poppy.'

'Can't we go on as before? We've been having a good time, Dennis. I don't want to get serious with anyone until I've finished my nurse's training. You do understand, don't you?'

He smiled ruefully. 'Rhett waited years for Scarlett. I guess I can give you as much time as you want, kid.'

POPPY WAS RELIEVED that she had to work on Boxing Day. It gave her a good excuse not to see Dennis and she had warned him that she might have to work over-time if they were short-staffed on the wards. She needed time and space to come to terms with the turmoil raging inside her head and the sensual longings that his kiss had awakened. She felt that she had grown up almost over-night, but although Dennis excited her physically and she enjoyed his company, there was something lacking. There was no magic spark to make her pulses race when he came into the room. She did not think about him when they were apart. In short, she was not in love with him. But he was not the sort to take no for an answer. There was a dogged determination in Dennis's make-up that was both flattering and exasperating. Sometimes she felt like telling him to go away and leave her alone, but that would be too cruel. She was trapped, but she needed him. Life without Dennis would be drab and boring. Mabel thought the world of him and so did Mrs Tanner, when she was not running him down and calling him a spiv.

In February the news filtered through that Singapore had fallen to the Japanese. Poppy was in agonies, wonder-ing what fate had befallen Amy. She wrote to Jean immedi-ately, asking if she had heard anything from Algy. The reply came a week later saying that Amy and her parents had left for Australia before the invasion, and as far as Jean knew they were safe and well. Poppy almost cried with relief. Amy had been wonderful to her when she was a fright-ened and lonely evacuee. She wished she could tell her how much she meant to her, and that she hoped it would not be too long before she was able to return to England and marry Guy. That was not exactly true, of course, but she had long ago faced the inevitable: her idol would marry his childhood sweetheart, and that there was no place for her in his life. Mrs Carroll had made it abundantly clear that a girl from the East End was not welcome in their family. Poppy knew she must accept her fate with as good grace as she could muster.

In April, the day before her sixteenth birthday, Joe turned up unexpectedly with a pass for forty-eight hours' leave. Mabel was ecstatic and Poppy had to put a pillow over her head that night to shut out the noises emanating from their bedroom, which was adjacent to hers. In the morning Mabel looked pale, tired and extremely happy. She said she had decided to take the day off sick and so what if she was given the sack. It would be worth it to spend some time with her husband.

Poppy herself would have liked to spend more time with Joe, but that would not have been fair on him and Mabel. Their married life so far had consisted of a brief honeymoon and then a long separation. In their joy at being reunited they had quite forgotten that it was Poppy's birthday. She went to work as usual.

Dennis was waiting for her when she left the hospital that evening, and for once she was pleased to see him. His face lit up when she greeted him with a smile, and he brushed her cheek with a kiss. 'Had a good day, love?'

She shook her head. 'Not really. We're rushed off our feet, short-staffed and I'm on the maternity ward. There were four babies born within minutes of each other.'

Dennis grinned. 'That's what the blackout does for you.' He shrugged his shoulders, holding his hands palms upwards. 'Well, it's true. I bet Joe's been making up for lost time with Mabel, lucky chap.'

'You make it sound so sordid,' Poppy said, turning her head away. 'They really love each other.'

He took her hand and linked it through his arm. 'Of course they do, sweetheart. And I'm going to take you up West and treat you to dinner to celebrate your birthday. The newly weds can have some time together, that's if the old battleaxe will let them.'

'That's really kind of you, but all I want to do is go home and have an early night.'

'I won't hear of it. No doubt Joe and Mabel will have something laid on for you later, but this evening is ours. We'll get the tube to Oxford Circus and I've booked a table in the Brasserie at Maison Lyons. I've got it all planned and I've been saving up for months. This is going to be the best birthday you've ever had, Poppy Brown.'

'But I'm not dressed for going to a posh restaurant. My clothes and hair smell of disinfectant and I look a mess.'

He snatched up a brown paper parcel lying at his feet. 'I've got it all sorted, ducks. This is part of the present. You can change in the ladies in the underground station.' Tucking the parcel under one arm, he took her by the hand. 'Come on, Poppy. I'm not taking no for an answer. This is going to be a night to remember.'

Getting changed in the confines of the cubicle was comparable to Houdini escaping from a strait jacket, but after a lot of wriggling and struggling with the tiny mother-of-pearl buttons that did up the bodice, Poppy emerged from the ladies to a loud wolf whistle from Dennis. The silk-taffeta dress in eye-catching scarlet fitted as if it had been made for her. The sleeveless, figure-hugging bodice was cut low, exposing rather more flesh than she would have liked, and the flared skirt ended just below the knees, but the overall effect was, she thought, the height of fashion. Silk stockings caressed her skin like gossamer, adding the finishing touch. She had never possessed anything so luxurious before and Dennis had gone so far as to include a pair of white sling-back sandals in the parcel. It must have cost a small fortune and she ought not to accept but it was her birthday. She took off the snood that she always wore for work and shook out her hair, allowing it to tumble about her shoulders in an abundance of curls.

'My little Scarlett,' Dennis said with a proud smile. 'You look absolutely bloody marvellous.'

Embarrassed but secretly delighted, she felt the blood rush to her cheeks. 'How did you know my size, Dennis? Everything fits perfectly.'

He ground his cigarette butt beneath the toe of his shoe. 'Can't take all the credit for that, ducks. Mabel gave me a list of your measurements, but I chose everything myself. You do like the dress, don't you?'

She kissed him on the cheek. 'I love it, but you shouldn't have spent such a lot of money on me. You must have used up all your coupons.'

He tapped the side of his nose and winked. 'I told you before, love. I've got mates. Anyway, let's get going. I'm starving, I don't know about you.' He draped her jacket around her shoulders. 'Pity about that, it kind of spoils the effect. We'll have to see about getting you a nice little fur coat for next winter.'

LYON'S CORNER HOUSE on the corner of Oxford Street close to Marble Arch was an imposing building. Poppy had been there once before when Mum and Gran had taken her up to see Father Christmas at Selfridges, and they had gone to Maison Lyons for afternoon tea to complete the treat. She had been so small that she had had to kneel on the chair in order to eat her Knickerbocker Glory, a sickly confection made with jelly, ice cream and tinned fruit, topped with meringue and whipped cream. Afterwards, on the way home on the Green Line bus which was travelling at a snail's pace due to the pea-souper fog, Poppy remembered feeling terribly sick. Worse still, Gran had told everyone that it was her own fault for scoffing something that was almost as big as she was. Tonight she had no intention of disgracing herself in such a manner.

Dennis led her through the huge food hall, past counters piled high with chocolate boxes decorated with enormous satin bows, although they were probably empty and just for show nowadays, Poppy thought ruefully. It had always been her ambition to be given one of those luxurious boxes filled with delicious chocolates, but Dennis was guiding her away from the opulent array towards the stairs leading down to the Brasserie.

The cloakroom attendant raised her eyebrows when she was handed the brown paper parcel containing

Poppy's old clothes and shoes, but she checked in their outer garments without comment. At the entrance to the restaurant a maître d' resplendent in a black swallow-tail coat greeted them solemnly and led them to a table beside a potted palm, while an orchestra consisting of rather elderly musicians played popular dance music. Dennis held out a chair for Poppy and she was about to sit down when someone called her name. She stood absolutely still, hardly daring to look round.

Chapter Fourteen

JEAN LEAPT UP from her seat and rushed towards Poppy, holding out her arms. 'It is you. I thought it was when I saw you come through the door, but you've grown up so much I can hardly believe it.' She embraced Poppy in a hug.

'What are you doing here?'

'I might ask the same of you.' Jean turned to Dennis with a friendly smile. 'And who is this?'

Poppy heard the words but they barely registered. Glancing over Jean's shoulder she could see Guy and Algy seated at the next table. 'Dennis,' she murmured vaguely. 'This is Dennis Chapman, my brother's old school friend.'

'Here,' Dennis said, chuckling. 'Less of the old if you don't mind, kid.' He held out his hand. 'How do, Jean. Pleased to meet you.'

'Hello, Dennis.' She shook his hand, but there was a trace of coolness in her smile. 'It's nice to meet one of Poppy's friends. Have you known her long?'

He opened his mouth to reply but Algy had risen to his feet and he moved to Poppy's side, giving her a peck on the cheek. 'Poppy, old thing. By golly, it's good to see you looking so – so fine.' He turned to Dennis, proffering his hand. 'How do you do? Since the girls have forgotten their manners, I'd better introduce myself. Algy Fenton-Jones, and the grim-looking individual seated at the next table is Guy Carroll.' He shot a meaningful glance in Guy's direction.

Dennis shook Algy's hand, but his expression remained neutral. 'Dennis Chapman. Pleased to meet you, squire.'

Jean was saying something but Poppy's gaze was fixed on Guy, who had risen slowly from his seat and was coming towards her, seemingly in slow motion. She had to remind herself to breathe. 'Guy,' she whispered.

He acknowledged Dennis with a brief nod of his head. 'Hello, Poppy.'

'Is that all you can say to the girl after all this time?' Jean said with a teasing smile. 'Just look at her, Guy. Can you believe that this is the same kid who helped out on the farm and was scared stiff of everything with hooves and horns?'

Algy slipped his arm around Jean's waist. 'Our food's getting cold, darling. Perhaps we can catch up later, and give these two people a chance to order their meal.'

Jean squeezed Poppy's hand. 'Of course. It's a special occasion, isn't it? We sent you a birthday card, that's if Mavis remembered to post it.'

Poppy shifted uncomfortably from one foot to the other. She did not have to look at Dennis to know that he was displeased. Resentment oozed out of every pore and if he had been a dog she was certain that his hackles would have been raised as he glared at Guy and Algy.

'I haven't forgotten your fourteenth birthday when we got you drunk on cider,' Jean continued, apparently oblivious to the tense atmosphere. 'D'you remember that evening outside the village pub, Guy?'

'That was a long time ago.'

Her pulses were racing and she was certain that her heartbeats could be heard above the tune the orchestra was playing. She wished that Guy would relax and smile at her, but his expression was stony. She turned to Dennis, forcing her lips into what she hoped was a cheerful smile. 'Dennis, I'd like you to meet Mr Carroll. His mother took me in when I was evacuated to the country.'

'It's Pilot Officer Carroll now, Poppy,' Algy said proudly. 'Guy was the first one to get his wings. I only made navigator.'

Guy and Dennis faced each other like opponents squaring up for a fight, but it was Guy who eventually broke the tension. 'How do you do?'

'Very well, mate. But don't let us keep you from your dinner.' Dennis hooked his arm around Poppy's shoulders in a proprietorial gesture. 'Best take a seat, love. The waiter wants to take our order.'

'We'll catch up after dinner,' Jean said cheerfully. 'I've lots to tell you, Poppy.'

'I can't wait to hear all the news.' Even as the words left her lips, Poppy realised that it was not what Dennis wanted to hear. She eyed him warily. What had started out as an exciting evening was turning into something of a disaster. Guy and Dennis obviously disliked each other on sight, which was something she could not fully comprehend, and it led her to make unfavourable comparisons between them. Guy with his athletic physique and fine features looked every inch the fighter pilot hero as portrayed on the silver screen, while the part of Heathcliff might have been written with Dennis in mind.

'We came here to eat, so let's order before they close the damned kitchen.' Dennis moved awkwardly to hold the chair for Poppy.

Some of the other diners were staring at him as people always did when they saw his odd shambling gait, and Poppy was torn between pity and exasperation. 'All right,' she said in a low voice. 'But there's no need to be rude.'

The waiter reappeared at Dennis's side. 'Are you ready to order, sir?'

'Almost. Give us a couple of minutes, mate.' Dennis opened the menu and stared at its contents, frowning.

Out of the corner of her eye Poppy could see the next table. Jean, Algy and Guy were laughing and talking as if they had not a care in the world. They were only sitting a couple of yards away from her but it might as well have been a mile.

'What will you have, love?'

She shook her head. 'You order for me, Dennis.' His pleased smile made the small sacrifice of her independence worthwhile. Despite his outward display of confidence she realised that he felt ill at ease in the company of two men he considered to be his superiors. But now, to her chagrin, he was ordering their meal in a loud voice and speaking to the waiter in such a patronising manner that she wished she could crawl under the table and hide. She stole a glance over her shoulder and found that Guy was staring at her with a question in his eyes.

The meal dragged on. Poppy ate the food put before her but everything tasted exactly the same. She tried to look as though she was enjoying herself but she was painfully aware that Dennis was talking too loudly, laughing at his own jokes and generally putting on a show which was not entirely for her benefit. She stole a glance at Guy every now and then but all she saw was his profile. He appeared to have forgotten her existence and it saddened her. She had felt attractive and chic in her new clothes, but it seemed that Guy could hardly bear to look at her. Perhaps he would like her better if she wore her old jodhpurs and sweater and smelt of the stables rather than the Californian Poppy perfume that Dennis had generously included in her magnificent birthday present.

'I'll finish off your apple pie if it's too much for you,' Dennis said, reaching out to take her plate. 'It's a crying shame to waste good food.'

'It was lovely, but I'm full. Thanks, Dennis, it was a lovely dinner.'

'Three courses and coffee for one and six,' he said with his mouth full of pie. 'I call that a bargain.' He raised his hand to beckon the waiter. 'Oy, mate. The lady is ready for coffee, and you can bring mine too. It won't take me long to clear me plate.'

Poppy rose to her feet. 'I'm just going to powder my nose.'

He nodded his head and continued shovelling pie into his mouth as if it were his last meal on earth. Poppy made her way between the tables to the ladies' room. She was joined moments later by Jean.

'Are you all right?' Jean asked anxiously. 'You look a bit pale.'

Washing her hands, Poppy dashed cold water on her face. 'It's a bit stuffy in there, and I'm not used to eating such a lot of food all in one go.'

Jean opened her handbag and took out a compact and a lipstick. 'Don't take this the wrong way, Poppy, but how well do you know Dennis? I mean, he's a lot older than you, and he's . . . well, I don't quite know how to put this, but I wouldn't have thought he was exactly your type.'

'Dennis is an old friend of the family. He's been really good to me.'

'I'm sure he's got a heart of gold, but you're just sixteen, little more than a child, and he doesn't look like the sort who would take no for an answer.'

'He's not like that,' Poppy said angrily. 'Why does everyone have to judge people on outward appearances? Dennis is kind and generous.'

'That's a gorgeous gown. Did he buy that for you, by any chance?'

'It was my birthday present.'

'Then he's generous to a fault.' Making a moue, Jean put on her lipstick. 'Just be careful, that's all I'd say if I were your big sister.'

'You've got him all wrong.'

'I hope so, for your sake, but it's obvious he's got his eye on you, love. Things can get out of hand if you're not careful. Do you understand what I'm saying?'

'I'm not a kid any more, Jean. Dennis knows that I don't want to get serious.'

'Then we'll say no more about it.' Jean turned away from the mirror, smiling. 'I've missed you, Poppy. We all have.'

'I've missed you too, and Squire's Knapp, but I'm probably better suited to nursing than I was to work on the land.'

'And is that what you want to do? Nursing, I mean.'

Poppy nodded emphatically. 'I'm back where I belong. I was always an outsider as far as Mrs Carroll was concerned.'

'Marina Carroll is a first class bitch, Poppy darling. She's the worst kind of snob, but she'll get her comeuppance one day, just you wait and see.'

Arm in arm, they returned to the restaurant to find couples dancing to the strains of 'A Nightingale Sang in Berkeley Square'. Algy claimed Jean and guided her onto the dance floor, and Poppy returned to her table. Dennis's chair was empty. She hesitated for a moment, looking around, but he was nowhere to be seen. He must, she thought, have taken the opportunity to freshen up and she was about to resume her seat when she saw Guy walking towards her. He held out his hand. 'May I have this dance?'

Her feet barely touched the ground as he led her onto the dance floor and took her in his arms. 'I'm afraid I'd forgotten it was your birthday, Poppy. I'm sorry.'

'It doesn't matter,' she murmured, lowering her gaze as she concentrated on her steps. He whirled her round to the strains of the waltz, but his silence forced her to raise her eyes to his face. 'Have I done something to offend you, Guy?'

'Whatever gave you that idea?'

'You've been treating me like a stranger. I thought you were my friend.'

His expression softened and this time the smile reached his eyes. 'I'm sorry if I gave you that impression. I suppose I was shocked to see the change in you.'

'Do I look so awful?'

'You're beautiful, but that dress isn't you, Poppy.'

'How can you say such a thing? It's the latest fashion, and anyway what do you know about women's clothes?'

'Not much, I admit, but it makes you look like a little girl dressed up in her mother's frock.'

Suddenly the lovely red dress seemed tawdry and cheap, but Poppy was not going to let him see how much his criticism hurt. 'I'm not a schoolgirl now, Guy. I'm a first year probationer nurse and I'm going to make nursing my career. I can't remain a kid just to please you.'

His breath caressed her cheek as they were caught up in the crush of the other dancers. 'I know, but I miss the old Poppy: the little girl with the lost expression in her eyes who fainted every time she saw a horse.'

His words made her heart swell with joy but his initial cool reception still rankled and she could not bring herself to forgive him so easily. 'I've grown up a lot since then.'

'You're still an innocent. You shouldn't be out alone with that fellow. He's too old for you.'

Poppy met his intense gaze with a defiant shake of her head. There was an edge to their conversation that was unexpected and strange. She had thought they would slip easily into their old companionable relationship, but something had changed and she was not sure what or why. 'You're wrong about Dennis.'

'You don't know what I'm thinking, unless of course you can read my mind.'

'I know you well enough to tell when you disapprove of something or someone.'

'He's a type, Poppy. And I don't like to see you with an older man who might take advantage of your youth and inexperience.'

'That's just not fair, Guy.'

'What's he been saying to you?' Dennis tapped Guy on the shoulder. 'The lady is with me, squire. In case you've forgotten.'

They were in the middle of the packed dance floor and had barely been moving. Guy stopped and turned his head to glare at Dennis. 'This is my dance.'

'And I'm cutting in.'

'Stop it, Dennis,' Poppy said in a low voice. 'You're making a scene.'

'Yes, this is ridiculous.' Guy placed himself squarely between them. 'Sit down and stop behaving like an idiot.'

'I've met your type before. You think you're above the rest of us. Well I can tell you now, mate – you ain't. Come along, Poppy. I'm taking you home.'

Without giving her a chance to argue, Dennis grabbed her by the arm. Taken by surprise, she did not resist as he led her off the floor, but as soon as they reached their table she broke free from his grasp. 'How dare you?' she hissed. 'You made a complete fool of yourself and of me too.'

Dennis glowered at her, breathing heavily. 'I was protecting what's mine. Any man would do the same.'

'I am not your property.' Poppy pushed past him, making for the exit.

'Poppy, wait.' Jean hurried to her side. 'Don't rush off like this. I'm sure it can all be straightened out.'

Poppy hesitated. Tears of humiliation and anger burnt the backs of her eyes. She doubted if she could ever look Guy in the face again and she was furious with Dennis. 'I'm going home,' she said, her voice breaking on a sob. 'Tell Guy I'm sorry.'

'It wasn't your fault. It was that oaf you came with.' Jean shot a venomous glance at Dennis, who was arguing with the waiter. 'He's haggling over the bill by the looks of things. He's not good enough for you, Poppy. Hold on a minute and Algy and I will see you home.'

'I'll be all right. I know my way home. I'm an East End girl born and bred.' Poppy fled from the restaurant, shutting her ears to Jean's protests. Having collected her jacket and parcel of clothes from the cloakroom attendant, she slung her gas mask case over her shoulder and hurried from the building, thankful for the blackout as it enabled her to disappear into the darkness. She made her way to the tube station just as the air raid siren started to wail. The sound of anti-aircraft fire echoed around the city like thunder as the searchlights cut into the velvet night sky. She bought a ticket and had to walk down several flights of stairs as the escalators had been switched off. The stench from the crowded platforms hit her even before she reached the dimly lit area which was packed with people in sleeping bags, lying on wooden bunks or simply huddled on the ground covered with their coats. It was hot and stuffy and she had to tread carefully so that she did not step on anyone as she made her way to the edge of the platform. White lines had been drawn so that those sheltering from the air raids did not obstruct the passengers waiting to board the trains. The man in the ticket office had warned her that the service ceased at ten thirty, and she had to ask the time from the man standing next to her.

'Ten fifteen, love. Let's hope we don't get stuck here all night.'

'But that last train goes at half past ten.'

'There's an air raid. Anything can happen. Remember Bank station in January? Fifty-six poor souls killed in one go.' He glanced round at the tightly packed bodies. 'Could happen anywhere.'

Poppy said nothing. At this particular moment her most pressing worry was that Dennis would turn up before the train arrived. She did not want to talk to him now, or possibly ever. It would be a long time before she could forgive him for the way he had behaved. She shifted her foot as a small child pushed past her carrying a cup of tea. The little girl carried it carefully along the platform and gave it to an elderly woman who was sitting on a battered cardboard suitcase. Families were huddled together in groups. Women were putting in their curlers and preparing to settle down for the night. From fragments of conversation that Poppy picked up it seemed that some of them had been down here for hours, staking their claim to a space big enough to spend the night in relative safety. She felt almost envious when she saw mothers and daughters making the best of the situation together. It was something she would never share again. Her entire family, except for Joe, had been annihilated by a German bomb in a matter of seconds. She shivered as a gust of warm wind preceded the rumble of the tube train as it emerged from the tunnel and ground to a screeching halt at the platform. The doors opened with a hiss and she followed the gloomy man into the carriage. He slumped down on the seat opposite and produced a folded newspaper from his coat pocket.

As the doors closed and the train picked up speed, Poppy caught sight of Dennis standing on the platform. She bent her head, hoping that he had not spotted her. She could not help feeling sorry that he had missed the last train, but she did not trust herself to speak to him. Her skin crawled with embarrassment as she recalled the moment when he had all but carried her off the dance floor. As the carriages were swallowed up in the dark maw of the tunnel, she settled down on the seat with a sigh of relief. She was exhausted physically and emotionally. What had started out as an exciting birthday treat had turned in a debacle, and Guy had made it plain that he disapproved of her new outfit. Red dress, no knickers, Gran used to say. Poppy's fingers plucked nervously at the scarlet silk-taffeta skirt. What she had thought was glamorous and smart now appeared cheap and tawdry. She realised with hindsight that she ought not to have accepted such an extravagant present. If she ever spoke to Dennis again she would tell him that this sort of thing had to stop.

She arrived home just before midnight. Her feet were sore from walking a long way in unaccustomed high heels and as she let herself into the house all she wanted was her nice warm bed. But a light was on in the kitchen and Mrs Tanner was standing by the gas stove stirring something in a milk pan. She put it aside, peering myopically into the dark hallway. 'Who's there?' Making a grab for her walking stick she advanced on Poppy with her flannelette nightgown billowing round her skinny frame like a bell tent, and her grey hair hanging limply around her face so that she looked like an agitated witch. 'Who is it?'

'It's me, Poppy. I'm sorry if I scared you.'

'What sort of time do you call this to come home?' Mrs Tanner hitched her glasses higher up on the bridge of her nose, staring at Poppy as she moved into the beam of light from the single bulb dangling from the kitchen ceiling. 'What are you wearing? You look like a tart.'

'You've never had a good word to say for me, have you?' Poppy's nerves had almost reached breaking point.

'It wouldn't matter what time I came in or what I was wearing, you'd find something to complain about.'

'Don't you speak to me like that, you trollop. I don't know where you got that outfit but you weren't wearing it when you left for work this morning.'

'If you must know, it was a birthday surprise from Dennis. He took me up West for a meal and we got separated in an air raid. I caught the last train home and I don't know where he is now. Are you satisfied?'

'You snooty little bitch.' Mrs Tanner clutched her hand to her chest. 'I'm having one of my turns and it's all your fault. I told Mabel not to take you in, but she's as soft as a boiled carrot.'

Poppy rarely lost her temper, but she was on the edge now. 'Well she doesn't take after you then, does she? You're a mean old woman and you run her ragged.'

Mrs Tanner shook her stick at Poppy. 'No one speaks to me like that. You wait until I tell Mabel what you said to me.'

Poppy shrugged her shoulders. She had had enough for one day and she made for the stairs. 'I'm going to bed. I've got an early start in the morning.'

'You're just like your mother,' Mrs Tanner said through clenched teeth. 'She was a hoity-toity cow when she was younger.'

Poppy paused with one foot on the stair tread. 'You leave my mum out of this. She was a wonderful woman.'

'I was in service with her years ago and she was no better than she should be. We all knew that she'd been having it away with the master's son.'

'That can't be true. My mum wasn't like that.'

'That's all you know. She had to leave when her affair with Harry Beecham became common knowledge and Sir Hereward found out. It was hushed up, of course, but Mary was sent packing and Harry joined the army soon afterwards.'

Disbelief and anger roiled in Poppy's stomach. 'That's a pack of lies, and it can't be true.'

'It didn't end there,' Mrs Tanner said with obvious satisfaction. 'When I left the manor house I took a job at the ABC teashop in the High Street. I used to see your mum all dolled up when she came there to meet Harry. They chose a table far from the window and sat staring into each other's eyes and holding hands. It fair made me sick. Especially when I knew that your dad was away in the army.'

'You're making it up.'

'Joe and Mabel were at the same school. I knew what was going on all right, but your dad only found out when it was too late. She was three months gone with you by the time he come home for good.'

'I don't believe you. You're a wicked, spiteful old woman.'

'It's God's honest truth,' Mrs Tanner called after her as Poppy ran from the room. 'You're a little bastard, that's what you are, Poppy.'

Racing upstairs to her room, Poppy shut the door and locked it before shedding the offending garment. Her hands were shaking as she placed it on a coat hanger. It would have been satisfying to give vent to her anger and rip it to shreds, but she could not bring herself to destroy such a pretty dress. She hung it from the picture rail as a reminder of her own folly, even though she had no intention of ever wearing it again. Too tired to undress completely, Poppy went to bed in her underclothes, but sleep did not come easily.

She did not believe a word that Mrs Tanner had said, but doubts niggled at her brain. Odd remarks made at home that she had not understood came to mind. Her father's obvious preference for Joe had been hurtful but Mum had explained it away by saying that dads always favoured their sons, and Joe was the first born. Not that her father had ever treated her with anything other than kindness, but there had always been a reserve between them, whereas Mum had spoiled her whenever she had the opportunity. She had always told her she was different from the other kids in her school. Perhaps that was why she had wanted her to stay on at Squire's Knapp. It was something Poppy would never know for certain.

Eventually, she slipped into a troubled sleep but she was awakened at the crack of dawn by the sound of horse's hooves and the rumbling of cartwheels. Dennis. She knew it was the dray even before she rose from her warm bed to peer sleepily out of the window. She blinked, rubbing her eyes as she took in the scene below. Dennis was not alone. Seated next to him was Mabel's Uncle Fred and behind them perched amongst the beer barrels were the two aunts, Ida and Dottie. Forgetting that she was not speaking to Dennis, Poppy slipped on her serviceable navy blue cotton skirt and a short-sleeved jumper.

Barefoot, she made her way downstairs to find that Mabel had opened the front door and was standing there shivering in her flannel dressing gown with her hair still in curlers.

Looking over Mabel's shoulder, Poppy saw Auntie Ida and Auntie Dottie making their way along the garden path. Auntie Ida was wearing her coney fur coat over her nightdress, and Auntie Dottie wore a hand-knitted woollen hat which did not quite conceal the rows of snail-like pin curls secured in place by hairgrips.

'Auntie Ida, what happened?' Mabel cried anxiously.

'I'm in shock, dear. The house went down like a pack of cards. If we hadn't been in the Anderson shelter we'd all have been killed.' She turned to her husband, who was struggling beneath the weight of something heavy. 'Have you got the strong box, Fred?'

'Of course I have, Ida. Go indoors before the whole street sees us in our nightwear.' Fred hustled Auntie Dottie into the hallway before setting his load down on the floor. 'Put the kettle on, Poppy, and fetch the brandy bottle, there's a good girl.' He stomped off into the front room, leaving his wife to her own devices.

'Thank you very much, Fred,' Ida said bitterly. 'Such a gent. You'd think a man would be concerned for his wife after she's lost absolutely everything.'

'And me,' Dottie added plaintively. 'Everything I owned was in your house since you persuaded me to move in with you, Ida. You aren't the only one who's been affected.'

'You poor things, but at least you're safe,' Mabel said, making an obvious attempt to sound cheerful. 'Why don't you both go into the front room and sit down?' She shot a desperate glance in Poppy's direction. 'Poppy will make tea and I'll fetch the brandy.' She went to close the front door, almost shutting it in Dennis's face. 'Oh, sorry, Dennis. I thought you were in already.'

He entered the house giving Poppy a sheepish grin. 'So you got home all right then?'

'It looks like it.' Poppy took in his dishevelled appearance with a cursory glance. 'What happened to you?'

'I don't know what's going on here,' Mabel said with a sigh. 'I thought you was going to see her home, Dennis, or I'd never have given you the go ahead to take her up West.'

'We got separated in an air raid and I caught the last train.' Poppy had no intention of going into details now or ever. Last night was something she wanted to forget.

'We'll sort this out later, but right now I've got more important things to do, and the first one is to break the news to Mum. The shock of hearing what's just happened might bring on one of her attacks.' Shaking her head, Mabel hurried into the dining room leaving Poppy and Dennis alone in the hallway.

'Why did you run off like that?' he demanded in a low voice. 'Anything could have happened to you.'

'You had no right to behave as you did. Anyway, I don't want to talk about it now. I've got to make tea for the aunts and Uncle Fred.' Turning her back on him, Poppy went into the kitchen and picked up the kettle to fill it at the sink.

He followed her, pausing in the doorway. 'I was worried sick about you.'

'I can look after myself.' Poppy struck a match and lit the gas, placing the kettle on the hob. Sending him a sideways glance beneath her lashes she could not help feeling a bit sorry for him. He was covered in brick dust from head to foot, and there were smudges of soot on his face. He looked more like a circus clown than the dashing young man he had been attempting to portray last night. 'What happened to you?'

'I missed the bloody train and I had to walk all the way to the brewery. I hitched up the horse intending to come straight here. I needed to make sure you'd got home okay, but the shrapnel was flying about and I had to wait for the all clear. Then, just as I was driving through Leytonstone, I saw that the Barkers' street had caught a packet. I went to see if I could help and found them standing outside a pile of rubble that had been their house. Nothing left. Not a thing.'

Despite the gravity of the situation and her own heartache, Poppy could not quite smother a hysterical bubble of laughter. 'I'm sorry,' she said, covering her mouth with her hand. 'But you do look like a clown, Dennis.'

He did not seem to appreciate the joke. 'I'm glad you think it's funny because I bloody don't. What were you playing at, running off like that? You might have been killed in the air raid.'

'You should take a look at yourself in the mirror,' Poppy murmured, turning away to search for clean teacups.

'I walked halfway home looking for you last night. I took Napoleon out in the dark because of you.'

Suddenly it was no longer funny. She whirled round on him. 'You had no right to behave as you did. You made a fool of yourself and of me. You embarrassed me in front of my friends.'

'I suppose I'm not good enough for you. That's it, isn't it? That's what it's been all along, and it's got nothing to do with you being too young or wanting to put your studies first. It's all about you thinking that you belong to that toffee-nosed set we met last night. Well, let me put you straight on that score, ducks. You don't fit in with them any more than I do. They'll be nice as pie to your face but behind your back I bet they call you that snotty kid from the East End.'

'I may be a kid to you, Dennis Chapman, but all the more shame on you for dressing me up like a tart. That's what Mrs Tanner called me when she saw me in that red dress, and that's what Jean was trying to tell me only she was too nice to put it in so many words. You're a hypocrite and you only do things to suit yourself. I'm sorry if you wasted your time looking for me, but you needn't bother another time. I don't want to see you ever again. D'you understand, Dennis? Never again.'

Chapter Fifteen

THE BARKERS AND Auntie Dottie moved in. Fred and Ida invaded the back bedroom and made it their own, giving Poppy no alternative but to offer her room to Auntie Dottie. It might only have been a tiny boxroom with a lumpy mattress and a window that did not fit properly so that the wind whistled about her head like a screaming banshee on stormy nights, but it had been her own private space. Deprived of that, the only place where Poppy could sleep was the saggy old settee in the lounge, but this meant that she had to wait until everyone else had gone to bed before making herself as comfortable as possible on a piece of furniture that had seen better days. She found springs sticking through the cushions in a different place almost every night. Mabel's sheets were worn and thin in the centre and Mrs Tanner said they ought to be cut and turned sides to middle, but somehow nobody seemed to have the desire or the energy to take on such a boring task.

The bombed-out aunts sat about all day complaining about the loss of their possessions and their homeless state. Mabel bore it all with her customary good nature, but Poppy's patience was stretched to the limit. She had to leave the room sometimes or she might have told them that they were lucky not to have suffered the same fate as her parents and grandparents. Uncle Fred still had his business, whatever that was, and shortage of cash did not seem to be their problem. In fact, the only time Ida and Dottie showed any spark of enthusiasm was when they collected the extra clothing coupons allocated to people who had lost everything in air raids. They went out on a spending spree, but Poppy noted grimly that they did not include Mabel or her mother in these forays into the West End, which included lunch at a swanky restaurant. They seemed blissfully unaware that their presence put a strain on everyone else in the house, and neither of them lifted a finger to help with the household chores.

Every morning Poppy folded up her bedding to make room for Ida, Dottie and Mrs Tanner. Each of them had their own special place where they sat all day, marking their territory with a magazine or an unfinished piece of knitting and woe betide anyone who unintentionally encroached on their space. Poppy made them tea and toast before slipping out of the house, leaving them huddled round a desultory fire like the three witches in *Macbeth*. She half expected them to start chanting 'Bubble, bubble, toil and trouble', but they were usually arguing about something trivial that had happened years ago in their youth, but for which they had borne a grudge until the present day.

Working on the wards was the only thing that kept Poppy sane. The hospital was filled to capacity. There were beds in the corridors and the walking wounded were treated in a marquee set up on the bomb site which had once been the casualty department. Staff shortages meant that probationer nurses worked even harder and were given more responsibility than they would have had in peacetime. Poppy was eager to learn but she found it almost impossible to study at home. The small house was hopelessly overcrowded and the air in the front room was invariably polluted by cigarette smoke and stale cooking smells. Mabel and Poppy were the only non-smokers in the house and sometimes it was difficult to see across the room through the manmade fog from Capstan Navy Cut and Passing Clouds cigarettes. Poppy thought that who-ever gave the latter product that name had never had to sit in a small room with three women puffing out smoke like factory chimneys. The fog never seemed to dissipate completely even if the windows were left wide open after everyone had retired to bed.

Although Poppy had tried to end her relationship with Dennis he seemed to have a skin as thick as an elephant's. He had kept away for several days after she had told him that she never wanted to see him again, but he turned up at the end of the week as if nothing had happened, bear-ing gifts for all. He brought flowers for Mabel, cigarettes for the smokers, a Havana cigar for Uncle Fred and a box of chocolates for Poppy, which she could hardly refuse without causing a scene. He complimented the two aunts on their new clothes and volunteered his services should they require any of the little luxuries in life. He had, he said, made friends with some of the American soldiers who were based at a camp not too far away, he could not say where of course for security reasons. But the Yanks were good fellows and they had chocolate, chewing gum and nylons. The ladies had only to ask.

Mrs Tanner called him a rascal and Auntie Ida said she did not believe in the black market, but Uncle Fred asked her where she thought the chops came from that they had eaten for supper. 'You've just had your whole month's meat ration in one meal, you silly cow,' he said, puffing on his cigar and winking at Dennis. 'Thanks, old chap. A fine Havana is what I miss the most.'

'Rolled on a luscious Cuban lady's thigh,' Dennis said, grinning.

Auntie Dottie stubbed her cigarette end out in her saucer. 'Shame on you, talking that way in front of ladies.'

'He's a bad 'un.' Mrs Tanner chuckled, jerking her head in his direction. 'You're a cheeky devil, Dennis. That's what you are.'

Dennis had been standing on the hearth rug with his back to the empty grate, but he knelt at Mrs Tanner's feet in a theatrical gesture. 'You love it, Maggie, me old china.'

She slapped him on the shoulder, smiling coyly. 'You are a one. Get up, you fool. Save your soft words for young Poppy.'

Poppy had been keeping out of the way as much as was possible in a room filled with bodies. She had perched on an upright chair by the door in readiness to escape to the kitchen should anyone ask for more tea, but now everyone was looking at her and Dennis had risen to his feet. He came towards her, holding out his hand. 'Perhaps Poppy would like to come for a walk. It's a fine evening and the nights are drawing out. How about it, girl?'

She was going to refuse but anything was better than sitting listening to Mrs Tanner and her sisters complaining about shortages and harking back to the good old days. 'I'll get my cardigan.'

She met him outside the front door. Spring was well and truly in the air. The birds seemed oblivious to the fact that there was a war on. They trilled their songs, made their nests and went about their short lives as they had done since the beginning of time. The scent of wallflowers filled the cool air together with the fruity smell of freshly turned soil where householders had dug up their front lawns in order to plant vegetables. Poppy hooked her cardigan around her shoulders as she followed Dennis down the path. He opened the gate and held it for her. She struggled to think of something to say. 'You're quite a hit with the aunts and Mrs Tanner,' she said with an attempt at levity.

'It's my personal charm. It works on almost all females, present company excepted.'

She fell into step beside him. 'I'm happy to be friends, Dennis. I just want to keep it that way.'

'I was out of order the other night, but it's only because I care about you, kid.'

'It's forgotten.'

'And forgiven?' He stopped, holding out his hand with a twisted smile that was impossible to resist. Poppy conceded with a nod.

'Yes, of course.'

He glanced at his watch. 'We're too late for the flicks. How about a quick one at the pub? Do you good to get away from the family for a while.'

'They're not my family. I'm the odd one out, and I can't stand sleeping on that settee for much longer.'

'Poor little Poppy,' Dennis took her by the hand. 'A glass of lemonade and a packet of crisps will cheer you up no end.'

DENNIS EDGED THROUGH the bar crowded with men in uniform and civilians enjoying a brief respite from their daily routine. Poppy had to admire the way he conquered his disability and managed somehow to carry two glasses filled to the brim, one with beer and the other with lemonade, without spilling any. He put them on the table and sat down, taking a packet of Smith's crisps from his jacket pocket. He took a swig of beer and swallowed. 'Look, Poppy. Going back to what you were saying about sleeping on the settee and it being crowded in Muriel's house.'

She sipped her lemonade. It was warm and sweet, tasting more like sherbet than lemons. 'What of it?'

'I've got a house all to meself, girl. I rattle round in there like a pea on a drum. You could have a room of your own if you move in with me.'

Shocked at the thought, she shook her head. 'Oh, I don't think so, Dennis. It's very kind of you, but . . .'

'No strings, love. I'd be a perfect gent, and you wouldn't be too far from the hospital.'

'Mabel would have a fit, and Joe wouldn't like it either. You must see that.'

'All right then. I thought you might say that, and I've got another suggestion.'

'What's that, Dennis?'

'That we get hitched. You're old enough as long as you get permission from your next of kin, and that's Joe. I don't think he'd have any objection.'

Poppy almost choked on a mouthful of lemonade. 'What?'

'I'm asking you to marry me, girl. I can't live without you, Poppy. It's as simple as that.'

Stunned into silence, she met his earnest gaze with a sense of shock. She had thought at first that he was joking. She could tell by his expression that he was not.

'I'd go down on one knee,' he said with an attempt at a smile, 'but I wouldn't be able to get up again. Say something, Poppy.'

'Oh, Dennis, I'm sorry. I can't marry you.'

'Why not? I'd be good to you, kid. I'd look after you and give you a decent home.'

'You make me sound like an abandoned pet.'

'I'm serious, Poppy. I've never been more serious in me whole life.' He reached across the table to lay his hand on hers. 'Think about it, love. You don't have to give me an answer straight away. Get used to the idea.'

'I don't have to think, Dennis. I know it's not right for me.'

'We get on well, don't we?'

'Yes, we do.'

'And I love you enough for both of us. You'd grow to love me too. We'd be a happy couple just like your mum and dad. My old man ran off with a waitress when I was two, and Mum had a string of boyfriends afterwards but none of them stayed for long. I always envied Joe having a proper family.'

There was no doubting his sincerity and for a brief moment she was tempted. It would be wonderful to be the centre of someone's existence, and sheer bliss to have a home of her own, but the shadow cast over her past by Mrs Tanner's spiteful revelations came rushing back to her. She curled her fingers around his hand. 'I'm going to tell you something very private, Dennis. Something I didn't know until recently, and I want you to promise not to tell anyone, and especially not Joe.'

'Swear to God.' Dennis crossed his heart and took another swig of his beer. 'Go on.'

'Mrs Tanner was in service with Mum years ago. She told me that my mum had an affair with someone while Dad was away in the army, and that man was my real father. Everything I thought I knew about my family was a lie.'

He withdrew his hand, his brows drawn together in a frown. 'It doesn't matter to me, love. I know who you are, and I wouldn't want to change anything about you.'

'It's not as easy as that. I can't explain it exactly, but I can't marry you or anyone until I find out who I am.' Unable to bear the hurt look in his eyes, Poppy jumped up from the table. 'I'm sorry, Dennis. Anyway, I'd best be going home or Mabel will worry. Don't come with me.' She pushed through the crowds, ignoring the wolf whistles and offers of drinks from the men in the bar. Outside the air was cool and fresh. She wrapped her cardigan more tightly around her shoulders and broke into a run. Dennis would not be able to catch up with her even if he tried. She glanced over her shoulder as she turned the corner but the street was empty. She walked on at a brisk pace, arriving home just as it started to rain.

Mabel was in the kitchen making cocoa. She glanced up and smiled when she saw Poppy. 'Well?'

'Well, what?'

'What did you say to him?'

'You knew?'

Mabel put the saucepan back on the gas ring, beckoning to Poppy. 'Come in and shut the door.'

'How could you?' Poppy demanded, closing the door. 'Why didn't you warn me?'

'I promised Dennis that I wouldn't breathe a word. He said that with Joe away in the army I was the closest you've got to family, and he asked me if I approved.'

'And you said you did? Why, Mabel? I'm sorry, but it's got nothing to do with you or anyone else.'

'Love, you're under age. You can't get married without your guardian's consent and I suppose that's me.'

'Well, you needn't have worried. I said no.'

Mabel stared at her with the heaped teaspoon of cocoa clutched in her hand. 'You turned him down?'

'Of course I did. I'm only sixteen, and I'm not even halfway through my training. I don't want to get married now or in the near future.'

'It's wartime, Poppy. Things are different, and Dennis is a good man. He'd see you right and he's got a nice little house. You could do worse.'

Poppy eyed her curiously. 'You know, don't you? Your mum told you.'

Adding the cocoa powder to a little cold milk in each mug, Mabel began stirring vigorously. 'Told me what?'

'About my mum and Harry Beecham.'

Mabel gave a trill of self-conscious laughter. 'Oh, that old chestnut. I'd heard something but it's just gossip, love. Take no notice.'

'So it's true. I thought as much.' Poppy snatched the saucepan off the heat as it was about to boil over. 'I want to find him, Mabel. I want to meet my real father.'

'That might not be a good idea, ducks.'

'I've got to see him. I need to find out where I came from and who I really am. Come on, Mabel, you know where they worked. Please tell me.'

THREE WEEKS LATER, on her first full weekday off, Poppy caught the train to Epping. Mabel had been persuaded to give her the address of Beecham House which was situated on the edge of the forest a couple of miles from the market town. They had kept her mission secret from Mrs Tanner and her sisters, and Poppy had set out with a degree of trepidation. Harry Beecham might be dead for all she knew, but she could not rest until she had found out as much as she could about the father she had never known.

After enquiring at the local post office, she followed their directions and walked the rest of the way. The trees on the edge of the forest were almost in full leaf and the hedgerows were lacy with fading heads of cow parsley, red and white campion and ragged robin. Poppy had become conversant with some of the wild flower names whilst living at Squire's Knapp and the scent of the countryside in May took her forcibly back to what seemed now like halcyon days. With every step she became more and more nervous. This might go horribly wrong. Her father was almost certain to be married with a horsey wife and numerous offspring. Until now she had been living in the make-believe world of the movies where the long-lost daughter turns up and is welcomed with open arms, tears of joy and finds a happy family waiting to embrace her. But when she came to the brick wall surrounding the property and the wrought iron gates secured by a rusty padlock, she knew that the reality was going to be very different.

Peering through the ornate scrollwork she could see the carriageway cutting a swathe through overgrown gardens knee-high in weeds and brambles. At the far end, the burnt-out shell of what must once have been a great country house stood out against the sky like a romantic etching of a ruin. She stared at the blackened walls in disbelief. The person behind the counter in the post office had failed to mention the fact that the house no longer existed, but then she had only asked its whereabouts.

Perhaps they had thought she was a sightseer or an artist who wanted to paint fallen masonry with moss growing all over it. But this was no ordinary pile of bricks and rubble. This was the house where her mother had fallen in love with a young man well above her station in life, and he with her. The irony of the situation was not lost on Poppy. It seemed that history had repeated itself when by chance Marina Carroll had picked her from the line-up of evacuees. The circumstances were not the same but she, like her mother before her, had been taken into a household far different from the one in which she too had been raised. She too had fallen in love with the son and heir, although there the similarity ended. Hers was an unrequited love; a childish crush, nothing more.

That did not alter the fact that the home of her forebears had been razed to the ground. Her bright dreams of being part of a family had once again been shattered to dust. She turned away from the scene of desolation, and was about to start walking back towards the town when she heard a sound behind her. She paused, glancing over her shoulder as a man riding a bicycle drew level with her. She could see by his dog collar that he was a man of the cloth. He stopped, steadying himself with one foot on the ground. 'Good morning. It's a fine day for sightseeing.'

'Good morning, vicar. Yes, I was just looking at the ruins.'

'Ah, yes, Beecham House. It was a fine building before the fire.'

'You knew the family?'

'Very well indeed.'

'My mother worked there a long time ago. I wanted to see the house.'

He held out his hand. 'Raymond Hayes. How do you do?'

'Poppy Brown. How do you do, sir?'

'Are you going back to town, Poppy? If so, perhaps you'd allow me to walk with you.'

'I'd like that, sir. Perhaps you could tell me something about the family?'

'I'm sure your mother has more interesting stories to tell.'

'My parents were killed in a bombing raid. That's one reason I came here. I wanted to see where she worked.'

'I understand, and I'm sorry for your loss. What would you like to know?'

By the time she reached Epping station, Poppy had learned the history of Beecham House and the Beecham family whose ancestor came to England with William the Conqueror. Poppy could not help thinking that if true it was one in the eye for Mrs Carroll. It was a pity she would never know that the kid from the East End had aristocratic forebears, even if she had been born on the wrong side of the blanket. The Beecham family, according to the vicar, had suffered many reversals of fortune through the centuries. One of their privateering ancestors had become fabulously wealthy and had built the manor house, but the succeeding generations had either gambled the fortune away or made huge losses on the stock market. In the nineteenth century, Sir Timothy, a sober-sided man determined to salvage the reputation of his once respectable family, had become an MP and had pulled the family back from the brink of bankruptcy. But once again, in the nineteen twenties, the money had been frittered away by Sir Hereward Beecham, who fancied himself as a film producer and had spent what was left of the family fortune making films of questionable artistic merit that had flopped at the box office.

At the station entrance, Poppy paused. 'What happened to the rest of the family? My mother mentioned someone called Harry.'

Raymond Hayes smiled. 'Harry was a delightful young man. Very good-looking as I recall, but quiet and unassuming, totally unlike his father who was what you might describe as larger than life. Harry left to join the army, quite suddenly and to the surprise of everyone, including the family.'

'Is he . . .' Poppy could hardly bring herself to frame the words. 'Was he killed in the fire?'

'No, he wasn't there when it started. They never did find the cause of the fire, but the gossipmongers said it was arson. Sir Hereward was accused of starting the conflagration with a view to claiming on the insurance but it was never proved. He died of a heart attack soon afterwards, and the estate fell into disrepair. The villagers always hoped that Harry would return one day, but so far he hasn't shown any signs of wanting to take over the reins so to speak.'

'What about the rest of the family? Do they still live round here?'

'There were two younger sisters, both of whom married well and moved away from Essex. I believe that

Sophia and her husband live in Northumberland and Margery married a Guards officer. I think they have a house in Chelsea, although my information is probably out of date by now.'

Poppy held out her hand. 'Thank you, vicar. It was good of you to spare the time to talk to me.'

He smiled, shaking her hand. 'Not at all. I enjoyed our little chat.' He was about to mount his bike but he hesitated. 'By the way, you didn't tell me your mother's name. I might remember her.'

'Mary Fitzpatrick. She was just a maid.'

'Mary, of course. I can see the likeness now. She was a very pretty girl and lively too. She was always smiling, as I recall.' His smile faded and he frowned as if another and less happy memory had clouded his vision. 'Well, I must be getting on, my dear. It was nice to meet you, Poppy.'

'Wait.' Poppy reached out to catch hold of his sleeve. 'There's something you're not telling me.'

'It's nothing. Just a bit of gossip that went round at the time. I'd forgotten all about it until now.'

'Won't you tell me? I think I might know already, but I need to be sure.'

'It was a long time ago and so I suppose I'm not breaking any confidences.' He smiled gently. 'I was fond of Harry and it was obvious to anyone who knew him that he was very much in love with Mary and she with him. It was common knowledge in the town as they'd been seen together on numerous occasions, walking arm in arm, oblivious to the world around them.'

'Why was that so wrong?'

'Things were different years ago. Sir Hereward had plans for his son that did not include his falling in love with a girl from a less privileged background.'

'But Harry loved my mother.'

'I think pressure was brought to bear on poor Mary. She left Beecham House quite suddenly. Harry was sent to Sandhurst and entered the army as a commissioned officer. As far as I know he never married.'

'Thank you, vicar. You've been very helpful.'

'Mary was happy though? I wouldn't like to think of her living a life of regret.'

Poppy nodded her head. 'I think she was content, although I can't be sure now. She was a good mother and I miss her every day.'

'Goodbye, Poppy, and good luck, my dear.' Raymond Hayes mounted his bike and pedalled off towards the centre of town, wobbling from side to side.

Poppy went into the station to wait for her train. As she stood on the platform she tried to picture her mother when she was young, before worry and hard work had worn her to a shadow of her former self. The plump, motherly woman in her saggy skirt and ill-fitting hand-knitted cardigan did not fit with the description of a pretty young thing full of life and laughter. She must have loved Harry very much to have given herself to him body and soul even though she was a married woman. What had she felt when she discovered that she was pregnant by him?

The train rumbled into the station. Carriage doors opened and passengers stepped out onto the platform. Poppy found a window seat in an empty carriage and settled down to mull over what she had learned from the vicar. The train pulled out of the station and she was on her way back to the metropolis, away from the place where her mother had lived, loved and lost. She stared out of the carriage window at green fields, hedgerows and farmland flashing past but it was just a blur. She would never know what had been in her mother's heart, but at least she had found out a little about Harry Beecham.

'My REAL DAD's an army officer, Mabel,' Poppy said in a low voice as they washed up in the tiny kitchen that evening after supper. She had been longing to talk about it ever since she arrived home, but it was almost impossible to get Mabel on her own. She seized her chance safe in the knowledge that neither Mrs Tanner nor her sisters would offer to help with the chores, although Auntie Dottie had been known to listen at keyholes if she thought there was anything interesting going on.

'And you saw the ruins of the big house?' Mabel stopped swishing the block of hard green soap around in the water in an attempt to make lather. She glanced at Poppy with shining eyes. 'How exciting. Was it a grand house before the fire?'

'I don't know, but the vicar said it was very old, so I suppose it must have been pretty imposing. Anyway, I'm not interested in the house, but I would like to find out more about Harry. I wish I'd thought to ask what regiment he was in.'

Mabel smiled triumphantly. 'I think I can answer that one. Joe told me ages ago that his dad was in the London

Rifle Brigade. He was batman to a Colonel Gerald Beecham and that's how he came to meet Mary. Colonel Beecham was Sir Hereward's brother and he was staying at the house. It's just possible that Harry joined his uncle's regiment after the affair was discovered and Mary was given the push.'

'It's something to go on,' Poppy said thoughtfully. 'But I don't suppose it will be easy to find any information about Harry until this wretched war is over. I'd probably be arrested as a spy and end up in the Tower if I started making enquiries.'

Mabel flicked suds at her, giggling. 'Don't do that, love. I'd be left all alone with the awful aunts and Uncle Fred. If he pinches my bum once again I'm telling Auntie Ida and hang the consequences.'

'He's caught me once or twice,' Poppy acknowledged, grinning. 'He pretends to be a respectable businessman but I'll bet he chases his secretary round the office, and he's probably got a couple of mistresses tucked away in seedy bedsits in Plaistow. I'd love to tell his clients what he's really like.'

'He's my problem, not yours.' Mabel pulled the plug out of the sink. 'Anyway, you've got two posh aunts of your own now if what the vicar said was true. You've got rich relations, Poppy girl.'

'Maybe, but they wouldn't be interested in me. I'd be one of those blot things on their escutcheon, or whatever you call it.'

'I dunno what that is but it sounds painful. You talk like you've swallowed the dictionary these days, Poppy, but I suppose that's what a fancy education does for you.' Mabel wiped round the sink with the dishcloth. 'You're too grand for the likes of us. I'm not being funny, ducks, but you was always a bit different even before you was evacuated. Now I know why.'

Poppy had no answer for that. It was no good arguing with Mabel. Once she had formed an opinion she was unlikely to change her mind. Poppy was putting the clean plates away in the cupboard when the doorbell rang.

'Who can that be at this time in the evening?' Mabel said, glancing at the wall clock. 'It's almost nine thirty.'

'If it's Dennis, I don't want to see him.'

Wiping her hands on her apron, Mabel shook her head. 'Don't worry, I won't let him in. I'll say you're on night duty or something.' She hurried out of the kitchen closing the door behind her.

Poppy waited, holding her breath. After the emotional and physical journey she had experienced during the day she could not bring herself to face Dennis. She could hear Mabel's feet pattering over the linoleum in the hallway and the door opened.

'There's someone to see you, Poppy.'

'It's not Dennis, is it?'

Mabel shook her head. 'No, it's a chauffeur. He says the lady in the car wants to speak to you on a matter of importance. That's his words not mine. He says it won't wait.'

Chapter Sixteen

EVEN IN THE twilight, Poppy could see that it was the Pallisters' limousine parked at the kerbside. Hector's chauffeur was standing by the rear door, holding it open.

Pamela's pale face stared at her through the window as Poppy hurried down the path. She climbed into the car. 'Mrs Pallister, you're the last person I expected to see here.'

'I must speak to you urgently.' Pamela dismissed Harper with a wave of her hand.

'Is there something wrong?' It was a rhetorical question as Poppy could see by Pamela's fraught expression that she was not the bearer of good news. 'It's not Guy, is it?'

'Guy?' Pamela's full lips formed a small circle of surprise. 'Why would it be anything to do with him?'

'I don't know, I just thought . . .'

'Just listen to what I have to say, Poppy. I haven't time to play games. It's a long drive down to Squire's Knapp and I have to return this evening.' She gazed out of the window, gazing abstractedly at the chauffeur's back as he leaned against the bonnet, lighting a cigarette. 'I'm not supposed to be using Hector's petrol coupons for private business but this is a matter of life and death. Daddy's car was in an accident during the blackout last night.'

Poppy laid her hand on Pamela's arm. 'I'm so sorry. Is he . . .'

'It's touch and go. He was on his way home from the court and I suppose he was in a hurry to get back to Mummy.' Pamela's voice broke on a sob. 'You don't know, of course, but Mummy collapsed at one of her meetings a week ago and was rushed to hospital.'

Poppy found it almost impossible to imagine Marina Carroll laid low by anything other than a severe blow to the head, but it was obvious that Pamela was genuinely upset. 'She's all right though?'

'Not really. Apparently she'd suffered a massive stroke and now she's paralysed down one side and can barely make us understand what she's saying. She's at home but she needs constant attention. We've hired a nurse but Mummy makes it obvious she loathes the woman and throws things at her. I'm at my wits' end.'

'I'm truly sorry, but without wishing to sound uncaring, what has this got to do with me?'

'I wouldn't blame you if you told me where to go, Poppy. I know we didn't treat you terribly well, but I was hoping that you'd come back with me and look after Rupert. He's running wild and I can't do anything with him.'

'But he's such a sweet little boy.'

'He was once, but he's really naughty these days. We've gone through two nannies since you left and with most of the village girls either in the forces or doing war work, it's almost impossible to find a reliable person who can cope with a lively four-year-old. Jean told me that you're a trained nurse and I thought you might help me look after Mummy as well as Rupert.'

'A probationer nurse,' Poppy said quickly. 'I'm not qualified yet, and I won't be for another three years.'

'Darling, that doesn't matter a bit. I need a helping pair of hands and someone with commonsense who knows the household routine and won't be upset by Mummy's little tantrums.'

'I'd like to help, I really would, but if I leave in the middle of my training I might never get another chance. What would I do when you no longer need me?'

Pamela grasped both her hands. 'We need you now, Poppy. If Guy were here he'd beg you to come down to Squire's Knapp and help out. If it's money you're worried about . . .'

'No.' The word escaped from Poppy's lips in a sigh of despair. She wanted to tell Pamela Pallister to go to hell, but invisible cords were tugging at her heartstrings. She remembered the way that Rupert used to cuddle up to her in bed, and wake her up by jumping on her and tugging at her hair. The nursery should be filled with children, not one sad and lonely little boy who would grow up to carve his name on the wooden desk lid, just as Guy had done all those years ago. Guy would expect her to answer his sister's genuine plea for help, and there was no doubting Pamela's sincerity or her deep distress.

'Please, Poppy,' Pamela whispered. 'We need you desperately. Apart from the land girls, there's only Mrs Toon left out of all the servants. She copes splendidly with the help of a daily woman from the village, but we need someone living in the house whom we can all trust, and who understands Mummy's little foibles. If you can't bring yourself to do it for Mummy and me, please think of Rupert. He needs you terribly.'

Staring out of the window, Poppy was suddenly alert as she saw Dennis lumbering towards the car. Harper stood to attention as if ready to ward off an aggressor.

Dennis was a complication that she could well do without. She was fond of him and that was the trouble. With his 'never take no for an answer' attitude she was afraid that one day she would simply give in, and in a moment of weakness agree to marry him. She came to a sudden decision. 'All right, Mrs Pallister. Give me a few days so that I can give some kind of notice at the hospital . . .'

Pamela shook her head. 'No, Poppy. You must come with me now. I simply can't cope, with Daddy at death's door and everything.' She fumbled in her handbag and brought out a scrap of lace that served as a hanky.

Not knowing what to say, Poppy gazed out of the window. Dennis had stopped and was speaking to the chauffeur. She could not hear what he was saying but she could tell from the set of his jaw that he was going to be difficult, and she knew that he would not let her leave without putting up a fight. The thought of a confrontation made her decision easier. 'All right, I'll come with you, but only if you write to the hospital explaining why I had to leave so suddenly.'

Pamela mopped her eyes leaving smudges of mascara on her cheeks. 'Darling Poppy, you won't regret this. I'll get Hector to have it written on government headed writing paper to make it look official. We'll be eternally grateful to you.'

'Yes, well, I'd better go indoors and tell my sister-in-law. I'll need to pack some things.'

'Yes, of course, but please hurry.' Pamela glanced up and recoiled as she saw Dennis peering at them through the window. 'Who is that fearful oick?'

In any other circumstances Poppy might have laughed outright at Pamela's shocked expression, even though she was appalled by this overt display of snobbery. 'Don't worry about him. He's an old friend of the family.' She opened the car door and stepped out onto the pavement. 'Come away, Dennis. You're frightening Mrs Pallister.'

'What's going on?' Dennis demanded as he followed Poppy up the garden path and into the house. 'Who's that posh bird in the Daimler?'

'I'm sorry, Dennis. I haven't got time to chat right now.' Poppy hurried into the kitchen and closed the door, leaving Dennis outside in the hall. 'Mabel, I've got something important to tell you.'

'What's going on?' Dennis banged on the wooden panels. 'I'm coming in.'

Poppy leaned her back against the door. 'Go away, Dennis. This has nothing to do with you. I want to speak to Mabel in private.'

'Good God, what's happened?' Mabel demanded. 'Shut up, Dennis. I can't hear myself think with you making that noise.'

'What's going on, Dennis?' Uncle Fred's voice echoed round the hallway.

'That's what I want to know.' Dennis gave the door one last thump. 'I'll be in the front room when you're ready to talk, Poppy.'

'You'd think he owns me,' Poppy said crossly. 'I thought I'd made it plain that there's no future for us, but he won't take no for an answer and that's another reason why I'm leaving tonight, Mabel.'

'You're what?' Mabel leaned against the sink, clutching a cup of tea in her hands.

'It's Mrs Pallister outside in the car. You know, Mrs Carroll's daughter.'

'What does she want?'

Poppy explained as quickly and simply as she could, but Mabel was at first shocked and then angry. 'How can you even think about going back there after the way they treated you?'

'I'm going for Rupert's sake as much as anything. He's a dear little boy and I love him. I can't bear to think of him shut up in that miserable nursery with a grumpy nanny who doesn't give a damn about him, and Mr Carroll was always kind to me. He's in a bad way according to Pamela.'

'But they'll treat you like a servant and the only difference is they won't pay you. She's taking advantage of your good nature. Anyway, you can't just walk out on your nurse's training. What will Sister McNally say?'

'Mr Pallister is going to write an official letter explaining why I had to leave without notice. It'll be all right, Mabel.'

'I don't know about that. I don't like it, and Joe wouldn't either. I doubt if he'd let you go.'

Poppy slipped her arm around Mabel's shoulders. 'I love you, Mabel, and you've been good to me, but we're packed in this house like sardines in a tin. It'll be much more comfortable with just you and your family.'

'That's it, isn't it?' Mabel's eyes glistened with unshed tears. 'This is all because you don't feel at home here, especially now you've found out about your real dad. Honestly, Poppy, it doesn't make any difference to me or Joe. He won't care if you're only a half-sister: he loves you and he'll be mad at me for letting you go.'

'Then don't tell him. I'll probably be back in a few weeks anyway. Once I've settled young Rupert and helped out with Mrs Carroll, I'll come home again. Hopefully Uncle Fred will have found them somewhere else to live by then, and I'll be able to go back to work at the hospital. I'm going to finish my training no matter what.'

'That's easy for you to say.' Mabel wiped her eyes on her apron. 'You might find yourself out of a job, or the Carrolls will keep you hanging on until you're an old maid with no chance of training for anything.'

'It won't happen like that. This is just a temporary arrangement until Mr Carroll is fit and well again after his accident. You'll see.'

IT WAS ONE THIRTY in the morning by the time the Daimler purred up the drive at Squire's Knapp. Pamela dismissed Harper with a casual instruction to garage the car in the coach house before turning in.

'Where will he sleep?' Poppy asked anxiously. 'You don't expect him to spend the night in the back of the car, do you?'

Pamela started up the stone steps leading to the front entrance. 'Heavens no. I wouldn't want Harper to put his size tens on the upholstery. Don't worry about him, Poppy. He's been here often enough to know the ropes. He'll wake Jackson and they'll muddle in together.' She rummaged round in her handbag and produced a key. 'I'm ready for bed, I don't know about you.'

The house was in darkness as Poppy followed Pamela indoors. A sliver of moonlight formed a pathway across the parquet floor ending abruptly at the foot of the grand staircase. The scent of beeswax and lavender polish was endearingly familiar.

'You'll have to use Guy's room,' Pamela whispered as they made their way upstairs. 'It's the only one with a bed that's been aired, although I doubt if the sheets have been changed since he was here a fortnight or so ago, but you won't mind for one night, will you, Poppy?'

'Can't I sleep in the nursery?'

'Not until I've given Miss Stokes the sack, unless you want to share a bed with her, and she has whiskers growing out of her nose and on her chin. I don't think she'd make a very exciting bedfellow.'

'Thanks,' Poppy murmured. 'I think I'll take Guy's bed.'

Pamela led the way to a room on the first floor. 'You'll have a nice view of the lake in the morning. I'm afraid there's no hot water. The beastly fuel shortages mean we only have the boiler going twice a week. It was miserable in the winter without the central heating, but I only came down a couple of times. Now it looks as though I'm going to be stuck here for the duration; such a bore. Anyway, goodnight, Poppy. I hope you sleep well.'

The door closed and Poppy was alone in Guy's room. The faint and achingly familiar scent of him assailed her senses. Moonlight slanted through the square window-panes, making trellised patterns on the carpet. She felt that she had walked into a surreal world where everything was painted in shades of silver and grey. The furniture was undoubtedly Edwardian: heavy, masculine and uncompromising. A desk stood against the wall between the two tall windows, and a leather captain's chair was set at an angle as if the person who had been sitting in it had risen and left the room without bothering to put it straight. Moving like a sleepwalker, Poppy went to the window and looked out at the ploughed field which had once been grassy parkland with the glassy shimmer of the lake beyond. A shadowy black shape slunk across the carriage sweep, its telltale brush warning that the fox was on the prowl for its supper. She drew the curtains and was instantly plunged into darkness.

Feeling her way across the room she switched on the light. The eerie dreamlike quality of moonlight was replaced by the glow of a hundred-watt bulb, and the room was suddenly bathed in colour. The soft shades of blue and old gold in the curtains, carpets and bed covers were exactly what she would have imagined in Guy's room. Whether or not he had chosen them for himself she had no idea, but the subtle hues suited his character: conservative, reserved and understated.

She undressed and slipped on her flannelette pyjamas before climbing into bed and snuggling down beneath the Egyptian cotton sheets that smelt even more strongly of Guy. As she laid her head on the pillow she found a comfortable hollow where his head must have rested on his last night in Squire's Knapp. She closed her eyes, wondering if she had just made the biggest mistake of her life in returning to a place with such mixed memories.

'POPPY, WAKE UP.'

Someone was calling her name and shaking her. Poppy opened her eyes, squinting against the bright light. 'What?'

'I've brought you a cuppa.' Jean put the cup and saucer down on the bedside table with a clatter. She perched on the edge of the bed, smiling broadly. 'So you came then. We didn't think you would.'

Poppy raised herself on one elbow. 'What time is it?'

'It's half past eight.'

Poppy sat up and reached for the tea. 'What about Mr Carroll? Is there any news?'

Jean's face crumpled. 'That's what I came to tell you, love. He passed away in the night. They telephoned from the hospital in the early hours.'

'No.' Poppy shook her head in disbelief. 'He can't have gone just like that.'

'Careful, you'll spill your tea.' Taking it from her, Jean put the cup back on the table. 'I know it's upsetting. He was a lovely man and it's been a terrible shock to all of us. It doesn't seem fair that he's gone and the old witch is clinging to life like a blooming limpet.'

Poppy stared at her in surprise. 'That's not like you, Jean.'

'You've been away from here for a long time. She's become more and more unreasonable. I think power had gone to her head.'

'How bad is she? Pamela was a bit hazy about Mrs Carroll's condition.'

'Bad enough, but I think the old cow is making the most of it. Anyway, I'll leave you to drink your tea. We can chat later but you're needed downstairs as soon as possible. Mrs C hasn't been told yet and the brat is playing up this morning. I don't envy you your task, I really don't.'

Poppy swung her legs over the side of the bed. 'All right, I'll get dressed right away. Is Pamela with her mother?'

'She went to the hospital first thing. She left a message saying we weren't to tell Mrs C anything.'

'I understand. What about Rupert?'

'He needs a firm hand, or a good spanking, I don't know which, but he's not the sweet little boy he was when you left. He's a four-year-old monster, and that's no exaggeration.' Jean made for the door. 'I'll leave you to it. Come down to the kitchen when you're ready and have some breakfast. You'll need all your strength if you're going to cope with the Carroll family.'

IN THE KITCHEN Mrs Toon was sitting at the table with an untouched cup of tea in front of her, her head bowed and her shoulders hunched. She looked up when Poppy entered the room and her eyes were reddened from crying. She rose to her feet and held out her arms. 'Poppy, thank God you came.'

Poppy crossed the floor to give her a hug. She had not expected such a welcome, but neither had she thought she would arrive to find the household teetering with the news of Mr Carroll's sudden death. 'Of course I came,' she murmured. 'Although I don't know what good I can do.'

Mrs Toon sank back on her chair and Poppy noticed that she had lost weight. The skin on her face and neck seemed to have stretched and hung in folds like old elastic. She took a hanky from her apron pocket and blew her nose. 'I never thought I'd say it, but I miss Olive and Violet. They weren't the most willing helpers but they did their bit even if I had to keep an eye on them all the time. I'm stretched to the limit these days, Poppy. What with doing invalid food for Madam upstairs and trying to make meals out of next to nothing, it's a nightmare. Then there's that new nanny. Don't get me started on her; she's an idle, stuck-up piece. You'd think she was a duchess, not a blooming nursemaid.'

Poppy refilled her cup with tea. 'I'm sure I'll be able to take some of the pressure off you, Mrs Toon. I'm not much good at cooking, but I can peel vegetables and do the running about for you.'

Mrs Toon raised the cup to her lips. 'You always were a good little girl, and now you're grown into quite a young lady. Jean tells me you're a nurse.'

'Only a probationer as yet, but I want to finish my training and then I'll be a properly qualified nurse.'

A bell jangled and Mrs Toon raised her eyes to peer at the board on the wall above the door. 'That's her in the nursery. Nanny Stokes. If she thinks I'm going up all them stairs to find out what she wants, she's got another think coming.'

The bell rang again. 'I'll go,' Poppy said firmly. 'I want to meet Nanny Stokes.'

'Best take your tin hat with you,' Mrs Toon said with a hint of her old spirit. 'She's got a temper on her, has that one.'

'So have I when roused,' Poppy muttered as she headed for the back stairs. She could hear Rupert screaming even before she reached the final flight leading up to the nursery. She raced up the remaining stairs and burst into the room without knocking.

Nanny Stokes had Rupert over her knee and was whacking him with a slipper. His screams were genuine and tears poured down his cheeks as he fought and struggled.

'Bite me, would you, you little beast?' Nanny Stokes lifted her arm as if to strike again but Poppy sprinted across the floor and snatched the slipper from her hand.

'How dare you hit that child,' she cried, tossing the offending item of footwear across the room. 'Put him down at once.'

Nanny dumped Rupert unceremoniously on the rug, rising to her feet and folding her arms across her chest. 'And who do you think you are, barging into my nursery and telling me what to do?'

Poppy bent down and picked Rupert up. He was heavy and she staggered beneath his weight, but he clung to her, sobbing against her shoulder. She held him in her arms, rocking him as she had when he was a toddler and had fallen and hurt himself. 'There, there, Rupert. Poppy's here.'

'P-Poppy,' he repeated, hiccuping. 'P-Poppy, she hit me.'

'Well she won't do it again.' Poppy glared at Nanny Stokes. She would have liked to take the slipper to the awful woman and beat her until she cried for mercy. 'I suggest you get your things together, because Mrs Pallister will send you packing the moment she gets home.'

'And who are you to lay down the law?' Nanny moved closer to Poppy, causing Rupert to scream with fright.

'Get away from him,' Poppy snapped. 'Touch him again and I'll report you to the police for child cruelty.' She hitched Rupert onto her hip and stalked out of the nursery. If she stayed a moment longer she would do something she would regret later, and anyway it was more important to look after Rupert than to argue with a sadistic old woman who should never have been allowed to look after a dog let alone a small defenceless child. No wonder Rupert had turned into a brat if that was the kind of treatment to which he had been subjected behind closed doors. She carried him downstairs to the kitchen and sat him on the table.

'Good Lord, what's the matter with him?' Mrs Toon rose to her feet, staring at the sobbing Rupert in dismay. 'He hasn't been told, has he?'

Poppy shook her head, sending her a warning glance. 'No, nothing like that. I caught the nanny beating him with a slipper. I've told her to leave, but of course I haven't got any authority and she knows it.'

A frantic thudding on the ceiling sent a shower of plaster floating down on them. Mrs Toon looked upwards, shaking her head. 'That's Madam. She's got a stick and she bangs the floor when she wants something. I can't manage them stairs again, Poppy. Could you run up and see what she wants?'

Poppy thrust Rupert into her arms. 'Mrs Toon will look after you for a moment, sweetheart. Poppy will be back in two shakes of a lamb's tail.' She kissed him on his hot cheek, and ignoring his outstretched arms with difficulty, she hurried from the kitchen for the second time.

She found Mrs Carroll in the drawing room, slumped in her usual chair by the fire, which had died down to embers and ash. Outside the sun was shining but there was a noticeable chill in the large room. Marina turned her head slowly, glancing at Poppy without any noticeable glimmer of recognition. Her handsome features were distorted on one side of her face and her left arm hung limply at her side.

Poppy approached her cautiously, not wanting to startle her, but Marina's expression remained impassive. 'Mrs Carroll, it's Poppy.'

Marina nodded wordlessly.

So far so good, Poppy thought, moving nearer. 'Can I get you anything?'

Again a nod.

Poppy had had a little experience of working with stroke victims, and she studied Marina's face. She was staring at the empty cup and plate on a table at her side. 'Would you like something to drink.'

Marina's lips moved but all she managed was a sound between a grunt and a hiss.

'Would you like a cup of tea?'

Marina raised her right hand and pointed to the plate.

'And something to eat?' Poppy noted the flicker of an answer in Marina's hazel eyes, and she was moved with a sudden and deep feeling of pity. The helpless woman seated in the chair was a mere shadow of the person who had treated her as an unnecessary encumbrance when she was little more than a child. Putting her feelings aside and adopting a professional approach, she laid her hand on Marina's with a brief comforting touch. 'I'll see to it right away, Mrs Carroll.'

EDWIN CARROLL'S FUNERAL took place on a warm, sunny morning in the village church which was filled to capacity. Dressed in black from head to foot, Marina was wheeled down the aisle to the front pew by Guy, who had been granted twenty-four hours' compassionate leave. Algy had also managed to get time away from the aerodrome, much to Jean's delight. Poppy could not help wondering what Marina thought when she saw them sitting together in the family pew. She would disapprove, that was certain, but trapped in her lonely inner world there was nothing she could do about it.

Following behind Pamela and Hector, Poppy took a seat in a pew on the opposite side of the aisle. She had been back less than a week but already she had assumed much of the responsibility for the running of the house as well as taking care of Rupert and attending to Mrs Carroll's more intimate needs. Pamela was prepared to sit with her mother and made an effort to keep her spirits up by endless chatter, which Poppy could see drove Marina almost to screaming point, but Pamela refused to do anything that entailed physical contact. It was left to Poppy to bathe and dress Marina and to help her on and off the commode. Such tasks came under the heading of nursing duties, Pamela said firmly. One did not embarrass one's parent by treating her as if she were a helpless baby.

Poppy might have resented Pamela's cavalier attitude had it not been for the fact that she was obviously deeply distressed by her father's sudden death. Leaning on Hector's arm she was weeping openly, although even in her grief she still managed to look as though she had stepped straight from the pages of *Vogue* or *Harper's Bazaar*. Rupert had been judged to be too young to attend the service and had been left in Mrs Toon's care. He had been a different child since Nanny Stokes' dismissal so everyone said, although to Poppy he was still the dear little boy she had known and loved. He followed her round all day and she guarded their time together jealously. They resumed their walks in the grounds and fed the ducks daily. When she could get away from the house, Poppy took him to help the girls with their chores on the farm, and he loved nothing more than being in the stables with the horses. Poppy had promised him that on her return from the church she would take him for a ride on Goliath, which would serve two purposes: it would keep Rupert amused and she would not have to face Guy.

After their uncomfortable last meeting she did not quite know how to treat him, and he had barely spoken more than a few words to her. He had arrived early that morning but had spent most of the time with his mother. Poppy had kept out of the way. She had Rupert to look after and Mrs Toon had needed help to prepare a buffet lunch for the mourners. Out of necessity it was to be a simple affair consisting of a couple of chickens that Edie had somewhat unwillingly surrendered for the meal, although the birds were past laying and likely to die of old age quite soon anyway. Growing up in the East End, Edie had never had contact with animals other than household pets, but since coming to Squire's Knapp she had developed a passion for the poultry in her care and protected them as if she were the mother hen.

'You'd think I'd asked her to sacrifice one of her children instead of a couple of old boilers,' Mrs Toon said as she basted the birds. 'I had to stew them for hours last night or they'd have been too tough to eat.'

Poppy listened sympathetically, but she was tempted to tell Mrs Toon that they lived like lords here in the country compared to city people who had to eke out their meagre rations every week. She sat Rupert on a stool at the table and showed him how to mix the potato salad, but even that did not pass without a comment from Mrs Toon.

'Bottled salad cream,' she muttered, eyeing the mixture in the bowl. 'Time was when we made mayonnaise with olive oil and egg yolks. I can't abide that shop bought stuff.'

'I'm sure no one will notice,' Poppy said, shaking her head at Rupert as he licked the spoon.

Mrs Toon sniffed and turned her attention to the egg and cress sandwiches. 'At least the bread is homemade.'

'Can I have one?' Rupert held out his hand.

Hastily wiping a telltale smear of salad cream from his cheek, Poppy gave him a sandwich.

'You shouldn't feed him between meals.' Mrs Toon removed the plate to a side table and covered it with a damp tea towel. 'It's as well Mr Carroll can't see what we're putting before the mourners. It's not like the old days, Poppy,' she said, wiping her hands on her apron. 'We'd have had a whole ham, an assortment of cold meats and poultry, and salads of every description, not to mention syllabubs, trifles and jellies made with champagne. This is the sort of spread I'd have done for the staff, not for the gentry.'

This conversation came back to Poppy as she stood dutifully by the table in the dining room while the guests filtered in to help themselves from the buffet. In spite of Mrs Toon's reservations it was an ample meal, elegantly served on silver salvers with white damask table napkins neatly folded by Mavis who had been called in at the last moment to help lay the table. Edie had elected to take Rupert to the stables, which robbed Poppy of her means of escape. Pamela and Guy were in constant attendance on their mother and Hector appeared to be doing his best to circulate amongst the mourners. Algy was moving about amongst the guests, his normal exuberance suitably subdued for the occasion. He had taken Poppy aside whilst they were waiting for the main body of mourners to arrive at the house, and had welcomed her return with such sincerity that it had brought tears to her eyes. Really, she thought, Amy and Algy were two of the nicest people she had ever met. He had kissed her on the cheek and told her that his sister would be proud of her, but his kindness only underlined Guy's chilly reception. She did her best to melt into the background but this was not difficult as most of the guests walked past her as if, like a well-trained servant, she was invisible.

The mourners continued to arrive. Poppy had not seen as many people in the house since Guy and Amy's engagement party, although the atmosphere now was subdued and the mood sombre. It seemed that everyone was here, from the town dignitaries and the members of the various committees that Marina had once chaired to the local doctor and the Carrolls' tenants from the village. The postmistress was drinking sherry with the vicar's wife and there was a fair representation of the Guppy family. Violet and Nancy were dressed to the nines in very short skirts, and unless Poppy was mistaken they were wearing nylons provided by generous American GIs.

'So you're back,' Violet said, reaching across Poppy to snatch an egg and cress sandwich. 'Couldn't keep away from the old place, I suppose.'

'How are you, Violet?'

Violet flashed her left hand in front of Poppy's face. 'Got engaged to a Yank. We're getting married next month and I'm going to live in Texas. Not bad for a village girl, eh?'

Poppy was about to congratulate her when she saw Guy heading towards them. His expression was stony and her heart sank.

'Poppy, can I have a word?'

Chapter Seventeen

VIOLET SHOT A knowing glance at Poppy. 'Still kowtowing to the boss, are you?' She sauntered off, teetering on ridiculously high heels.

Poppy eyed Guy warily, wondering if she had done something wrong. 'Yes, Guy?'

'Not here. Wait for me in Father's study. I'll just make sure that Pamela is coping.'

'All right.' Poppy watched him as he strode off towards the drawing room where Marina was holding court from her wheelchair. As Poppy made her way to the study, she wondered what it was that could not be said in public. She hesitated before entering the room. It had been Mr Carroll's private domain from which he conducted all his business and it seemed like trespassing to go in without seeking his permission. Plucking up courage she opened the door and went inside.

Edwin's desk was still neatly laid out exactly as he liked it and there was a pile of unopened correspondence on the blotter. She caught a faint whiff of the bay rum he had used on his hair and the Acqua di Parma aftershave that he favoured above all others. He might be dead, but the room was still patently his. She paced the floor, feeling like a schoolgirl waiting for the headmistress to chastise her for some minor misdemeanour. It seemed like hours but the grandfather clock in the corner showed that she only waited for five minutes before the door opened to admit Guy.

He smiled apologetically. 'Sorry, Poppy. I got waylaid by one of Father's friends. It's been a terrible shock for everyone.' He perched on the edge of the desk, motioning her to take a seat.

She remained standing, clasping her hands behind her back. 'What did you have to say to me? I really ought to get back and help.'

'They can look after themselves.' He paused, staring at her intently. 'What are you doing here, Poppy?'

Taken aback, she blinked and swallowed hard. 'I–I came because Pamela asked me to.'

'I know that, and she had no right to impose on your good nature. What bothers me is that you've given up your nursing training to come down here and act as an unpaid servant. My sister hasn't given you a salary, has she?'

Poppy shook her head. Cold fingers clutched at her insides, squeezing her stomach so that she felt sick. So this was business after all. 'I came as a friend. Your family took me in and looked after me and I . . .'

'That's rubbish and you know it. My family treated you like dirt.'

'You didn't, and Amy was kindness itself.'

'Amy has a good heart but I'm as much to blame as anyone else. I saw what was going on and I was too wrapped up in my own affairs to do anything about it.'

'You encouraged me to ride.'

A wry smile curved his lips and his expression softened. 'Even that was based on self-interest, Poppy. I needed to have my horse exercised and you were the perfect answer.'

'I could have ridden Romeo. Why are you talking like this, Guy? Have I done something wrong?'

He stood up and walked to the window. 'Only to yourself. Why did you let Pamela persuade you to come here in the first place? I thought you were happy and settled with your family and your – your friend.'

'If you mean Dennis, that's all he is – a friend. I know he behaved badly in Lyon's Corner House, and I told him so, but that's just Dennis. As to my family, well, Mabel is my sister-in-law but it's not the same as . . . oh, you know what I mean.'

He stared resolutely out of the window. 'I'm beginning to and I've no right to feel sorry for myself when I think of what you must have gone through. Losing your family when you were little more than a child must have caused you unimaginable pain.'

'It did, but I'm grown up now.'

He turned slowly, meeting her troubled gaze with a steady look. 'I can see that, which is why I don't want you to make a dreadful mistake. You shouldn't have given up everything for us, it's all wrong. My family will suck you in and spit you out as it pleases them.'

'I don't believe it. You're not like that or we wouldn't be having this conversation now.'

'Beware of the Carrolls. We're a self-centred bunch used to having our own way. I don't want to see you taken in.'

'I don't know what you're talking about, Guy. I came here of my own free will. I want to help you, I really do.'

He hesitated, gazing at her with a perplexed frown as if seeing her properly for the first time. 'I should be packing you off to London to continue your training, but the truth is that I'm glad you're here, and not just for Mother's sake.'

Suddenly it was difficult to breathe. 'So you want me to stay?'

'Of course I do. More than you could possibly imagine, but . . .' He hesitated again. 'How old are you, Poppy?'

'Sixteen, but I'll be seventeen next April. I'm perfectly capable of making up my own mind.'

'I know you are, and I also know that you love Squire's Knapp as much as I do.'

'I do, don't I? It wasn't until I returned to London, that I realised how much I was going to miss Rupert and everyone.' She dropped her gaze, unable to look him in the eyes in case he guessed her secret.

'Even Mother?'

His smile was infectious and Poppy could not help smiling back. 'Even Mrs Carroll. She was good to me in her way, and I hate to see her laid low by the wretched stroke.'

'You know too that you're the only one who can deal with her, and you've got young Rupert eating out of your hand. I don't know how you do it Poppy Brown, but my family is suddenly dependent on you.'

This made her laugh outright. 'Who'd have thought it? But seriously, Guy. What do you want me to do? Am I to be a sort of housekeeper cum nurse, or what?'

He moved swiftly round the desk to take her hands in his. 'Just be here for them, and for me. You're very young and I know I shouldn't ask this of you, but I'm certain that Squire's Knapp will be as safe in your hands as in my own.'

WHEN THE LAST guest had left the house Poppy began clearing the table in the dining room with the help of Jean and Mavis. Edie, as usual, was out tending to the livestock.

Mavis piled plates on a tray, scraping leftover scraps into an enamel dish to feed to the pigs. 'That went well, I suppose, as far as wakes go.'

Poppy was only half listening. Her mind was fully occupied with what had passed between Guy and her in the study. It was not so much what he had said, but the look in his eyes and the timbre of his voice had made her feel wanted, needed and – if she dared admit it – loved. It was impossible, of course, but for a few short minutes she was convinced that she had felt something pass between them.

'You haven't been listening,' Mavis said in an aggrieved voice. 'You were miles away, Poppy. What's up?'

Jean cut a slice of sponge cake and passed it to Rupert, who had been allowed into the house now that the mourners had departed. Pamela had gone to her room to lie down, and Hector had retired to the conservatory to smoke and chat to Guy. Algy had been left to keep Marina entertained.

'You look very serious,' Jean said, watching her intently. 'What did Guy have to say to you? We saw you both going into the study.'

'I know,' Mavis said, grinning. 'He's asked her to marry him, so that she'll work here for nothing.'

This drew a reluctant smile from Poppy. She had been wondering how she was going to tell them. 'Actually, he asked me to look after things for him while he's away.'

'No wedding ring?' Jean handed a linen napkin to Rupert. 'Best wipe the jam off your face before your mummy sees you, sunshine.'

'Don't be daft,' Poppy said, bending down to pick up a half-eaten egg and cress sandwich. She hoped they would think her red cheeks were from exertion and not due to blushing.

'I hope he's made it worth your while,' Mavis said tartly. 'We thought that Mrs P was taking the mickey when she dragged you away from London to wait on her mum and the proverbial little pitcher with big ears.' She jerked her head in Rupert's direction, but he seemed more interested in his cake than in their conversation. 'If you're giving up your career for the Carrolls then you jolly well should be paid for it.'

'Hear, hear.' Jean picked up a tray laden with empty glasses. 'I'll take this lot down to the kitchen. Mrs Toon's already up to her armpits in hot water.' She turned to Rupert. 'Coming, Rupie?'

He shoved the rest of the sponge cake into his mouth, nodding furiously.

'We'll chat later,' Jean said, making for the doorway with Rupert trotting along behind her. 'Come to the dorm and we'll hear all the gory details over a mug of cocoa.' She was about to leave the room when Algy appeared in the doorway, grinning broadly.

'Jean. I was looking for you, darling.' He took the tray from her hands. 'I thought we could go for a walk, if the girls don't mind my spiriting you away for an hour or two.' He shot a pleading look in Poppy's direction. 'I hear that you're in charge of things now, Miss Brown. May I have permission to take one of your staff away from her duties for a while?'

Poppy screwed up a napkin and lobbed it at him. 'Trust you to make a joke of it. I'm not in charge of anything.'

'Well, whatever you like to call it, I'm glad you're staying here,' Algy said seriously. 'You're a great girl, Poppy. You were too good for that chap you were out with in London. Ouch.' He turned to Jean, who had elbowed him in the ribs. 'What was that for?'

'Shut up,' she said, frowning. 'Put the tray down and come away before you put your foot in it for a second time.' She bent down to drop a kiss on Rupert's blond curls. 'Stay with Poppy, sweetheart. Auntie Jean will come and play with you later on.'

Algy replaced the tray on the table with an apologetic smile. 'Sorry, I didn't mean it to come out like that. All I meant to say was . . .'

'Tact was never your strong point, darling.' Jean linked her hand through his arm and dragged him out of the room.

'He didn't mean anything by that,' Mavis said hastily. 'Trust Algy to say the wrong thing.'

Poppy shook her head. 'No, he's right. Dennis isn't for me.'

'You're too young to get serious anyway. There are plenty more fish in the sea.'

'He wanted to marry me, but I refused.'

Mavis's eyes opened wide. 'Did you really?'

'Even if I wanted to get married, which I don't, I'd found something out about myself, Mavis. It was an awful shock and I'm still trying to work it out.'

'Do you want to talk about it?'

'I think so, but do you mind if I wait until we're all together this evening? It's not an easy thing to tell anyone.'

Mavis picked up a pile of dirty plates. 'Looks like I'll have to be patient, doesn't it?'

THE WARM CHOCOLATEY scent of cocoa filled the girls' sleeping quarters above the stable block. Poppy sat cross-legged on a cushion at the foot of Jean's bed, waiting for the full impact of her news to sink in. She gazed over the rim of her cup at their astounded faces.

After a moment of stunned silence, Jean was the first to speak. 'So you're related to royalty? I always knew you were different from the rest of us, Pops.'

'They're not royalty. Their family home was burnt to a cinder and as far as I can gather they lost all their money, but I doubt if the Beecham family would want to be associated with the illegitimate daughter of a servant.'

'But Harry Beecham is still alive, isn't he?' Edie lit a roll-up cigarette. 'He's entitled to know he has a kid.'

'The vicar I met in Epping told me that Harry joined the army years ago. Finding out about me might be a terrible shock. He could deny the whole thing and there's no way of proving it either way.'

'There are blood tests,' Mavis said seriously.

Poppy shook her head. 'This is getting silly. I'm never likely to meet Harry Beecham so it's not going to happen. I don't even know what regiment he's in.'

'Yes, you do,' Jean said eagerly. 'Your father was his uncle's batman, you said so, and he was in the London Rifle Brigade. So that's where you'd find Harry Beecham.'

'I'm not sure I want to meet him. It might be an awful disappointment to both of us, and if he didn't want anything to do with me, that would be even worse.'

Jean slid off her bed to give Poppy a hug. 'Darling, he'd love you. You're a poppet.'

'A real honey,' Mavis added, smiling.

'Oh shucks!' Edie drawled. 'You don't have to talk the lingo, Mavis. We all know you're stepping out with Yankee Doodle Dandy.'

Mavis lobbed a pillow at Edie's head. 'Shut up. Don't make fun of Lester, he's lovely.'

'You're just jealous, Edie, because Farmer Giles doesn't give you nylons and chocolate.' Jean heaved herself back onto her bed, stretching out her long legs. 'You're nearest the stove, Edie. Is there any cocoa left in the saucepan?'

'Get up and see for yourself,' Edie retorted crossly. 'And for your information, Mavis, Howard is very generous, and he treats me like a lady.'

'He's got it wrong there then,' Mavis giggled, dodging the pillow that Edie tossed back at her. 'Anyway, this doesn't solve Poppy's problem. What are you going to do, love?'

Poppy scrambled to her feet. 'Right now I'm going back to the house to check on Mrs Carroll and see if she's ready for bed.'

'Can't Mrs P do that?' Jean protested. 'It's her mother who's sick after all, not yours.'

'I know, but Pamela will want to spend her last evening with Hector before he returns to London, and Mrs Carroll doesn't play me up. She doesn't dare because I won't let her bully me, and Pamela gives in to her all the time.'

'The tables are turned,' Jean said with a wise nod.

'Serves the old bitch right if you ask me.' Edie stubbed her cigarette out in a saucer. 'I'm going to make some more cocoa. At least milk isn't in short supply if you happen to do the milking. There have to be some perks to the job to make up for the fact that we live like pigs and work like donkeys.'

'Speak for yourself,' Mavis said, picking up a hairbrush and shaking her long sun-streaked brown hair free from its snood. 'Goodnight, Poppy. Don't think you've heard the last of this, though. We'll find your dad for you if we have to go to Monty himself.'

'Night, night, girls.' Leaving them to their precious rest time, Poppy climbed down the ladder into the tack room. She let herself out into the cool May evening, inhaling the familiar smells of the stable yard mixed with the scent of May blossom and the purple lilac tree just beyond the brick wall. It was dusk and the clear sky was a luminous shade of duck-egg blue tinged with palest orange at the horizon. Bats fluttered erratically overhead and a cool breeze fanned her hot cheeks.

'Poppy.'

She turned with a start at the sound of Guy's voice. He emerged from Goliath's stable with a rueful grin. 'Sorry if I scared you. I was just saying goodbye to the old chap.'

She was suddenly breathless, as though she had been running. 'When are you leaving?' Her voice shook despite her attempt to sound casual. No matter how much she might pretend that he was returning to a safe desk job, she knew in her heart that this could very well be the last time she saw him.

'Jackson's driving Algy and me to the station first thing.'

'What time do you want breakfast? I'm always up early.'

'You don't have to wait on me, Poppy.'

'But you and Algy will have a long journey ahead of you. You won't be able to get anything on the train.'

'You're always looking after other people, aren't you? And I know I've taken advantage of your good nature, but I've asked Pam to make sure you're paid a decent salary.'

His rueful smile made her heart ache. She knew how much he had loved his father even though there had never been any outward display of affection between them. She sensed his deep distress now and she longed to give him a hug, just as she might have done to Rupert when he was unhappy. She laid her hand on his sleeve. 'It's all right, Guy. You're not imposing on me; I want to stay here and help. There is a war on, you know,' she added with an attempt at a grin. If she stopped smiling she knew she would cry.

The air around them was silent and still and his face was in shadow, but she felt the muscles in his lower arm tense. 'Poppy, I . . .' He broke off, moving his arm gently from her grasp. 'Never mind.' He leaned over and brushed her cheek with a whisper of a kiss. 'Take care of yourself, Poppy.'

'You too, Guy.' She knew now what girls in the films meant when they said, 'I'll never wash that cheek again.' It was corny and trite but that brief, sexless caress, such as might have been bestowed upon a much-loved child, meant more to her than all Dennis's passionate kisses. She wanted to fling her arms around him and feel his lips on hers, but she knew she was blushing like a schoolgirl. Scarlett O'Hara would have known what to do. She would have turned the situation to her own advantage, but this was life and they were not actors in a movie. 'I'll say goodnight then, Guy. See you in the morning.'

She was about to walk away but he caught her by the hand. 'Don't get up early on my account, Poppy. I hate goodbyes; it just makes leaving home all the more painful.' He closed the stable door. 'You'll look after Goliath for me, won't you?'

'Of course I will.' She started off towards the house. She wanted him to follow her but she hoped that he would not. The sound of his footsteps hastening over the cobblestones was pleasure and at the same time pain.

He caught up with her. 'Will you write to me, Poppy? I mean, I'd like to know how Mother is, of course, and you could keep me up to date with the gossip in Barton Lacey.'

She shot him a surprised glance. 'You want me to pass on tittle-tattle?'

'Of course. I'm not such a stuffed shirt that I don't enjoy a bit of scandal. It'll keep me up to date so that when I do return to Squire's Knapp I won't feel such an outsider.'

'You're coming back here to live? What about your studies? I thought you were going to be a doctor.'

'I think my future has been decided for me. I wasn't expecting Father to die, but someone has to take over the estate, and I suppose I always knew it would fall to me one day. It's just happened sooner rather than later.'

'What would Amy think about that?'

Guy hesitated, pausing at the bottom of the steps leading up to the house. 'No one else knows this, Poppy, not even Algy. Amy broke off our engagement before she went to Singapore. She said we both needed time to think about the future.'

Shocked, Poppy could only shake her head. 'I–I'm sorry.'

He shoved his hands deep in his pockets, staring abstractedly up at the darkening sky. 'I could have prevented her from leaving. If I'd promised to bring our wedding forward she would have stayed, but I think I knew deep down we were both making a big mistake. Childhood sweethearts grow up and change. Experiences alter us and shape who we are. I'm very fond of Amy, but she wasn't my life. I realise that now.'

'I don't think you ought to be telling me all this,' Poppy murmured, shivering. 'Maybe you'll feel different when she comes home after the war.'

'You're cold. I shouldn't have kept you out here selfishly unburdening myself to you.' Guy took her arm and led her up the steps. 'Go indoors and get warm. I'll stay out here for a while and smoke the last of Father's cigars while I make my peace with Squire's Knapp for deserting it in time of war.'

She paused on the top step. 'You talk about the place as though it were a real person.'

He smiled. 'If you love something it becomes real. Goodnight, Poppy. I won't say goodbye because I intend to come home eventually.' He turned on his heel and walked towards the lake.

'Come home to me,' Poppy whispered as she watched him stop to light the cigar. The tip glowed and then disappeared as he walked into the darkness.

IT WAS LATE by the time she had helped Pamela put her mother to bed in a small sitting room at the back of the house that had been hastily converted into a bedroom after Marina's stroke. When Poppy finally went upstairs to the night nursery, she was relieved to find that Rupert was sound asleep in the single bed that had replaced his cot. His tumbled blond curls spread out on the pillow and in sleep he resembled a Botticelli angel. She smiled to herself thinking that this cherubic look would vanish the moment he opened his eyes. Master Rupert was growing up to be quite a handful. Poppy drew the quilt up to his chin and dropped a kiss on his forehead. She went into the bathroom and had a quick wash in cold water before undressing and putting on her pyjamas.

She climbed into bed, exhausted both mentally and physically, but her mind was racing. Guy's revelations had shocked her to the core. She had thought him to be deeply in love with Amy and she with him, but now it seemed that theirs had been a shallow relationship based on an outgrown childhood romance. She was distressed and at the same time pleased, although she was ashamed to admit it even to herself, but she was also scared. When she had thought Guy was with Amy he was safe from the attractions of other women, but now he was free to fall in love with someone else. There must be any number of attractive unattached young women with whom he was in daily contact at the aerodrome. He lived in a different world now, filled with educated girls from good families whose jobs gave them an understanding of the risks he took daily. There might be young widows of comrades he had lost who needed a shoulder to cry on. Poppy's imagination ran riot over the possibilities until she drifted into a troubled sleep.

She was awakened by Rupert jumping on the end of her bed. Sunlight was streaming through the window and she snapped into a sitting position, reaching for the watch that Dennis had given her last Christmas. It was seven thirty. She almost fell out of bed, much to Rupert's amusement who seemed to think it was some sort of game. He chased her across the room as she went to the window to look out. There was no sign of the Bentley and she knew that she was too late. The first train to London left at six thirty each morning. Guy and Algy would have left over an hour ago.

Rupert tugged at her pyjama top and she was about to turn away from the window when she realised that there was someone standing outside the front entrance. She could only see a shadow but it was definitely male. Perhaps Guy had missed his train or had decided to take a longer leave. 'Stay here and don't move,' she told Rupert sternly. 'I won't be long.' Grabbing her flimsy cotton dressing gown, Poppy raced from the room, hurtling down three flights of stairs barefoot and struggling into her wrap. She wrenched the door open.

Chapter Eighteen

'Hello, Poppy.'

'Dennis!' She stared at him in disbelief. The shock of seeing him again temporarily robbed her of the ability to move. 'What are you doing here? Is something wrong? Has anything happened to Joe?'

'Hold on, girl. Don't panic. Joe is fine. He's still down in Kent somewhere and Mabel is okay too. She gave me a letter for you.' He reached inside his jacket and extracted a crumpled envelope from his breast pocket.

She took it from him with trembling fingers. 'Did you come all the way here just to bring me a letter?'

'No, ducks. I came because Joe and Mabel are worried about you. They think that the toffs are taking advantage of your good nature.'

'That's not true,' Poppy said angrily. 'I came because I wanted to.'

'That's as maybe, but you can't blame Joe for being concerned. He feels responsible for you and so does Mabel.'

'But why send you all the way down here?'

'I offered to come. I needed to see you again.' His eyes darkened. 'You walked out on me, but I can't believe that it's over between us.'

'Dennis, this is ridiculous. I didn't walk out on you. I left because Mrs Pallister needed me. You were the one who made a fuss.'

'I thought we had something special.'

Exasperated and not knowing quite how to handle him, Poppy shook her head. 'You know how I feel. I like you as a friend, and that's all.'

He shrugged his shoulders. 'I can't turn off my feelings. It doesn't work that way.'

'I'm sorry, but you shouldn't have come. I thought we'd sorted all this out before I left.'

His face was pale beneath his weathered tan and there were dark circles beneath his eyes. He seemed to shrink before her eyes, but all she felt for him was pity. It was not enough. She moderated her tone. 'How did you get here so early, Dennis?'

'I came on the mail train. Sat up all night in the guard's van with a couple of Yanks returning to their base, but what do you care?' He eyed her moodily. 'Do you want me to push off? If you do just say so.'

She had thought she could deal with Dennis in any of his mercurial moods, but she had never seen him tired and dispirited. She held the door open. 'You'd better come in for a while and rest, but that doesn't mean we're back together.'

He stepped over the threshold. 'You always kept part of yourself locked away from me, Poppy. I knew that all along.'

'Come through and please don't make a noise. Mrs Carroll is a light sleeper.' She led the way to the baize door and opened it, but Dennis was dawdling along, looking about him in awe.

'This is some place you've got here. No wonder you didn't think much of the house in Ilford.'

'I never thought about it like that, but it was Mabel's home, not mine.' Allowing the door to swing on its hinges, she left him to his own devices and hurried downstairs to the kitchen, praying that Mrs Toon had not yet risen from her bed. She was angry with Dennis for putting her in such an impossible position, but she could not simply turn him away and he knew it, which only added to her feeling of resentment. She went to the Aga and raked the embers until flames licked round the coal. She moved the kettle onto the hob, turning her head as she heard his footsteps on the flagstones behind her. 'I'll make you some breakfast, Dennis, but then I'm going to have to ask you to leave.'

He pulled out a chair and took a seat at the table. 'Just like that?'

'What did you expect?'

'I thought I might make you see sense, but obviously you know when you're well off.' He spread his hands in an expansive gesture. 'I understand now why you were so eager to get back here.'

She picked up the teapot, resisting the temptation to throw it at him. 'You're being horrible, and I don't deserve that. I'm sorry if you got the wrong idea, but I tried to tell you how I felt so many times I've lost count.'

He ran his hand through his hair. 'So you want me to go back to London and forget all about you?'

'Yes. I'm sorry, but that's just about it. You've got to let me lead my own life.'

'Next thing you'll be telling me I'll meet someone else.'

The hint of humour in his eyes made her respond with a sigh of relief and a smile. 'Well, you will. You're a great chap and I'm . . .'

He held up his hand as if to ward off a blow. 'For God's sake don't tell me that you're fond of me. I can't think of anything worse.'

'All right, I won't, even though it's true.' She made the tea and set it to brew while she cut slices off a loaf.

Dennis sat back in his chair watching her every movement. 'Don't spoil me or I'll never want to leave. If you change your mind, Poppy . . .'

'Don't, Dennis.' She patted his shoulder as she walked past him to fetch the butter dish from the larder. 'I don't want a fight. I'd like us to part as friends, please.'

He had just finished his breakfast when Mrs Toon entered the kitchen with her hair still in curlers. She stared at Dennis open-mouthed before turning a fierce gaze on Poppy. 'I thought better of you than this.'

Realising that she had jumped to the wrong conclusion, Poppy was torn between laughter and embarrassment. 'You've got it all wrong, Mrs T. This is Dennis. He's my brother's best friend and he came all the way from London to make sure I was all right and to give me a letter from my sister-in-law.'

'Best not let Mrs Pallister see him or she'll think the same as I did. You know that gentlemen callers aren't allowed.'

Dennis rose to his feet with a theatrical bow. 'It was a pleasure to meet you, missis. But I've got a train to catch. Now I know that Poppy is in good hands, I'm going back to London.'

'Well, I'm sure any friend of Poppy's is a friend of mine,' Mrs Toon said stiffly. 'I'll have a cup of tea if there's any left in the pot.'

Poppy saw Dennis to the door. There was an awkward pause as he stood looking at her, apparently at a loss for words. She put her arms around him and kissed him on the cheek. 'I am truly sorry and I'll miss you, Dennis.'

'But not enough.'

'No. If there was anything . . .'

He brushed her cheek with his fingertips. 'Don't say it, girl. I've always got Napoleon for company.' Twisting his lips into a smile, he gave her a mock salute and turned to make his way down the steps.

She closed the door, gulping back a sudden rush of tears. She hated herself for hurting him, but she was relieved that he had left without any further attempts to influence her decision to remain in the country. She put her hand in her pocket feeling for her hanky and her fingers closed around Mabel's letter. She had almost forgotten it in her attempts to deal with Dennis. She sat down on a Victorian hall chair and opened the envelope. The letter contained little news, apart from the fact that they were all well in South Road, and Joe was counting himself lucky not to have been sent abroad. With little enthusiasm, Mabel wrote that the Barkers and Auntie Dottie were unlikely to be moving out until the house in Leytonstone was rebuilt and no one knew when that would be. There were a couple of lines about how people at the hospital had reacted to Poppy's sudden departure, and in particular Sister McNally, who had not taken the news at all well. In a postscript, Mabel apologised for Joe's tactlessness in asking Dennis to travel to Dorset to make sure she was all right. She hoped that his impulsive action would not make things difficult and she signed off with a row of kisses.

Folding the letter and tucking it back in her pocket, Poppy rose from her seat. She felt sorry for Mabel having to put up with a house filled with carping relatives, but she was certain that Joe would stand up to them when he next came home on leave. At least she had the comfort of knowing that he was safe for now at least, and she knew she could trust Mabel to break the news gently to him about their mother's affair with Harry Beecham. Joe was strong, like his dad. He would take it on the chin.

Resolutely putting the past behind her, Poppy went upstairs to the nursery to get Rupert up and dressed. She found him in the day nursery, still wearing his striped

pyjamas and playing with some lead soldiers that had
once belonged to Guy. Having helped him put on his
day clothes she took him down to the kitchen where Mrs
Toon had his breakfast set out on the table. Poppy left
him in her care while she took a tray of tea to Marina's
room.

'I'm sorry I'm a bit late . . .' She ducked her head in
order to dodge a missile thrown with considerable force.
The glass whizzed past her left ear and hit the wall, splin-
tering into tiny shards.

'Where?' Marina demanded, making an obvious
effort to get the word out. 'Where?'

Poppy had grown used to interpreting Marina's
monosyllabic attempts at conversation. 'There was a
stranger at the door – asking the way to the village. I had
to give him directions and then I had to get Rupert up.'
She placed the tea tray on the bedside table.

Marina's mouth worked but no sound came from her
lips, only a drool of saliva from the corner of her mouth.
Her eyes filled with tears which slid silently down her
cheeks. Poppy took a clean handkerchief from a pile on
the rosewood side table and placed it in Marina's hand.
She pretended not to look as Marina dabbed ineffectually
at her mouth and cheeks.

'I'll give you time to drink your tea,' Poppy said gently.
'And then I'll help you get dressed. Miss Pamela will be
down soon, and she'll have breakfast with you, as usual.'

Marina lay back against her pillows, her face drained
of colour. She raised her good hand feebly and closed her
eyes. Poppy sighed. She had never had cause to like Mrs

Carroll, but she would never have wished such an igno-minious fate on anyone, and from what she had seen on the wards she could only guess that the prognosis was not good.

LATER THAT MORNING Poppy went to the study to put the call through to the butcher for the weekly order, although even using the points from all their ration books com-bined, the amount of meat that would be delivered was barely enough for one decent meal. She sat behind Edwin's desk but her mind was filled with thoughts of what had passed between her and Guy in this room just hours ago. She rested her head on her hands. Why did she have to be sixteen? She was not too young to fall in love and she was certainly old enough to know her own mind. A wave of sadness washed over her. She had said goodbye to Guy for what might possibly be the last time, and she had sent Dennis away. Even though he had put a brave face on it, she knew that she had hurt him. All that remained to her now was Squire's Knapp. She would do her best to keep it in good heart for Guy when he returned from war.

She dialled the number and gave the butcher the order that Mrs Toon had written out for her. He had a couple of rabbits, he said, brought in that very morning and reserved for good customers like Squire's Knapp. Poppy told him that Mrs Toon would be delighted and she was certain that Mrs Carroll would be very pleased. She had just replaced the receiver in its cradle when Pamela entered the room.

'Poppy, I've been looking for you.'

'I was just ordering the meat from the butcher.'

'That's not what I wanted to talk about.' Pamela toyed with the silver inkstand on the desk. 'I've decided to return to London. My husband has a very important job to do and he needs me at his side.'

Poppy nodded her head. 'I suppose so.'

'So I'm leaving this afternoon, but Rupert will remain here where I know that he'll be safe from the air raids. I've spoken to the headmistress at the village school and she said he can start right away. He'll remain there until he's old enough to take his place at prep school.'

'You're leaving him here?' Poppy could hardly believe her ears. Rupert would to all intents and purposes be an evacuee, as she had once been.

'Yes, as I said. He'll be happier here and I trust you to look after him. We'll pay you a wage, of course, as well as the salary that Guy promised you. I wouldn't expect you to take on the position of nanny without some remuneration. Hector will see to that, and we'll visit him as often as we can. That goes without saying.'

'Yes,' Poppy murmured. 'I understand.' She did, after a fashion, although she knew that if Rupert were her child she would never leave him – not in a million years.

She hoped that he would not be too upset, but when his mother left Rupert seemed to take their parting in his stride. He clutched Poppy's hand tightly as the big black limousine drove off through the tunnel of copper beeches. Pamela's white-gloved hand could be seen waving gracefully through the rear window and Rupert raised his small hand in response.

'She'll come and see you often,' Poppy said softly.

Rupert raised his face to smile up at her. 'Can we go to the stables now? I've got an apple for Goliath.'

THE HAY HARVEST was helped by good weather and the Dutch barn was filled with enough fodder to keep the cattle fed all winter. Poppy's daily routine fell into a pattern. She took Rupert to school, where he was apparently a model pupil. According to Miss Morris, he had mastered his alphabet and could write his name in block capitals, and the unfortunate incident with one of the Guppy children on his first day was all but forgotten. Rupert had proved surprisingly handy with his small fists and the Guppy boy had gone home with a bloody nose, but since that time they had become the best of friends. Poppy had felt like giving Rupert a medal, but she had given him the usual lecture about not fighting unless it was absolutely unavoidable, and turning the other cheek. She could have added that this did not apply to the Guppy family, but she managed to hold her tongue.

After a few weeks she felt that she had reached an understanding with her difficult patient. She refused to put up with tantrums, even though she knew that it was frustration that caused them. She borrowed books on stroke management from the village library and she did her best to initiate some kind of physiotherapy.

When she was not involved in caring for Mrs Carroll and Rupert, Poppy spent as much time as she could helping the girls with their work on the land, whether it was harvesting the wheat or ploughing the fields for the subsequent crops. She toiled in the vegetable garden and helped Edie with the milking. She gave herself little time to think about anything other than work. She was able to sympathise sincerely with Jean when she agonised about Algy's safety, but she could not admit even to her close friends that she was equally concerned for Guy. Edie spent her free time helping Howard on his farm, and Mavis's GI, Lester, would swoop into the drive on his motorbike to carry her off for romantic trysts whenever he could get away from the aerodrome.

Poppy had not heard from Dennis, although she did not expect to, and it was Mabel who kept her informed of his gradual return to his old self. By the beginning of December, Mavis was pleased to inform her that he was going out with the girl from the shop at Gants Hill that sold horse and whale meat. She was, Mabel said, a peroxide blonde with an ample figure but she was good-natured and made Dennis laugh. Who could ask for more? Poppy was glad for his sake and relieved that he had found someone who could make him happy. She just hoped that Napoleon had not ended up on the butcher's slab.

By Christmas Marina was beginning to show definite signs of improvement. Her speech was still impaired but she was able to walk with the aid of a stick and had regained some use of her left arm. Pamela and Hector arrived on Christmas Eve. Rupert seemed mildly pleased to see his parents, but having greeted them dutifully he followed Poppy to the kitchen where she was helping Mrs Toon to prepare the festive meal for Christmas Day.

The silver had been cleaned and the best dinner service washed and set out in readiness for the feast, although Mrs Toon shook her head over the two boiling fowls that were to replace turkey.

Atkins, the estate manager, had been busy sawing up logs and the whole house smelled delightfully of burning apple wood. He had felled a large pine tree. It was smaller than the ones Poppy remembered from the past, or perhaps she was taller, she was not certain which, but Rupert was delighted and had been eager to help decorate the tree.

Poppy could not help thinking of her first Christmas at Squire's Knapp. She had been such a child then; impressed by the lavish food and drink and the glamorous lifestyle of the Carroll family. Everything was different now, although on Christmas morning Pamela still managed to look as though she had stepped off a Hollywood film set and Hector was immaculate as ever. Marina's silk gown was two sizes too large for her now, but she insisted on wearing her triple row of pearls and matching earrings. As Poppy dressed her hair in a Victory roll she noticed that there were more strands of silver in Marina's chestnut locks but she was still a handsome woman, and some of her old indomitable spirit was returning.

Edie, Mavis and Jean had been invited to join them for lunch. Dressed in their best clothes, they trooped into the dining room to sit rather awkwardly at the huge table with Marina at the head and Hector at the far end with Pamela at his side. Rupert had to sit on a pile of cushions in order to reach the table, but all he wanted to do was to play with the train set that his parents had given him for Christmas. He fidgeted throughout the meal until he was scolded by his father, which made him cry. Poppy had to restrain herself or she would have jumped up from her seat to comfort him. She glowered at Hector, but there was nothing she could do other than wait until the meal was over. When the family rose from the table, Pamela helped her mother to the drawing room, and Poppy gave Rupert a comforting hug and a whispered promise to play games after she had helped clear the table and wash the dishes. Jean gave him the bar of chocolate that Mavis's boyfriend had sent for each of them as a small gift, and Rupert sat on a stool in the kitchen munching his treat while Edie washed the dishes and Poppy wiped them. Jean and Mavis put everything away and Mrs Toon sat with her feet up drinking a glass of the port that Hector had provided for the staff.

'One bottle of port between all of us,' Edie said, grinning. 'How very generous.'

'I bet he's got a cellar full of the stuff in London,' Mavis added. 'I expect she bathes in champagne, the snooty cow.'

'He wants to see me in the study,' Poppy said thoughtfully. 'I wonder what it's about.'

Edie flicked water at her. 'You seem to make a habit of meeting men in the study. Are you sure they only want to chat?'

Jean laughed but Mavis frowned, jerking her head in Rupert's direction. 'I expect Mr Pallister wants to tell Poppy how to put the train track together, or something like that.'

'Of course he does,' Edie said, grinning. 'That's what I meant.'

Mrs Toon held up her empty glass. 'That's a lovely drop of port. I wouldn't mind another.'

Jean snatched up the bottle and filled her glass. 'You've earned it, Mrs T. That was a splendid Christmas dinner. The best I've ever tasted.'

Mrs Toon's already flushed face deepened to a shade of puce. 'You're just saying that. Why, I remember a time . . .'

Poppy took the opportunity to slip away unnoticed. She found Hector sitting in Edwin's chair, smoking a cigar. The scent of Havana tobacco reminded her of the last time she had seen Guy and the Christmas spirit seemed to evaporate within her. 'You wanted to see me, Mr Pallister?'

'Yes, Poppy. Come in and close the door. I don't want anyone else to know until it's absolutely necessary.'

Nervously, Poppy perched on the edge of a chair. 'What is it?'

'It's top secret at the moment, but this house has been requisitioned by the army. I don't want you to say anything for now, but I want you to prepare the gatekeeper's lodge. You will move there in two weeks' time with my mother-in-law and Rupert.'

Poppy stared at him, hardly able to believe her ears. 'You want Mrs Carroll to live in that cottage? She won't like it.'

A grim smile lit Hector's pale eyes. 'No, I'm afraid she will dislike it enormously, but this has come from the very highest source, and what goes on here may well affect the outcome of the war. I can't say any more, but I'm going to have to leave Marina to you.' He leaned forward, fixing her with a determined stare. 'In fact, Poppy, I'd say you are the only person, apart from Guy, who could undertake such an onerous task. I'm not pretending it will be easy, or that you will live as you have in this house, but it is absolutely vital or I wouldn't ask it of you.'

Poppy's mind was racing. 'What about Mrs Toon? Will she come too?'

'I believe there are three bedrooms in the lodge, and I'm sure you wouldn't mind sharing with Rupert, as you always have done.'

She was not about to argue. 'And the land girls?'

'Will go on as before, but I'm taking Jackson back to London to work for me. My chauffeur wants to retire to the country to live with his sister, and the Bentley will have to be laid up for the duration. Have you any questions, Poppy?'

She thought quickly. 'What about the family heirlooms and the silver?'

Hector frowned. 'I want you to make an inventory and I'll arrange for them to be packed, collected and stored in a repository. I'll telephone you in a few days' time and you can let me know when things are ready to move.'

'But I'll have to explain why I'm doing all these things. I won't be able to keep it secret for long.'

'Keep it quiet for as long as possible. I leave everything in your capable hands, Poppy, my dear.'

JEAN WAS THE first to guess that there was something major afoot when she met Poppy coming out of the lodge two days later on a bitterly cold and frosty morning. Poppy took her back inside, swearing her to secrecy before telling her what Hector planned. 'But he doesn't realise how much work it entails,' Poppy said, glancing round at the empty living room. The wallpaper was hanging off in patches and cobwebs festooned the ceiling. A tracery of ice patterns decorated the insides of the small-paned windows and the bare floorboards were covered in mouse droppings. 'I've got to get this place habitable in less than a fortnight as well as making an inventory of all the valuables in the house so that they can be collected and stored somewhere safe. I just can't do it, as well as everything else.'

Shoving her hands deep in the pockets of her corduroy trousers, Jean followed Poppy's gaze. 'What's it like upstairs?'

'It's just about the same, only with a few damp patches where tiles have come off the roof.'

'You'll have to tell Edie and Mavis, but we'll help you. If we can get this place cleaned up and the chimneys swept before you move in, it'll leave you free to make a note of the stuff in the big house. We need to get the old girl moved in here before they come to take her treasures away or she might think we're flogging them and pocketing the cash.'

Poppy blew on her numbed fingers. 'You're a brick, Jean. What would I do without you and the others?'

'Dunno, love. But I tell you one thing: when I marry Algy I'm never going to get my hands dirty again.'

'You're engaged and you never told us?' Poppy could hardly believe her ears. 'You dark horse.'

Jean slipped her finger beneath her shirt collar and pulled out a fine silver chain on the end of which dangled a diamond ring. She held it out for Poppy to see. 'It's half a carat set in platinum,' she said proudly.

'It's beautiful. But why didn't you tell us?'

Jean pulled a face. 'It's supposed to be kept secret from Algy's old Aunt Jane. She's the one who holds the purse strings, apparently. She thinks she can pick the woman he'll marry but Algy has other ideas, I'm glad to say. I think she must be a terrible snob and a bank clerk's daughter wouldn't be good enough for her precious nephew.'

Poppy wrapped her arms around Jean, hugging her until she protested. 'Then she's a silly old woman. If anything you're too good for him. But when did all this happen? I don't know how you kept quiet about it.'

'It was after the funeral lunch. He asked me to go for a walk.'

'I remember that, but you didn't say a word.'

'We didn't think it was the right time. I'm sorry, Pops. I desperately wanted to tell you and the girls.'

'Anyway, it's wonderful news. I'm so excited for you and Algy. You must tell Edie and Mavis or I won't be able to look them in the face.'

'Okay. I'll tell them my secret but only if you tell them about the army taking over the main house. We've got to stick together.'

THE MOVE TO the lodge went surprisingly easily, although it was impossible to keep the secret from Mrs Toon and the daily woman, since their help was essential in making the place habitable. The chimneys were swept, the floors scrubbed and the windows flung open to air the musty building. Pamela, who seemed to be delighted not to be involved, had given permission for them to take anything they needed, and Poppy scoured the rooms for objects that would make Mrs Carroll feel at home.

It was only when Marina was told of the impending move that Poppy encountered any opposition. In the end she was compelled to telephone Pamela and beg her to reason with her mother. When this failed it was Hector who took over the telephone call. After a long conversation he finally managed to persuade his mother-in-law that there was no alternative other than to allow the army to occupy the family home. Poppy had no way of knowing what it was he said that convinced her that the move was imperative to national security, but it was obvious that Squire's Knapp was going to hold an important strategic position in forthcoming events.

WITH EVERYBODY PITCHING in, the lodge was ready for occupation just in time. Small household items were transported in the farm cart, but when it came to moving bigger items of furniture that were too heavy for the women to shift on their own, help was called in from outside. Howard brought his tractor and trailer over and Lester was able to take time off from his air base at Warmwell to lend his considerable muscle to furniture moving. If the adults had reservations about leaving the main house and setting up in the lodge, Rupert seemed to think it was a great adventure. He told Poppy that it was like the gingerbread house in the story of Hansel and Gretel, and she could understand its appeal to a small child. With lattice casement windows and a tiled porch over the front door it was a pretty place even in the depths of winter, but in summer there would be roses rambling up the walls and hollyhocks growing in the small front garden. At the back of the house was a well that could have come from the illustrations in one of Rupert's nursery rhyme books, and a vegetable garden that would provide them with much-needed food. Rupert might be happy and Mrs Toon was resigned to the move, but Poppy was only too well aware that Mrs Carroll might view her new accommodation in a less enthusiastic light.

The move was accomplished on the day that the army was due to arrive. A wheelchair had been purchased for Marina and Poppy pushed her along the avenue of beeches, their bare branches forming intricate patterns against a cool azure sky.

'Walk.' Marina held up her hand as they reached the garden gate. 'Walk.'

Poppy knew better than to argue. She helped her from her chair and unhooking the ever present walking stick she placed it in her hand. Marina walked slowly up the path to enter her new home with her head held high. Poppy had never felt such admiration for anyone. She was pushing the wheelchair round to the shed at the side of the cottage when she heard the sound of approaching motor vehicles. Overcome by curiosity, she hurried to the front gate. A faint sound from the house caused her to glance over her shoulder and she saw Marina standing in the doorway. Poppy could only imagine what was going through her mind as the first staff car swept through the gates which Atkins had left open in readiness for their arrival.

To Poppy's surprise the vehicle stopped and a soldier leapt out to open the rear door, holding it for the officer who emerged from the vehicle. He came towards her, tucking his hat under his arm. 'Good morning. Is this Mrs Carroll's residence?'

Poppy nodded her head. 'Yes, it is now, thanks to you lot.'

'And you are?'

'I'm Poppy Brown. I look after Mrs Carroll. She's not well and mustn't be overexcited.'

'I understand, Miss Brown. But the Brigadier would like to have a few words with her, if convenient.'

The familiar sound of dragging footsteps made Poppy turn to see Marina making her way slowly back down the path. She hurried to her side. 'The Brigadier wants to meet you, but if you don't feel up to it . . .'

Marina clutched Poppy's arm, squeezing it with surprising force. 'Feel fine.'

'Captain Fellows at your service, ma'am.' He snapped to attention, inclining his head in Marina's direction. 'Brigadier Beecham presents his compliments and wonders if you could spare him a few moments of your time?'

Chapter Nineteen

Everything seemed to be moving in slow motion as Poppy watched Brigadier Beecham step out of the car and walk towards them. If this man was really her father, surely she would recognise her own flesh and blood? But as he drew closer she was even more confused. He was not much above average height and hardly an imposing figure, but he had an indefinable air of authority. If she had hoped to see a mirror image of herself she was disappointed. He was fair-haired whereas she was dark like her mother, but as he drew closer she realised that his eyes were a similar shade of green to her own. He was smiling, but there was no instant flash of recognition as he met her gaze for a brief moment before turning his attention to Marina.

Captain Fellows cleared his throat. 'May I introduce Brigadier Beecham, ma'am?'

'How do you do, ma'am? I'm delighted to meet you in person. Hector has told me so much about you, and I wanted to tell you in person how much the British Army appreciates your sacrifice in allowing us the use of your home. I will personally see to it that your property remains in the same state when we withdraw as it is today.' He took Marina's hand and bowed in a gallant old-fashioned gesture.

Marina met his gaze squarely with a determined lift of her chin, but Poppy could feel her trembling. 'I think I'd best get Mrs Carroll indoors,' she said firmly. 'She's not used to being outside in such cold weather.'

'This is Miss Poppy Brown, sir,' Captain Fellows said hastily.

'How do you do?' Brigadier Beecham shook her hand. 'You're quite right, Miss Brown. It's too cold to stand about out here.' He proffered his arm to Marina. 'Allow me. Wait for me in the car, Fellows, there's a good chap.'

Together, Poppy and Brigadier Beecham managed to get Marina into the house and settled in her chair by the fireside, watched anxiously by Mrs Toon who was hovering by the kitchen door. 'She shouldn't have gone out without her coat. I'll put the kettle on to make tea. Poor soul, she looks frozen.' She disappeared into the kitchen, closing the door with a disapproving thud.

'Will Mrs Carroll be all right?' Brigadier Beecham asked in a low voice. 'I could get our medical officer to give her the once-over when he arrives.'

'She just needs rest,' Poppy whispered. 'It's not easy for her. Coming to live here, I mean.'

'I do understand.' He moved towards the front door, pausing to give Poppy a searching look. 'You're not from these parts, are you, Miss Brown?'

'No, sir. I was born in West Ham and evacuated here.' She felt her heart rate quicken as she met his intent gaze. If she had had any doubts about his true identity they were dispelled in that moment. Despite the fact that they had just met, she felt she knew him already. This was the man her mother had loved and it was easy to see why. He was not what she would call handsome, but he had strong features and the telltale laughter lines at the corners of his eyes hinted at a sense of humour even when he was not smiling.

'From West Ham, you say. Your family must miss you very much, Miss Brown.'

Poppy shook her head. 'My mother and father and my grandparents were killed in a bombing raid, sir. I decided to stay on here and look after Mrs Carroll and her grandson.'

'You're very young to have so much responsibility thrust upon you.'

'I'll be seventeen in April, sir.' Even as the words left her lips she had the feeling that she was answering an unspoken question.

'Excuse me, sir.' Captain Fellows poked his head round the door. 'The convoy has just arrived at the gates.'

Brigadier Beecham nodded briefly. 'I'm coming.' He smiled at Poppy. 'If there's anything that Mrs Carroll needs please don't hesitate to come and see me or my aide, Captain Fellows.'

'Thank you, sir.'

Captain Fellows shot her a smile as he closed the door, and she could hear the sound of their leather-soled shoes crunching on the frosty brick path. Running to the window she was in time to see them climb into the staff car. It moved off, followed by the convoy of army vehicles.

'What?' Marina's strident voice made Poppy turn away from the window.

'Yes, Mrs Carroll?'

'What's the matter?'

The expression on Marina's face was enough to convince Poppy that she would not be satisfied until she had wormed the truth out of her. She went to sit beside her on a footstool. 'I know I can't keep anything from you, Mrs Carroll. I think that Brigadier Beecham could be my real father.'

Marina nodded vigorously, tapping the floor with her stick. 'More.'

She had to tell someone or she would burst. Poppy told her everything she knew about her mother and Harry Beecham. 'It could all be a huge coincidence but he looks familiar even though I've never seen him before in my whole life.'

Marina seemed about to try to speak but was prevented from doing so by Mrs Toon who bustled into the room carrying a tray of tea. She thumped it down on the burr walnut occasional table that they had brought from the main house. 'I don't know how I'll manage on that silly little electric cooker, and the boiler needs more coke, Poppy. Go out and fill the hod, there's a good girl, and bring some logs in for the fire. Atkins said he left a good supply in the lean-to.'

Poppy rose to her feet. 'Yes, of course.' As she bent down to pick up the log basket, Marina patted her hand.

'Good,' she murmured, smiling her lopsided smile. 'Good girl.'

Poppy squeezed her fingers in return. For the first time since she arrived at Squire's Knapp, a frightened little girl far from home, she felt that she had reached a definite understanding with Marina Carroll, and that they were now on the same side. She was as close to being considered one of the family as anyone who had not been born a Carroll.

THE DAYS WENT by and Poppy hugged her secret to herself. She could not bear to tell Jean or the others in case she was proved wrong, and Brigadier Beecham was not her father. She did not know if his name was Harry, and even if she dared ask the question she lacked the opportunity, as the house was always surrounded by tight security. It was off bounds to everyone except the military and most of the grounds had been turned into a giant army camp filled with khaki tents and overrun with soldiers. The farm work continued although there was little to do in what fields were left until the ground was soft enough for ploughing and spring sowing. It was a similar story in the gatekeeper's lodge. Mrs Toon managed the house and Marina was growing more independent with each passing day. The doctor was pleased with her progress, but had warned Poppy not to expect too much. Mrs Carroll, he said gravely, was unlikely to recover completely, but strength of character and determination could work wonders and Marina Carroll had these traits in abundance. He arranged visits from a physiotherapist whom Marina disliked on sight, but Poppy decided that this was probably a good thing as it provided her with another incentive to overcome her disability.

After Poppy had taken Rupert to school each morning she was able to spend more time helping Jean, Edie and Mavis with work on the farm. Her hopes of getting to know the brigadier a littler better were dashed when she discovered that he had been recalled to London. She was left in limbo, not knowing when or even if he would ever return to Squire's Knapp. She bitterly regretted her lost opportunity. If only she had said something to him on that first day. As the weeks went by she became resigned to the fact that she might never know the truth.

Life fell into a set routine, and it really was a case of 'make do and mend'. Food was scarce, rationing was strict and new clothes were out of the question. Even if they saved their coupons there was little choice in the Fairford shops. Edie and Mavis showed Poppy how to redden her lips with beetroot juice and old clothes were cut up and restyled. Poppy became adept with a needle and thread and struggled to master the art of knitting. In her spare time she exercised Goliath, riding out into the country lanes and occasionally following the route she had taken once with Guy. She felt quite jealous when Jean received letters from Algy, who was an excellent correspondent, and as he often flew as Guy's navigator there was usually something in the contents that was of particular interest to Poppy. Jean only read out the bits that were not too personal. It was obvious when she came to the more romantic passages as her cheeks would redden and she turned the page saying, 'Censored. And that bit too – censored. Sorry, girls.'

At least Poppy knew that Guy was alive and well. She convinced herself that she could not expect him to write to her, and it might look strange if she wrote to him. One day, hopefully quite soon, he would come home unscathed. He would take up his position as head of the household and Mrs Carroll would be reinstated in her rightful position in Squire's Knapp. Rupert would either return to his parents in London or be packed off to boarding school. The sad truth was that she herself would no longer be needed. She would be free to do whatever took her fancy, but she knew that she would never be entirely free from Squire's Knapp and Guy Carroll. Her heart would always be here and, like the glass pendant that hung round her neck, it had been given to the one she loved most in the whole world.

She had passed her seventeenth birthday in April and it was now early autumn, but her feelings were not like the seasons; they did not change and she knew that if she lived to be a hundred she would always love Guy. She wondered if her mother had felt like that about Harry and if, in fact, the high-ranking officer she had met briefly was that same man. Brigadier Beecham had not made a return visit to Squire's Knapp and perhaps he never would. Even if he were to discover that he had a daughter, would he want to know her? It was a question that she feared might never be answered. She did her best to get on with the day to day routine of simply keeping things going.

Autumn mists had followed long days of double summertime. The harvest, such as it was with half the fields taken over by the army, was gathered in and Poppy was just about to set off to help Edie in the milking parlour when she saw the telegram boy cycling into the drive. She froze. They weren't nicknamed angels of death for nothing. He stopped at the gate, putting one foot on the ground to balance himself.

'Who are you looking for?' Her voice sounded strange even to her own ears.

He studied the envelope. 'Mrs M Carroll.'

Moving like an automaton, Poppy held out her hand. 'I'll take it to her.'

He frowned. 'I'm supposed to give it to her in person.'

'She's an invalid. Give it to me and I'll make sure she gets it.' Without giving him the chance to argue, Poppy snatched it from his hand. Turning her back on the startled boy she ripped the envelope and extracted the telegram. Her breath caught in her throat as she saw Guy's name in print and the dreaded words danced before her eyes – *missing in action, presumed killed*. She read it again and again as if hoping she could change its meaning by sheer willpower.

'Bad news, is it? I'm sorry, miss.'

She nodded wordlessly.

'No reply then, miss?'

She shook her head. Her mind seemed to have detached itself from her body. There must be some mistake. If anything had happened to Guy she would have known instinctively. She realised that the boy was watching her anxiously. She was quite calm; ice cold in fact and completely numb. 'No reply, thank you.' She walked slowly back towards the house and went inside with the telegram clutched in her hand. 'Mrs Carroll, I need you to be very brave.'

THE DAYS THAT followed were like a waking nightmare to Poppy, but somehow she managed to function. Marina had taken the news with typical stoicism and without any outward display of grief for her son. Poppy broke the news to Rupert as gently as she could but he did not seem able to grasp the fact that death was final. He seemed to think that Guy was simply somewhere else and might turn up at any moment. Poppy found this oddly comforting and she was happier in Rupert's company than with anybody else. Jean was sympathetic, but try as she might she could not quite hide the fact that she was overjoyed that Algy had not been the navigator on that particular mission as a bout of influenza had laid him low and he had been unfit for duty. Deep down Poppy refused to believe that Guy was dead, and she prayed for a miracle.

Gradually and almost imperceptibly, the landscape changed from the rich colours of autumn to the monochrome of frosty winter days and freezing nights, but it was warm and cosy in the lodge. Mrs Toon said it was the first time she had not suffered from chilblains caused by the bitter chill rising from the flagstone floors in the kitchen at the main house. Maybe the army would pay compensation to the family for requisitioning their home and a decent central heating system could be installed. Poppy listened without comment. She could not think that far ahead. Her world had been turned upside down and inside out by that fateful telegram.

Christmas was of necessity a low key event. Pamela telephoned to say that Hector was unable to leave London as there was something massive and totally hush-hush being planned, although of course she could not say any more. Poppy could not imagine Pamela spending Christmas in the cottage with its one tiny bathroom and outside lavatory. She suspected that this might have had something to do with the fact that she was not coming down to see her son, but Rupert did not seem to mind. He had made friends with some of the soldiers camped in the grounds, and when he was not with them he spent his time in the stables with the horses. Poppy took him out riding as often as the weather permitted. When she was exercising Goliath it brought Guy close to her. He had loved that horse and had not been afraid to demonstrate his affection for the animal, whereas with people he was often reserved and appeared to be distant.

In February, Jean was a winter bride. Algy had two days' leave and the wedding took place in the village church. Poppy had been thrilled for Jean but she had dreaded the moment when she must face Guy's old friend. She had been afraid that she might resent him for simply having survived, but the moment she saw Algy on the eve of his wedding, Poppy knew that she had worried about nothing. His friendly smile and his warm embrace banished any lingering resentment she might have felt. 'You loved him too, Poppy,' he said in a low voice. 'I know that, and I know he loved you.'

She sniffed and reached for her hanky. 'You're just saying that.'

Algy took her by the shoulders. 'No. I wouldn't make up such a thing. He told me how he felt just before the last op. It was almost as if he knew that his time was up.' He smiled apologetically. 'Sorry, I don't mean to make things worse, but we never kept anything from each other. It wouldn't have worked with my sister, and she realised that in the end, which is why she broke off their engagement. I don't think he saw it coming until it was too late, but he certainly adored you, Poppy.'

'He didn't tell me. Not in so many words, anyway.'

'He wouldn't. He thought you were too young for him, but I told him time would sort that out, and that you'd always worshipped the ground he walked on. That wasn't wrong, was it?'

Poppy gulped and swallowed hard. 'N-no, but how did you know that?'

Algy grinned, touching her cheek with the tips of his fingers. 'Jean told me, and I may not be brightest chap when it comes to matters of the heart but I'd seen the way you were with him.'

'Was it so obvious?'

'Only to those who love you.' He kissed her on the forehead. 'Chin up. He'd want you to be happy, always remember that.'

THE WEDDING WAS a quiet affair in the village church. Algy's Aunt Jane had declined her invitation using the excuse of poor health, but she had paid for the wedding breakfast in the village pub, which pleased Jean immensely, as she said the last thing she wanted was to cause a rift in Algy's family. Mrs Toon had made the cake, but even with their combined sugar rations they did not have enough points for icing sugar, and the cake sat beneath a cardboard cover, painted white, with a slightly battered sugar paste bride and groom that one of Mrs Toon's cronies in the village had unearthed from their store cupboard and loaned for the occasion.

After the final toasts were drunk the bride and groom said goodbye to their guests as they prepared to leave for Weymouth in Atkins' pony and trap. Algy had booked the honeymoon suite in a hotel on the seafront.

'We'll have a lovely view of the beach through barbed wire and scaffolding,' Jean said, smiling.

Edie nudged her in the ribs. 'You won't spend much time looking out of the window, ducks.'

Mavis frowned, jerking her head in Poppy's direction. 'Don't be crude, Edie.'

'The kid is almost eighteen. She's a grown-up now, Mavis.' Edie linked her arm through Poppy's. 'Come on, girls. Let's wave the bride and groom off and then I'm going to get Howard drunk and perhaps he'll propose.'

'Lester already has,' Mavis murmured, blushing. 'I'm going to be a GI bride.'

'No. Are you really?' Poppy gave her a hug. 'How lovely. Will you go and live in America?'

Mavis chuckled. 'His family own a hardware store in Texas. I can't wait to meet them. I'll be Mrs Lester Grover. Isn't it exciting?'

'Yeah,' Edie said, angling her head. 'All those nuts and bolts and oil cans. You'll be like Dorothy in *The Wizard of Oz*.'

'Well, if you're half as happy as Algy and me, you'll be ecstatic,' Jean said, kissing each of them in turn.

Algy strolled over to them, having just shaken hands all round as he took his leave of the guests. 'Your carriage awaits, Mrs Fenton-Jones.' He tucked her hand in the crook of his arm.

Jean smiled up at him. 'Mrs Fenton-Jones. Doesn't that sound grand?'

Everyone followed them outside and they left in a shower of confetti and ice-cold rain. Poppy wiped her eyes, thankful for once for the bad weather which disguised the fact that she was crying. She looked down as a warm little hand clutched hers.

'Don't be sad, Poppy,' Rupert said, squeezing her fingers. 'I expect he misses us too.'

He was too big to scoop up in her arms and so she did the next best thing, which was to give him a hug. 'You're a special boy, did you know that?'

'Yes,' he said, grinning impishly. 'I did as a matter of fact.'

JEAN'S RETURN FROM honeymoon was bittersweet. She was deliriously happy with Algy but parting from him so soon was deeply upsetting. She tried to make light of it, describing the dire food served up in the hotel, which was filled with American army officers. She said that they had not seen the sea. The bay was crammed with vessels of all types so that you could have walked the length and breadth of it jumping from ship to ship.

Even if Jean had not told them about the frantic activity on the coast, it was obvious that something important was going on at Squire's Knapp. More troops arrived and there was a constant stream of staff cars filled with high-ranking British and American officers. Poppy had given up hope of meeting Brigadier Beecham again and had almost managed to convince herself that he was not the man who had fallen in love with her mother. It was a mystery that she was unlikely to solve. Heartsore and still mourning privately for Guy, she did what was demanded of her daily and tried not to think of the future.

At the beginning of June it was obvious that some major offensive was about to begin. Convoys of tanks roared along the road into Weymouth, and the skies were filled with a seemingly endless stream of planes towing huge gliders escorted by swarms of fighters. It was only after the news of the D-Day landings was announced on the wireless that Poppy realised why Squire's Knapp had played such an important role in the Allied invasion of France.

It seemed that the dark days of war must come to an end soon, but although the tents were deserted there was still a military presence in the main house. Poppy had just returned one morning from taking Rupert to school when she heard the sound of a car engine in the lane. She paused by the garden gate, her curiosity aroused. She watched as the army staff car swung through the gates, and was surprised to see it slow down and come to a halt in front of the lodge.

The driver leapt out to open the rear passenger door and suddenly she had a feeling of déjà vu as Captain Fellows climbed out of the car, followed immediately by Brigadier Beecham.

'Good morning, Miss Brown.' Captain Fellows saluted her smartly.

Brigadier Beecham came towards her and Poppy was suddenly uneasy. Visits from high-ranking officers usually meant only one thing – what further bad news could he possibly bring? Her hand flew to the pendant hanging round her neck. She fingered it nervously. 'What can I do for you, Brigadier?'

His smile froze as his eyes rested on the glass heart glistening in the warm June sunshine.

'What?' Poppy asked nervously. 'Why are you staring at me like that?'

'Where did you get that pendant?'

Surprised by the sharpness of his tone, she dropped her hand to her side and the glass heart felt suddenly cold against her bare skin. 'My father gave it to my mother and she gave it to me.'

'Mary,' he murmured dazedly. 'It was Mary. I knew you must be her daughter, but I hardly dared to hope . . .'

Captain Fellows cleared his throat. 'May I suggest we go into the house, sir?'

'Not now, Fellows. Give me a moment.' Brigadier Beecham caught Poppy by the shoulders, looking deeply into her eyes. 'Mary Brown was your mother?'

Poppy nodded wordlessly.

'I gave her that pendant. My God, you're so like her, but I didn't know – she didn't tell me about you.'

'You're Harry.' Poppy caught her breath on a sob. 'You are Harry Beecham. I knew it. I mean I felt it.'

'She told you about me?'

His eager expression made him look suddenly younger and vulnerable. Poppy could hardly bear to disappoint him. 'No. I found out by chance. As a matter of fact it was a spiteful old woman who told me that my mother had been sacked from her job because she was having an affair with the son of the house.'

Harry winced. 'It wasn't like that, Poppy. Your mother and I were very young and we fell deeply in love. I wanted to marry her but I was entirely dependent on my father. He sent her away, forbidding me to see her again. That was before I joined the army.' He touched the glass heart with the tip of his finger. 'This was my parting gift to her, and you say that she gave it to you.'

'It was the last time I saw her.' Poppy paused, blinking away tears. 'She didn't have a Christmas present for me. She said that my father had given it to her, and she'd worn it ever since.'

'We swore to love each other forever,' he said, smiling sadly. 'It seemed like a miracle when we met again years later and realised that nothing had changed between us.'

Poppy held her breath. She knew now why the glass heart had been so precious to her mother.

Harry turned to his aide, who was hovering anxiously at his side. 'I know I can trust you to be discreet, Edmund.'

Captain Fellows nodded emphatically. 'Absolutely, sir.'

'Wait in the car, there's a good chap. I'd like to speak to my daughter in private.'

Poppy opened the gate. 'Come into the house. Mrs Carroll is out walking with Mrs Toon. She manages very well these days.' She held out her hand and felt the warmth of her father's fingers as they curled around hers.

In the cottage, his presence seemed to overpower the small living room and she felt suddenly shy. 'I wish that Mum had told me about you, but I suppose she couldn't because of Dad. She was very loyal to him and he was good to me.'

'I'm sure he was. I only met him once but I know that he was a fine man. If I'd only known that Mary was pregnant I would have fought for her no matter what the consequences. But she finished with me because she couldn't bear to hurt her husband or abandon her young son. I left because I loved her too much to want to see her suffer in any way. I want you to believe that, Poppy.'

'I do,' she murmured. 'And I'm glad I've found you at last.'

He stood with his back to the empty grate, gazing at her as if he could not bear to look away. 'You are so beautiful, just like Mary. I knew there was something familiar about you when we first met, but I could never have imagined the truth. You must think me a terrible fellow.'

'No,' Poppy said slowly. 'I know what it is to love someone with all your heart and soul. Losing them is the hardest thing to bear.'

'I think I can guess who it is you love with such a passion.'

'I don't see how you could. I mean . . .'

He took her hand and held it in a firm grasp. 'The reason I came here today was to bring Mrs Pallister some wonderful news. Hector rang me in the middle of the night to tell me that Guy was discovered by the Allied troops in a German field hospital near Paris. He'd been there for months. Apparently he was plucked out of the sea by the crew of a French fishing boat and taken to hospital suffering from a broken leg and exposure, which turned into pneumonia.'

'He's alive.' Still clutching his hand, Poppy sank down onto Marina's chair. 'Guy's alive! You don't know how happy that makes me.'

He squeezed her fingers. 'I think I do, my dear.'

'But why didn't Mr Pallister let us know sooner?'

'The news had only just filtered through to him, Poppy. In the grand scheme of things it was not the most urgent communication between the landing forces and London, which accounts for the delay.'

'Mrs Carroll must be told. She'll be overjoyed, although of course she won't show it. She never does.' Poppy knew she was babbling but she was so happy that it hurt. She felt like throwing her arms around her father and dancing round the room, but she was still a little shy of him.

'Hector thought it best if Mrs Carroll was told in person. He's well aware of her delicate state of health, and he didn't want to risk anything that might cause her a sudden shock.'

'He couldn't have told you that I had feelings for Guy. How did you know?'

He smiled gently. 'Watching your face just now when you spoke of undying love – it wasn't hard to put two and two together, my dear. You're so like Mary. Your eyes will always give you away. Besides which, Guy has been asking for you, which is another reason why Hector asked me to come here in person. I think he too is quite capable of putting two and two together, Poppy.' He raised her gently to her feet, wrapping his arms around her. 'Might I be permitted to give my daughter a hug?'

She slid her arms around his neck. 'Yes.' She smiled shyly. 'May I call you Dad?'

'Oh, yes.' His eyes were moist and he hugged her so hard that the brass buttons on his tunic pressed into her flesh, but it was a sweet pain.

'Dad,' she repeated. 'Or Father, if you prefer it.'

'You may call me whatever you please, my darling. I can't begin to tell you how happy I am to have found you, and to be the bearer of such good news too.'

Dazed with happiness, Poppy felt her heart swell inside her like a balloon about to burst. 'Where is Guy now? Will he be allowed to come home soon?'

Harry chuckled. 'One question at a time, Poppy. He's been transferred to a hospital in Cherbourg, and he'll be brought over to Weymouth on the first available ship. Of course he'll have to spend a day or two in hospital being checked over, but I gather he was on the mend when they found him.'

Poppy brushed tears from her eyes, but they were tears of happiness. In the space of a heartbeat she had found her father and been given the news that Guy was alive and well. All her prayers were answered and she vowed she would never bother God again as long as she lived.

'Perhaps we'd better go and find Mrs Carroll,' Harry said softly. 'She needs to know that her days of grieving for her son are over.'

'How dreadful. I almost forgot poor Mrs Carroll,' Poppy said, fumbling in her pocket for her hanky. 'I'm so happy and excited I don't know what I'm doing.'

JEAN WAS ECSTATIC when Poppy told her that Guy was safe and on his way home and she rushed off to tell Edie and Mavis. That evening they celebrated by sitting round the pot-bellied stove drinking mugs of cocoa and eating some of Mavis's store of chocolate given to her by her adoring Lester.

'So you really are going to end up as lady of the manor,' Edie said, licking her fingers one by one. 'I hope you'll invite us all to the wedding, Poppy.'

'He hasn't asked me yet,' Poppy said hastily. 'I mean, he might take one look at me and decide that it was all a huge mistake.'

Jean snorted with laughter. 'Have you taken a look in the mirror recently, kid? Apart from the fact that you're one of the sweetest people I've ever met, you're absolutely gorgeous. He'd be mad to let you get away.'

Unused to such fulsome compliments, Poppy covered her hot cheeks with her hands. 'Stop it, Jean. You're making me blush.'

'It's poor old Dennis I feel sorry for,' Mavis said, grinning. 'He never stood a chance.'

'He's okay,' Poppy said, smiling ruefully. 'According to Mabel he's engaged to the girl from the horse meat shop. She's a peroxide blonde who wears bright red lipstick and loves cream cakes. I'm sure she'll make him much happier than I ever could.'

The next few days were spent in a flurry of activity and anticipation. The army had all but vacated the big house, but Harry and Captain Fellows remained there with just a few key officers and a skeleton staff to attend to their needs. Marina and Poppy were invited up to the main house and entertained by Harry and some of the visiting top brass. At first Poppy had thought it might be too much for Marina, and she was worried that the house might be in a parlous state which would cause her even more distress. But the moment she set foot in her old home, Marina seemed to positively bloom. Apart from her need for a walking stick and her hesitant speech, she assumed the mantle of gracious hostess, completely turning the tables on the assemblage of high-ranking military men who now found themselves outranked and outflanked. Marina Carroll was in her element, and Poppy felt that life had come full circle.

Harry made time for her in his busy schedule and Poppy saw him every day. Discovering a mutual love of riding, they exercised the horses every afternoon. Poppy was able to show her father the extent of the Carrolls' estate and some of the surrounding countryside that she had grown to love. These were moments of shared peace and tranquillity snatched in between the business of war that still occupied much of Harry's waking hours. It gave Poppy pleasure to see him mounted on Goliath and handling the horse with the same expertise that Guy had always demonstrated. All she needed now was for Guy to return home and her happiness would be complete.

IT ALL HAPPENED suddenly. One minute Poppy was hanging the washing on the line in the cottage garden and the next she was in the staff car being driven to Weymouth. She sat in the back seat holding her father's hand. 'I'm scared,' she whispered. 'What if he's changed his mind? What shall I say to him, Father?'

Harry raised her hand to his lips and brushed it with a kiss. 'You'll find the right words, my darling. Trust me.'

LEAVING HARRY STANDING in the atrium of the hospital, Poppy made her way up two flights of stairs to the male wards. The receptionist had told her where to find Guy but Poppy was suddenly stricken with shyness. The fast-moving events of the day had left her reeling slightly, but now the initial feeling of euphoria had worn off she was tense and nervous. It was many months since she had last seen Guy, and despite what Jean, Mavis and Edie had said, he might find the young woman she had become quite different from the girl he had left behind.

She made her way to the nurses' station, waiting patiently for the sister to finish writing up her notes. 'Yes?' The sister's demeanour was not encouraging.

'I've come to take Pilot Officer Carroll home.'

The sister pointed her pen at a bed in the far corner where the curtains were drawn. Slowly, Poppy crossed the floor, acknowledging the cheeky remarks of the less sick male patients with an attempt at a smile. She hesitated, clearing her throat. 'Guy?'

With a rattle of brass rings the curtains opened and Guy stood there, thinner, paler, but his smile was enough to make her feel light-headed. 'H-how are you?' she murmured, glancing over her shoulder to see if the man in the next bed was listening, but thankfully he was lying with his eyes closed and appeared to be sleeping soundly.

'Poppy. You came.' He drew her to him and she tilted her face, thinking he was going to kiss her on the forehead as he had always done in the past, but his mouth sought her lips in a kiss that was tender and yet filled with desire and longing. A round of applause from the rest of the ward made him release her with an apologetic grin.

'Give her one for me, mate.' The man in the bed opposite raised himself on his elbow, blowing a kiss to Poppy.

'Find your own girl, mate,' Guy said, laughing. He snatched up a brown paper parcel from the foot of the bed and slipped his arm around Poppy's waist. 'Let's get out of here, darling Poppy. I've got so much I want to say to you.'

Before she realised what was happening they were in the narrow corridor leading away from the ward. Guy stopped outside the sister's office and took her in his arms. 'If I've overstepped the mark please tell me. I've been away for a long time and if it wasn't for Algy I wouldn't have dared to think that you cared for me.'

'You've known all this time?'

'It's what kept me going in the long hours when I was floating about in the drink with nothing but my Mae West for company. Eventually I was rescued by a French fisherman. It's all a bit hazy after that but I ended up in a German field hospital.'

'I thought you were dead,' Poppy whispered, close to tears. 'We all did.'

'I was as good as for a while apparently, but I don't remember much about that. When I began to recover it was the thought of you waiting for me and not knowing I loved you that gave me the will to survive. I had to come home and tell you that I love you with all my heart and have done for a very long time. My darling girl.'

Ignoring the two nurse probationers who were in the sluice next door and had stopped washing bedpans to stare at them, Poppy slid her arms around his neck. 'I've never loved anyone but you, Guy.'

He kissed her again, holding her to him as if he would never let her go. 'I thought I'd lost you when I saw you with that erk, but I was a jealous fool. I'm going to spend the rest of my life making it up to you.'

She laid her finger on his lips. 'Is that a promise?'

'It is. Most sincerely and from my heart, Poppy. It's a promise.'

Continue reading for an excerpt from
Lily Baxter's thrilling historical fiction saga,

THE SHOPKEEPER'S DAUGHTER

*In World War II-torn England, a young woman must
fight to keep her family together, whatever the cost.*

Ginnie Travis has been working in her father shop for
the past five years trying to keep it afloat. When scandal rocks her family just as relentless Nazi raids threaten
their very lives, Ginnie and her sister are forced to flee
and stay with their aunt in the north of England. The last
thing she expects to find in the quiet countryside is love,
especially with an American soldier. A soldier who has
secrets of his own.

Tragedy strikes, the horror of war rages on, and Ginnie will do whatever she must to protect everything she
holds dear.

Available now from Avon Impulse!

Chapter One

East London, June 1944

GINNIE HAD RISKED leaving the safety of the air raid shelter when Fred Chinashop suffered one of his funny turns. Despite her father's protests she had returned to the small office at the back of their furniture store, and was about to add a generous spoonful of her precious sugar ration to a cup of tea when she heard the dreaded rasping buzz of the doodlebug. The cup rattled on its saucer and the floor beneath her feet started to vibrate.

The deathly silence when its engine cut out made her hold her breath, closing her eyes as she prayed that the bomb would fall on fields or wasteland, anywhere but on the crowded suburban streets. The explosion when it came was too close for comfort, and she felt the repercussion of the blast shaking the foundations of the building. Large flakes of plaster fell from the ceiling and the air was thick with dust. Her hand was trembling as she picked up the cup and saucer. They had been lucky this time, but somebody somewhere must have bought it.

The all clear siren was blasting out its monotone wail of relief as she let herself out into the back yard. Sidney Travis emerged from the Anderson shelter red-faced and bristling with anger. 'You stupid girl. You might have got yourself killed.'

'I'm all right, Dad. How's Fred?'

Her father shook his head. 'He'll live, but you could have been dead and buried under the rubble if there'd been a direct hit.' He gave her a clumsy hug. 'Give the silly old devil his tea. I'm going inside to see if there's any damage.' He hurried indoors and Ginnie could hear him exclaiming in annoyance, and cursing the Jerries. She hesitated, gazing anxiously at the surrounding buildings, and breathed a sigh of relief when she realised that the parade of shops in Collier Lane had escaped the worst of the blast.

Purpose-built before the war, the box-like units had been designed with living accommodation above and a functional but drab service road at the rear. The concept, Ginnie had always suspected, might have looked stylish and ultra-modern on the architect's plans, but surrounded by a hinterland of small factories and uniform streets of Edwardian terraced houses in one of the poorer suburbs of East London, the Utopian dream had rapidly deteriorated into a shabby mass of concrete and glass. Most of the windows were now criss-crossed with sticky tape and sandbagged, but Sidney had steadfastly refused to have his shop boarded up, declaring that it was bad for business, and Hitler and his Luftwaffe could take a long walk off a short pier for all he cared.

Ginnie knew that they had been lucky this time. They had survived, and she could only hope that no one had been killed when the bomb landed. She hurried into the shelter, wrinkling her nose at the pervasive smell of damp and sweaty bodies. Fred Chinashop was still sitting on the wooden bench looking pale and dazed. She gave him his tea. 'I hope it's sweet enough for you.'

He managed a wobbly smile. 'Ta, love.'

Ginnie glanced anxiously at the only other occupant of the shelter. Ida Richmond lived in a flat above the shop and had been administering her version of first aid to Fred, which consisted of making encouraging noises and fanning him with her handkerchief. 'Is he all right, Mrs Richmond?' Ginnie asked in a whisper.

Ida nodded vigorously, causing her hairnet to slip over one eye. She adjusted it with a practised tweak of her fingers. 'It'd take more than a Jerry bomb to finish our Fred Chinashop.'

Fred nodded in silent agreement and sipped his tea. His real name was Fred Brown but Ginnie's dad had a penchant for giving people nicknames. Fred Brown had become Fred Chinashop in order to distinguish him from Fred Harper, also known as Fred Woollies, the manager of the Woolworth's store situated a little further along the parade. 'I'm fine now, ducks.' Fred raised the cup in a toast. 'Sweety, weaky and milky – just how I like it.'

'He's all right now.' Ida picked up a willow pattern plate piled high with her latest attempt at baking. 'Nelson squares. Try one of these, Fred.' She wafted the cakes under his nose. 'You need building up, love. You're all skin and bone.'

'I won't say no.' He took one and bit into it. 'You're too good to me, Ida.'

'I was just using up the crusts of bread and some dried fruit that had been on the shelf since last Christmas. My hubby doesn't have a sweet tooth and I have to watch my figure.' She beamed at him through the thick lenses of her horn-rimmed spectacles. 'You bachelors don't know how to look after yourselves properly. I dunno why you never got married, Fred. You must have been quite a good-looking feller years ago, before you went bald and lost all your teeth.'

He swallowed the last morsel and took a mouthful of tea. 'I feel better now, Ida. Ta very much, but I'd best get back to my emporium and see if there's any damage. The blast might have shattered what little stock I've got left. It's hard to get hold of decent crockery these days.' He put his cup and saucer on the wooden bench and struggled to his feet, steadying himself with one hand on the wall. 'Thanks for the cuppa, Ginnie.'

'Any time, Fred.' She stood aside to let him pass as he made his way out of the shelter.

Ida rose to her feet. 'That man needs a wife. He lives on tea and toast. No wonder he hasn't got any stamina. My Norman is twice the man he is. He'll scoff this lot in one go.'

'It's very kind of you to share them with us, Mrs Richmond,' Ginnie said, smiling. She was fond of Ida, who had always taken a motherly interest in the Travis family. With no children of her own to care for and a husband who worked long hours on the railways, Ida had nothing to do other than clean her tiny apartment and she was always popping downstairs with samples of her cooking.

'But you haven't tried them yet, love. Norman won't miss one more.'

Ginnie shook her head. 'No thanks. They look lovely but it's nearly lunchtime and I'll be in trouble if I don't eat everything on my plate. Mum will have been slaving away all morning to make something tasty out of next to nothing.'

'You're a good girl, Ginnie. It's a pity your flighty sister isn't a bit more like you.'

'Shirley's all right, Mrs Richmond. She's just high-spirited, that's all.'

'And you're very loyal, ducks.' Ida stepped outside, squinting in the sunlight. 'Let's hope the war ends before you get called up or have to work in the munitions factory like your sister. How old are you now, dear? I lose track.'

'I'll be nineteen in August.'

'At least you've got another year before you're called up. The war might be over by then, God willing.'

'Let's hope so, Mrs Richmond.'

'Your dad would be lost without you, Ginnie. I dunno how he'd manage the shop if you weren't there to give him a hand.'

'I enjoy it,' Ginnie said stoutly. 'Maybe it's not what I'd set my heart on when I was at school, but I've learned how to keep accounts and I know almost as much about carpets and furniture as my dad.'

Ida patted her on the shoulder. 'You're a treasure.' She ambled across the yard and let herself out into the service lane. 'TTFN, ducks.'

Ginnie collected a dustpan and brush from the outside lavatory and hurried into the partitioned off area at the back of the shop that served as an office. She had not been lying to Ida when she said she enjoyed working for her father, but there was a part of her that wished he would allow her to enlist in one of the women's services and do her bit for her country. In a year's time she would be conscripted anyway, or else she would have to do war work like Shirley, but she did not relish the idea of slaving away in the munitions factory or volunteering as an ARP warden.

Shaking the plaster dust from her dark blonde hair, Ginnie brushed it back from her face and fastened it in a ponytail with a rubber band that she found in the bottom of one of the desk drawers along with a stick of sealing wax and an empty Fisherman's Friend tin. A stray strand tickled her nose and she secured it in place with the aid of a kirby grip, checking her reflection in the scrap of fly-spotted mirror balanced on a pile of account books, before setting to work, sweeping and dusting until everything was cleaner than it had been before the bomb fell. She had just finished when she heard her father talking to their local ARP warden, Tom Adams, whose stentorian tones were unmistakeable.

She hurried through to the shop. 'Where did the bomb land, Mr Adams?'

'We was fortunate this time,' Tom said solemnly. 'It came down in the park and smashed the cricket pavilion to smithereens, but it's lucky it wasn't Saturday or it would have taken out half of the home guard and the team from the munitions factory in Dagenham.'

'That's where Shirley works,' Sidney said with a disapproving downturn of his mouth. 'That girl was top of the class in school. She'd have done well for herself but for the bloody war.' He shot an apologetic glance at his daughter. 'Excuse my French, but it makes me blooming mad.'

'Can't stay here chatting all day, Sid. Got my duties to perform.' Tom saluted and ambled towards the door. 'Abyssinia.'

'Maybe I'll see you in the King's Arms later,' Sid called after him. He turned to Ginnie with a sigh. 'The shop window's cracked. I suppose I'll have to give in and board it up, although it goes against the grain.' He bent down to heft a roll of linoleum upright. 'The blast tipped these over, Ginnie. Give us a hand to put them back up, there's a good girl, and then you'd best get home for your lunch. You know how Mum worries if you're even a minute late.'

GINNIE SET OFF at a brisk pace to walk the mile or so home. Situated in the middle of a large estate of identical 1930s semi-detached houses, Cherry Lane was a tree-lined suburban street. It was not the poorest part of town but it was on the edge of the industrial area where the gasworks sat cheek by jowl with the glue factory and the abattoir. The station with its sooty sidings and noisy shunting yard was nearby, and small businesses plied their trade beneath the railway arches.

Ginnie had been aware from an early age that the girls who lived on the other side of town, notably the posh Monk Avenue area, came from homes where they called their parents Mummy and Daddy and not Mum and Dad. Their fathers were professional men, and their mothers played bridge or socialised while charwomen did their housework. The houses in Monk Avenue were set in large gardens shielded from the road by high walls or hedges, with the golf links at the rear and the grammar school only two streets away.

Shirley might have aspirations to live in Monk Avenue, but Ginnie was fiercely loyal to her roots. There was nothing wrong with number ten, she thought as she approached the house. The exterior was pebble-dashed and the lounge and master bedroom had the benefit of curved bay windows. There was a good-sized garden at the rear and a smaller one at the front, separated from the pavement by a low brick wall. Ginnie paused at the gate, looking up at the small triangular window behind which was her personal domain, cluttered with her most prized possessions, including a silver-backed dressing-table set that her paternal grandparents had given her on her sixteenth birthday. They had been killed in the Blitz, although it was still hard to believe that Hitler had got the better of Granny Travis. Ginnie still missed the old lady, with her acerbic tongue and wicked sense of humour. Her maternal grandparents had succumbed to heart attacks within weeks of each other when Ginnie was twelve years old, leaving her with nothing but happy memories of Christmases and summer holidays spent in their bungalow at Frinton-on-Sea.

She took her front door key from her handbag and let herself in. 'Mum. Hello, it's only me.'

Mildred Travis bustled out of the kitchen, wiping her hands on her floral pinafore. Snail-like pin curls had escaped from the scarf tied turban-fashion around her head, and her cheeks were flushed. 'Did you hear that doodlebug go over, Ginnie? I was in the Anderson with Mrs Martin from next door, and when it stopped my heart was beating so fast I thought I was going to pass out with fright. Thank God you're all right. D'you know where it landed?'

'In the park, Mum. Mr Adams said the cricket pavilion copped it, and the shop window's cracked, but Dad's going to board it up.'

'About time too. I keep telling him that he should have done it years ago, but will he listen to me? No, of course he won't. Your father is the most stubborn man I've ever met.' Mildred shot back into the kitchen, reappearing a moment later with a saucepan in her hand. 'Just caught the spuds before they boiled dry. I'll serve up right away.'

Ginnie tossed her handbag and gasmask case onto the hall stand and peeled off her gloves. Although it was a hot day she would have been nagged to death had Mum seen her less than immaculately turned out. War or no war, standards had to be maintained. Ginnie took her seat at the table and waited for her mother to bring in a steaming plate of Woolton pie. It was Wednesday and meals were served on a strict rota, so at least she knew what to expect, although a salad would have been more welcome.

'Flaming June,' Mildred said as she brought the plates to the table, placing one in front of her daughter. 'It's too hot to spend the day slaving away in the kitchen, but your dad likes his midday meal, and I've never let him go one day without a proper cooked lunch since we were married.' She nodded, sighing. 'That'll be twenty-four years ago in July.'

'Yes, Mum.' Ginnie picked up her knife and fork. 'You've done wonders. This looks really tasty. I'm sure Dad will love it. I'll go back early and relieve him so that his dinner won't be dried up.' She sampled a mouthful and swallowed manfully. It was stodgy and salty with an overriding flavour of onions, but it was hot and filling and she would not have hurt her mother's feelings for the world. 'Lovely.' She washed it down with a sip of water.

'At least you've got a good appetite, not like your sister.' Mildred pushed a piece of potato round her plate, eyeing it with distaste. 'She's been looking very peaky recently. I blame the chemicals in the munitions factory.'

'Yes, Mum.' Ginnie continued to plough her way through the plate of food. Shirley was probably eating in the works canteen and listening to *Workers' Playtime* on the wireless, surrounded by her friends and colleagues. It was impossible not to envy her sister's independent spirit. Shirley had refused to help their father run the shop when she left school and had made a feeble and unsuccessful attempt at job-hunting. She had spent most of her time at the tennis club, but this had ended abruptly when the government decreed that single women over the age of twenty would be compelled to enlist in one of the armed forces or take up war work. The munitions factory had not been Shirley's idea of a perfect job, but she had chosen not to enlist, stating that all the uniforms were hideous and unflattering and she would not be seen dead in any of them. Ginnie smiled to herself. Blessed with impossibly good looks and irresistible charm, Shirley could probably commit murder and get away with it.

'Are you listening to me, Ginnie?'

Her mother's voice cut across her thoughts and Ginnie looked up. 'Yes, Mum.'

'I was saying that I'd have taken you girls to stay with your Auntie Avril in Shropshire at the start of the war if it weren't for your dad and the perishing shop.' Mildred sighed and pushed her plate away. 'But I couldn't leave him to look after himself. He can't boil an egg, let alone cook a decent meal.'

'But I thought you didn't get on with Auntie Avril, Mum? You've always said she was no better than she should be.'

'I never did.' Mildred dabbed her lips with a gingham table napkin. 'I just said that Avril's way of life wasn't my cup of tea, but at least she's calmed down a bit since her last husband died.'

'She's only had two, Mum.'

'And both of them dead before their time. That's what comes from living the high life, but she's still my sister and it would be her duty to take us in.'

'You wouldn't enjoy living in the pub. You don't even like the smell of beer.'

Mildred sniffed and set her knife and fork down at a precise angle on her plate. 'Anything would be better than waiting to be blown to bits by a buzz bomb. Anyway, it's a lovely part of the world. Your dad and I spent our honeymoon in Shropshire, only Sid took to fishing and I spent most of my time standing on the riverbank being bitten by gnats.'

'Poor you.'

'Why are you grinning?' Mildred demanded, eyeing her suspiciously. 'It wasn't funny, and we had to eat fish for dinner every night. I hate trout and I've never touched it since.'

Ginnie dabbed her lips with her napkin. 'That was delicious, Mum. I'd better get back to the shop now and let Dad come home to enjoy a feast.'

'But you haven't had your dessert.'

'I'll have it for tea, Mum.'

'But it's strawberries from the garden. I picked them this morning.' Mildred pursed her lips. 'You'll suffer from dyspepsia like your dad if you're not careful.'

'I'll take them to work with me, Mum. I'll have time to enjoy them later.'

'Shirley's bringing a young man home for tea, so make sure that you leave the shop on time, and tell your dad not to stop off at the pub. We don't want to create the wrong impression.'

'Which boyfriend is this?'

'Don't say things like that, dear. It makes it sound as if Shirley's flighty. She's a very pretty girl and she can't help it if she attracts a lot of attention.'

'She's had more boyfriends than I've had hot dinners. Anyway, I thought she was going steady with Charlie Crisp.'

'Charlie's a lovely fellow, but I think Shirley deserves more in life than to marry a man who works for the water board.'

Ginnie knew very well that in reality Charlie's job was at the sewage works, but to mention it at the table would offend her mother's delicate sensibilities. 'So who is she bringing home today?'

'Olivia Mallory's brother. Shirley was at school with Olivia and the family are very well-to-do. Olivia introduced Shirley to the tennis club.'

'I remember her,' Ginnie said, frowning. 'I always thought she was a snooty cow and she treated Shirley like dirt.'

'Her father is a solicitor and he's on the council. He's a magistrate too, so I believe, and they have a house in Monk Avenue. I've seen Mrs Mallory in church, but I've never spoken to her. She has some lovely clothes, Ginnie. I daresay she bought them in posh shops up West.' Mildred sighed and smiled. 'Some people have it all. Anyway it's Olivia's brother, Laurence, who's coming round tonight. He's in the Navy. He's an officer.'

'That must make him a very nice chap.'

Mildred shot her a suspicious look. 'Are you laughing at me, Virginia?'

'Of course not, Mum.' Ginnie rose from her seat and dropped a kiss on her mother's turbaned head. 'Bye. See you later.'

AT SIX O'CLOCK that evening Ginnie was standing outside the bathroom, banging on the door for a second time. 'Hurry up, Shirley. I want to wash the plaster dust out of my hair before tea.'

'I won't be long.' Shirley's voice was accompanied by the sound of running water.

'Are you washing your hair, Shirley Travis? If you've used the last of my precious Amami shampoo I'll never forgive you.' Ginnie waited anxiously until at last the door opened and Shirley breezed out of the bathroom with a towel wrapped round her head.

'I think I might have used the last drop. Sorry, love, but I'm sure your friend Fred Woollies will let you have another bottle.' Shirley sailed past her, leaving a waft of Amami shampoo and Lifebuoy soap in her wake.

Speechless and knowing that it was useless to argue, Ginnie took a deep breath and counted to ten. Even so, she was still angry and she followed her sister into the large, airy back bedroom. 'You selfish beast. You might have asked first.'

Towelling her hair, Shirley looked up and smiled. 'I know, I'm a cow sometimes, Ginnie, but you are a sweet little sister and you wouldn't begrudge me my big night, would you?'

'What are you talking about?'

Shirley let the towel fall to the ground and stepped into her parachute silk camiknickers, fastening them at the waist with a single mother-of-pearl button. 'I want you to be nice to my new chap.'

'It's only Olivia's big brother. I never liked her; she's stuck-up and she used to get you in trouble. What's so special about Laurence Mallory, anyway?'

'Don't say nasty things about Olivia. She was my best friend at school and I had a bit of a crush on Laurence. We met again at a tennis club dance a couple of weeks before Easter when he was home on leave. He made me feel like one of the Monk Avenue set and it was lovely.'

'Don't, Shirley. You sound snobby, just like Mum.'

'I'm not a snob. Laurence is super and I know he really fancies me, but his leave is up tomorrow and he has to return to his ship, so I want him to take fond memories of me back to sea.'

'But what about poor Charlie? He's totally devoted to you.'

'I know, and I'm very fond of him too, but it only takes a moment to fall in love, Ginnie. You'll know when it happens to you.' Shirley made a moue and tossed her head so that her strawberry-blonde hair formed Medusa-like curls around her face. 'You'll love Laurence, but only in a sisterly fashion because he's mine.'

Ginnie rose to her feet. 'Well, good luck. That's all I can say.'

'He's tall and blond, and he has deep blue eyes with little crinkly lines at the corners from constantly staring out to sea.' Shirley reached for her bra and put it on, struggling to do up the hooks and eyes. 'Give me a hand, Ginnie. This wretched thing must have shrunk in the wash or else my boobs have got bigger. Come to think of it they've been a bit tender recently. Perhaps I should see a doctor.'

Ginnie clipped the two ends together. 'Mum said you'd been looking a bit peaky.' She let the elastic go and it snapped against her sister's back, making her yelp.

'Ouch, that hurt.'

'Sorry.' Ginnie stood back, eyeing her sister thoughtfully. 'You haven't had any other symptoms, have you, Shirley?'

'I hope you're not insinuating anything improper, my girl.' Shirley snatched the dress she had laid out on her bed and slipped it over her head. She tugged at the zip fastener, pulling a face. 'I'm definitely putting on weight. It's all that hateful stodgy food we're forced to eat in the works canteen.'

'Are you sure about that?' Ginnie gazed at her sister's voluptuous figure with a sinking heart. 'You haven't done anything silly, have you, Shirley?'

'I don't know what you mean. Ouch.' Shirley's eyes filled with tears. 'I've pinched my skin in the blasted zip. That really hurts.'

'Breathe in.' Ginnie held the material together with one hand and eased the fastener into place. 'Just don't eat much at tea or you'll burst the seams.'

'It's not funny.' Shirley did a twirl, examining her reflection in the mirror on the front of her wardrobe. 'I'm getting fat.'

'How long is it since you had the curse?'

'That's none of your business.'

'It will be if you're up the creek without a paddle.'

'I can't be. Charlie took care of that side of things and with Laurence it was . . .' Shirley clapped her hands to her flaming cheeks. 'I mean, it's simply not possible.'

Ginnie shook her head. 'It might be a false alarm. You'll have to make an appointment to see the doctor.'

'Yes, I will.' Shirley dashed her hand across her eyes. 'The last thing I want is to have to beg Charlie to make an honest woman of me.'

'At least he won't get blown out of the water by a U-boat torpedo,' Ginnie said grimly. 'I hope you know what you're doing.'

Shirley moved swiftly to her dressing table and seized a hairbrush, dragging it through her tangled curls. 'I'll be all right. I know what I want out of life and it isn't a terraced house close to the sewage works.'

'I feel sorry for Charlie. He's crazy about you. Isn't that enough?'

'I can hear Mum calling you,' Shirley said, pointing to the door. 'I expect she wants some help with the meat paste sandwiches or whatever she's laid on for tea. Let's hope we don't have to eat them in the Anderson shelter. That would be the last straw.'

'I haven't had time to wash and change yet,' Ginnie protested. 'You're nearly ready. You go down and help with the food. It's your chap who's coming, not mine.'

'That would be difficult considering you haven't got a boyfriend.' Shirley slumped down on the dressing-table stool, turning her head with an apologetic smile. 'Sorry. That was bitchy. I didn't mean it. Please go downstairs and keep Mum happy, and I'll shift heaven and earth to find you another bottle of Amami.'

'I'll do it, but only if you promise to see the doctor tomorrow.'

'Cross my heart and hope to die, although not literally, of course. It's just a false alarm. It's got to be.'

GINNIE HAD JUST reached the foot of the stairs when the doorbell rang.

'Answer that will you, Ginnie?' Mildred called from the kitchen. 'I'm just taking the scones out of the oven.'

Ginnie opened the door. She had not seen Laurence Mallory since she was a child, but the smiling young man in naval uniform simply had to be her sister's latest conquest. 'Hello,' she said, smiling. 'You must be Laurence. Do come in.'

'And you must be Ginnie. You were just a kid when I last saw you.' He took off his peaked cap and tucked it under his arm as he stepped over the threshold. He handed her a bottle wrapped in brown paper. 'It's gin. I'm afraid I couldn't get anything else, but perhaps I should have got some fizzy pop for you. I'm not very good at this sort of thing.'

She frowned. 'How old d'you think I am?'

His cheeks reddened beneath his tan. 'I'm awfully sorry. Have I put my foot in it?'

She caught a glimpse of herself in the hallstand mirror. Thanks to Shirley, she had not had time to change out of the open-neck blouse and slacks she had worn to work, and her face was innocent of make-up. With her hair still tied in the ponytail she realised that she could have passed for a schoolgirl and it was her turn to blush. 'I'm older than I look, but thank you for the gin.' She ushered him into the front room. 'I'll call Shirley. She won't be long.'

'I am sorry if I embarrassed you just now.' He smiled, and Ginnie noticed that his eyes did crinkle rather attractively at the corners, just as Shirley had said.

'That's all right. I don't always look such a mess, but the blast from the doodlebug brought some of the ceiling down at the shop and I haven't had time to change.'

'You look fine as you are. I was afraid you might all be dressed up and it was going to be terribly formal.'

'What would you like to drink, Laurence?' She opened her parents' much prized cocktail cabinet and realised her mistake when she saw the row of empty shelves. 'Oh dear, I'm afraid there's no choice. It's going to be gin and water or just gin.'

He grinned appreciatively. 'I'll take gin and water, but only if you'll join me.'

'Thanks, I will.' She selected two glasses and poured a measure of gin in each. 'I'll fetch some water.'

In the kitchen she found her mother red-faced from the heat as she took the second batch of scones from the oven. 'What's he like, Ginnie? Where's Shirley? She should have been the one to greet the poor man.'

'She's getting dolled up, of course. He's nice, Mum. You'll like him and he's brought a bottle of gin. I just came to get some water.'

'He's obviously a gentleman. Shirley could do worse.'

'She's only been going out with him for a short while.'

'I'd only known your dad for three days and I knew he was the one for me. That's all it takes sometimes, dear.' Mildred tipped the scones onto a cooling rack. 'Mrs Martin gave me her last jar of strawberry jam so that we could have a proper tea. Take the water and keep him company, while I finish up here. Your dad should be home soon.'

Ginnie filled a jug with tap water and took it to the front room where she found Laurence looking at a framed photograph of herself and Shirley on the beach at Frinton. 'I was nine there,' she said, adding water to their drinks. 'And Shirley was twelve.'

'This is how I remember you,' he said, grinning. 'You've both changed quite a lot since then.'

'Shirley said that you're going back to your ship tomorrow. That's a pity. I mean it would have been nice to get to know you properly.'

He raised his glass to her. 'I'll drink to that, Ginnie.'

The door opened and Shirley swanned into the room, arms outstretched. 'I'm so sorry I wasn't here to greet you, Larry darling.'

He put his glass down and stood up to give her a brief embrace. 'That's quite all right, Shirley. Your sister has kept me entertained.' He met Ginnie's amused gaze with a hint of a smile. 'I'm afraid I was a bit early.'

Ginnie was about to offer Shirley a drink when a movement in the front garden caught her eye and she saw her father running up the garden path. 'Here comes Dad, and he's in a tearing hurry.'

'Is that gin?' Shirley said, eyeing the bottle. 'I'd love a drink, Ginnie. Pour me a stiff one, there's a dear.' She sent her a warning glance. 'Please.'

Ginnie was about to pour the drink when the door opened and Sid burst into the room. He came to a sudden halt when he saw Laurence. 'Oh, you're here already, son. I'm afraid you've arrived at a bad time.'

Mildred had followed him into the room and she clutched his arm. 'Not now, Sid. Whatever it is can wait until after tea, can't it?'

'I don't think so, love.' Sid patted her hand. 'This concerns you mostly, Shirley. During the air raid this morning a buzz bomb fell on the sewage works. I'm afraid there were casualties.'